PILGRIM

Book Two of the Sojourner Saga

Martin Halbert

Eposian Publishing
Greensboro, North Carolina

Pilgrim: Book Two of the Sojourner Saga

Copyright © 2026 Martin Halbert

All rights are reserved. No part of the book may be reproduced without prior permission of the author, Martin Halbert.

This is a work of fiction. Any resemblance of names of characters to actual persons, living or dead, is coincidental.

ISBN: 978-1-970664-01-0

Publisher: Eposian Publishing LLC

First Edition, Version 1.6: February 2026

Dedicated to

All my Readers, Reviewers, Advisors, and Friends that helped me create this book. Thank you all!

Contents

Openings 1

Chambers 48

Births 102

Partings 138

Consequences 181

Resurrections 212

Answers 267

Returns 317

Openings

Brother Apprentice Greymalkin Thomas of the interstellar monastic Sojourner Order stood on the surface of the planetoid, ankle-deep in the lemon-yellow sulfur-dioxide snow, his feet and exposed hands freezing, his thoughts paralyzed with fear at the sight of the mountain-sized golden Abyssal rising into the sky. Seen clearly in the brilliant light of the blazing yellow-giant star above them, the golden cyborg was terrifying, a flying mass of technological cliffs and hard-edged scarps that must have massed hundreds of millions of tons. Despite its inconceivable bulk, the vast being was accelerating faster and faster as it flew across the surface of the planetoid toward him. And the huge weapon aperture in what appeared to be the thing's head was now opening to fire.

The young monk looked up at his two allies, the slowly morphing black form of the liquid-stone protean Bruno and the ferociously jagged-toothed alien form of the Sylphid Tatterdemalion. But both of them seemed to also be frozen in fear at the sight of the rapidly approaching Abyssal. Greymalkin communed desperately to both of them through the shadow jewel suspended in hyperspace within his brain. «Tatter! Bruno! Snap out of it! Get out of here!» When they did not respond, he tried to slog through the stinking sulfurous snow toward them, but found that his feet were now frozen solid, and his entire body had become rigidly immobile. *Wait*, he thought in confusion, looking at his bare feet and ankles buried in the dirty yellow snow. He looked down at himself and realized he wasn't wearing a void suit. In fact, he wasn't wearing *anything*. He was standing frozen in the snow, helplessly naked. *But, this is impossible. I'd already be dead if I* was on the surface in the vacuum without a void suit. He heard a deafening inchoate roar, and looked back at the charging Abyssal. Then he frowned in frightened confusion. *How can I <u>hear</u> it? There's no atmosphere on this planetoid.* But then he saw the monster's primary weapon charging as it prepared to fire. He looked back to his two friends in anguish.

They'll both be killed! I've got to save them! I've got to do <u>something</u> to help them! He struggled to move, but was still paralyzed. Then he heard a tremendous pulsation, and saw that the golden monster's now-glowing weapon had finished charging. As the weapon discharged with a blast like the end of the universe, he screamed... and woke up.

His head jerked up in the darkness as he cried out in fright. The young Sojourner monk tried to thrash, but realized that he was still inside his cocooned void suit. His suit had been encased in thick web-like bindings when he'd been seized by the hulking owl-like Crotani slaves of the golden Abyssal. After the Abyssal had questioned him, the Crotani had taken him deep within the fortress and cocooned him there in a dark cell. All of his limbs were restrained, wrapped tightly by the bindings, and achingly numb. Greymalkin groaned inside the helmet, realizing exactly why he'd been helplessly immobile in the snow of that lurid dream. He shook his head painfully to try to throw off his fatigue and wake up completely.

It was just a nightmare; it wasn't real. I must've passed out. But I <u>was</u> captured, and I'm still stuck here alone, tied up. As he finally regained full consciousness, he remembered everything that had happened, and the horror of his situation flooded back in on him. He was in pitch blackness, alone within a prison cell deep inside the fortress of an incomprehensibly powerful golden alien Abyssal, a fortress that was buried beneath the cold snowy surface of an isolated planetoid in the remote Eta Carinae region of the Sagittarius Arm of the Galaxy. He'd journeyed across thousands of light-years to reach the Carinae, losing his fellow Sojourner monk colleagues Bora and Soren in the process when they'd been murdered en route. No one was coming to help him, and he would likely be killed soon by the Abyssal. Greymalkin's head hung down in despair as he dangled helplessly in the bindings, and he sobbed quietly by himself in the darkness for a time. Finally he threw off the despair, grit his teeth in anger, and struggled again against the bindings. But it was no use; he had been secured very tightly. He again thought through the final disastrous moments of their battle with the gigantic gold alien Abyssal.

Greymalkin's head was still aching with the echoed agony he'd felt through the sensory communication link when that final blast from the golden monster had evidently put an end to the reckless alien cyborg that had called itself *Bruno*. He contemplated that horrific ending sadly. Even if he had not completely trusted or always liked Bruno and his antics all that much, the protean had been his ally and a loyal companion. And Bruno had *died* trying to rescue him. He thought mournfully about Tatterdemalion, the half-human half-Sylphid alien who he'd befriended in the main human expedition base of the Carinae, and Royce, the living cyneget starship that he'd freed from a cruel Burani dock-master at the base. He had no idea if Tatter or Royce had survived or not, but given the destructive power that the golden Abyssal monster had demonstrated, it seemed unlikely. Now Greymalkin was alone, with nothing before him but the hideous prospect of being dissected alive, the fate that the evil golden alien had promised him.

At first he'd simply felt despair, both at the memory of the phantom pain he'd experienced in Bruno's annihilation and his guilt over his friends' deaths because of his bad decisions. But then he shook off the despondency. *They aren't dead, they can't be,* he vowed to himself again furiously. *And I have to focus or I'm never going to be able to figure out a way to help them.* At last he composed himself and did what he always did when he felt completely lost in the hopelessness and cruelty of the

Carinae. There in the pitch blackness, Greymalkin prayed alone, reciting the Sojourner Great Vow to himself to remember what he believed in, what the core of his faith had always been. The Vow was simple. It was the personal affirmation of the principles of the Great Commitment to which all Sojourners adhered. Greymalkin recited the words slowly, breathing in time to the chant.

I will seek discoveries with clarity. I will save the Bereft with compassion. I will share information with humility. I will sustain knowledge with diligence. And I will sojourn through life with courage.

The avowal stirred him then, as it usually did. Somewhere deep inside him, determination rose up in wrath and defiance to drive off the sense of despair that had overcome him. *I may as well be dead, but I'm not giving up while I'm still able to think and plan.*

He tried once again to see if he could move his arms or legs, but they were constricted so tightly that his limbs had gone from numb to cramping spasms because of the bindings. The pain scattered his thoughts, so he took a moment to concentrate and calm himself again with an internal Sojourner meditative chant and steady breathing to keep from panicking. *What assets do I have?*

He still had the mysterious golden multi-tool, but while the Crotani slaves that had bound him had not removed it from his suit harness, they had nevertheless coated it and most of the other gear on his harness with the mysterious web-like muck that prevented him from communicating with any of it. He thought about what had been on his harness when he'd been captured, and squirmed in the bindings to see if he could reach anything. He could feel something like a small hard brick-shape on his belt by his left hand, and wondered what it was for a second. Then he remembered that he had stuck Constance's databloc on his belt. It had apparently not been coated with the Crotani muck, because it activated when he sought for it mentally. *Okay, here is knowledge. I can definitely use that. Access to information is the greatest weapon anyone can possess.*

He began to rifle through Constance's data, looking for anything that might be remotely useful. There were endless excised snippets of information that Constance had stashed away from various sources in her mnemotome, but she had been so busy collecting it she'd not had time to index it. As a result he had to rummage through her links and cross-references in a maddening hunt for anything helpful. And it was hard to guess what might be helpful in this appalling circumstance.

He found no obvious additional bits of information on the Abyssal that had captured him beyond the main reference which had led him here, and which Constance had jotted down herself. Eventually he decided to simply scan for more information on the star system he was in. There were many catalog entries for the yellow supergiant star, especially in the old Xenocorps survey entries. He noticed that Constance had cross-linked some of those, so he skimmed through the links. Apparently, the same wide ranging survey scout team that had studied the manticore husks on the surface had spent a great deal of time in the same star cluster where the yellow supergiant was located. One member of the scout team had left the group before its last mission, and had survived long enough to write up reports on events and phenomena the team had encountered in the cluster. The reports were written in a scattered manner that suggested to Greymalkin the same haste that both he and Constance had experienced ever since arriving in the Carinae. But as he raced through the entries, one leaped out at him.

The Xenocorpsman of the mission three centuries ago had been named Alexander Borgess, and in one of his entries he described an encounter the scout team had with an enormous golden Abyssal that had pursued them and nearly destroyed their ship with an incredibly powerful beam weapon. *That definitely sounds like the grotesque fellow in charge of this place,* Greymalkin thought grimly. He quickly read through the rest of the hastily written entry. The Xenocorpsman had given the Abyssal a nickname, the *Aurelian*. Greymalkin knew the name simply meant "Golden One", but it certainly had appropriate precedents in the history of Old Earth. What was even more interesting was that Borgess and his crew had also briefly contacted the equally powerful being in the center of the Keyhole Nebula, which he had also given a nickname, the *Clavisian*, before it disappeared as well.

But the most interesting details were recorded in a small attached narrative by Borgess within the centuries-old entry. The first interesting point was that the two immensely powerful beings were apparently enemies, or at least unfriendly to one another in some way.

That's right, Greymalkin thought to himself, now remembering the idea that had occurred to him before he'd passed out. *Try to contact the other one and see if it will help, or at least take some action against the Aurelian. And it makes sense that they'd oppose one another, at least in this madhouse of a region. Even back among human civilizations, neighboring powers are often rivals. But the concept of mutual assistance doesn't seem to exist at all here in the Carinae. It's just everyone versus everyone else.*

He read further, and found a second detail that was the most surprising of all. Borgess had written that he'd learned the Aurelian had not originally been an Abyssal at all. Rather, the creature had been one of the *Risen*, a lesser being that had been exponentially improved in intelligence and other capabilities through technologies found here in the Carinae. Originally, the Aurelian had been a *Crotani*, one of the odd owl-like sapients Greymalkin had encountered repeatedly throughout the Carinae, the same sort of creatures that had cocooned him in the cell he was imprisoned within.

But this particular Crotani had somehow not only been improved mentally and physically, but had also gained control of incredibly advanced Abyssal technology. Greymalkin had encountered several of the Risen, and they were all deeply unsettling, even the friendly ones. The unfriendly ones simply seemed like terrifying forces of nature to the young monk. He wondered for a moment what it would be like to have an intellect like that, to be transformed into a being categorically and radically beyond human capabilities. He had to admit that there was some tiny part of him that envied those capabilities. But the thought of such a profound transformation seemed simultaneously enticing and horrifying. *Would you still have the same identity? Or would you change into someone else?*

Greymalkin skimmed through the rest of the entry eagerly looking for more information about the Aurelian, but was frustrated to find that the rest of Borgess' entry was simply stellar survey prospecting data. *I guess the Xenocorps were interested in financial gain, not cultural details.* Greymalkin was still methodically skimming through Constance's notes for any other clues when brilliant light flooded the dark cell. The metal door was thrown open with a harsh clang that reached him as vibrations through his bonds in the silent vacuum of the cell.

Burly Crotani in void suits poured into his cell and manhandled him again as they cut his bonds. As they seized his arms and legs with unnecessary force, Greymalkin blinked in the bright light and glanced down sadly where he had seen the fragment of Bruno drop into a puddle. To his surprise, there was nothing there. He started to look around the cell floor, but the Crotani slammed him against the wall, dazing him before they proceeded to drag him down a very long hallway. Greymalkin tried to disassociate and not think about the physical pain, but it wasn't possible. All he felt was violent and agonizing sensations smashing against various parts of his body, along with the return of the horrible synesthetic stench of rotting flesh that had been resonating with his shadow jewel ever since he'd entered the star system of the yellow-giant. By the time that all the shoving and punching from the aliens stopped, whatever mental focus he'd had was shattered and he couldn't think clearly. Then he became aware that something was looking down at him from high above. Greymalkin lifted his head. It was the vast form of the Aurelian.

«Your guardians are either destroyed or have fled. It is time for your vivisection.» The gigantic bulk of the alien cyborg once again loomed down closely over him like a falling building. Greymalkin crouched on the metal floor for only a second in terror before throwing himself backward and trying to scuttle away like an insect about to be squashed. A massive grapple-limb came down on him, and before he knew what was happening he'd been scooped up and lifted high off the floor. He looked up and saw that an orifice had opened in what loosely appeared to be the cyborg's "head". The huge creature was actually *placing him inside the opening*. Greymalkin screamed as he saw what appeared to be writhing maxillae inside the maw. The implied perception that he was being *eaten* was unavoidable and he screamed again as he felt the squirming graspers close around him, pulling him in.

It was when the thrashing maxillae closed around him that it finally happened, what Greymalkin had been anticipating, another of the bizarre hallucinations that always seemed to overcome him when he came into direct contact with one of the Risen. Given the tremendous size of the Aurelian, the young monk had feared that the sensation would be shattering, but instead it came on with a surprisingly *enfeebled* impression.

In the hallucination, Greymalkin seemed to be wandering through vast empty ruins, a cold wasteland of abandoned alien structures. Then he once again smelled the same fetid corpse-stench, and heard a faint sound like an animal gasping for air. He followed the odor and faint sound until he rounded a corner and saw something utterly revolting. There was some kind of feebly crawling mass that lay on the top of an enormous pile of delicate artifacts that seemed ancient. The rasping breaths of the flabby creature were ghastly. As Greymalkin watched in loathing, the nauseating thing quivered and clutched at the strange relics it lay on top of, and then weakly lifted what appeared to be a head. There were multiple eyes in the thing's disgusting face, watery animal eyes that blinked at him in pain and distress. It seemed to extend a rotting limb toward him slowly, but Greymalkin flinched back in revulsion. The hallucination faded, and he was suddenly back among the frenzied maxillae closing on him like row upon row of gruesome teeth.

It definitely *felt* like the Aurelian was trying to eat him, as the razor sharp maxillae graspers roughly tried to tear him into pieces in the darkness. However, wherever the maxillae tore at him, the golden void suit stiffened. He wound up simply being thrown around bodily for a few moments. The rough treatment certainly *hurt*, but the maxillae apparently could not penetrate the material of the suit. After a pause, the graspers threw him a meter down onto a surface, and blinding spotlights and other probing beams of energy came on all around him. Then, one of the strangest conversations of Greymalkin's young life ensued.

«Your integument is sturdy. Too sturdy for my assay chamber dissasemblers.» The Aurelian's thoughts and the synesthetic illusory stench of rotting corpse-flesh were both unbelievably intense at this close range, and left Greymalkin gasping. The cyborg was obviously annoyed at not being able to immediately rend him apart. He saw lenses and sensors like clusters of moist black eyes and antennae descend close around him from the assay chamber walls. «I will examine you until I can discern how to defeat your armor. If nothing else is effective, I will place you on the surface and use my primary weapon to annihilate you at close range. However, that may simply *atomize* you.»

«Wait!» Greymalkin pleaded in a desperate tone. «I did not order the others to attack you! They made the choice themselves. I say again, I came here for *dialogue* with you, nothing more!»

When the Aurelian responded, Greymalkin thought he could detect a kind of dry amusement in the alien's thoughts. «You are a very strange organism, with absurd conceptions. You surely must know where you are, and why the very nature of this realm reveals all of your lies as impossible and irrational.»

«No! I do not!» Greymalkin found himself shouting the words inside his helmet as he communed them. «I am *new* to this place. I *only* want to communicate with you. I do not understand why you are so *violent*.»

There was a long pause. Greymalkin was being held spread-eagled, but the maxillae were no longer trying to tear him to pieces. When the Aurelian finally responded, its thoughts seemed tired and exasperated. «Human, your ignorance is tedious. And I find it hard to believe that you know nothing at all of this realm.»

«I only know that it seems hellish and perverse. But *why*?» Greymalkin put all the frustration that he had experienced in the last few months into the plea. The Aurelian's exasperation changed back to dry amusement.

«I do not know those words in your language, but I sense your meaning. You find this region frightening, human. But it is a realm of *wonder*. Yes, the stars here are bright and blazing, shedding so much radiation that only the strongest beings can survive here. But the wealth of this realm is similarly great, for the most beautiful star gems and highest quality materials are created *only* inside these stellar furnaces. And of course, the greatest prizes are the *Forge* and the *Nexus*.»

«Although I do not know what those objects may be, I remember you mentioning them previously.» Greymalkin was still shaking, but he felt a glimmer of hope. That was the longest coherent series of thoughts the Aurelian had shared with him yet. Amidst his panic, Greymalkin wondered if the arrogance that he sensed in the cyborg could be stoked to get it to share more information. «But whatever those objects may be, your behavior and the behavior of the other powerful beings here seems illogical. Why is this area characterized by so much violence? Cooperation always makes more sense than trying to murder one another!»

The lenses and other sensors were moving around Greymalkin now like revolving clusters of black eye-orbs on stalks. When the Aurelian communed its response there was a distracted sense of diversion in its thoughts. «Those of your kind that came here in your last invasion were not so appallingly stupid. The ones I captured before admitted before they died that the wealth of this realm in star gems and supernal riches were what attracted them here. Obviously this is true, just as these resources have attracted other lesser beings, and just as the *true* wealth of this region attracted much wiser beings before them. But all such seekers of wealth inevitably come into conflict.»

I've got him talking to me, Greymalkin realized, followed by another terrified insight. *Now I've got to keep him talking.* «Why? Because of their greed and avarice?»

The alien cyborg seemed genuinely puzzled in its musing response, but he could also tell it was not paying a great deal of attention to the conversation. The Aurelian was primarily absorbed with figuring out how to tear open his void suit and kill him. «I again do not know those words in your language, but I sense that you are a very young member of your species and do not understand many basic behaviors of sapient beings. The powerful among all sapient wealth seekers always wish to claim and control as much territory, information, and resources as they can. War breaks out among them. It was the same among my own people when we first came here.»

Greymalkin hesitated, thinking very carefully before making his next statement. «You were once much like your followers, were you not?»

«Why do you ask that?» The Aurelian's response to that statement was hot and angry.

It must be the truth! Greymalkin thought. *He was angry that I knew this about him! This frightful monster was once a mere <u>Crotani</u>, but now he is Risen. And it angers him that I know! Why? Shame? Fear that it makes him appear weak? Maybe I can get him to reveal more.* The young monk decided that Sojourner honesty was usually the best policy, even when duplicitously trying to trick an enemy. «A human named Alexander Borgess made that claim long ago.» Greymalkin held his breath as he communed his next question. «Is it true?»

The Aurelian snarled an incomprehensibly vicious thought, and then continued more understandably. «*Borgess* again. I almost caught and killed that vermin very recently, but he escaped once again by submerging beneath a shadow channel into a subchannel conduit. He is incredibly elusive and difficult to catch.»

Greymalkin felt disoriented. «Wait! The man I am referring to was among those of the first human expedition here. That was long ago. He can't possibly still be alive.»

«You are such a stupid kit! He is still roaming loose in this region to this day. But I will kill him eventually, just as I will kill you momentarily.» The Aurelian's thoughts had gone back to being distracted as it studied its instruments. Greymalkin was very confused, but decided to float the other bit of information he had gleaned from the old records.

«Please do not kill me! I may be able to help you... *resolve* your differences with the other powerful being in this immediate vicinity. The one at the center of the—» Greymalkin communed an image of the central star in the huge Keyhole Nebula where the creature called the Clavisian was supposed to be. All the moist eyes and other sense-organs on stalks abruptly stopped moving.

«Yes, you previously let slip that you know of the Prosecutor. But, *what* do you know of him? You will tell me!» The Aurelian's thoughts were flat, but felt very tense. Greymalkin hesitated again, wondering what to say.

«I only know that there is conflict between it and you.» Greymalkin waited to see if he had angered the monstrous cyborg.

«It is very good that I have you here with me, then.» The thoughts of the Aurelian seemed almost fearful now. «*Nothing* must attract the attention of that one to me at the moment! Nor even my overlord, the Tenax, at least not before I retrieve your data caches.»

That's right, Greymalkin thought. *He's afraid of both the 'Prosecutor' entity in the Keyhole Nebula and this mysterious 'Tenax' entity that apparently rules over the region.* The young monk thought back to the bizarre image that he'd detected in the mind of the Aurelian when it had first mentioned the Tenax. The impression had juxtaposed a strangely familiar vista of coiling tentacles overlaid by what seemed to be a memory of Rodolfo Flavopallio, the evil man that had initially ordered Greymalkin killed by Burani operatives, but who had later tried to recruit the young monk. *How is Rodo mixed up in all this? And what does he have to do with this Tenax thing that the Aurelian apparently works for?*

The oily black lens-orbs and sensors began moving again, systematically studying every centimeter of Greymalkin, and clustering around his helmet. The Aurelian's communed thoughts formed an irritated growl once again. «This shadow aureate shell of yours is as impregnable as my own armor, but I begin to understand how to disassemble it without atomizing your cephalic organ.»

Greymalkin struggled to understand what the monster was conveying. «Wait, do you mean my *head*? Yes, please don't atomize my head!»

«Not immediately, no.» The Aurelian seemed pensive, but encouraged. «To fully recover the data troves, I must extract the shadow jewel while you still live.»

Greymalkin cringed, not wanting to think about his shadow jewel being ripped out of his brain. «You referenced these... *data troves* previously. But believe me when I say that I do not know what could possibly be of value about them, or why you would wish to extract them.»

The Abyssal's thoughts seemed incredulous for a moment. «You surely must have stolen these troves? I am quite familiar with such theft, myself! You must be trying to deceive me now, even though I can detect no trace of deception in your thoughts. But even a creature as ignorant as you must be aware of the nature of the massive data troves layered onto the resonance structures of the shadow jewel in your cephalic organ? And their *purposes?*»

Greymalkin tried to guess what the monster meant, but he was as in the dark as ever. «We call these information structures *covenants*. But... they aren't data troves, they're....» His thoughts trailed off. He recognized that he actually knew *nothing* for certain about what had been placed in his shadow jewel, first by the Velan, and then by Kuanian through the device she had given him. In fact, he wasn't even sure if they actually were covenants or not. He'd long assumed that the implanted data structures had been the same as the cybernetic coercive covenants used by the Burani, complex programs to enslave a mind. But he had started wondering whether they might actually be some kind of assets or resources that the two powerful beings had given him. Apparently that was the case, given the Aurelian's thoughts. He decided to simply ask. «Well, what exactly *are* the purposes of these 'data troves', then?»

The Aurelian was amused once more. «You truly do not know? *Ah, I understand.* You are being used as an unintelligent animal courier to carry important information.»

Greymalkin was first outraged, but then faced the fact that what the Aurelian was claiming was actually true. It made him even angrier. «So, what's in these precious troves I'm carrying, then? Do you even know?»

«You would not comprehend the meaning of such data treasures.» The Aurelian sounded dismissive in the extreme. «Although, I think your powerful guardian, the protean one that I destroyed with my primary weapon, *that* one must have known the nature of what is encoded in your shadow jewel. Some of the data must have been promised to the guardian as a reward for safeguarding the troves. Your protector was powerful indeed. There could have been no other motivation that would cause it to serve as guardian for an ignorant larva such as you.»

Greymalkin did not respond. He felt unsure of many things now. Bruno had, by the protean's own admission, been motivated exactly as the Aurelian claimed. And what had the Velan and Kuanian placed in him, anyway? He began to wonder how many larger schemes there were that he was obliviously unaware of in his actions. *Maybe I was simply an idiot to trust Kuanian in the first place when I decided to come to the Carinae.* But that conclusion still felt wrong to him. *And even if I am being manipulated, I still want to know what's going on here.*

The Aurelian startled him when it abruptly communed another terrifying snarl of frustration. «Nggarh! It will require some time for me to construct the necessary apparatus to disassemble your armor; it is too well constructed by those who chose you as an animal courier. Slaves, come! Take him back to his cell for now!»

Greymalkin found himself ejected from inside the Aurelian and then seized again by the Crotani servitors. They hauled him protesting all the way back to his cell, whereupon they proceeded to truss him up once more and leave him suspended from the ceiling again. He found that this time they had bound him perhaps even more tightly than before, leaving him barely able to breathe. And in an abundance of caution, his Crotani jailors had now coated his entire suit harness with the communication inhibiting muck. He cursed inside his mind for most of an hour, trying to reach the multi-tool or anything else potentially useful on his harness or scrape the stuff off. But it was useless. He was stuck firm in the bonds and helpless. He tried to mentally fiddle with the controls to the golden suit itself, but the only significant thing he could potentially do was to reconfigure it into a garment other than a void suit, which would simply kill him in the vacuum of the cell. He struggled mightily in the bonds for a time until he became faint with exhaustion and hunger. After hanging dizzy-headed in the bonds for what seemed like ages, at some point he fell asleep.

* * *

Greymalkin found himself wandering through nightmares again. This time his nightmares featured the corpse-stench of the Aurelian pervading throughout armies of skinned Crotani corpses staggering after him in pursuit while he ran in slow motion across the blindingly bright yellow surface of the planetoid. After a seemingly endless terror-stricken chase, the corpses closed on him, and he screamed in the dream as they reached for him. Whereupon the undead Crotani simply vanished, and he abruptly found himself wandering through the abandoned halls and chambers of the main expedition base among the thousands of strangers there, none of whom acknowledged his existence. He found the evil dockmaster Trauerstrom, but the man lay dead, crushed and bloodied where Bruno had seized him at Greymalkin's command. Then the dead man slowly rose to his feet and began to stagger towards him. The young monk fled from the corpse, looking for Tatterdemalion's tavern. When he found it and began to worm his way through the crowd, all the Canisian miners appeared to be changing into animated corpses. When Greymalkin finally seated himself at a table, he realized that sitting across from him was the eerie man named Lex that he had met weeks ago, an old man with close-cropped blond hair and an artificial mind inside his skull. The old man stared at him with a ghastly death's-head expression and said, "Join me."

The young monk screamed in the nightmare and stumbled away in fear, finally finding himself standing alone in a dark space. Something abruptly felt profoundly different. He had the unnerving feeling that he was being watched from all sides in the dream. He looked around pointlessly until he finally thought to look up. There, stretching across the entirety of the dark sky above him in the dream, was the enormous and bizarre form of the Velan, becoming larger and larger, then sweeping down around and past him.

As the vast bulk of the incomprehensible entity came down on him and he began to scream once again, he felt an eerie presence communing with him, asking a question. «Why are you distressed?»

Greymalkin gasped in the darkness, looking up at the asteroid-sized being descending on him, and tried to commune in response. «What's happening now? You didn't commune with me before!»

«That was my elder colleague, not me, human. Do not be afraid. I will assist you in your distress.» The vast communed thoughts echoed in his mind like the opposite of an explosion, as if it was spreading an endless calm across a chaotic ocean instantly. In a moment, Greymalkin felt completely at peace and tranquil.

«...Thank you....» Greymalkin now seemed to be lying motionless, floating on a perfectly still and dark sea within the dream, looking up at the endlessly morphing form of the entity that he had thought to be the Velan. But he saw now that the slowly morphing shape that filled his vision was different from the Velan in subtle ways, large, but not as overwhelmingly vast as the other being had been. He felt confused once more, trying to hang onto clarity of thought even though he was in a dream. «If you are not the Velan, who are you?»

«Borgess calls me the Clavisian.» The thoughts of the huge being were tranquil and soothing. Greymalkin struggled to remember why that name sounded so familiar as it continued communing. «I am one of the designated authorities of this realm representing the Central Authorities, we who are termed the *Pellucids*.»

«I was afraid.» Now Greymalkin's thoughts were lazy and distracted. The vast thoughts drifting down on him were so soothing. He felt like he was drifting away. «So afraid. But now I can't remember why. Tell me? Why am I here? And why have *you* come here?»

«I was notified of your situation by your companion, who sought me out. You are being held prisoner by the one that Borgess calls the Aurelian. But delaying you is not permitted.» The enormous presence had settled all around him, like a peaceful blanket. Greymalkin struggled again to keep his focus and not drift away. *I'm dreaming, but something is happening. Wake up! I have to wake up.*

«Why is it not permitted?» Greymalkin asked the question, even though he had already forgotten what the great, tranquil Voice in his mind had said was not permitted.

«You bear the mark of my elder colleague.» Now the echoing Voice briefly seemed stern, but the anger was directed elsewhere. «You must not be hindered. You must be set free.» As the last of the enormous thoughts echoed into the darkness around him, Greymalkin drifted away into unconsciousness for what seemed like only a single, peaceful moment of rest.

And then the vibrations of an explosion somewhere very near him woke him up as he bounced back and forth in the bonds, screaming in fright once again. Light was now shining through fissures and cracks in the wall of his cell. Greymalkin came fully awake and looked around in desperation. *What in blazes is happening?* Then he sensed an all too familiar communed bubbling signal from his shoulder, bubbling that signified laughter.

«Ah, you are finally awake again!» Bruno's thoughts were very ebullient, and very much not dead. After a moment of disbelief, Greymalkin craned his neck around to look at his shoulder. At first he thought nothing was there, but then he saw a tiny, inconspicuous black splatter like a pinprick.

«Bruno! You've been alive all this time? Why didn't you let me know!» Greymalkin felt both relieved and furious, but his angry tirade was interrupted by another explosion so close that he could *hear* it distantly through the vibrations reaching him through his bonds. Most of one wall of the cell actually blew away, revealing gas spewing into the corridor outside from the walls and igniting as it hit other burning clumps of liquid on the floor.

«It would not have been advisable, boss!» Bruno's cackling thoughts seemed jubilant, but also staccato again, as if the protean was being pummeled. «After I recovered myself, I had to shrink my fragment down to a sufficiently small size such that it would not be detected. Your captor put you through quite the examination!»

«What's going on!» Greymalkin was thrown back and forth again as another explosion reverberated through the walls and his bonds. This time he swung so far back and forth that he painfully bounced off one of the remaining walls of his cell. Instead of answering, Bruno simply activated the sensory link once again, and Greymalkin gasped at what he saw.

Bruno was again in combat with the immense form of the Aurelian above the surface of the planetoid, but this time he was not charging alone towards the monster. Greymalkin was stunned to see a gigantic shape passing by Bruno in the sky, a bizarrely morphing form very like the Velan but much smaller. *It wasn't a dream!* he realized. *That thing was communing with me while I slept!*

The being called the Clavisian swept past Bruno, fantastic extensions and arches appearing and vanishing smoothly in and out of visible space for kilometers around its central form. The Aurelian had turned and was quickly accelerating away from it towards the horizon, but not quickly enough. An incomprehensibly complex *twisting* shape extended from the Clavisian and speared through the huge golden form of the Aurelian in sundering violence. The giant golden Abyssal crashed into the ground and disintegrated into a brilliant fireball of destruction across the sulfurous sludge of the surface.

After a few seconds, Greymalkin felt what must have been the shockwaves of that crash jolt through the walls in the most violent explosion yet, throwing him careening and bouncing off the walls so brutally that the bonds holding him suspended in the middle of the cell snapped. He was flung through empty space and hit something hard, stunning him.

He came to full awareness as he sensed a warm communal presence approaching him quickly. He felt a shuddering impact in the floor near him, and was then lifted off the ground by enormous limbs, all the while feeling the deliriously pleasant sensation of his tight bonds being severed and removed. He stretched his painfully sore arms and legs, and looked up to see that he was being held with tender care in Royce's now fully regrown grapple-limbs. The cyneget hovered over him in the corridor, protectively moving its three ovoid hulls around him to shield him from falling debris. Greymalkin felt choked with a sense of gratitude. Somehow, *unbelievably*, the loyal cyneget had jammed itself all the way through the maze of corridors searching patiently, and had actually managed to find him.

«*Royce.*» Greymalkin's head was spinning, and he could barely focus enough to commune. «Get us out of here. This place is collapsing.» As he looked up at his own distorted reflection in Royce's curved mirrorshell hull, he could see reflections of rock and big metal fragments falling all around them. The cyneget sent him a nonverbal high-pitched whining, a communal thought which Greymalkin had learned was a signal for concern from the cyborg. It was accompanied by a data stream of bodily signals from his void suit. Greymalkin saw from the void suit readings that he was bleeding badly from various internal injuries, and had several fractured bones. «Yeah, I'm not doing too well, Royce. *Let's go.*»

The cyneget carefully lifted him up and placed him inside the airlock blister of the central ovoid hull of the three that formed the cyborg's body. Greymalkin dizzily crawled into the main compartment toward the secondary cockpit space in the central hull. Royce quickly activated the helm link, and he saw through Royce's sensors that the living starship was cautiously moving back through the collapsing corridors and tunnels, even as they continued to crumble. As Royce passed through some of the larger tunnel junctions, Greymalkin could see that hundreds of Crotani slaves in void suits were running in all directions trying to escape the destruction of their base. Although he felt a spasm of angry resentment toward the aliens because of the way they had beaten him, he couldn't help feeling pity for them as well. Whatever else the foul lair had been, he knew it had been their home.

Greymalkin dizzily thought about trying to save some of them as Royce paused in a collapsing junction, seeking a way through the wreckage. But then several of the Crotani pulled out weapons and began firing at Royce, and the cyneget flew away through the debris shower that thudded and clanged noisily against the cyborg's hull just meters above Greymalkin. *Thank Providence for this loyal creature,* he thought. *I'd be dead if Royce hadn't found me.*

Then, just as he was painfully clambering into a seat to strap himself in, Royce accelerated into a huge ruined space, and Greymalkin saw the bright light of the yellow supergiant star through gaps. The enormous metal doors that he had seen through the sensory link with Bruno were ahead of them, but now lay ajar and smashed. Just as the mammoth roof of the entrance began to slowly collapse, the cyneget shot forward, dodging segments of conjoined rock and metal that must have massed hundreds of thousands of tons apiece. Some of the smaller debris inevitably struck the cyneget and the cabin shuddered around him forcefully, but by now he had strapped in, and the jolts were cushioned.

With a tremendous lunge the cyneget vaulted into the black starry sky of the planetoid, soaring high above the endless field of sulfurous hills and volcanoes. Greymalkin gasped a painful sigh of relief. Bruno communed with him then, in rather unconcerned thoughts.

«Good, your cyborganic vehicle was able to retrieve you before you were crushed.» The tiny black splatter on his shoulder gradually grew larger until it was the size of his hand. «Come and see what we have discovered in the crash site of our opponent.»

Greymalkin grit his teeth, and belatedly activated the emergency medical subsystem in the void suit. He began to feel internal prods as the trauma systems began attempting to treat his worst injuries. There was a prick of a dermal injection in his neck and the pain began to go away, but his thoughts began to feel very fuzzy as a consequence. He'd hesitated to activate the medical system for exactly that reason; he'd been afraid it would sedate him. He shook his head, trying to throw off the haziness, and steered Royce across the sky of the sulfur-world in the direction Bruno indicated.

«Is Tatter okay?» He had still not seen or heard from the Sylphid-human hybrid since the first battle and was terribly fearful of what that meant. His mood brightened when her communed thoughts came to him over the link he shared with Bruno.

«I'm okay.» Tatter's thoughts were subdued. Sad even. «This Aurelian guy is not quite what I thought.»

«Why?» Greymalkin was scanning the horizon, and began to see the wreckage of the Aurelian's crash site coming over the horizon of the planetoid. It was awe-inspiring. A tremendous splattered path of sulfurous sludge littered with smoldering wreckage stretched away for kilometers. He saw the slowly morphing form of the Clavisian on the surface at the end of the debris field, and brought Royce down to hover nearby.

As Greymalkin scanned the horrific vista he saw that the Clavisian seemed to be carefully extracting something from the ruin of the Aurelian's enormous body. As he cautiously brought Royce closer, he saw a familiar form near the center of the wreckage. Even in her towering Sylphid shape, Tatter looked tiny in comparison with the Clavisian and the remains of the Aurelian. Greymalkin hovered Royce closer, magnifying the image of what the Clavisian was extracting. At first he could not understand what he was seeing, and then he gasped.

The Clavisian was carefully pulling a golden pod out of the wreckage. The golden pod had transparent panels, and Greymalkin could see that it was full of some sort of amber-tinted oily liquid. Something malformed and misshapen floated in the pod, festooned with penetrating tubes. He realized that the omnipresent stench of rotting flesh was emanating from the pod, which Greymalkin sensed was still very much *functioning* as it generated an intensely vibrating preservative field of some kind that was the source of the strange synesthesia. What made Greymalkin gasp was that he finally recognized what the pallid shape floating in the center of the droning golden pod was. It was the body of a Crotani, hideously decayed to the point of resembling a corpse. This wasted thing was the Aurelian, or at least what remained of its ancient and barely surviving corporeal body.

A weakly communed groan of agony emanated from the half-alive Crotani in the golden pod. The enormous, calm thoughts of the Clavisian came to Greymalkin as the pod was lifted up and began to vanish into the complex shifting form of the Abyssal. «This creature has prolonged its life far, far beyond what is natural for its species. But now its time of passing has finally come. By means of technology that it stole from us it has clung to its mortal existence from a time long before your people began to first journey into space, human.»

Greymalkin could feel the terrible pain the Aurelian was in as the creature's moaning thoughts continued to commune on the same channel it had used to interrogate him. Despite the fear it had inspired in him, he felt nothing but pity for the dying thing in the reeking pod. «Is that why you killed it? Because it stole technology from you?»

«I did not kill it.» The calm presence of the Clavisian was again reassuring. He could almost sense a tenderness in its thoughts toward the ancient, dying Crotani wretch in the pod. «As I told you, the inevitable time of its passing had arrived. I have known this being for its entire span of years. I harbor no ill will toward it. I merely wished to ease its passing. And also as I told you, you bear the mark of my elder. You must not be hindered. When your companion alerted me that you had been captured, I knew it was time that I intervened.»

«Thank you for saving my life.» Greymalkin timidly plucked up his courage, fighting to stay awake against the numbing anesthetic flooding his body and relieving his own pain. «But, why did the Aurelian cling to its existence here so long? Did my kind come here long ago? I have so many questions about this region! May I accompany you to learn from you?»

The overwhelming peace that the Clavisian radiated was soothing him further, and Greymalkin felt his eyelids drooping as the vast being communed with him. The last glimpse of the golden pod disappeared into the Clavisian's bulk, and the foul synesthetic stench of the Aurelian disappeared with it. In the sudden absence of the oppressive reek it was almost as if a gentle aromatic incense had surrounded them. The Clavisian began to rise into the dark starlit sky.

«No. Even I may not deter you. You must continue on the way. Have no fear. You will find your path.» The warm presence of the

Clavisian faded as the huge being dwindled at an improbable speed into the stars, and Greymalkin fell into an untroubled sleep.

In an altogether too brief time, someone was shaking him awake. A female voice was calling to him close to his ear, although the sound of the voice was muffled by his helmet. He groggily came awake, and found himself staring into Tatter's concerned brown eyes a few centimeters outside the helmet. "Grey! You're awake! We can't get the void suit off you. Can you deactivate it? I need to get you into the medical pod!"

"Yeah, give me a moment..." He found the correct mental command, and the helmet retracted back over his head and the frontal suit seal came loose down his chest to his waist. He started to fumble at the lapels feebly, but Tatter seized him and efficiently stripped the golden suit off of him in a second, and then startled him by peeling off all his undergarments in the next second. She lifted him up with one hand and stuffed him into the medical pod, unceremoniously snugging the connectors manually onto various places all over his nude body with her other hand even before the pod could attach them itself. Her touch in intimate places left him tingling. Greymalkin cleared his throat, and lifted his eyebrows.

"I take it that you've had medical training—" he began pointedly, before Tatter firmly shoved an oxygen tube down his throat and a breathing mask over his mouth, cutting off his statement. She had applied all of the connectors proficiently and was already adjusting the various pod settings manually.

"Luckily for you!" she snapped. "You're bleeding out inside, dummy. I don't know what in all space that void suit's made out of, but you might seriously consider giving me the release codes for it in case this happens again. It's way too tough to cut open. I tried."

Since he could no longer speak, Greymalkin communed blearily. «I didn't know you were the designated medic here.»

Tatter snorted and put her warm hand on his forehead for a second, still looking at the pod controls. "*Somebody* needs to fix up you two lunkheads when you're too stupid to dodge, and I guess it's going to be me." She glanced to the side in irritation at Bruno where the glossy black rock form of the protean floated silently, and then back to the pod controls.

Greymalkin's eyebrows went up and he looked over at Bruno, remembering when the protean's fragment had turned into a puddle on the floor. «What!? Was she actually able to heal *you* when you got blasted?»

"More like collected all the crispy remaining *chunks* and got him out of there before they could finish him off," Tatter said. "You two idiots don't have enough sense to stay out of trouble." She shut the cover of the medical pod over him, and her voice became muffled again. "You know, all you have to do is run in the *opposite* direction from what's trying to kill you, not *toward* it. It's really not a terribly difficult strategy, you ought to try it sometime."

Bruno's heavy, low growl was stiff and annoyed when the protean finally spoke. "Your assistance was indeed timely, Sylphid. I have already complemented you."

Tatter stood with her hands on her hips scowling at the protean. "How about a '*thank you*' then? Seriously, Grey, your monster here is just rude."

Amen to that, Greymalkin thought. The pain of his injuries had been numbed, but he forced himself back to full wakefulness for a moment and tried to mentally sort through everything that had just happened. Tatter sat down next to the medical pod with her arms and legs crossed, looking from him to Bruno in annoyance before leaning back in the seat.

"So was it worth it?" she asked scornfully. "Did you find out anything from that lunatic nightmare? Or was it just a waste of time and a set of near death experiences for everyone?"

«It was worth it. I *think* it was, anyway.» Greymalkin lay in the pod feeling numb all over except inside, where the needle sensations of micro-runcible probes were lancing through his organs and deftly mending injuries. He bit down on the oxygen tube and tried to ignore it. Tatter evidently caught sight of the twinge, and looked worried.

"Do you want me to put you under again?" she asked. He thought he could hear genuine concern in her voice.

«No, I've slept enough.» He frowned and began a centering prayer to focus his mind, but Tatter kept talking, somewhat nervously.

"I don't understand any of this. What *was* that thing on the planet? An Abyssal? Really? Why did it try to kill us?" She looked at Bruno again, with a questioning expression. "And what in all space was that *other* thing that you contacted? Was it the other Abyssal that Grey was talking about before? How did you know to do that, to contact it?"

"You accuse *me* of imprudence, Sylphid," Bruno rumbled. "But I pay attention. The monk gave me the idea. When he was first captured he said that we should have approached the *other* being, the one in the big nebula, and *not* the aggressive one in that fortress. And then, after I recovered from the attack of the aggressive one and went to spy surreptitiously as it was interrogating the monk, I overheard it confess its *fear* of the one in the nebula."

Greymalkin mulled over what the Aurelian had said to him again. He had been so petrified with fear when it had been questioning him in the assay chamber that he had not fully absorbed the things it had said. But now the cold words amid the rotting stench of the Aurelian's innards rang in his mind.

«It was paranoid.» Greymalkin felt nothing but disgust remembering the creature and its thoughts. «It was paranoid, afraid...

and *greedy*. Incredibly greedy and grasping. It wanted to hold fast everything it had taken here. That big yellow star... the Aurelian was mining a huge amount of shadow aureate and jewels from it. And it was collecting other things as well, secret things. Those images were behind all of its thoughts, an obsession with its 'treasures'. I've never felt such avarice in another being. It was in so much pain, but all it cared about was clinging to what it had taken. The star. Its slaves. Its wealth. Its dominance. And its miserable life. It was so *old*....» Greymalkin thought about the terrifying and shocking extent of the miserly obsessions he had sensed in the thoughts of the Aurelian. *It had such a huge mind, and yet it was so preoccupied with such pointless greed.* The thought sickened him.

And there had been something else lurking in the thoughts and statements of the Aurelian. The Aurelian had been *desperately* interested in the covenants in his mind, even more so than the star, its resources, or its slaves. That lurking desire was linked to its thoughts about the obscure secret treasures it had mentioned, the *Forge* and the *Nexus*. If anything, that craving had seemed even more frenzied than its other grasping desires. Greymalkin didn't understand what it meant, at least not yet, but somehow those memories bothered him more than anything else about the Aurelian.

"Hmph. He just sounds like *most* of the goons I meet around here," Tatter grumbled, scowling and folding her arms even more tightly. "And it also doesn't sound like you learned much of anything from him."

«That's not true.» Greymalkin felt a grim kind of depressing satisfaction. «There were impressions in its thoughts, images and details that I have to sort through to fully understand them. It was obsessed with two things that it called the *Forge* and the *Nexus*. I don't have any idea what those things are yet, but I learned one thing that's *immediately* useful. There's apparently a fellow that's actually been creeping around here for *three centuries*. The Aurelian hated him, but even with all of its power the Abyssal somehow couldn't catch this man. I want to seek him out. I think he may have some answers to my questions. I just have to find him, now.»

Tatter looked intrigued. "Wow. Okay, you've got my attention. So, who is this secretive person anyway?"

«Some Xenocorpsman named Alexander Borgess. His entries and observations are all through the Xenocorps records of their expedition three hundred years ago. Somehow he's apparently still alive after all this time, but Providence knows where he is.» Greymalkin felt a sinking sense of exhaustion. How could he find one man in all of the Carinae?

"Borgess?" Tatter had a puzzled look. "I think I might know that guy, or at least I think I've heard people use that name for a man that came in my tavern every once in a while."

«What!» Greymalkin ruefully wondered why it should surprise him that Tatter would know the man. A tavern keeper as chatty and sociable as Tatter would likely know almost every human in the entire region. «Well, where is he? What do you know about him? You actually know this man Borgess?»

"He goes by a lot of different names," Tatter said thoughtfully. "I've also heard people call him Xander, and he introduced himself to *me* as Sandy. But, yes, I remember that sometimes they called him Borgess as well. He's a weird guy. Uh, see, his head is really odd..."

Greymalkin grimaced and suddenly felt incredibly exasperated. «Wait, don't tell me. He has an artificial brain.»

Tatter looked astounded. "How did you know that? I thought you said you didn't know him!" Greymalkin groaned inside the medical pod. His entire body felt numb now with anesthetic, and his own head was swimming.

«I think I've met him as well. He told me his name was *Lex*. Yeah, strange fellow.»

Bruno spoke up then, the protean's almost subsonic growl reverberating through the cabin, "I recall that encounter, monk. The individual you reference was indeed unusual. It appeared to be a human being superficially, but it had a tremendously extended set of shadow space chambers surrounding it, linked through its cranium. I thought it remarkable."

«I didn't sense that!» Greymalkin felt annoyed with Bruno again. «You observed all *that* and didn't even comment on it to me?»

"I have no idea what you can and cannot discern, human!" Bruno growled. "I definitely thought that this individual was worthy of further investigation, but you were in need of funding at the time, and I became engrossed with the ill-advised scheme to threaten the Sylphid."

"Gee, well-done you stupid rockhead!" Tatter snapped. Greymalkin sensed Bruno bristling with anger and felt irritated at both of them. Royce whined over the helm link at the increase in angry emotions inside him.

«Will you two stop arguing! We're finally onto something here!» Greymalkin was glad to see both of the aliens subside. «Now, Tatter, where is this Borgess, Sandy, Lex, or whatever he's calling himself?»

"I don't know exactly where he goes," Tatter said, thinking it over. "But I remember that a lot of the miners said that when they see him leaving the main base that he heads away toward the big channelway, you know that huge one on the other side of this cluster. Nobody knows why though. He's a big mystery."

«I thought you said you never saw anyone go prospecting alone and come back?» Greymalkin felt increasingly woozy with the anesthetics coursing through him. And he ached in places he hadn't known were inside of him.

Tatter shook her head. "He doesn't go prospecting, or at least I don't think he does. He never sells any jewels, shadow flux... or *anything*. He just comes in occasionally to resupply and then goes out again. Nobody knows who funds him, and he doesn't make much sense when you try to talk to him. He keeps to himself, mostly."

«We've got to find him.» Greymalkin started to open the medical pod, but found that he was so dizzy that he could barely move now. Tatter saw him moving weakly, and jumped up to put her hand on the lid of the pod.

"Oh no you don't! You just sleep. I can pilot our buddy Royce here," she said, glaring at him through the transparent cover. Greymalkin thought about the absurdly complex path he'd taken to get to the system and shook his head.

«It's too twisted a path out of here through the cluster. You got lost before, you won't make it.» He scanned outward, trying to figure out where they were, but shadow space simply whirled through his perception incomprehensibly. *I can't pilot like this*, he thought in frustration. Tatter touched something on the pod controls, and he began to feel even more sleepy.

"Rest now," Tatter said assertively. "Rockhead and I will figure it out." The cabin spun around him even more and Greymalkin slid into restless unconsciousness.

For a long time he drifted in and out of fitful sleep. His synesthesia woke him up occasionally when he sensed particularly violent stellar radiation coursing outside Royce's hull. The pseudo-sensations were like blasts of frigid wind, and they frightened him into brief wakefulness every time, with the associated pseudo-sight confronting his shadow sense of a glittering multi-colored plane sloping downward at an insane slanting angle for light-years ahead of them. He could sense Tatter in the helm link with Royce, and he could tell she was not particularly comfortable steering the ship across, up, and down the treacherous shadow planes of the Carinae. Royce could sense her hesitation as well, and there were many times that the cyneget shuddered through a sloped shadow surface or even balked completely when Tatter tried to urge him across a particularly acute plane. It felt terrifying to wake up in the middle of a whirling emergency spin, wondering if Royce's manifold was about to be annihilated. He only slept soundly when Tatter brought them out of shadow space to catch some sleep herself. He could feel Bruno's sullen presence in the cabin as well, and had a suspicion that the protean was still recovering from the Aurelian's attack. It made for a very unsettled recuperation period.

* * *

There finally came a day when he felt well enough to climb out of the medical pod, painfully pull on the golden void suit, and then weakly limp through the cabin to where Tatter sat dozing in the cockpit seat. She woke up at his approach, and he saw the shadows of exhaustion under her eyes as she simply looked at him with silent fatigue. Although they were parked temporarily in normal space, Greymalkin wanted to know their situation, so he scanned their surroundings with his shadow sense.

He stifled the urge to gasp in fright. Royce was perched on a tiny hyperspatial location that was barely stable enough for them to have a prayer of regaining a hold on the nightmarish topography of the shadow plane surfaces around them. When Tatter saw his reaction she simply looked defeated and said, "Yeah. I think we're stuck here. I can't find a way through all these crazy risky inclines and paths. I'm not even sure I can get us back the way we came. I think it's your turn now."

Greymalkin refocused his eyes, looking down at her hunched and weary shoulders, and he suddenly felt guilty. While he'd been uselessly recuperating, she'd been doing her best to honor his request and help. She stood up and pointedly sat down in the copilot's seat, looking at him in resignation. After a moment, he nodded slowly and carefully stepped into the pilot seat, wincing as he did so. Even with the medical pod working on him for several days, although his broken ribs had more or less healed they still ached a bit whenever he inhaled deeply. He connected with the Helm Link and checked Royce's subsystems. The cyneget was extraordinarily fatigued as well, but the cyborg's attention perked up at the touch of his mind.

"I can take it from here," he said, quietly feeling ashamed at having left so much of the difficult passage to Tatter. *I'm supposed to be the pilot here, and the whole thing was my idea.* He studied the planar potentials around them, analyzing the possible paths down toward the huge channelway he could see not too far in the distance. "Where's Bruno?"

Tatter gestured over her shoulder, and Greymalkin saw the protean packed into a corner of the cabin like a compact black boulder. She said in a low voice, "He hasn't moved at all for more than a day. I think he was a lot more damaged in that fight than we knew."

The low rumble of the protean's voice issued from the boulder like a distant mountain quake, "I can hear you conversing about me, Sylphid; you must be aware of that."

"Fine!" Tatter snapped back. "So, what's the story, then? Are you back in the game or what?" The black boulder seemed to shudder and then ooze toward them both, finally assuming the half melted, vaguely humanoid form that Bruno sometimes took when the protean felt like talking. It was only the height of a child, but the massive limbs stuck out on either side of it in a way that looked menacing even when it became almost motionless.

"I was... slightly affected by the Abyssal's weapon; it was far more powerful than any I have encountered in a very long while. But, I have recovered," Bruno growled finally. "Where are we going next, monk?"

As he continued methodically checking Royce's organs and systems, Greymalkin was also scanning the length of the gigantic channelway in the two directions that it stretched away from them. He tried to gauge how big its core radius was, but the readings he got didn't seem possible. It was by far the biggest shadow space channel he'd ever encountered. "Have either of you ever navigated that channel?"

Tatter seemed taken aback, saying, "No way! I'm not even a pilot, really. I mean, I can steer Royce here, at least a little. But I generally try to stick to civilized areas that aren't going to immediately kill me. My personal multimodal shadow space drive is pretty limited. That channel looks... awful."

Greymalkin grimaced and nodded. *I can't fault her for that*, he thought, and turned to the slowly simmering protean. "What about you, Bruno?"

"What do you mean?" the protean's voice reverberated. "You know that I was imprisoned for an inordinate amount of time after being subdued in a different part of the galaxy. In any event, my ability to travel between the stars is constrained to the shadow plane and the shadow volume. I am unable to traverse shadow space channels."

Greymalkin's eyes widened. "That's right, I forgot. But Royce's drive is configured *solely* for planar movement in shadow space. That means...." He looked back to Tatter, who looked incredulous.

"Oh, you have got to be joking!" she snorted. "I have to bail you guys out again? You want me to go transit that huge channel with my crappy little personal multi-modal unit?"

"Uh, it may be worse than that," Greymalkin said apologetically, thinking back to what the Aurelian had said. "Apparently this guy we're looking for can submerge deeper into shadow space channels, all the way down into the subchannel dimensions. Ah, can you do that?"

Tatter glared at him for a moment, before rolling her angry brown eyes to the side. "If I *have* to," she finally said. "But my multi-modal is even *slower* in subchannelways. Do you really need this guy that badly?"

Greymalkin thought about it, and then shrugged. "Never mind. You've already done more than your share. I'm just not sure what else to try...."

"Oh, *stuff* that!" Tatter barked at him. "I'll go find your mystery man. That is, if you can even get us from here all the way down to the edge of that big channel."

Greymalkin grinned appreciatively and said, "*Thanks, Tatter!* You're the best! I owe you *another* one. Okay, then; away we go! Hold onto your rear ends!" He urged Royce into shadow space, and the cyneget dutifully launched itself without any hesitation. He marveled again at how loyal the cyborg was to him. Then he was totally occupied with navigating the mind-boggling shadow planes of the Carinae.

The transit down through the chaos of paths was terrifying, but he'd fully linked with Royce now and their minds were operating virtually as one mental process. After only a few moments of the frenetic pace, he simply closed his eyes tightly to concentrate on his shadow sense. Because the shadow space synesthesia of the transits were bewilderingly distracting, he had to force himself to focus solely on finding the proper shadow paths with his mind, sorting through and interpreting the brilliant colors, deafening sounds, and other illusory resonance sensations from the shadow jewel in his head.

He was only able to make sense of the resonance signals from the shadow jewel because he had trained as a pilot from childhood. His psyche was instinctively translating the subtle energy differences and transit potentials of the shadow space around them as intuitive concepts like *cliffs* and *drops*, even though it was all just hyperspatial transit potentials. Although normal human senses could not even perceive shadow space, to his shadow senses it felt as if he was urging Royce to deliberately leap down insanely plunging paths through the blazing cerulean blue lights and roaring winds of shadow space that the big jewel in his head revealed to him.

Greymalkin knew that not long ago he would never have even considered attempted these kinds of absurdly risky planar transits. What was different now was the way that he and Royce had bonded and now trusted one another. It amplified their perceptions and confidence. There were several times over the next few hours that he could distinctly hear Tatter shriek in fear or curse a blue streak in her own language as they shot across gaps or down energy inclines. He found that he was grinning maniacally through much of it, even as he gasped in pain from his ribs whenever he flinched involuntarily during a drop or plummet that threatened to shatter their manifold and disintegrate them all. When he finally brought the starship to a halt next to the big shadow channel and opened his eyes to the cabin again, Tatter looked positively panicked.

"Remind me to never try a steeplechase with you," she muttered. "For a human, you're out of your ever-loving mind."

"Thanks, Tat!" he said with a wide smile, and then sobered as he looked at the roaring violence of the channel current. "Uh, are you *sure* you still want to go out into that?"

"Feh!" Tatter exclaimed. "It'll be a relief after your driving!" She stood up and began changing into her alien form, rapidly shrugging out of her jumpsuit. By the time she crossed the short distance to the airlock she was so big that she could barely fit inside the cabin. Then a stray thought crossed Greymalkin's mind.

"Hey, Bruno," he called over his shoulder to the seemingly inert protean. "Can you do your sensory linking trick to keep us in communication with Tatter?"

The protean wordlessly shed two small black splatters, each of which flew to perches on his shoulder and Tatter's head. She showed her monstrous fangs to them both as she hefted the runcible she used as a weapon. When she spoke, her voice had become garbled through her alien jaws and deepened with her much larger torso, to the point that it was almost as low as Bruno's heavy growl.

"*Wish me good hunting,*" Tatter growled, and shut the airlock behind her with an immense clawed hand almost as wide across as his outstretched arms.

"Yeesh, that's our girl," Greymalkin winced, and watched through the view port as she flew away from the ship toward the torrent of stars, and then vanished into her own shadow space manifold. He watched her as she shunted through shadow space until she hit the edge of the big channel, at which point her manifold accelerated to a superluminal speed and she became hard to follow in the distance. Greymalkin quickly realized that they would need to follow her as best they could on the shadow plane near the channel or risk completely losing track of her. As he took Royce into shadow space, racing along behind her on the closest shadow plane he could find, he decided to try the communications relay through Bruno. «Hey, Tatter! Are you receiving? That channel is awfully big and fast; we don't want to lose you out there.»

«Receiving you fine, Grey.» Her thoughts were very tense, and he was surprised to find that Bruno's relay link could still transmit full sensory perceptions. He could feel the tug of vacuum across her armored skin and even some of her synesthetic perceptions through shadow space, which he realized were very different from his own. Greymalkin knew that his own synesthesia was very atypical in that he sensed temperatures in an inverted manner; the hotter a star was, the *colder* it seemed to his synesthesia. But Tatter felt and heard the blazing heat from all the stars she was passing like brightly thrumming furnaces around her. Her reversed synesthesia was all the more disorienting to him. As he tried to follow her flickering manifold in the huge channel, he realized she was pulling away from them. The transit potential in the big channel was giving her a large speed advantage over Royce on the plane.

«Tatter, can you heave to? You're leaving us hard up.» Greymalkin was starting to worry about even keeping track of her in the distance.

«Heave what? *All of these monk-spacers use weird jargon...*» Tatter's thoughts were so distracted that he could sense side-thoughts that she hadn't meant to transmit to him. He realized that he'd lapsed into arkspeak in his own distraction.

«I mean, *slow down*! You're leaving us with a problem; we're way too far behind you to be able to follow you!» His shadow sense followed a logarithmic scale of perception which allowed him to focus on objects billions of kilometers or even light-years away in shadow space, but Tatter was quickly growing more and more distant.

"I will be able to follow her more effectively in the shadow volume," Bruno rumbled. With that, the protean vanished into shadow space from inside the cabin. His communed thoughts continued, in his usual supercilious tone. «Besides, I'm much faster than either of you. If she leaves the channel she may require assistance.»

Greymalkin always found it impressive whenever Bruno transited through shadow space. As he watched the protean speed ahead through the shadow volume after Tatter's distant signal, Greymalkin could momentarily sense some of the protean's true mass, which was gigantic. The fact that Bruno had simply vanished into shadow space rather than leaving through the airlock was another reminder of the protean's capabilities. Greymalkin mulled on the enormous technological differentials between himself and his companions. The only objects humans were able to shift into shadow space were entire ships, and the transition was tricky even there. He still found it hard to believe that Tatter had a personal shadow space *pouch*. And Bruno's ability to arbitrarily shrink or grow his amorphous form into and out of shadow space was baffling. At times like this he felt quite primitive in comparison with the two aliens. He refocused on the daunting task he now faced of tracking *two* rapid targets transiting through different shadow spaces. Royce was racing along at a tremendous rate, but both Tatter and Bruno were *still* pulling away from him. Greymalkin urged the cyneget forward, dodging up and down to follow the contours of the shadow plane.

«I can't slow down!» Tatter's thoughts were still very agitated. He could tell she was casting her own shadow sense awareness around her, looking everywhere she could. «The current in this channel is too strong. And how in blazes am I supposed to find this guy out here? The channel goes on for parsecs!»

Bruno's steely thoughts rattled through them both, and Greymalkin noted with alarm that the protean's barely contained emotions had once again become intent and murderous all of a sudden. «I believe I have acquired his scent-trace. The monk was correct, you must transition into the subchannels, Sylphid.»

«Bruno, remember that we want to talk to this guy, not attack him!» Greymalkin once again felt frustrated by the protean's mindless aggression. The alien cyborg was almost as much of a liability as an asset.

«Do not worry, human.» The protean's thoughts bubbled with amusement. «It is very entertaining to observe your surprise every time we suffer unprovoked assaults. Sylphid, you are approaching the locus of the traces I am detecting. You must submerge now.»

«Gotcha, rockhead.» Tatter's thoughts were barbed and taunting toward Bruno, but she was still on edge as she plunged deeper into shadow space. Greymalkin's anxiety grew as he realized that he had now completely lost her signal in his shadow sense, even though he was still linked to her thoughts through Bruno. He could feel the way that the stars faded around her in her shadow sense. She felt much as he had when he'd descended to reach her in the mine, with an oppressive sense of crushing depth around her.

«Okay, I'm in the subchannel.» Tatter said, glancing around her. «I don't sense anything here, though. Bruno, are you sure... wait a minute. My manifold feels strange. I feel like... well, as if something is near me in shadow space or something....»

«TAKE EVASIVE ACTION!» Bruno's roaring thoughts startled Greymalkin, but Tatter instantly dodged sideways in shadow space, just as something enormous emerged from shadow space *into her manifold around her*. Greymalkin could not make out what the shape was. It didn't seem to register in Tatter's synesthesia at all, and looked utterly bizarre to her visually, as if it was and was not there. Greymalkin belatedly realized that Tatter could apparently see in *infrared*. Visually, the shapes were black against the black field of the inside of her manifold, but in the infrared she could see geometric composite shapes like the claws of a huge grapple hundreds of meters across snatching at her.

«*Yeeoowr!*» Tatter's thought was somewhere between a screech and a snarl in her mind as she twisted wildly in her manifold, kicking at the closest of the huge claws coming at her. Through the link, Greymalkin felt the same sensations that Tatter did, the metallic *clang* that rippled heavily up through her leg as her armored foot slammed into the nearly invisible grasping talon. The impact slammed her away from the clutch of the thing for only a moment. Whatever it was, the thing was *inside* her shadow space manifold with her, clenching around her with a vise-like grip that she would not be able to avoid.

«Tatter! No-no-no....» Greymalkin felt horrified as he felt her desperate lunges. *I should never have asked her to go down there! That thing's going to grab her!*

In the split second that she had before the sharp edges of the claws closed on her, Tatter desperately thrust the long alien runcible in the direction of the immense invisible hand, and touched the extension control that sent the invulnerable blade around and through shadow space into whatever was on the inside of the grappling claws. The huge geometric claw seemed to ripple for an instant and then simply vanished.

«*Crap! Sarding crap! What-is-it, what-is-it, what—??*» Tatter's thoughts were panicked, and she was dodging furiously in random directions in shadow space, coming back up into the main channel and trying to reach the edge so that she could escape from the powerful current that was hurling her forward. Just as she reached the edge of the channel the dark claws emerged out of shadow space from the inside of her manifold around her once more. She snarled, kicking them away and trying to jab the runcible into the center of the claws once again. But this time, two of the claws smashed together on the runcible, fixing it at an angle directed away from the center of the hand. Greymalkin gasped, trying franticly to think of something, *anything*, to do to help Tatter.

Then Bruno's overwhelming communal roar startled him again, and the protean emerged inside Tatter's manifold just in time to crash against the giant claws before they closed on her. The protean had also swelled into mammoth dimensions, and charged past Tatter to collide with the grapple-limb, throwing it back into shadow space. Tatter wasted no time, skimming back across the shadow plane to where Royce and Greymalkin were barreling toward her.

Greymalkin kept his attention partly on her, partly on the treacherous shadow plane contours that surged up and down unpredictably as Royce tried to maintain speed, and partly on the savage wrestling match going on in shadow space at the edge of the huge channel. The geometric shapes of the pitch black claw were dissolving and reforming in a chaotic swirl with Bruno's similarly morphing form. It was virtually impossible to understand anything that was happening visually as the chaos of complicated glowing black boulder outlines that made up Bruno smashed violently against the shifting granular shapes of his opponent inside the darkness of Bruno's manifold. Then the claws disappeared once more, and Bruno was first left flailing against nothing and then consolidating into a defensive mass. Greymalkin could tell Bruno was keenly peering around through shadow space seeking for the claw.

Greymalkin scanned ahead with his synesthesia, looking for the protean's manifold against the trillions of kilometers of the channel's dazzling hyperspatial span. He could spot the remote form of Tatter's manifold fleeing back towards him, but even his acute synesthetic senses could not make out anything else against the havoc of the channel. Yet, he could feel every bit of Bruno's fury through the communal link, and knew the alien cyborg was eager to fight.

«Bruno, *stop*! We're trying to talk to this guy! He probably thinks we were trying to kill him.» Greymalkin tried to think of a way to send a signal through all the shadow space noise being generated by the channel.

«I *am* trying to kill him!» Bruno's thoughts bellowed. «The coward has dared to attack me, but lurks there in the channel where I cannot reach him!» The protean had rapidly scanned through an incredible range of shadow space senses that Greymalkin had not known Bruno possessed, and had actually succeeded in spotting his opponent, a vague blur now deep in the subchannel once again.

«Bruno, for the last time, *will you please stop!*» The vehemence of Greymalkin's thoughts surprised even Bruno, and the protean stopped flitting back and forth along the edge of the channel and simply glowered toward where their unknown assailant was somehow circling, out in the flow of the subchannel. Tatter arrived skimming next to Royce, and breathlessly re-entered the little rover starship through the airlock. When she emerged from the airlock in human form, once again clad in Bora's old jumpsuit, she looked disheveled and shaken. She jumped into the copilot seat next to Greymalkin, and pulled up her knees with her arms.

"I'm not going out there again," she said, her voice wobbly and rattled. She looked so frightened that Greymalkin impulsively put his arm around her shoulders and gave her a reassuring hug. She turned her wide brown eyes to him. "I've never seen *anything* like that before," she muttered. "It was like... fighting a ghost that wasn't even *there*."

Greymalkin nodded, frowning as he thought. As he considered possible next steps, Royce finally slowed to a halt and dropped out of shadow space near the literally fuming Bruno. Greymalkin could see the waves of angry heat pouring off the protean. He'd learned enough to give the alien cyborg's temper a few minutes to subside before trying to reason with it again. Then he started with something simple. «Hey, Bruno. Can you direct a communal signal at our spooky friend in the channel that's strong enough to reach it through all the channel noise?»

The protean whirled toward Royce's hull. «You wish to communicate with it?! After what it almost did to the Sylphid, stupid as she is?»

Greymalkin looked at Tatter. For once she didn't snap back at Bruno, but only managed to give him a faint and distracted smile in return. Where he still held her arm, he could actually feel her trembling, and he asked in genuine concern, "Are you okay, Tatter? Are you hurt?"

"Well, no," she answered, and then shuddered even more. "I'm not hurt. But that thing tried to kill me!"

"Let's find out," Greymalkin said. "Maybe it was just trying to capture and question you." As Tatter started to protest, he communed again with the protean. «Bruno, open the signal, please.»

The alien cyborg growled angrily for a moment, but then Greymalkin felt Bruno open the link. Greymalkin tried to fill his thoughts with cheerful feelings. «Greetings to the being in the channel! By any chance, are you Alexander Borgess? And, uh, do you perhaps go by 'Lex'?»

After only a moment or two, crisp thoughts responded. «Who wants to know?»

Greymalkin smiled. «I am Brother Greymalkin Thomas of the Sojourner Order. I believe we've met? At the main expedition base? You were kind enough to give me the table.»

Nothing came through the communal link for seconds while Greymalkin held his breath. Then thoughts that seemed surprised came back in response. «You're that kid I met? What are you doing all the way out here?»

«Looking for you! I just want to talk to you. Sorry for any misunderstanding.»

«Who was that Sylphid? Why did she come poking around in my subchannel? She damaged several of my storage lockers.» The communed thoughts seemed guarded, but not angry. Tatter, on the other hand, communed an angry response before Greymalkin could say anything to quiet her.

«Hey, pal, you tried to kill me! What did you think I'd do?» Tatter still looked shaken up by the encounter.

«I certainly was not trying to kill you, miss!» The communed thoughts seemed surprised again. «But... I can see why you might have misinterpreted that enclosure maneuver. However, listen to me, you can't be too careful with unexpected visitors out here.»

Before Tatter could compose a spluttering rejoinder, Greymalkin sent a cheery response. «You know, my friend Tatterdemalion here says the same thing to me all the time, mister Lex! I bet you two would get along well.»

«Is that *Tatter*? The young lady back at the tavern?» The communed thoughts seemed incredulous. «She's really a Sylphid? I always thought she was a human.»

«I'm not in the tavern business anymore.» Tatter folded her arms next to Greymalkin, scowling as she communed. «And I'm only *half* Sylphid, and you shouldn't *scare the living crap* out of people, and—»

«I'm really sorry to have scared you, miss. You were always nice to me when I visited. But why are you out here? And what is that other thing that attacked my lockers? That thing like a tornado of rocks?» The communed thoughts seemed somewhat guarded once again.

«That's just Bruno, and he can't help it, he's a reprobate.» Greymalkin hurriedly continued as the protean bristled. «But he means well; he was just concerned about Tatter's safety. Hey, I've got a bunch of questions. Can we talk?»

«Did you say you were a Sojourner?» The thoughts seemed very sharp around the last word, and Greymalkin silently prayed that the man was not opposed to Sojourners for some bizarre reason.

«Uh, yes, I did.» Greymalkin found himself tensing again. «You see, I was sent here by this woman named Kuanian—»

«*Kuanian* sent you?» The man's communed thoughts suddenly changed in tone and seemed hopeful. «She's why I came back here after all this time. And I'm a Sojourner as well. Or at least I used to be. I left the Order a long time ago. Sure, I'd be happy to talk to you kid, as long as your friends aren't still upset with me.»

«Great!» Greymalkin felt the tension lifting off his shoulders, although he was still confused. Lex was a *Sojourner*? «Will you come out and meet with me? I'm in a cyneget rover and can't enter the channel.»

«Yeah, sure. Give me a minute....» The communal link cut off. Bruno circled around Royce's hull, obviously still agitated and suspicious.

«Do you actually trust this individual?» The protean's thoughts growled with barely subdued wariness.

«Bruno, do *not* cause any more conflicts!» Greymalkin held his forehead for a moment, but then sensed that the angry energy had leaked out of the protean as quickly as it had boiled up when the fight had started. It amazed him how quickly the alien cyborg's emotional state could change. Greymalkin communed his thoughts. «This is the first potentially helpful contact we've made! I wonder what kind of starship he has....»

They watched for long moments. Then what appeared to be a barely discernable black dot emerged from the channel and came toward them rapidly. Greymalkin scanned it in confusion as the tiny black object drifted toward Royce, right up to the front airlock. It was hard to make out the shape of the small geometric box-like object against the black of space except when it crossed in front of the brilliant stars and nebulae. After scanning it with his amplifier, Greymalkin finally understood that it was a pitch black rhombic dodecahedron, a box with diamond-shaped facades. But the thing was *less than two meters across.*

«Permission to come aboard, Brother Thomas?» The thoughts of Lex were still crisp, and very polite. Greymalkin blinked.

«Uh, sure, I guess. I mean, yes, please come aboard!» Greymalkin opened Royce's airlock uncertainly. Tatter jumped to her feet and glanced at him uncertainly.

"Are you sure about this?" she almost whispered to him. Greymalkin cautiously got out of the pilot seat, wincing at the pain in his ribs.

"As sure as I'm going to be about anything anymore," he muttered. "C'mon let's go meet this guy." As they walked to the airlock hesitantly, Bruno appeared in the cabin, once more in his slowly morphing child-height form.

"It will be most entertaining if this individual kills you both when you meet in person, human," the protean rumbled. Greymalkin glared at Bruno, but then limped to the airlock. It had already cycled, so he opened it and went in. The black box was sitting on the deck as they approached it uncertainly. Greymalkin stood looking at it, wondering what would happen.

Then the black box simply faded away as if it had never been there, leaving behind a man sitting in a meditative pose on the deck. Greymalkin took half a step back, stupidly wondering where the box had gone.

The man stood up and stretched. He was recognizably the same man that Greymalkin remembered meeting in the tavern, with the same weathered features, close-cropped blond hair, and ancient flight suit. He stood slightly taller than Greymalkin. The young Sojourner noticed now that the man had a set of cryptic, unfamiliar tattoos on his temples.

"Good to see you again," the man said, gazing down at Greymalkin, Tatter, and Bruno with a slight, almost sad smile. "What did you want to talk about, then, kid?"

Greymalkin looked at the deck again, in bewilderment at where the box no longer was, and then at the strange fellow who very much looked as if he might have just stepped out of three centuries ago. *Finally, someone that wants to <u>talk</u> to me and not kill me*, Greymalkin mused. *Well, this is progress....*

Chambers

Greymalkin nodded and took another slightly limping step forward, all the while looking over the tall man uncertainly. Out of the corner of his eye he noticed that Tatter, still spooked, had actually stepped behind him and was peeping over his shoulder at Lex. That struck him as funny, given that she was a hundred times more physically capable of dealing with any threat than he was. Then Greymalkin simply stepped up to the man and purposefully put out his hand. He had a strong suspicion that this strange individual was yet another of the Risen. Knowing by now what would likely happen if he physically touched Lex, Greymalkin grit his teeth and thought, *I may as well get this part over with....*

The high forehead of the man wrinkled in skeptical curiosity, but he put out his hand and clasped Greymalkin's in a firm grip.

The young Sojourner grimaced and, as he had anticipated, there came a brief moment of disorientation when the airlock around him vanished. He found himself on the surface of an airless, dead planet surrounded by craters beneath a black sky crowded with magnificent blue and white stars. There was a human in an old-style void suit lying before him, weakly trying to push itself up out of the regolith. As the helmet angled up to look at Greymalkin, he saw that it was the man Lex, his eyes gaunt and trickling blood from his eyes and nose. The expression on his face was one of resigned despair as he communed shaky thoughts. «All right, I give up. You have a deal.» Lex collapsed back into the dust and his own shadow. Following a sudden instinct,

Greymalkin looked down at the shadow he was casting across the dead surface in this hallucination. Just before the vision faded, Greymalkin saw that his own shadow was growing, spreading out toward the collapsed man on the ground, and was not the shadow of a human being but something gigantic and monstrous.

Greymalkin shuddered, coming back to himself, and released Lex's hand. The older man peered at him for a moment, but made no comment. Instead, he looked beyond Greymalkin and then stepped up to Tatter. He smiled gently, but Tatter glared at him and backed away further.

"Susan Scrofa Shelley," he said, making the name sound like a pronouncement. "I definitely owe you an apology. I'm very sorry."

Tatter's eyebrows went up, and then she scowled. "I don't use that name anymore. How do you even know it? I'm *Tatterdemalion* now. And what in all space were you trying to do to me out there, anyway?"

"Just trying to restrain you," Lex said amiably, folding his arms. Then his smile went away. "I don't get many visitors. Anyone I find out here... well, believe me when I say that simply *restraining* someone is me being *friendly*. Again, sorry. No hard feelings, please, miss."

Tatter glared at him, but then shrugged and nodded. Lex turned to study the floating mass of Bruno, and squinted at the protean for a moment before blinking and standing up straighter. He slowly walked around the morphing stone clusters of the alien cyborg, staring.

"So it *is* you," Lex said in a sour, disapproving tone. "I didn't recognize you at first; you aren't quite like the old accounts describe you. And you've been gone for a *very* long time. But now you're loose again, God help us all."

"What is your complaint?" Bruno rumbled. "You were fortunate that I did not kill you. We have never fought before today, and most do not survive their first battle with me." Lex sniffed slightly, and shook his head.

"No, I doubt they would," Lex said. "And I agree, I was lucky. I hope I never have to fight you again. But then, you're following this young man, I see." He turned his attention back to Greymalkin and walked up to him once more, peering intently at Greymalkin's forehead. Lex's expression slowly changed to one of fascination, and when he finally spoke it was in a voice of puzzled wonder.

"Greymalkin Aquino Teilhard Thomas?" Lex said, in a tone of voice as if he was reading in dim light. The young Sojourner gaped and then frowned, shaking his head.

"I don't have any middle names," he said. The older man tilted his head, looking from Greymalkin's eyes to his forehead.

"Well, you apparently did once upon a time," Lex said, putting his hand to his chin. "The encoding is old, faint, and it's buried under the mass of those two huge cybernetic structures that are laid on top of your shadow jewel now. But that name was evidently what someone gave you when you were born."

Greymalkin felt light in his head, as if the atmosphere had leaked out of the airlock. "What... do... you... *mean*?" he said, his voice becoming more strident with each word. Lex seemed surprised.

"Has no one ever told you that?" the older man asked in disbelief. "I was reading from the beginning of a longer message that was encoded on your shadow jewel years ago, probably when they put it in you. The first line is all that's still coherent now, but that statement was very deeply imprinted on your jewel. Somebody, evidently one of your parents from what it says, wanted to make sure that line survived no matter what. I suppose it's logical that those around you never talked much about it, given what the *remainder* of the legible words say, but I'm surprised they never even *told you*!"

Greymalkin was pale and trembling as he said, "It's considered very bad manners to put a person's shadow jewel under close scrutiny. Well, in civilized space, that is. But even when I've had medical exams in the Order, no one ever told me about a message on my jewel."

"That encoding was buried pretty deep, long before those new layers on your jewel," Lex said thoughtfully. Then he fixed Greymalkin with a cold stare. "Sorry if that was rude to scan your jewel like that, but I've become cautious about knowing who I'm talking to over the years."

"What does the surviving sentence say, then?" Greymalkin asked. His mouth felt dry, and his voice came out raspy. Tatter stood behind Lex now, looking at Greymalkin while holding her hands up to her mouth in astonishment. Lex stared intently at Greymalkin's forehead again.

"To the Sojourners who will find my son," he began, speaking the words slowly, "please care for him, take him to a place of safety, and tell your Abbott, who will know what to do, because my son, named Greymalkin Aquino Teilhard Thomas, is at great risk for the following reasons." Lex looked down sadly to Greymalkin's pleading eyes. "That's all. The rest is too scrambled and faded for me to even guess at. And I'm rather good at guessing secrets."

Greymalkin's lower lip trembled, and then he cursed as violently as he ever had. No one said anything. He finally stopped and found there were tears in his eyes.

Lex was watching him with solemn expression, and finally broke the silence, "Those who raised you may well have kept the message from you for good reasons, because of whatever it originally said. But you are here now, and no longer with the Order? No one else has examined you or your shadow jewel and commented on any of these facts?"

"I haven't left the Order!" Greymalkin said fiercely, and the heat in his words surprised him more than anyone. "I just... I've been on my own for a while. I had to leave my ark to come here...." His mind was racing. He now wondered who among the brothers and sisters of the *Dragon King* had known but kept this information from him. And then something that Trystia had said to him when she had awoken came back to him, something that had struck him as odd at the time. *She said to me, 'perhaps it will be time for you to make some decisions of your own, about what to do with your life and to <u>learn some things</u> about yourself.'* And Trystia was one of the Sojourners that found me abandoned on that Bereft world as a baby.

He met Lex's gaze, noting the older man's sad but stern expression, and asked in choked words, dreading the answer, "Is it possible that the entire message could be recovered?"

"Not by me," Lex said. "Not with any instrumentality that I have, or that you are likely to gain access to." Greymalkin caught hold of the implication in the statement, like someone drowning and reaching for a lifeline.

"But such capabilities do exist?" Greymalkin pressed. When Lex hesitated, Greymalkin felt a pleading stream come out of his mouth uncontrollably. "There *are*, aren't there? Lex, Brother Borgess, whatever you would have me call you, please know how grateful I am for you telling me these basic facts that have been kept from me all these years. And I have so many questions for you on so many other matters, for instance, your own incredible story and what you have learned of the Carinae, all of which I am desperate to hear as well! But I am begging you, if you know of some way to recover the full message from my parent or parents, please help me! I know we've only just met, and I doubt I have anything to offer you that you would find of value. But, *please help me*!"

The eyes of the older man were emotionless, and again Greymalkin felt as if he was looking into two deep pools that had been long undisturbed. The gruesome hole in the man's head, where a living mind should have been, was disturbing to Greymalkin. It felt as if he was talking to a skull and not a man. But then Lex tilted that skull, and said quietly, "There may be a place. I can take you there, but...." Doubt seemed to cross the older man's face.

When Lex hesitated for long moments, Tatter spoke up while frowning and asked, "What? Is it dangerous or something?"

"No," Lex said hesitantly. "Not to me, and not to you. But there are reasons I have not gone there in years. It is a place of many secrets and hidden things, but also many answers to many questions."

"It sounds ideal, then!" Greymalkin said, excitedly. "Will you take us there? Perhaps we can talk on the way? I have so many questions for you! What—what then do you want me to call you, sir?"

"Lex will be fine," the older man said, still appearing doubtful. "And yes, I will show you the way."

"Do you want to come with us, here inside my cyneget, Royce?" Greymalkin asked. "Or do you want to travel in your.... I'm sorry, what exactly is the nature of your... conveyance?"

Lex smiled gently again as he noticed a twinge from Tatter once more. "My *lockers*. I have them with me, always, but I will be pleased to travel with you inside this handsome creature. Shall we, then?"

Greymalkin led the way out of the airlock to the cockpit, grinning madly, his mind still spinning from everything he had just learned. Tatter seemed to pluck up her courage and walked beside Lex, asking in her sweetest tone, "Yes, about those 'lockers'; what *are* they exactly? Did you say you have them with you? And please would you tell me, what do you keep *inside* them?" Lex only looked at her with puzzled amusement. She hit the airlock button, almost sealing Bruno inside. But the protean followed close behind the group, silently shrinking in size.

"My lockers are a special series of endlessly replicating stabilized shadow space manifolds, miss." Lex seemed distant as he spoke. "They can tessellate into virtually any shape, like the big claw I tried to grab you with. They can also fold up on top of each other, along with all their contents, into the prime locker that I arrived in. The lockers were created long ago in the very same place of many secrets where we are going. Once, I thought of the people there as my friends. They gave me the lockers when I became as I am now, but... perhaps for their own reasons."

"So where is this mysterious destination that we are going to, then?" Greymalkin asked Lex brightly while hopping into the pilot seat. He winced at the motion, because his ribs were still sore. Lex came up beside him, but did not sit down in the copilot seat. Instead he communed a progressively more detailed series of star charts, zeroing in on a bright blue star with an odd satellite, a swollen purple star.

"That's it," Lex said. "*That's* the destination. They may be able to assist you there." Greymalkin and Tatter looked at the strange purple star, and glanced at each other uncertainly.

"That star looks... odd," Tatter said with a troubled look. "The color seems slightly... *off* somehow." Greymalkin stared at the star, not saying anything. He'd never seen a star that color. In addition to the peculiar color, there actually seemed to be a variegated, subtle *pattern* in the star's light.

"I've amplified the image in this view," Lex said. "It's quite dim in comparison to its sister star there to the side. You wouldn't even notice it unless you were actively looking for it."

Tatter plopped into the copilot seat, watching Lex closely. "You said 'they' could help Grey?" Tatter asked. She was clearly suspicious now. "Who is 'they'?"

Lex studied her, and then Greymalkin. "There are four individuals there. They are specifically occupied with looking for *secrets*. If anyone can help you, they would be the ones."

"We've had some... *difficulties* with Abyssals recently," Greymalkin said in a subdued voice. "Is this destination safe?"

"They are not Abyssals," Lex said, shaking his head slightly. "And they're safe to approach. Well, as safe to approach as anyone here in the Carinae. I worked with them, in a manner of speaking, long ago. You see, we were all part of the last Xenocorps expedition."

Greymalkin blinked at that and hesitated before asking anything else, thinking carefully first. Instead, he went about launching Royce onto the path across the shadow plane that led to the strange purple star. The distance was not so great, but the end of the path gave him pause as he scanned ahead. His synesthesia began to show the luminous surface of glowing blue hues sliding past them as Royce accelerated diligently, a frigid pseudo-wind from the bright stars ahead blowing across his face.

He could tell several things from the way his mind interpreted the reversed sensations from his shadow jewel resonance signals. The fact that the illusory 'wind' he seemed to feel blowing in his face was so unbelievably cold meant that the stellar winds in normal space which Royce's manifold was skimming across were actually blazingly *hot*, hotter than anything they'd encountered yet. In the Carinae, that was saying a great deal. The stellar nurseries they were approaching must have terrifically energized levels of ionization in the nebulae there. He settled into the pilot seat, dividing his attention between the hazards of the shadow plane and Lex.

"So, it's really true?" Greymalkin asked. "You were a member of the first expedition?"

Lex looked down at his feet with a stony expression. Then he walked around the cockpit seats and sat down facing Greymalkin and Tatter, his knees up and his back against the bulkhead under the main viewport. He nodded, and said, "Yes. That was a very long time ago, but yes, I was a member of the mission crew."

"I was told that everybody in the original expedition *died*," Tatter said, rather bluntly Greymalkin thought in irritation. She was watching Lex keenly.

Lex did not look at them, but leaned his arms onto his knees and stared at nothing. "Not everybody," he said stoically. "But it's true that *almost* everybody was killed when the Carinans flooded back into the area. We didn't know anything about their pilgrimage migration cycle back then. They'd been gone for more than two years, and nobody had any reason to suspect that they'd return. But they came swarming back without any warning. We just weren't ready."

"How did you survive?" Greymalkin asked gently. Lex didn't respond at first, but finally took a slow breath and spoke.

"I'd made a mistake. Ironically, that mistake turned out to be what saved my life," he said. "I had misaligned one of our observation arrays, rather badly, actually. My commanding officer almost chewed my head off before sending me out alone to fix it. I was out in the middle of nowhere when the Carinans returned. They overwhelmed the main expedition bases and slaughtered everybody. All my friends. Everyone I knew or cared about. My sister and brother were there. They were the only family I still had at that point. It was...." The older man paused. His eyes and the device-filled skull looked very dead indeed. "Well, it was quite an experience. Losing everyone and everything. I didn't think I'd keep going. But I was Xenocorps, and the Corps drilled survival into us, even when we stopped *wanting* to survive."

"That's horrible," Tatter said quietly. Greymalkin said nothing. *So Lex lost everybody he cared about as well.* He tried not to think about Bora and Soren, but couldn't help it. He focused on avoiding a panic attack that would incapacitate him. Lex only cocked his head to the side and shrugged.

"Like I said, it was a very long time ago," he muttered. "And they all died quickly, I suppose. I think what happened afterwards was much worse for those of us that made it through the first few days. It's not worth talking about. Nothing but fear and suffering."

"The surviving expedition galleons made emergency departures, obviously. Those of us that were left behind knew that nobody could come back to pick us up. The last any of us saw, it was a running battle with the forward wave of the Carinans. I never knew about the one ship of survivors that made it all the way back to the Orion Arm. Well, not until much, much later. You asked me how I survived. Well, the Carinans hunted down almost everybody left behind and killed them brutally. Some groups made last stands at the outposts, but...." Lex shrugged again. "The only ones that survived were the ones that were lucky enough to be isolated like me, and who then became very good at hiding. For decades."

"You hid here... *for decades*?" Greymalkin asked in disbelief. He had only been in the Carinae for a few months, and had almost died repeatedly. And the Carinans weren't even here! He looked at Lex with a mix of sympathy and awe.

"Most of the survivors that tried to band together just attracted attention," Lex said. "I saw that early on, and stayed alone, avoiding most of the other survivors. I knew there were primitives here like the Crotani, old populations of Bereft aliens. I survived by seeking them out and learning how to avoid the Carinans from them. There were a few para-human groups in the expedition that could survive in vacuum and hid by just abandoning most of their technology. They also survived, but at a cost. They quickly became scattered, uncivilized Bereft tribes."

"I met a tribe of para-human Scorpians when I first arrived here," Greymalkin said, thinking about how he *still* hadn't returned with supplies to thank Bokin and the other Scorpians.

Lex's wooden expression broke in a rare moment when he actually seemed interested. "They're still alive then? Good. I haven't heard from them in many years."

"They saved my life," Greymalkin said. "But, yes, they had become Bereft. They'd forgotten where they came from, or who they even were, and they had no shadow space drives."

Lex appeared sad and looked down again. "Yes, that was the whole point. I suppose it *worked*, sort of, anyway. They became savages, but at least they lived. It was one way of surviving. The Carinans don't bother primitive cultures that lack interstellar capabilities. That's the same way the Crotani endured after journeying here a long time ago, although they can't survive in the vacuum. They live stranded inside ancient feral Nemora meta-tree environments, scattered here and there around the region, just like the one the new expedition took over."

"But how did you survive until *now*?" Tatter asked, persisting. "You still haven't said."

An even more distant look came into Lex's eyes. "A very few of us survived by... *other arrangements*. Arrangements that involved making *bargains* with the more powerful locals. I resisted that option for as long as I could, but it was finally the only option left to me. You see, although I had survived for many years on my own, finally I became ill and was dying. This is much too hazardous an environment for normal humans. Too many enemies, and far too much radiation. I had contracted a neurodegenerative malady that my very old and malfunctioning medical pod could not cure."

Greymalkin looked at the man's head again and could see where the story was going. "What did you do?" Greymalkin asked softly.

Lex gestured to his skull with a wan smile and said, "I came to an *arrangement* with one of the Abyssals called the Aurelian in exchange for advanced preservative neuro-technology... and *other* modifications. As individual neurons in my brain died, they were replaced with *synthetic* ones. Eventually... well, you see how it ended up eventually."

Tatter looked thoughtful, and said, "At least you're still here."

Lex glanced at her. "*Something* is still here, miss. I'm not exactly sure whether it's still the same person or not."

"What about the rest of you?" Tatter asked, blunt as ever. "I mean, your body?"

"The Aurelian knows of many strategies for obtaining biological longevity," Lex said. "That is his specialty. I was too stubborn to agree to his terms until my brain had greatly deteriorated, but once I made my bargain with him, he... *did things to me* that have, in addition to increasing my intelligence and many other abilities, preserved the rest of me ever since." Lex shrugged again, this time with a scowl.

Greymalkin wondered when or if he should share the news about the Aurelian. "Ah, do you still have your arrangement with the Aurelian?"

"No," Lex said. "In exchange for what he had given to me, he made me his *slave*. That went on for a long, long time. I had to adjust my mind to be a bit less emotional about things, or I certainly would have taken my own life." Lex said this in a completely flat tone. *That's... ghastly,* Greymalkin thought. "Eventually, after many years, I escaped him and the Carinae by buying passage on a Jotun hoard-lair that cycles through the Carinae periodically. The Aurelian never forgave me. He's tried to kill me ever since."

Bruno reminded them that he was still there by speaking, his profoundly deep voice rattling through them all, "I doubt that the creature will pose a problem for you any longer."

Greymalkin sighed as Lex turned an inquisitive expression toward him, and proceeded to tell the story of their encounter with the Aurelian, and the Abyssal's sad ending. By the end of Greymalkin's tale, Lex looked somber.

"So the old schemer is finally gone, then," Lex said. There was a morose note in his voice. "That's too bad. I suppose I should celebrate, but I stopped hating him years ago. Continuing to evade that evil old miser was one of the few interesting things that kept me mentally occupied."

"But you said you escaped with *Jotuns*," Greymalkin said, wondering momentarily if it could have been the same hoard-lair starship he'd traveled on. "Where did you go?"

"Home," Lex said, still glum. "I wanted to go home. At least, I thought I did. But when I finally got back to the Orion Arm...." He looked at Greymalkin with his frozen blue eyes. "I should have realized that it wouldn't feel like home anymore. Everyone I'd ever known was ancient history. I thought I might usefully pass on the information and... *other* assets I'd gathered. I still haven't told you everything about my lockers, but I'll get to that. Anyway, that was the time period when I sought to join your Order, the Sojourners. This must have been... hmm, almost seventy years ago."

"Uh, about that," Greymalkin said, reluctantly feeling skepticism creep into his mind. "The Order does *not* accept beings with synthetic minds to take vows."

Lex nodded. "That I well know! It took me fifteen years, and I had to take my petition to join the Order all the way to Vernalis, to the leaders of the Order. They finally granted me dispensation to be accepted as a brother advisor, based on the wealth of information I could offer the Order. But by then I was losing the will to continue doing much of anything." Lex had a numb, almost vacant expression. "I became an anchorite, a hermit in a remote eremitic skete. I probably would have eventually decided to die there some day, but I was approached by a woman and a man from Sadoria."

Greymalkin rubbed his eyes and groaned, "And the woman's name was Kuanian?"

"Indeed. From what you said earlier, I suppose she must have recruited you as well. We have this in common at least," Lex said, his wan smile returning. He stood up then and turned in the direction of their travel. "Look, there! We are approaching our destination."

Greymalkin had been watching as they grew closer and closer to the strange star. Now he had Royce drop out of shadow space at the edge of the system. As they all stared at the bizarre star, Greymalkin brought up his amplifier, adjusted the filters, and studied the star. He immediately saw what was making the star look so odd and gasped. Tatter glanced at him in confusion, and asked, "What? What's wrong?"

Greymalkin stared incredulously. "That star... it has a layer of objects orbiting closely around it. *Artificial* objects." As Tatter made a choked sound of disbelief, he used the amplifier again to magnify his shadow sense and examine the star from a distance. The strange speckled distortions were obvious now as dark shapes slowly transiting the star in myriad ordered patterns. Although the shapes looked tiny at this distance, the fact that they were discernable at all meant that they must be colossal beyond reckoning. The orbiting shapes were so thickly layered that he realized almost all of the star's reddish light was being obscured, making it appear purple from a distance. He looked to Lex, who simply stood there with his arms folded, evidently lost in thought. "Who are these individuals that we're seeking here, then? What are all those things in orbit around the star?"

Bruno rumbled impatiently in his basso profundo voice, "Obviously they are absorbing energy from the star. Whoever constructed this array has balanced the equilibrium of the resulting system carefully. The radiance reflected inward has changed the star, expanding it into a red giant that is easier to use as a radiant source of energy."

Greymalkin looked at the tableau again, trying to wrap his mind around what he was seeing. *Someone is using a star as a source of energy. An entire star....* He'd heard tales of similar feats by the Builders in distant locales, but it was still hard to believe it even though it was there in front of his eyes.

"My former colleagues' abode is there, in a shadow space suspended above the star," Lex said, bringing up the topography image again. Greymalkin studied the location in the chart and then scanned the area of shadow space with his jewel.

"We can't reach it," he said, looking at Lex and wondering why the man had brought them all this way for nothing. "*Obviously*. Royce's shadow space drive is configured for planar travel, not volume transits to reach spaces like that."

"Their location is undeniably quite secure, but we can reach it," Lex said with certainty. "We need to go to that location, *there*, and then I will ask them for admittance. They have a small star bridge conduit that we can then traverse."

Greymalkin thought about it. *A star bridge situated in that location would make a lot of sense, actually. It gives them a controlled access point, like a drawbridge in an ancient stone fortress.* He sent Royce into shadow space again, and directed the cyneget forward along the path Lex had indicated. As they approached it, he felt uncanny sensations in his synesthesia from the strange purple star. He could smell the crisp, fresh scent of terpenes, as if a forest of conifer trees was nearby. And there seemed to be subdued waves of rhythmic sounds from the star, like insects chattering in vast numbers. Greymalkin had never heard anything remotely similar arising from his synesthesia before. As they drew closer to the spot Lex had indicated, the sensations became steadily stronger. He realized that the sensations were oddly pleasant, almost intoxicating. He brought the ship to a halt and looked to Lex expectantly.

The tall man communed then, sending some kind of coded message forward toward the almost invisible nexus of distortions displaced in shadow space above the star. Greymalkin could now sense that something was there, but it was hidden in the synesthesia phantasms thrown off by the subdued boiling energy of the purple star that was now so close to them. Then they all sensed eerie communed thoughts emerging from the nexus. The mind generating the thoughts was that of a mature human female, but Greymalkin uneasily felt that the thoughts seemed too perfectly still and serene to be those of an actual woman.

«You've returned, Lex. Good. Have you finally decided to join us? And who are these others you've brought? What an interesting group.»

Lex looked as stoic as ever when he replied. «May we come up, Calypso?»

The answer came in the form of the star bridge being extended. When the artificial shadow space conduit had finished forming, Greymalkin eased Royce into it. The cyneget seemed gingerly hesitant at first, but then moved into and across the displacement zone. His sensations of the strange purple star and virtually all of normal space faded away as they entered the nexus of distortions, and Greymalkin found that Royce had arrived in an isolated manifold like a vast darkened spatial enclosure. He immediately became aware of a large structure in the center of the manifold. It was a huge pale ship.

Guardedly, Greymalkin steered Royce toward the immense vessel, which was recognizably human in its design, although grander in size than anything he'd ever seen, even surpassing the *Dragon King* itself. In form it was a huge torus kilometers in diameter that surrounded a central sphere with a projecting shadow space drive array. He quickly realized that the giant ship's drive array was arranged in a Roc configuration, the largest possible configuration of shadow volume starship. That explained how it had traversed the shadow space volume to reach this baffling shadow space location. Lex wordlessly indicated where to dock the comparatively tiny cyneget living starship. As they approached the dock, Greymalkin was again shocked, this time by what he saw on the white hull. There was a name inscribed there, the *Vlieger*, but it was the symbol by the name that shocked him.

The symbol was the familiar stylized barred galaxy 'S' shape of the Sojourner Order.

After Royce thudded gently into the docking cradle, Tatter was the first one to break the silence. "That big symbol on the hull, it's the same one that's on the monastery compound at the main expedition base. Right?" she said, looking from Lex to Greymalkin quizzically.

"This is a memory ark," Greymalkin whispered in awe, thinking of the magnitude of the huge vessel. He looked at Lex in wonder. "But it's even bigger than the one I served on, the *Dragon King*, and that was a cathedral-class ark, one of the largest in the Order. This vessel... what *is* this vessel?"

Lex studied him silently with his ancient, pale blue eyes. He finally said, "You saw the name when we docked; have you never heard of the *Vlieger*?"

Greymalkin frowned, searching his memories, and then his eyebrows shot up. "I recall now! That was the name of the ark that was specially constructed for the Order by the Xenocorps expedition sponsors three hundred years ago. But, it was lost with all the other expedition ships...." He inhaled sharply. Lex nodded, and went to the airlock entrance.

"As you can see, it was not lost," the older man said. "But the Roc drive was much too slow to escape with the galleons, so most of the surviving Sojourners abandoned it and left with the Xenocorps ships. However, there were four Sojourners that refused to leave, including the Abbess. They stayed behind, because they had decided to die with their ark. But they *didn't* die." Lex scowled slightly as he cycled the airlock. "Instead, they came to an *arrangement*."

"Surely not with the Aurelian!" Greymalkin exclaimed, following Lex into the airlock. He felt the familiar plop on his shoulder of Bruno in his tiny form. Tatter crowded in behind them all, and Greymalkin sealed the airlock as he checked the conditions on the other side. Sure enough, there was a normal oxygen atmosphere there. He unsealed the airlock door, and Lex stepped out into a dim corridor.

"No, they had far more luck and common sense than I did," Lex said. *Is there a trace of bitterness in his voice?* "They came to an arrangement with the *Clavisian*." He began to walk down the corridor, and after a moment of hesitation, Greymalkin followed him.

* * *

The air on the ark felt cold and totally stale. Dead. To Greymalkin, it was obvious that the atmospheric circulation had not been in full operation for a very long time. The lights in the corridor had been set to a very dim illumination, and only activated for motion detection. Barely a few meters of the corridor were lit in front of Lex as he strode forward into a seeming black void. But the older man walked without hesitation, leading them through a short maze of turns until the corridor opened out onto a larger space.

Greymalkin stepped out of the corridor and peered around, trying to make out his surroundings. He could tell he was in an almost freezing temperature large open space, but the dim illumination strips they stood on revealed almost nothing beyond the pale white stone path on which they stood. He felt uneasy at the darkness, and then even more so when he heard faint sounds of movement nearby in the gloom. "Bruno?" he whispered. "What's out there?"

Greymalkin could vaguely sense the protean floating above him in the darkness watchfully. The alien cyborg did not speak, but communed with him privately. «We are standing on the main interior deck of the great torus. It is fashioned in a manner that appears to resemble a human city. There are a scattering of automata moving in the streets and buildings around us.» After Greymalkin had digested that for a moment, his anxiety increased when Bruno added one more comment. «One of the automata appears to be watching us closely. It is standing a short distance ahead of us in the main 'street' of this abandoned city.»

Greymalkin moved over to stand next to Lex, whose dim form he could barely make out. "Is there some reason why the interior is so cold and dark?"

Lex sighed. "Their servitors don't need heat or light. Let's go speak to the one that's looking at us. I think it's the welcome committee, such as it is." Lex walked forward into the darkness, and Greymalkin and Tatter followed him. He heard Lex ask, "Could you increase the illumination? It's too dark for some of our party."

A pale light slowly grew around them, and Greymalkin could now make out the faceless white form of a robotic servitor standing a few meters in front of them. Slowly becoming visible in the gloom around them, he could see what looked like elegant white marble buildings made of valicrete with crisp lines and appointments. The pale stone buildings stood in ghostly streets that stretched away into the frigid darkness. He felt an involuntary shiver run down his spine and turned up the warmth in his golden void suit. "Where is everybody?" he asked Lex. The older man glanced at him in confusion.

"Who do you mean?" he asked. "There's nobody here except for the servitors. Well, and the four people I mentioned. Let's go talk to them." He strode forward after the servitor, which had begun walking away from them down the center of the empty street. Greymalkin and Tatter followed him nervously, and Bruno continued drifting along behind them vigilantly.

"This is creepy," Tatter volunteered. She didn't seem affected by the cold, but obviously found the dark deserted streets unnerving. "You're saying this whole giant ship is empty?"

"It's hardly empty," Lex said. "Can you not hear that? I mean, *sense* it?" he gestured to the buildings, and Greymalkin frowned. Now that Lex had mentioned it, there was something....

He looked at the buildings around them. They seemed to have walked into a small plaza. He studied the structures around them and finally realized what had struck him subliminally as odd. The plaza was graceful and picturesque, and they were surrounded by various enigmatic empty troughs. As he gazed at the barren stone cribs around them, he saw they were actually long empty *planters* that should have held verdant flowers and other growing things. The dry chutes were water sluices for a huge circular cup that should have been a spraying water fountain in the center of the plaza. But everything was long abandoned and dead.

But there was something else profoundly disturbing. He concentrated and thought he sensed something indistinct, like *murmuring*. He stood still and listened. Slowly it struck him that there was no sound, and that he was not hearing anything at all. Rather, his *shadow sense* was detecting faintly communed whispers. He stepped closer to the entrance of one of the pale white buildings and cautiously looked through the open doorway. His eyes widened.

There were shelves of mnemotomes from floor to ceiling. And he quickly realized that the books were disturbed, and talking to one another. As he focused more keenly, he caught the proper communed frequency, and what he had only sensed subliminally came to him in a rush. There was actually a dull *roar* of communed whispers all around him. He walked across the plaza and looked in another door. What should have been a Sojourner refectory with places for meals was again packed floor to ceiling with memory volumes, all whispering intently to one another as he came near. He looked around, aghast. Even on the *Dragon King* he had never heard a clamor of books like this. Now that he had picked it out, the noise of the communing books was overwhelming. It began to feel threatening.

Lex and Tatter came up behind him, and he turned. "Why are there books *here*? This is a Sojourner memory ark; there surely must be many galleries and areas for mnemotome stacks?"

"There certainly are," Lex said, and Greymalkin thought he detected a feeling of unease in the older man. *At the presence of the whispering mnemotomes?* He tried to focus on the torrent of whispers around him, and felt an unsettling subcurrent in the books of this strange ark, as if they were invading his mind like the strangling creepers of a huge vine-system. He recoiled in fright and tried to force out the invading thoughts of the mnemotomes, but found that they simply returned and encircled his mind from some other direction.

As Greymalkin struggled with the feeling that the vast ranks of books were invading his mind, Lex continued, "*Too many* stacks and archives for my taste. There are countless books here, and they don't like to be disturbed. That's part of why I don't like coming here. Come, let's go." Lex walked away down the empty street after the servitor. Tatter looked uncertainly at Greymalkin, and then they both followed Lex down the wide, central street of the empty city inside the ark, leaving the angry books behind them. Greymalkin felt the cloying sensation clutching at his mind again, and quickened his pace.

The small group walked past block after block of gaunt and vacant white marble streets in the darkness. He looked up into the blackness above them. Had there once been a fanciful projected 'sky' provided for the monks here? Greymalkin had never heard of such an extravagantly configured ark, made to provide the illusion of a city on the surface of a planet.

As they walked past a grand and stately building, he noticed that it had the Sojourner symbol for a museum above the entrance. The doors stood open and despite his uneasiness, he couldn't resist the urge to see what the unknown monks that had once tended this strange ark had decided to exhibit inside. "Give me just one minute," he muttered to Lex, and darted inside before the older man could call him back. As he glanced back, he saw Tatter following after him with a worried expression.

He had been concerned about the lack of light, but the dim illumination came up around them as they entered a large cold chamber. And once again he saw that the big room was utterly crammed with books in racks that ran all the way to the high ceiling. Even for a memory ark, this was extreme. He wondered how this ark could possibly have collected so many volumes in the short time it had been in the Carinae.

Greymalkin walked up to the closest range and pulled out a volume at random. Where a normal mnemotome could easily be held in one hand, this volume was so massive he could barely lift it with both arms. He tried to access its contents with his mind, but it seemed to contain nothing but dense gibberish. He heard Lex coming after them into the chamber, just as Tatter gasped. He whirled around to see that she had approached and lifted the lid of an eoncrystal display cabinet in wonder. He walked up to her, looked down, and gasped as well.

Neatly arrayed in jammed precision across the cabinet's interior were thousands of shadow jewels. The jewels were all huge and seemingly perfect. Tatter picked one up, marveling at the size and clarity, her eyes sparkling at the beautiful glimmering radiance in the darkness. Greymalkin saw there were many more cabinets, all packed with a riot of gems.

Lex came up next to him and silently gestured upwards with his chin, whereupon Greymalkin tensed and grabbed Tatter's arm. She was still inspecting the jewel, and had started to reach for another as he said in a hushed voice, "Tat... look." She did look at him, still beaming, and then glanced upwards. Her grin vanished.

In the galleries above them, servitors were motionlessly watching them. As he looked around, Greymalkin saw that there were many, many more servitors in the dark archways, all watching them alertly in complete silence. Tatter looked down at the jewel held in her suddenly shaky fingers and then, very cautiously, placed it back precisely in the space it had been and closed the crystalline lid of the cabinet. Greymalkin carefully returned the big volume to its place on the towering rack. Lex led them back out onto the dim street, and the three of them began breathing again. No servitors followed them as they began walking down the street once again, but now Greymalkin could see them standing here and there in the side streets watching.

"What the blazes was that about?" Tatter hissed under her breath. "I mean, I was just taking a peek. And you didn't tell us that this place is a mad treasure house!"

"The shadow jewels are the least important treasures here," Lex said quietly. "Those gems are just specimens. They had me gather many of them myself, along with a lot of other sundries. That's why they gave me my lockers, to store all the things I brought to them here over the years. I've still got thousands of lockers jammed with all the stuff they don't have room for."

Greymalkin gradually turned his head around in a circle, taking in the rows of buildings that stretched away into the freezing darkness, and then the massive vaults and filled spans that he could vaguely sense beneath them through the deck of the gigantic ship with his shadow sense, and said, "They don't have *room*? Here??"

Lex chuckled. "If you think this memory ark is big, you should see all the archives they've got hidden away in the shadow spaces around this system. And they *still* can't store everything they've got." He began to stride away down the dim street even faster. Greymalkin, his mind a whirl of questions, hurried to catch up with him. He still felt the cloying sensation in his mind.

"What's happening here, then?" Greymalkin asked. "What kind of mnemotomes were those? I couldn't even understand their access metadata. And why were they so large?"

Lex looked pensive as he paced along, and then said, "Yes, the books in this library ark are much larger and far more advanced than those you are familiar with. The information in each of them is heavily compressed with advanced algorithms. A handful of them could store all of the information on your *Dragon King* ark."

Greymalkin's mind spun as he looked at the buildings around them, all packed with the dense volumes. "But that's ridiculous! Where did all this data come from? I thought the Xenocorps expedition was cut short? They couldn't possibly have collected so much information in the short time they were here before the Carinans attacked. And even if these four Sojourners were busier than spinning demons throughout the entire three hundred years they've somehow survived here according to your story, they couldn't have generated this much information! And who could possibly have built that power-absorption swarm around the entire star? Sojourners couldn't have done *that!*"

Lex paused for a moment in the street, and even in the dim light Greymalkin could see how troubled the older man appeared as he said, "It's very complicated. It's hard to even know where to start." He seemed to search for words, looking up at the pitch blackness above them. Greymalkin got the impression he was gazing out at the stars beyond the strange pocket dimension where the *Vlieger* was hidden. He finally sighed, began walking again, and said, "You are of course aware of the Homunculus Nebula just a few parsecs from here, and Eta Carina, the giant star that generated that nebula."

Greymalkin shrugged and nodded. "Obviously. It's the center of the Carinae and the most prominent thing in the entire region. You can't help but see the big hourglass shape of the nebula anywhere you go around here, it's light-years wide."

Lex nodded, and then said hesitantly, "What you probably don't know, what almost *no one* knows even now, is the *purpose* of it."

Greymalkin frowned. "What do you mean, 'the purpose'? Nebulae and stars don't have a purpose. They just are."

Lex looked at him somberly, steadily. "You say that, even after you've seen the star we're above right now."

Greymalkin was first simply confused. Then, as Lex's words began to sink in on him, his face became pale, and he whispered, "That's absurd. Eta Carina was the site of a series of near supernova explosions, some of the most violent stellar detonations in the history of the Galaxy. Are you saying...." When his voice cracked, he cleared his throat, and forced the words out. "Are you saying somebody... *caused* that to happen? For a... *purpose*?"

Lex kept walking for long moments before Greymalkin saw his shadowed profile slowly nod. Trying to wrap his mind around what the older man was saying, Greymalkin felt as if his insides were fluttering indistinctly. He knew intellectually that there were very powerful species in the Galaxy and that they were capable of feats that were astonishing in human terms. But this idea was on a scale that was hard to even hold clearly in his head.

"What was the purpose?" Tatter asked in an eager, slightly breathless tone. Greymalkin glanced at her and could see her exhilarated eyes twinkling in the darkness. *It's like she found a new toy or something,* he thought. Greymalkin, however, thought the idea was utterly terrifying.

Lex looked back at her, silhouetted in the gloom. Then he gestured around them at the cold white marble buildings, and said quietly, "Information. Knowledge."

Greymalkin gave a shake of his head, and sputtered, "Wait, what? Okay, maybe at some point you can try to convince me that the Eta Carina supernovae that have happened over thousands of years were, what, *artificial*? And maybe, in a fever dream, you can convince me that it served some sort of controlled purpose, but surely that would be for the generation of inconceivable amounts of *energy*, not *knowledge*, right?"

"This was not energy as we are accustomed to thinking of it," Lex said. "This was something else. Something on a scale that's hard to understand. *Power*. Do you know that the Eta Carina detonations made the star system so bright that in the ancient sailing days of Old Earth mariners navigated by its light? And that was at a distance of more than two and a half thousand parsecs! Like I said. *Power*." Lex's deep set eyes were in shadow. Greymalkin couldn't even be certain if his eyes were open or not, even while the man was steadily striding forward.

Lex's voice now sounded as uncanny as the dead city around them. "If that's too abstract, then let me try this approach. You know that formal axiomatic mathematical theorems are endless, right? There are always more that can be generated and proven eventually. It's as if there's an infinite ocean of math and therefore unending discoveries which that infinite ocean of math make possible, far, far beyond anything that we humans have ever even imagined. And that's just *math*. Or let's talk about physics instead for a moment. If you have Sojourner training in the history of science, you must have read about how the ancients were confused at how to reconcile quantum phenomena, gravity, relativistic effects, and other basic physics?"

"Yes, sure," Greymalkin said, still frowning. "They hadn't discovered shadow space yet, and many other fundamental aspects of their environment. But what does that have to do—"

"It led them into philosophically confused interpretations of the environmental effects they were seeing, such as the 'many worlds' idea that was once held. In that concept, all of reality, what we would now call the normal space manifold continuum within the larger environment of shadow space, was constantly splitting into infinitely many versions of itself in every moment. "

"But that was just an old misunderstanding of what quantum field equations imply," Greymalkin said, beginning to feel impatient. "And I still don't understand what any of this—"

Lex held up his hand. "Yes, I know, I know, the unified field theories of Galliman and Appleton sorted out all that confusion a long time ago." Lex came to a stop, looking up. Greymalkin and Tatter stopped as well; the street had ended. They stood at the base of a palatial structure of ghostly white spires that stretched up into the darkness.

Lex turned and faced them. "But like I said, math just goes on and on. And maybe you remember that in the past there were old self-referential metaphors of math and physics being like fractals, mathematical patterns that repeat unpredictably and indefinitely in various ways? They were called *strange loops*. Well, the Builders explored that concept extensively. While we were apes in the Pleistocene era on Earth, and Sylphids were forming their first primitive civilizations, the Builders had already figured out how to go way, way past all the unified field theories that we proudly, *eventually*, developed. They found that those theories are, again, just generalizations of what is *usually* true, in *most* situations. But not *all*. They identified mathematical simulations that led them to... *unusual* physical conditions in which those old ideas of infinitely branching realities were quite... *real*. Alternate realities that can be *studied*, and *mined* for information. They became interested in that for a time. But it requires... *Power*."

Greymalkin felt like a blind man that had encountered a chasm in a confused dream. "The Builders? You're saying *they* caused the supernova explosions of Eta Carina? What does that have to do with this ark? And all the books here...."

Lex looked at him sympathetically. "The ones responsible, the ones that conceived of these ideas and then designed the works here in the

Carinae long ago, were the last of the Builders in this part of the Galaxy before they... sort of got bored and departed. But they left behind their assistants to finish up the actual implementation of the designs, beings like the Clavisian. And the Clavisian in turn was amused to eventually recruit and train little monkeys like us to assist in *performing* the work. Here, for example. On *this ark*."

Tatter squinted with one eye and raised her other eyebrow. "Hunh? What's 'the work'?"

"The Builders discovered that with a very large, but not *infinite*, amount of energy they could generate... *actual* infinities of information. They tried it. Here in the Carinae."

"So, the power-absorption swarm around the star," Greymalkin said slowly, trying to understand. "*That's* what it's doing? Generating 'infinite' information?"

"No," Lex said. "The Builders generated, well, *simulated* would be the more correct term, an information *Nexus*, a very complex artifact that recovers information from an indeterminate number of alternate realities. Consequently, because there are an unending number of such alternate realities, it effectively provides access to an *infinite amount of information*. They accomplished this by means of the greatest tool that I am aware of anywhere in the Galaxy."

Lex communed an image of the hourglass shaped Homunculus Nebula, and indicated the two spinning stars at the central constriction. "That's where it is, the tool that enabled them to create the Nexus. It's an artifact they made that uses the energy generated by the two gigantic stars in the center of the Eta Carina system there, stars that we in the previous expedition called the Hammer and the Anvil. They designed a system that would effectively use the power of those two interacting stars as a *supernova Forge*."

Greymalkin's eyes widened. *So that's what the Aurelian was talking about. The 'Forge' and the 'Nexus'. Good grief, no wonder it was so obsessed.*

Lex continued with his explanation, "The two giant stars that power the Forge collide on a regular cyclic basis, you see. When they do, the impacts generate incomprehensible power, almost as much energy as a supernova depending on the particular cycle. They created this tool many thousands of years ago. But the power grid here? Around the star where we are...." He shrugged. "It's nothing in comparison, just a normal star. It barely generates enough power to kickstart the *unpacking* process for the data Nexus. Only a little toy in comparison to the Forge, it's just a little ancillary part of the whole array of facilities that make up the entire system. But that ancillary process is the purpose of this place and its dwellers. The four Sojourner survivors here on the *Vlieger* were made Risen, their intellects lifted up by the Clavisian, precisely to handle that tedious chore of unpacking the output of the Nexus. They've been at it for three centuries. And they've scarcely gotten started." Lex looked up at the towering structure of ghostly white spires. "Shall we go in, and I'll introduce you to them?"

Lex led them, stunned, into the palatial structure, which Greymalkin finally recognized as a variant of a standard Sojourner temple design. Most of the huge spaces and halls were again packed with towering stacks of mnemotomes, but narrow paths had been preserved through the endless piles of books in the temple's primary halls. They made their way through and eventually emerged into a dim space that was recognizably a grand chapel. There were still white marble shelves of memory volumes lining the multiple high stories of the perimeter, but the central space had been left open. Greymalkin saw that several figures were kneeling in meditation on the central raised dais of the chapel, evidently waiting for them as they approached. Lex walked up to stand a few meters away from them and folded his arms. Greymalkin approached cautiously, and studied the group on the dais.

There were four figures kneeling on the dais, wearing beautiful black and gold brocaded Sojourner hooded robes. One was clearly the leader, as she was on a platform elevated above the other three. Her face was shadowed by her gold and sable-black hood. All that he could see were her thin but elegant lips and pale chin. Greymalkin was struck by the richness of the group's robes, which were drenched in elaborate designs of shining gold brocade of shadow aureate. He was accustomed to the much humbler robes worn on the *Dragon King*. The leader noticed his glance and spoke abruptly in a resonant voice full of the senior patrician command inflections of an Abbess.

"You do not wear your robes, little Brother?" she asked. "Are you not on Duty Watch?"

Greymalkin belatedly realized she was right. He was on an ark, and he still very much considered himself a loyal Sojourner. But he'd not worn his robes in months, and had left them packed away inside Royce. Then he remembered that the remarkable void suit that he wore, the same garment that had been a gift from Kuanian and was made of the same golden shadow space aureate that these strangers wore, also had a setting that he had forgotten which conformed to Sojourner formal robes. He had been wearing the garment in the form of a void suit so long that he had forgotten the other forms it was capable of taking. Feeling self-conscious as everyone watched, he changed the garment's form. It quickly morphed into an even more dazzling version of the ostentatious robes that the four on the dais wore. For a moment he felt embarrassed, wondering if they would think him pretentious. But the Abbess nodded in approval.

"That is the proper form, little Brother," she said, and her perfect lips formed a lush smile. "Just as we designed it to Kuanian's specifications."

"What!" Greymalkin couldn't help exclaiming. "You know Kuanian? And *you* crafted this garment?"

All four of the Sojourners on the dais now had faintly amused expressions as the leader nodded again, and said, "Indeed, we did. We labored long on its design, as well as the design of your *vajra*, to ensure that these gifts would meet your needs in all the circumstances, both general and specific, that we could envision. We are pleased to finally meet the one chosen by Kuanian to receive them."

As Greymalkin was absorbing her words, the woman and the other three each began inclining their heads in polite greetings. The Abbess continued, "I am Mother Advisor Superior Calypso. These three are my crew: Sister Gizem, Brother Ammon, and Brother Janus. You and your companions are most welcome here on the Sojourner ark *Vlieger*. In fact, we hope that you will all consider staying with us and assisting us in the great work we are engaged in here."

Greymalkin and Tatter simply stared at the Abbess in surprise, but Lex chortled and said, "You waste little time before commencing your recruiting efforts, Calypso. I see nothing has changed with you."

The Abbess had a droll and mildly affronted air as she said, "I am pleased to see you again as well, Alexander. Have you reconsidered our offer, Brother Borgess?"

"I am no longer with the Order. And, no, Calypso, my answer is still the same," Lex said. His tired features told Greymalkin that this was an old conversation. The Abbess smiled at him mildly, and looked above Lex's tall form to where the orbiting rocks of Bruno floated silently.

"I see that you have freed the great *monster of memory*," she said, not sounding pleased. Although her hood still shadowed her eyes, Greymalkin could see that her previous smile had disappeared, and her lips had become a chiseled line straighter than the marble shelves of the chapel walls. "We advised Kuanian against this course of action, Lex. The creature was to be freed only as a last resort."

Now it was Lex's turn to appear affronted. "I had nothing to do with freeing this nightmare. It's almost killed me once, and may succeed at some point, I suppose."

"I, uh, was the one that freed Bruno," Greymalkin admitted. "And yes, it *was* a last resort. But Bruno has proven to be quite helpful."

"No doubt," the Abbess said. "Given the restraint codes and bait-reward that we also gave Kuanian for the purpose." The Abbess looked down at Greymalkin, and he could now make out her luminous eyes within the shadows of the ornate golden hood. He nervously thought her stare was becoming ever more intense as she studied him. "We gave her many gifts in consolation of the fact that we would not assist her fully as she wished, although neither would she join us as *we* wished. But now I see that you, little Brother, seem to have received much of what we provided her with for her 'expedition'. And you have *such* an interesting shadow jewel, with *such* a fascinating assemblage of data constructs imprinted on it." Greymalkin briefly wondered if he would again be shamed by the presence of the covenants.

Then Bruno's loud, low growl surprised everyone as its echoes rumbled off the walls, "So it was *you* that provided my master code restrictions to these humans. I find this interesting. How could you possibly have obtained them?"

The Abbess and the ornately clad Sojourners all smiled again. "We know many secrets," she said curtly, and something about the way she said it troubled Greymalkin profoundly. He bowed to her and said what was on his mind.

"Abbess Calypso, please accept my deepest thanks and appreciation for all the gifts that you have provided in your largess," he said, his words rushing out. "I have done my utmost to use your gifts to my very best ability as an avowed member of the Order. But there is a great deal that I do not understand." Greymalkin looked first at the Abbess, and then his gaze swept around the vaulted marble and valitanium arches of the chapel, and across the serried ranges of memory volumes crammed into every shelf. "The collections of this memory ark are like no other. To the limited degree that I understand the lore of this place from Brother Borgess, I mean, *Lex*, it seems that you have far more knowledge here than any other ark of the Order. Why then... why then have you not *shared* it?"

The Abbess smiled even more broadly now, revealing rows of flawless white teeth like pearls, and lifted her face up out of the shadows of her hood to look down at Greymalkin in an even more penetrating manner that raised the hair on the back of his neck. Her features were mature, but stunningly beautiful. She had high cheekbones and starkly outlined eyes of the palest icy blue that seemed to tunnel through him. *Can she really be three centuries old?* he wondered again. He glanced at the other three smiling monks, and they all seemed to be in the prime of life. When the Abbess spoke, her lush voice sounded almost seductive. "What an astute question, little Brother! The short answer is that we are prevented by something called the *Tenax*. But it would take a very long time to explain the Tenax to you, and to answer your question fully. Would you like to stay with us and learn all about our mission and work?"

"But, surely you can give me some brief account here and now? What is the Tenax?" Greymalkin asked. He felt his stubborn determination asserting itself, and he said with certainty growing in his voice as he spoke, "I, like you, am a Sojourner. We are all sworn to the Great Commitment, *to share information with humility*." Greymalkin frowned. "Why have you not?"

The *Vlieger* monks all continued to smile at him in a friendly manner, but a stray thought struck him how odd it was that none of them ever appeared to blink. The Abbess clasped her hands in her lap, and said with a dimpled grin, "Very well, little Brother; I will explain it to you. The simple answer is that while the Tenax does not allow us to share the information we collect, it does not prevent us from preserving it so that it may *one day* be shared. And I can provide you with the full story of what we do here. What our mission is all about. Go and pick up that book, there." She unfolded her palm and gestured with long fingers toward a prominent stone reading table to his left where one of the countless mnemotomes lay.

Greymalkin stepped to the table and picked up the heavy volume. He tried to scan it, however all he could make out in the densely encoded text was the prominent title. But that seized his attention instantly. *Mission Algorithm*. He returned to stand before the Abbess, who spoke in her almost hypnotically textured voice to him again.

"You may take that copy with you to read," she said. "It explains everything with which we are concerned. Now, let me take a look at you, my dear young Sylphid!" The Abbess faced Tatter with a delighted smile. As Tatter took a flouncing step forward, she had, if anything, an even more gleefully laughing grin than the Abbess.

"Hi there!" Tatter said. "You have a gorgeous place here!"

"Not so gorgeous that it would not be improved with your presence!" the Abbess said cheerfully. "And we are well aware of the many talents of Morganans! Might you be interested in joining us here?"

Tatter almost squealed with excitement as she responded, "Why, as it so happens, I'm between jobs just at the moment! But, uh...." A doubt seemed to cross her face. "This ship, um, seems a little bit lonely. Are there really only the four of you here?"

"You might be surprised what good company we make," the Abbess chuckled. "And you would definitely liven this place up! What do you say?"

Greymalkin felt as if his insides were falling out of him. He had not known Tatter for a very long time, but he was certain that he would profoundly miss her company if she decided to stay in this eerie place.

Tatter seemed unsure as well, and he noticed her begin to turn towards him momentarily before she stopped and responded, "Uh, can I think it over for a little while?"

"Certainly!" the Abbess exclaimed. "You all must be tired and hungry. Would you like to inspect our ship's provisions? We set out with food reserves in stasis for a crew of fifty thousand! Even after all the time we've been here we still have plenty of delicacies. Take whatever you like."

"Oh, I *am* famished!" Tatter said. She turned to Greymalkin and Lex. "How about it, guys? Are you hungry too?"

Lex looked somberly at Greymalkin and said, "I promised you I'd do what I can to decrypt that shadow jewel of yours. I've got my scans...." The older man faced the Abbess. "Calypso, may I use your labs? I know I haven't cooperated with your wishes, but –"

"You are welcome to use the labs, old friend," the Abbess said fondly. "And what about you, little Brother? Will you go and research your remarkable gem as well?" And then Greymalkin caught a very small and subtle reaction in the Abbess. It was such a slight shift in her expression that he would never have caught it if he hadn't been observing her so closely. When she'd mentioned his shadow jewel she'd glanced ever so slightly at his forehead, right where the jewel was embedded in the shadow space just above his prefrontal cortex inside his skull. It had only been for a split second, but her face had tensed with some kind of... *coiled* emotion. *What was that? Fear? Anger? Recognition? Or... confirmation?*

It made Greymalkin hesitate, and he thought carefully for a moment before responding. He certainly longed to know if anything about his past could be recovered, but he felt an almost unbearable curiosity about the enigmatic Sojourners of the *Vlieger*. "I... first want to try to read the book you've given me. I want to understand your mission, even if it's complicated."

"Spoken like a Sojourner," the Abbess said. "Very well, the servitors will take you back to your ship, little Brother. Lex, you know the way to the labs. Young lady, I will personally escort you to our galleys and food storehouses." She squinted again at Bruno. "Where away with you, then, monster?"

"I believe I will accompany the Xenocorpsman," Bruno rumbled. "I find that I am curious about the history of the monk's shadow jewel as well."

The Abbess sniffed, and her perfect features became hard and cold for a second. "I see. Do try not to destroy anything, hmm? We take our work here very seriously." Then she turned away from the protean, gave Tatter a sunny smile, and linked arms with her, saying, "Very well then, will you come with me, my dear young lady?" Tatter nodded eagerly.

The tall Abbess led the bubbly young Sylphid away through a side exit of the chapel. Greymalkin followed Lex and Bruno out the way they'd entered. A silent faceless white servitor stood waiting, evidently for Greymalkin. The young Sojourner pulled Lex aside for a moment before leaving.

"Lex, can we trust these people?" Greymalkin asked quietly. Even as he asked the question he wondered why he was asking Lex. He hadn't known the man any longer than the *Vlieger* crew, but he instinctively felt significantly greater faith in the man.

"They're Sojourners like you," Lex said tiredly. "You don't trust them?"

"They aren't like any Sojourners I ever met," Greymalkin said. "Why wouldn't the Abbess just answer my questions? Why give me a *book* to read instead?"

Lex shrugged. "They've never threatened me, if that's what you're asking."

"Why didn't you want to join them, then?" Greymalkin asked pointedly. Lex took on the distant expression that he seemed to fall back into as a default.

"For a long time it was because I was a slave to the Aurelian," he said grimly. "They helped me escape from him, but even so... I suppose I just didn't care about their... *project*." Something about the way he said it made Greymalkin think that Lex found the grandiose project foolish, despite its incredible nature.

"And what *is* the project? I mean, beyond all of the incredible things you told me about. What precisely are they trying to accomplish? Do you know?" Greymalkin pressed. Lex yawned, and gestured at the endless memory tomes around them and then the one in Greymalkin's hands.

"You tell me, you've got the answers there, apparently. It all seems pointless to me, for the same reason that you pointed out: they're hoarding the information here and not sharing it. But then again I've *never* really understood what they were doing completely." After clenching his jaw for a moment, Lex added in a bitter tone, "The Clavisian picked *them*, not me. Look, I'll catch up with you tomorrow. I've scanned that jewel in your head and have the recordings with me, but it's going to take me a while to find out anything useful about it."

Greymalkin touched the older man's arm and looked him in his old faded blue eyes. "Thanks, Lex. I *greatly* appreciate your help in this."

"Thank me if I actually find anything out," Lex muttered, and then looked up at Bruno's drifting mass above him. "C'mon, monster. You can help."

* * *

Greymalkin followed the servitor back through the lonely streets of the ark to the dock and Royce. The cyneget was deliriously happy at his return, communing a blast of pure joy to him when he stepped through the airlock. Royce's welcome cheered Greymalkin up considerably as he plopped down to dig into the big mnemotome.

Several hours later he was still sitting cross-legged with the book in front of him, but now feeling thoroughly frustrated. He got up, stretched, and began pacing in a circle through the small cabin spaces around Royce's core. With great difficulty he'd made some progress with the mnemotome, but the complexity of what it described was much too advanced for him. Greymalkin felt reasonably confident in his command of mathematics and physics, but the big memory volume was far beyond anything he'd ever seen, much less understood.

He had just sat back down with the huge book, wondering if the Abbess had given it to him simply as another way to dodge answering his questions, when a clatter in the airlock announced Tatter's return. He was surprised to see her enter the room in new clothes, hauling in several tons of food containers on a big autocart. She carried a big crate over and dropped it next to him with a thump. Kneeling down, she opened the crate while crowing, "Look at all this stuff they gave me! All kinds of fabulous food and other things!" She pulled out some kind of snack and began eating it enthusiastically.

"Un-hunh," Greymalkin said halfheartedly, leaning his chin on his hand as he morosely regarded the cryptic book the Abbess had given him. *I'm never going to figure this thing out.* Tatter followed his gaze and pursed her lips as she chewed.

"No luck with that thing, hunh?" she asked. When he nodded dourly, she laughed as she sat down next to him on the crate, slapping her hand on her thigh as she crossed her legs. "Oh, come on now; things are looking up! We've finally got some decent food! We found these Sojourners here, and they seem to have everything we need, right? And, *hey*, what do you think of these clothes they gave me? Not as fancy as those robes that you got from them, but maybe not so bad?"

He finally gave up on the tome and took a closer look at what she was wearing. After his eyes bugged, he quickly sat up a little straighter and looked away to keep from gawking. The outfit she now wore was composed of some sort of richly sparkling and wildly multi-colored fabric that clung to absolutely every curve and protrusion of her body so tightly that, shape-wise, the garment simply might not have been there at all. She kicked her leg up and down excitedly while grinning at his averted gaze, and said, "Can you believe they had Erisian couture?"

"Uh, *wow*, it, ah... *suits* you," he said after searching for a remotely appropriate word, and tried to keep his eyes directed anywhere else before they popped out of his head. "I, um, guess you won't have to wear Bora's old jumpsuits anymore." Tatter laughed deep in her belly, stood up, and reached down with both hands to pull him up next to her playfully.

"They have fantastic stores of food!" she said, gesturing down at the crate of packages in elation. "*Look* at all this delicious stuff they gave me! I've only *heard* of some of these dishes. And the gnari cellar they have is full of incredible vintages!"

Greymalkin looked at the containers doubtfully. "Most of these foodstuffs are three centuries old. Are you sure it's safe to eat?"

"It was all preserved in stasis fields," Tatter said happily, peeling open a long package with a pop that spilled a sharp tang of spices and cooked meat into the cabin. She took a bite and rolled her eyes, holding it out to Greymalkin. "Here, try this, it's fabulous!"

The scent of the food got his attention, but he shook his head, remembering standard Sojourner convictions about avoiding meat. "I don't eat anything that had a face or a mother."

Tatter sighed, and said, "Neither do I, dummy. *This* was grown in a Brentasian meat forest. It's their major export, and they take great pride in producing it. Nobody slaughters animals anywhere except on those primitive planets you monks insist on visiting."

"Bleh," he said, still shaking his head. "Brentasians! Composite sentients that grow and sell parts of themselves are weird and gross. Even if that's how they trade with each other." Tatter was standing so close to him that her thigh was pressed against his. He took a nervous step away, all too aware of both her tightly clinging garment and the roasted meat she was holding under his nose.

Tatter shook her head with a sigh, bent over the opening in the crate, and began rummaging through the containers, all while wolfing down the big roasted fillet. She began pulling out vegetarian delicacies, ripping them open, and setting them out triumphantly on the top of the big crate in an array. As she opened package after package, the tantalizing scents of seemingly freshly baked bread, savory sauces, and dishes both familiar and unfamiliar instantly made his mouth water. He looked through the items, trying to identify them all. The fresh bread scent came from a delicate, yeasty Peretian curl-loaf that Tatter set down beside an aromatically steaming container of hot Erisian soup. Next to the soup was a piquant Sadorian curry, then a container of luscious Crucian truffles, a tub of fragrant saffron Compostelan rice, sautéed Kabdhilinan medleys of bright tubers, verdures, and squash... and Tatter was *still* opening containers one after another.

Greymalkin sat down next to the crate, staring at the sumptuous food. He hadn't had a hot meal in weeks, and he looked up at Tatter in mild astonishment. She was looking at him uncertainly with lifted eyebrows, clearly hoping for some response from him. He was struck again by how expressive her big brown eyes were, and he felt totally lost in them for a moment. Then, with an excited grin, he gratefully stammered out, "Th-thanks, Tatter!" He looked at the banquet she'd set out on the crate. "I... don't think I've ever had a meal this nice in my whole life." He meant it.

Tatter's face lit up with a brilliant smile and she sat down across from him, squeezing her shoulders up and down with a delighted shiver.

"Fantastic! Let's eat, then!" But Greymalkin reached out and shyly touched her warm hand as she reached out for the food. Tatter met his eyes with an abruptly... *interested* expression at the contact, and he flinched.

"L-let me say a blessing first?" Greymalkin said. "All this food is something to be grateful for." Tatter nodded, looking intrigued. He briefly wondered what meals were like in Sylphid households, realizing he knew almost nothing about her species and wanting to ask her about their customs. Instead, he reached out to hold both of Tatter's hands, and said the simple Sojourner meal blessing over the food while looking back and forth earnestly between her two deep brown eyes.

"We are grateful for this nourishment, and pledge to not forget those who hunger for both food and knowledge," he said, reciting the blessing with the most sincerity he'd felt in a long time. "May this meal inspire us to act with greater compassion, to sustain not only ourselves but to share our bounty, both physical and intellectual, with humility. For in giving, we find our greatest strength. Let it always be so." He smiled, letting go of her hands and eagerly tucking into the food. Tatter watched him thoughtfully for a few moments, and then went back to eating her big roast somewhat slower.

"I like that," she finally said. "You monks seem really decent. And you're right, it's good to be grateful." She looked at the food, seeming lost in thought. "People never said blessings like that in my tavern. But then, I didn't serve anything this nice."

"I liked the food you served," Greymalkin said. "I always looked forward to eating at your place. People were happy there. You always brightened up everybody's day."

"Yeah?" Tatter said, beaming again at him. "It wasn't what I planned when I came out here, but I had a lot of fun running that place." Then her face fell. "Too bad it ended the way it did."

Greymalkin swallowed, feeling guilty. "I'm sorry that Bruno ruined everything."

Tatter shook her head, looking down. "No, that was all on Jamie. I still can't believe he could stab me in the back like that." A cloud of bitterness passed over her face. "But then, why should he be any different than anybody else I ever cared about?" She opened a tube of some pungent alcoholic drink and took a long swallow. Greymalkin paused and looked at her sad face, abruptly wondering not only about what Tatter's life in the expedition base had been like before he met her, but all the years before. *She's so open and cheerful most of the time, but then she seems so guarded every once in a while... as if she's been through really terrible experiences.* The food was delicious but now he felt unhappy, wondering about all the awful experiences Tatter must have been through before he'd met her.

"Still, I'm very sorry about what happened," Greymalkin said. "I wish I'd known about that stupid plan of Bruno's before he went off on you. You didn't deserve that." Tatter shrugged, drained the rest of the drink tube, and finished the roast with one big bite.

"Thanks, Grey. I've been around so many mean people for so long, I like being around you. You're... *kind*, do you know that?" Tatter said slowly, a rueful smile spreading across her face once more. She watched him that way so long that he nervously looked down in embarrassment. She chuckled warmly at that, and pointedly put her hand on his arm until he looked up at her again. Then she said softly, "The big black blob was just trying to help you. And what he did wasn't *your* fault, Grey. I know that now." She only let go of his arm when he finally nodded at her.

"Where is Rockhead, anyway? And Lex?" Tatter asked after ripping open another big package of Brentasian steak. Greymalkin watched her tear into the roast, astonished as always at the amount of food she could devour. By observing her over time he'd discovered that she could metabolize not only human food in addition to Sylphid nutrients, but half a dozen other types of alien fare. It hadn't seemed possible to him at first, until he began to understand how complex her adaptive alien biology was. He now knew she could eat almost anything that was from a remotely carbon-based life-form. But then he thought again about the sheer size and power of her muscled Sylphid form. *Her anatomy is orders of magnitude larger than mine, how can she even fuel herself with just food alone? Does she consume shadow flux when I'm not watching?*

"I guess they're both still in the lab," he said. Although the food was amazing, he found he could not help stealing glances at the even more amazing sight of Tatter's perfect figure in the diaphanous Erisian garment. But, interestingly, he also found he could not avoid mentally picturing the giant and terrifying form of the folded Sylphid body that he knew was hidden away in the shadow space all around her. The enigmatic way that her stunning human form concealed that tremendous alien physique still fascinated Greymalkin. *How did her species evolve that ability? And... why?* There was so little that he actually understood about Tatter. He was intensely curious about her, but knew how much it annoyed her whenever he asked direct questions about her species.

Tatter caught him looking at her then. As she always did, she just grinned at him lasciviously as he looked down blushing. She took another huge bite of food, and then seemed to remember something. While she chewed, she pounced on a sturdy crate behind her on the autocart. The heavy crate reminded him of the containers he had seen her unloading back at the main expedition base. She pried it open and triumphantly pulled out a static suspension bottle.

"Look what I found in their cellars!" she crowed. "Three centuries old Lochaber gnari! Do you know how expensive this stuff is? And they just *gave* me a case of it!"

Greymalkin frowned. The suspension bottle certainly looked extravagant. He'd heard of Sojourner sects that created rare consumables as a way of funding their operations, but never the substance known as gnari. From what he'd read, it was a very powerful psychogenic drug. And the Lochaber culture was a semi-outlaw civilization on the remote lawless border between the Alban Realm and Erisia. He wondered again about the strange Sojourner ark *Vlieger*. The script and language on the bottle was archaic even for a centuries old Sojourner ark. He could make out the words *Gnaritas Viva Autonoma*.

He watched as Tatter cracked the bottle open and poured out a glistening glass-full of the stuff, saying, "Okay, you have to try this! You never came by my tavern when I had any gnari on hand. And this is the really, *really* good stuff!" She set the glass down on the table between them. Greymalkin eyed it skeptically, wondering what would happen if he drank it, and if he'd be able to make any more progress on the cryptic book that Calypso had given him.

But the meal with Tatter had distracted him, and he was certain he wouldn't make any more progress on the mnemotome anyway. He also suspected that Tatter would pester him until he tried it. *Okay, I trust her. I'll drink it.* While she took the bottle back to the crate and fiddled with resealing the suspension seal, he sighed and, mustering up his most incautious impulses, drank the glass down. The substance slid down his throat slickly. The taste first seemed simply tart but then set off a delayed reaction on his tongue that was like a buzzing flame that strangled him.

Greymalkin looked at the glass with appalled shock and set it back down, trying to catch his breath and already regretting the reckless impulse. *Oh well, that'll probably knock me out for the rest of the night.*

Tatter came bouncing back and looked at the glass in confusion. "What happened to the gnari?" she said, looking at the deck as if it must have spilled. When she saw Greymalkin's choked expression her eyes widened. "Oh, *crap*! Did you drink it *all* just then? That was for both of us! And you're supposed to sip it gradually over time!"

Greymalkin felt mortified, and rubbed the tears out of his eyes. "You might have warned me!" he gargled. Tatter watched him with a mildly concerned expression as she went back for the bottle, and Greymalkin hastily ate some more food to try to stop the burning on his tongue. When she returned with another, smaller glass of the lustrous fluid she pointedly set it down on her side of the crate that was serving as their table.

"Well, at least you didn't drink all that on an empty stomach," she laughed, and took a small sip along with several more bites of food. Greymalkin looked at her askance.

"You actually like that stuff?" he muttered. His throat was still burning, and now his head felt light. Tatter smirked at him and took another sip.

"Let's see what you think of it in a little while, you lunatic," she chuckled. "And it has a milder, different effect on Sylphids than humans. Remember, I've got a much wider tolerance for volatiles than you. One of the benefits of being a Morganan."

A thought streaked through Greymalkin's increasingly spinning head. "Hey, Morganans are supposed to be a lot smarter than humans, right? You should be the one reading this blasted book that Calypso gave me! I'm never going to figure it out."

Tatter hooted with laughter. "That's your thing, Grey! And I'm *celebrating*, not working tonight." She took another deeper drink of the gnari, and after finishing off the food on her plate stood up. "Do you want some more of these vegetarian goodies?"

Greymalkin had thought he would feel intoxicated by the burning drink, but to his surprise he found that his mind was suddenly racing with sharper thoughts. His fingers seemed to be tingling with electricity as he ran them along the crate, and the aches in his ribs had vanished.

Wow, I feel great. Distantly, he felt Royce send a strange chuffing communed signal to him that he couldn't understand. For a second he sent his awareness flashing through the ship's cyborganic systems, but everything was nominal. Greymalkin wondered what was agitating the cyneget. "No, I'm full now," he said and then paused, startled. His voice had sounded weirdly different. *Is it slowing down? Or speeding up?*

Tatter giggled at him, a strange distorted sound that echoed. He looked at her and blinked. Had she been wearing that Erisian garment before? How long had it been since he'd last seen her wear that multi-colored raiment? Her voice also sounded echoing and distorted as she said, "Looks like that gnari's already hitting you."

He glared at her. It sometimes annoyed him that even after the many years he'd known her, Tatter could still somehow manage to instantly get under his skin with a smug comment like that. He stood up unsteadily and wobbled back over to the big mnemotome. He sat down in front of it and focused doggedly. Behind him, Tatter chortled, and her voice was *still* changing.

This time, when he scanned the memory volume, the incomprehensible equations that had been gibberish to him before seemed obvious. He skimmed through the dense information blocs, assembling the different pieces of the algorithm rapidly. A stray thought continued to bother him though, *Why did this seem so cryptic to me before?*

Royce chuffed again in alarm, but he ignored the extraneous signal and focused on the content of the book. The mnemotome had a gigantic amount of information, but now he could grasp that the thing was made up of three modules that built on one another in a linked system.

He could hear Tatter talking somewhere, and was surprised at how her speech seemed to be speeding up dramatically, as well as his responses. He paused for a moment, puzzled. Had they been talking for minutes? Or hours? How long ago had that meal been? As time went by, he started picking up stray communed thoughts from Tatter that he could tell she hadn't intentionally meant to send. Eventually, he couldn't help blushing, even while he tried not to smile. Her increasingly explicit thoughts about him were starting to spill out around the sides of her now very *taut* consciousness. He was very familiar with the mood that gnari always put her in. But he had to get through the book while it still made sense. He picked up the heavy mnemotome, clenching it in his left hand and focused with closed eyes. He'd raced through the first of the three modules when he felt a warm and very strong hand on his right shoulder. Aggravated, he opened his eyes and looked up. Tatter's pupils were only centimeters away from his, and so dilated that there was only a thin rim of encircling brown remaining.

His head swam, and he suddenly felt confused. When had she returned? She'd been gone for months, hadn't she? He tried to go back to the book, feeling a desperate need to finish it while he still could. But Tatter's hand now held his chin very firmly. She licked her lips just as the huge tips of the dagger-like teeth of her Sylphid form started to emerge.

He smiled fondly at her, and reached up unhurriedly with his right index finger to affectionately rub the spot on her cheek just under her ear in the way that always helped her to stop changing. She looked startled for a second, an expression of pure pleasure overtaking her face, and then she let go of his chin with an effort. The razor-sharp fangs withdrew, and her normal brilliant white human teeth flashed at him again as she laughed briefly with unexpected delight.

Even as he beamed back at her, he found she'd taken his breath away once again. *Teeth or fangs, I don't care. She is so...gorgeous.* Tatter closed her eyes and leaned into his hand as he cupped her warm cheek. The sensation of her face and then her soft lips nuzzling his hand was electric.

He felt her lips on his palm, and then couldn't stop himself from slowly extending his hand back into and through her thick mane of soft and curly chestnut hair, feeling the thick satiny mass of it run through his fingers. *My heart is pounding so damn hard, what....*

Then she leaned down again and opened her hugely dilated eyes, staring at him with that *intent* expression. *It's her instinctive Sylphid arousal response. But she's trying to resist the change.* He grinned and peered back into her eyes in utter fascination, eyes that he knew from experience were hovering right at the edge, striving to *not* become *totally* black and then disappear completely back into her armored Sylphid skull. *I need to help her come back to me.* He couldn't stop laughing a little at his own tense excitement as he again touched the precise required spot there at the junction of her cheek and neck below her ear, stroking her slower and more intensely, in just the right way to pull her mind back to its human side. *I've had years of practice at this, though....*

Her back arched for a second in surprise, but now her big dark brown irises swelled back around her pupils. She was breathing raggedly as she leaned down even closer to stare into his pupils, black spaces that he knew must be hugely dilated as well, surrounded by the narrow silvery-grey rims of his irises. He knew she liked his eyes, and he simply smiled at her fondly once again. *Gnari. This stuff always does this to us....* The heavy mnemotome fell to the floor, and he found that he didn't *want* to look away from her face anymore. His left hand was on her waist unexpectedly, and then sliding *around* her waist. Inhaling deeply, he breathed in her distinctive *Sylphid* musk-scent; it seemed to reach down into him and squeeze parts of his anatomy deliciously. Her lips were now so close to his that he could smell and almost *taste* the tantalizingly tart and sparkling flavor of the gnari in her mouth. He realized just how urgently he *wanted* to taste her, then.

"Damnation," she whispered in a husky voice, "this gnari... it's so stinking *strong*... Hey, just tell me one thing, will you, Grey? Do Sojourners take chastity vows or anything like that?"

"Sojourners?" He felt even more confused than before, and felt the last few threads of the equations falling away. But he was already unable to remember why he even needed the calculations as he looked from her lips to her wide eyes. "You mean... those information monks that live on the big ships? No. No, they don't. I don't think so, anyway. They're scientific, not *celibate*, at least from what I remember about them. But why would you ask about...?" Then he felt very dizzy indeed as the cabin began to tilt and spin. *Wait,* he thought, trying to get his bearings again. *I know a lot about Sojourners... don't I? What else is it about Sojourners that I know?* He made a last desperate effort to throw off the dizziness, but it was impossible to take his eyes off her now. His right hand slid out of her thick hair down to the back of her neck. *Her skin is so hot....*

She slipped her arms around him quickly, smiling savagely. "*That's what I wanted to hear...*" With one smooth motion, she lifted him onto his feet up against her soft curves with one hand, slipping the other around his head to pull his face down to hers. He felt her long tongue sliding up into his mouth hungrily, and one of her legs wrapping around him.

He could no longer laugh with her tongue practically down his throat, but he peeped at her closed eyes and happily held her tightly in his arms. He knew what to expect from her in this mood. He could hear a disturbance in the distance, a chuffing sound of increasing distress. The signal was distantly disorienting. *Wait, wait, wait, what mood? What just happened?*

Then *all* he could focus on was her tongue as she kissed him. He felt her sliding her garment off and then pushing the robes off of him. They began to topple over, and she abruptly threw him down on the bunk and got on top of him before he knew what was happening. He felt her lush lips, strong arms, and lithe body surge onto and around him. Then a long period of violent havoc ensued as they enveloped and twisted tightly against each other in exquisite passion, before an even longer period of deep blank sleep took him. At some point he found himself in a dream.

He was lying on a warm shoreline in green grass, the sound of water splashing nearby. When he opened his eyes he could see that he and Tatter were lying naked next to each other, although she was sound asleep. He lifted his head and felt everything spinning again. He was on the side of a sculpted cliff in one of the vast aeries of the distant Peretian realm, waterfalls dancing through the sky of the habitat. Floating through the air above him was a strangely out-of-place anachronism, an ancient pre-space sailing ship made from the trunks of organic Old-Earth trees. He could see the Abbess watching them from the stern of the ship as it sailed away. He tried to find his voice to call out to her, but felt frozen. She saw his distress, and said, "Don't worry. I think we'll meet again, little Brother." The ship dwindled into the clouds of the aerie.

Then Greymalkin's head and ribs were both pounding with pain. *I'm awake,* he thought. *It hurts too much for me to be asleep.* He groaned, but then froze stock still. A smooth, warm, soft, and very bare body was wrapped around him within his sleeping sack. The dimmed lights of the cabin responded to his wakefulness and brightened. He opened his eyes and was immediately lost in the landscape of Tatter's forehead, eyebrows, and tousled brown hair. She was softly snoring. His heart began hammering, and he jerked slightly. Her eyes blinked open sleepily, and for a moment she smiled. Then she saw his panicked reaction and it seemed to trigger panic in her as well. They tried to separate, but there was nowhere to go inside the sleeping sack.

"Uh, good morning?" Tatter said uncertainly, taking in his reaction. Then a stricken look came over her face. "Grey, are you alright? Oh, no...." She seemed to be searching her memory indecisively, but then she only looked at him with even greater panic and spoke in a soft voice. "Crap, I always get so carried away and rough when I'm on gnari.... Grey, did I... hurt you? Did... did I *force* you, or...?"

He stared at her in profound confusion, sorting through what little he remembered, and more prominently what he *felt*. All of his limbs were bruised, his ribs seemed like they might have additional cracks now, and he felt *quite* raw and sore in some *very* unexpected places. But all of these pains were nothing compared to the way his head was ringing with what he assumed must be a gnari hangover. With an incredibly awkward attempt at a reassuring smile he shook his head very slowly and painfully, although he had the feeling that the smile came off more as an agonized rictus. "No. *No*, you didn't, Tatter. That was... very consensual."

She looked his face over apprehensively, and asked with a weak smile, "What's wrong, then? That was... nice." She slowly put her arms around him again, but felt how he unconsciously tensed because of the pain in his ribs. Trying to mask her anxiety with patter, she said lightly, "And, ah, you absolutely *have* to tell me how you knew about that spot on my neck... and, um, some of the *other* things you knew how to do...." Seeing the continuing consternation on his face, she became serious. "Grey, I *did* hurt you didn't I? How badly? I'm so stupid, I forgot you were already injured, and humans don't heal as fast as I do. Or... just tell me, what's *wrong*?"

He tried to work through the confusion of what he remembered, but the memories were fading rapidly. "I felt like... I was someone *else*. Or some-*when* else. Or, well, I just felt... so *different*." He looked at the disordered cabin around them, and saw the big mnemotome lying on the floor where he'd left it. He accessed it for a second and found that the book had simply become gibberish again. He looked back at Tatter, and at the curve of her neck. It had felt so... *natural* to touch her there when she had started... changing. Now he could not get the terrifying image of huge glistening fangs emerging from her lips out of his mind. It had been frightening, but *also* very expected and even... *enticing* as well? *But, what would have happened if I hadn't somehow known how to handle that moment?*

Tatter saw the way he was staring at her mouth, and wriggled out of the sleeping sack away from him, nervously chattering again. "*Sure* you felt different, that's just the gnari. It hits humans like that. You feel like somebody else for a while. Most regular humans tell me they find it pleasurable. I can't say, it doesn't have that effect on me. It just makes me feel goofy, and, uh...I get really...um....really..."

She looked down at her naked body, flustered. Greymalkin didn't avoid looking at her this time. She utterly took his breath away. Tatter gazed back at him with a sheepish expression before turning away and looking around for her clothes.

It took her a full minute of searching through the tumbled cabin for Tatter to locate her Erisian garment, but then she began putting it on quietly. Greymalkin saw his golden robes thrown against the crate. He climbed out of the sleeping sack and picked the robes up off the ground. After a moment he folded them and put them away in his locker, instead putting on one of his regular jumpsuits. But then his face went slack with disbelieving shock, and he spun around despite the pain, extending his shadow sense. "*Where's the ark?*" he cried in dismay. "Royce is drifting in normal space!"

Tatter looked equally surprised, and they both dashed toward the cockpit. Greymalkin opened the hatchway to the cockpit, and they piled through together. Lex was snoring in a sleep sack on the floor, but he jerked awake as they came in. He immediately turned his head to the main viewport and frowned, asking, "Why did you undock us? We're back in normal space."

"I didn't do that!" Greymalkin exclaimed, and leaped into the pilot seat. Even though his head was still splitting with pain, he linked with Royce. The cyneget greeted him with jittery signals, and Greymalkin saw that they were drifting in a distant orbit around the strange purple star. The *Vlieger* and its peculiar pocket space was gone. Mystified, Greymalkin turned to Lex and asked, "Where did they go? What happened?"

Bruno's massively deep voice rumbled out of the corner where the protean had been packed away unobtrusively, "The large ship undocked while you were all sleeping and departed, dropping us out of shadow space in the process. It is no longer within my observation range."

"Why didn't you wake us up?!" Greymalkin yelled. Bruno's response bubbled up with amusement.

"The Xenocorpsman was soundly asleep. And you two were... *actively indisposed*."

"I'll say they were," Lex said to no one in particular. "It took me a while to fall asleep in here after I came back, what with the ruckus that was underway on the other side of the ship."

Tatter simply grinned to the side, but Greymalkin found himself blushing deeply and angrily asked, "Why did the *Vlieger* leave?"

"Probably because Calypso was quicker than I was to translate the very *top* statement on that whopping-big shadow jewel in your head," Lex said sternly. "The message is emblazoned on the larger of the two data constructs there, the giant one that everybody thinks is a covenant. It took me a bit to recognize and translate the Builder glyphs that are on the top level. I've only seen glyphs like those a few other times, always on really ancient Carinae monuments and ruins. But Calypso could probably read it right away; she's a fully Risen Sojourner and she can likely read any language that *can* be read. But then again, who knows; it might have taken even her a minute. There's a *lot* jammed into your head, kid."

"Well, what does it say?" Greymalkin cried. His head hurt much worse when he yelled.

Lex looked very old as he stepped up to Greymalkin to gaze into the shadow jewel and slowly read what was there in a solemn tone. "The Inscripted bearing this dictum is charged with and has accepted commission requiring and granting the right to travel through all territories unhindered and unimpeded. All local officials and authorities along the path of the Inscripted will render assistance and supplies, and will not delay safe passage under any circumstances."

As Greymalkin stared at the older man with wide eyes, Lex added, "It's sealed with a Glyph that everyone with any wisdom knows to take about as seriously as death itself. Translated, the inscription is signed *By order of the Galactic Central Authority*." Lex looked down at Greymalkin and said quietly, "You sure as blazes are in some *really* deep shit, kid."

The silence in the cabin was profound. Lex's words rang through Greymalkin's pounding head like echoes of incomprehensible thunder. The tall blond Xenocorpsman looked around the cabin, first at Bruno's silently boiling mass, then at Tatter's frightened face, and finally back at Greymalkin. Then Lex cracked a grim smile and said, "Is *every* day with you three this interesting? I think I'm going to come along with you after all."

BIRTHS

If he had been able to scream, Greymalkin would have done so. But the agony was paralyzing. He had thought he'd experienced significant pain before in the moments when he'd been beaten or injured seriously, but those incidents now seemed like nothing at all. His muscles spasmed again against the restraints, and then he eventually collapsed back into the medical pod in aching exhaustion. The waves of pain were starting to subside, but still left him immobile.

He opened his eyes to look out through the haze of pain. Greymalkin could see Lex outside the medical pod, still studying the indicators with an impassive expression. As the agony slowly diminished to a bearable level, he took a deep, grateful breath. He could think and move again. Without speaking, he rapped his knuckles on the side of the pod. Lex got up and opened the lid. The oxygen mask and restraints retracted, and finally the mouthpiece that prevented Greymalkin from grinding his teeth or biting his own tongue off. Lex helped him sit up.

Greymalkin said nothing for a time, simply appreciating the absence of the generalized neuropathic seizure. He finally climbed out of the big medical pod unsteadily while leaning on Lex and looking down at the cushioned, sweaty interior of the pod where he had spent so many miserable hours over the past two weeks. Lex's medical pod was much more advanced than the smaller scavenged model on Royce. Greymalkin shut the lid behind him and sat down on the pod unsteadily, asking, "Did you find out anything more this time?"

Lex was not looking him in the eyes, just looking into the distance again. *This can't be good,* Greymalkin thought. The older man eventually said simply, "Yes. I did."

Greymalkin had a feeling that he didn't really want to know what Lex had discovered but at length asked, "Well? Is it the same kind of neurodegeneration that you originally developed?"

Greymalkin's migraines had exploded into agonizing seizures not long after the *Vlieger* had departed. The interval between the seizures had steadily decreased from days at first to only hours. At first he'd tried to not think about the seizures, and they had sought out the next target he'd been given by Sister Constance. The site was on yet another unremarkable airless planetoid, but this time they'd found something more substantive than ever before. Greymalkin looked out through the tessellated side of the surface structure Lex had assembled from his miraculous lockers. Lex could make the lockers transparent from the inside, and they looked out onto the vast and barren surface of the planetoid. But what lay there was wondrous. The ancient hull of a large spacecraft was partly buried in the colorless regolith of the planetoid, a spacecraft almost three thousand years old. A human spacecraft of unmistakable origin and make.

"No, it's not the same as the neurodegenerative condition that I contracted," Lex said. Greymalkin wanted to feel hopeful at that, but something about Lex's manner told him not to bother. The older man turned to him, his gaunt face and artificial mind still seeming so much like a death's head to Greymalkin, and said quietly, "It's much, much worse. You're dying."

Greymalkin felt a sense of stillness creep over him. Then he asked, "How long, then?"

Lex cocked his head. "I don't know, Greymalkin. I'm not a doctor. But from the speed at which the condition is progressing, it could be any time. Soon, one way or the other."

"Why do you think this is happening to me? Why can't the medical pods...." he said, trailing off as he gestured to Lex's pod.

Lex shrugged. "From what you've told me, you've experienced a variety of concussions and destructive radiative trauma since you arrived here in the Carinae. Medical pods are limited in what they can do. Maybe, if you had been placed in a good hospital back in civilization? But even then it might not have mattered. And while that advanced golden void suit has excellent radiation protection, you also told me you haven't always been wearing it when you were undertaking EVA. And even though you had the gold suit on when the Aurelian had you...." The older man finally met Greymalkin's eyes with the eerie shadowed blue gaze that was always so unnerving, and said with icy anger, "That bastard didn't care one little bit about anyone but himself. Who knows what kind of scans he subjected you to? Your gold suit is good, but—"

Greymalkin closed his eyes and recited the Great Vow slowly in his mind. When he came to the final assertion, he held onto it. *I will sojourn through life with courage.* He appreciated as never before the recurring admonishment of the Proctors as he was growing up. *Your life will end. All mortal life ends. The only thing that gives it meaning is that which you believe in and to which you fully commit yourself.*

"Thank you, Lex," he said sincerely. "Thank you for telling me directly and concisely. I need to collate my final notes for Sister Constance. Would you take them to her after I'm gone?" When Lex nodded silently, Greymalkin continued hesitantly, "And... I know you left the Order, but you remember the core practices, still? Would you perform the *Journey's End* rite when I'm gone? I would really appreciate it, if *you* would do that."

Lex nodded, and gently said, "I will." Greymalkin marveled over how peaceful the older man's voice sounded, and thought about how sad it was that Lex had not stayed in the Order.

"The timing of this happening to me right now is ironic," Greymalkin said. "Tomorrow is my nineteenth birthday; did I tell you that? Well, probably not my *real* birthday, just the day that the Order *assigned* as my birthday, that is. I was found abandoned as an infant; nobody knows exactly when I was born. But I've heard it said that sometimes dying people will stubbornly stay alive just long enough to see their next birthday. Maybe I'll live till tomorrow, then. But the way I feel, though... well, I guess we'll see what happens." The pensive young monk looked around the enclosure, and asked, "Anyway, where are Tatter and Bruno?"

"They departed with your ship some time ago, when your seizure began. Tatter was quite distressed at your pain. She said that she and Bruno would retrieve the best medical pod available from the main expedition base."

Greymalkin placed his palm over his face, and wondered what kind of trouble Tatter would stir up with this futile effort. "I wish she hadn't done that. The medical pods on the base are surely no better than this deluxe model of yours."

Then Lex folded his arms as if he'd made up his mind about something, and said, "Grey, I agree that what she's doing is pointless, but I'd like to propose one other, quite *different* course of action. Would you hear me out?"

Greymalkin frowned. "I've accepted what's happening, Lex. You, more than most, know that in the Order we contemplate impermanence and prepare for this. It's an inevitable aspect of committing to a way of life that can lead to dangerous missions and lost lives."

"And that is a very good and proper thing," Lex said. "But let me tell you about a... most *unusual* place here in the Carinae. A place that I never wanted to see again, but that I think it may be worth taking you to at this point."

Greymalkin felt a strange premonition of fear at Lex's tone, but then dismissed it. *What do I have to lose at this point?* "Sure, tell me about it. But could you be brief? I really do want to record all my notes for Constance. It's the one useful thing I can still accomplish now."

"Perhaps that's not the only useful thing that you can do," Lex said, his jaw tightening slightly in a facial tic Greymalkin had never before noticed. "I told you that the Aurelian did things that improved my intelligence and longevity, but I did not tell you *what* he did to me. He took me to a place, one of the oldest inhabitations in the Carinae. It almost certainly dates all the way back to the time of the Builders."

The premonition of fear was now growing in Greymalkin's mind. "What's special about this place, then? What's there?"

Lex paused, clearly reluctant to talk further, but then went on, in a voice not much above a whisper at first. "There is a... *Tree*. It is truly gigantic, another of the Builders' notorious experimental cybernetic marvels. But to my knowledge it is the only one of its kind that was ever created by the Builders, as I have never heard of another such creation anywhere. It is called the *Genibrata*. It grows... an extremely unusual kind of fruit."

Greymalkin squinted skeptically. "A fruit. You want me to consume a fruit?"

Lex shook his head. "More the other way around. But I'm getting ahead of myself. You first have to understand that the Genibrata was just one more subsidiary experiment that made up the grand design of the information-generating Nexus here, and the underlying Forge that powers it. All of these and more, the grand *array* of Builder experiments found in the Carinae, were developed for the same reason the Builders created so many of their experiments throughout the Galaxy, as instrumentality to enable them to undertake their twisted investigations. The pods which grow on the Genibrata were designed by the Builders as a way of satisfying their perplexing curiosity about a peculiar sort of question concerning life and death. You see, you do not consume the fruit of the Genibrata, *they consume you*."

"Carnivorous...fruit?" Greymalkin asked. His skepticism and revulsion was growing by the moment. Lex smiled grimly and shook his head.

"Not carnivorous," Lex said. "The fruit are very complex cyborgs designed to serve as *symbiogenic* chambers." When Greymalkin looked baffled and started to ask questions, Lex held up his hand and said, "Wait, let me explain what that means and what it entails. The individual fruit are custom grown for specific species, and they take a *very* long time to grow. It literally takes thousands of years for one of these giant pods to fully develop. They are *that* complex. But they enable *wonders*. Given the effort that went into creating the Nexus, the Builders wanted to explore questions about the radically different types of information and *beings* they could extract from it. You already know that the Builders created myriad types of cyborg designs for various purposes. The Genibrata uses filters to sort through the unending information that emerges from the Nexus to find unusual and advanced new intelligent species, and then zero in on the premier individual specimens from such species. *Wonders*. The Builders always sought to *build* on wonders to create *new* wonders. It was their defining characteristic and motivation. The Genibrata was designed to take wonders retrieved from the Nexus and recombine them with exemplary sapient beings of our galaxy to create unique new beings with great abilities."

"What do you mean by 'recombine'?" Greymalkin asked warily.

"The biological term is symbiogenesis," Lex said. "Merging two separate species into something greater. The primary example we're familiar with from Old Earth was the creation of eukaryotic multicellular organisms billions of years ago when two different types of single cell organisms merged in a symbiotic relationship. That single evolutionary transformation was very basic, but it was foundational to the history of life on our world; it led to most forms of life on Old Earth, humans among them. With that in mind, understand why the processes the Builders designed into the Genibrata are so much more provocative. The artificial symbiogenic process that occurs in the Genibrata chrysalis cases is far more controlled, deliberate, and thorough than random evolutionary chance. The processes that take place there merge characteristics of the beings identified in the stream from the Nexus with the subject placed in the pod. It produces a wholly new being that superficially acts and looks the same, at least initially. But the new being has many characteristics inherited from whatever being was selected from the Nexus as well."

"That sounds utterly grotesque," Greymalkin said with distaste. "The chimeric life forms produced from such a process surely would not be viable. Do most of them die?"

"No," Lex said. "Not only do they not die, the resulting metasymbionts are always significantly improved in terms of intelligence, vitality, and adaptations. Sometimes incredibly so. I understand your skepticism. I don't understand it either. Recombining sentient life forms in this way, to this degree of subtlety, is far beyond human technology generally. It was complex even for the Builders; that's why the individual pods take so long to grow. *But it works.* Why do you think so many Risen have appeared here in the Carinae?"

"*Risen?*" Greymalkin said with alarm. "You mean, *this* is the process that produces the individuals I've heard referred to as Risen?"

"This is one such process," Lex said. "I know there are other processes which lead to similar results that are used in the Orion Arm. For instance, the xenogenesis process whereby Sylphids interbreed with Humans and other alien species. From what I learned from the *Vlieger* crew, the Sylphids themselves were created by the Builders long ago by means of earlier transformation processes similar to those of the

Genibrata. The Builders symbiogenically created the Sylphids by combining a simpler species of arboreal predators they discovered with other more advanced cyborganic species they had encountered. As a result, all Sylphids are Risen. Tatter is not only more intelligent, but quite a bit more advanced in her biology than any normal human being. So are all of the Risen."

As Greymalkin thought about it, something occurred to him. "That's interesting, Lex. Every time I've physically touched one of these 'Risen' individuals for the first time, well, I get strange impressions and sensations." Greymalkin looked at Lex with creeping uncertainty. "It happened with you, too. When I shook your hand that first time. And you say that the Aurelian put you through this process?"

Lex nodded, scowling. "Yes, but in my case I think the process was stunted. By the time I went into the pod virtually all of my brain cells had already been replaced with cybernetic substitutes. I was maimed." His face took on the distant expression again as he spoke in a stoic voice. "The rest of my body was improved, no doubt. For instance, it hasn't aged at all since I went into the pod. But the pod couldn't fully operate on me, not all of me, that is." The older man shrugged. "I hope it will be different with you. You've been injured, yes, but you're still fundamentally intact, for the most part."

Greymalkin slumped against the back of the medical unit, and said, "What you're describing doesn't sound like a cure for my ailments, Lex; more like a randomized way to commit suicide. Or worse."

"I will admit that, from a limited perspective, it might be understood simply as death," Lex said grudgingly, and then continued in a gentler tone again. "At least, you will not continue in your current form. But that which dies has continuity with something far greater that lives. And, Grey, one way or the other, your current body is about to die. However, *transformation is not death*. You will be fundamentally different physically, but you will still have your memories. I hold onto the belief that memories are the most important aspect of identity. And I thought a Sojourner would be more receptive to possibilities for a changed existence that enhances you. The Order's doctrine holds that life is a continuous process of change."

"I should have died already," Greymalkin said bitterly. "It should have been Bora or Soren that lived to undertake this mission. I'm just an inept and inexperienced acolyte. I've bungled every effort I made here."

"You forget," Lex said, and once again his voice sounded stern, "You can't simply give up and die, you agreed to volunteer for an undertaking of great importance. The inscription on your shadow jewel says that you accepted a commission from nothing less than the Galactic Central Authority."

"I have absolutely no idea who that is, or what that phrase even means," Greymalkin said. He could already feel the early symptoms of the onset of another neuropathic seizure. Part of him dreaded the pain that was coming so much that death seemed like a welcome release.

"You said you encountered a being called the Velan," Lex said, patiently now. "And that after the encounter was when you became aware of this complicated cybernetic construct that is inscribed on your shadow jewel. What did you agree to do? What was the commission you accepted?"

"I don't know what I agreed to do, or even if I agreed to anything," Greymalkin admitted. "That encounter and entity were far beyond my understanding. But the only way I felt that I could survive was to accept its assessment of me, including how I would answer a question or questions that it apparently couldn't ask me for some reason it couldn't tell me! It was all very confusing. Absurd and surrealistic, really. But nothing was communicated to me about anything I'd agreed to, and I'm also very certain there was no mention of a 'Galactic Central Authority'."

"That's what the Builders became when they withdrew to the central Galactic regions," Lex said, rubbing his chin in thought absently. "Now, I'm finally putting this together myself. You told me before that the Clavisian referred to the Velan as an 'elder colleague'? The Clavisian is the only local representative of the Central Authority in the entirety of the Carinae. That would make the Velan the ranking representative in this entire region of the Galactic hinterlands...."

Greymalkin sighed in irritation. "Lex, this is too much, I'm sorry. Even if I accept all that you say about some 'Authority' which I've never heard of, how should I understand what you've said about the inscription as well? And even if what you've said is accurate, it may simply boil down to exactly how the Aurelian described me and my role."

Lex folded his arms and scowled frostily. "Please, by all means, tell me what the old rascal said to you."

"He said that I was 'being used as an unintelligent carrier of information', basically that I was an animal being used as a courier," Greymalkin said. He still felt angry at the thought, particularly because it seemed like the most plausible explanation for everything that had happened. "In primitive human cultures they used birds with homing instincts to carry messages. I think that's exactly the purpose to which I've been put."

Lex looked incredulous, and snapped, "Oh, I see. Well, please, tell me where your homing instinct is directing you."

Greymalkin felt the first pangs of the oncoming seizure start to lance through his head and winced before saying, "Exactly nowhere. Whatever the Velan's plan was, it was a fool's errand. And I'm the fool."

Lex studied the obvious signs of neuralgia crossing Greymalkin's face, and then glared at him. "Neither stupidity nor self-pity become you, Grey. I can assure you that beings like the Velan do not set foolish plans in motion. Let me propose a mechanism for settling the matter."

"Fine, just do it quickly!" Greymalkin barked. He was realizing that he'd already lost what little opportunity he'd had for collating his notes to Constance.

"Let us speak to the caretakers of the Genibrata," Lex said, while coming over to strap Greymalkin back into the medical pod. "We will explain your dire medical condition, and I will point out the inscription to them. They are... *well-versed*, and adept in such matters. If they do not accept the injunctions of the inscription, that will be proof enough that I'm either lying or misguided. But if they agree to help, and are willing to provide us with a chrysalis fruit from the Genibrata for your use, you will undergo the process, yes?"

Greymalkin clenched his teeth as the outermost waves of the seizure began to come on. The moments of pain were indescribable. "You said that the process would merge me with a being drawn from this supposed Nexus? Is the being living or dead?"

Lex was adjusting the controls of the medical pod and inspecting the indicators. "What an odd question you've posed. But I'll answer it. The beings the Genibrata selects for the process always seem to be long-dead, legendary exemplars of their respective species."

"And therefore unable to agree or disagree to participate in the process," Greymalkin said crossly. "So, this process requires the unwilling merger of two beings that have either died or are dying? To create a new entity that could potentially be monstrous in its nature? This hardly seems like a process that recommends itself, Lex!"

"The chrysalis fruit are themselves intelligent beings, Grey," Lex said. "They live only to successfully create new masterpieces, and they will not proceed with the symbiogenesis if the two beings selected are unwilling."

Greymalkin laughed cynically. "Even worse, *three* intelligent beings must die to create one monster!"

Lex looked down at him sadly. "Please tell me that you'll at least consider it?"

"You said that either way, it won't be me anymore. I won't survive, whether I simply die or am transformed into something else." Greymalkin bit off the words, just as the seizure began and agony began to leap through his mind. "As a result, it hardly seems that it should matter to me either way."

Then Greymalkin's universe dissolved into pain again, nothing but sheets of horrific agony that made everything go away. At some point he found that he could feel Tatter embracing him, and he saw her desperate brown eyes looking at him from just above his face. He heard her arguing with Lex, and felt himself in a new pod that did nothing at all. The pain became his entire universe, waves of a storm that constantly beat on the shore of his mind. He tried to meditate, but the agony simply swept away any attempt he made at chants, rhythms, or any other effort to reclaim an ordered intelligence.

* * *

At some point he heard words again, and tried to hold onto them. "This is pointless." The words had Lex's dispassionate tone, and Greymalkin knew that the older man said nothing but the truth. "We have to take him to the Genibrata while there's still time."

"You keep talking about that thing, but what will it do to him? Actually? Specifically?" Tatter's voice sounded so upset. Greymalkin thought how odd it was that he could hear tears in her voice and didn't have to see them. He wanted to focus on her voice, but it drifted away out into the sea of pain. Later he could feel Royce skimming across the shadow plane, and tried to extend his shadow sense to see where they were going. In the synesthesia from his shadow jewel he could only sense a bitterly cold wind through the waves of mind-obliterating pain. When it finally began to subside, he quieted his mind and sensed a communing conversation going on nearby. Lex seemed to be debating communally with an unfamiliar, angry pair of individuals. Their thoughts were like a thatched barrier of thorns.

«Examine the inscription on this boy's shadow jewel!» Lex was communing the message with demanding intensity, but the response was alien and skeptical. Greymalkin recognized the thoughts of a Crotani, or something that resembled a Crotani. He could discern that the creature was standing on a dock platform just beyond the airlock, arguing with Lex.

Weakly, Greymalkin released his own restraints and pushed the lid up off of the medical pod. He sat up then, even though the movement felt like acid splashing across his spine and brain. It no longer mattered. Now everything in his mind was measured in finely accounted degrees of agony, and the new aches were trivial. He climbed out of the pod and staggered toward the airlock, his bare feet hitting the cold deck with slaps. After a few moments or an eternity he found himself stepping out of the front of Royce's airlock, stark naked, taking slow steps forward. He could sense Royce chuffing behind him in agitation, but he reassured the cyneget with communed thoughts. *It's going to be okay. Somehow, it will be okay.*

There was a small tableaux on the dock in front of Royce. Lex and Tatter faced two large Crotani that were wearing elaborate garments that gave him the impression of ceremonial robes. He could not see Bruno, but he felt the cyborg's presence. As he haltingly stepped up to the tense group, the Crotani saw him and faced him, their beaks clamped in hard lines. He could see that they'd made up their minds about whatever the dispute was. Tatter turned and was shocked, looking at him up and down. Lex glanced back at him with a grimly satisfied expression. The tall man reached back and pulled him forward by the arm.

«Read the inscription on his shadow jewel, you fools.» Lex pushed Greymalkin forward and he looked up into the alien eyes of the Crotani that faced him. Like all of the Crotani he'd met, the creatures displayed no emotions that Greymalkin could interpret physically, but unexpectedly glowing inside their brains were shadow jewels, much like the minds of all the men and women he had known on the *Dragon King*. The presence of the creatures burned brightly in their jewels, and Greymalkin thought they were angry and offended.

These aliens have shadow jewels; they're civilized. Perhaps I can converse with them. Greymalkin tried to commune, but found that his mind was too scrambled by the pain to form any intelligible message. The biggest Crotani stepped closer to him and Greymalkin now found himself face to face with the alien, it's array of four eerie eyes stared out of a broad, flat face of starkly patterned brown and white fur. *Or are those feathers?* He saw that the creature was inspecting his shadow jewel. The many eyes blinked rapidly, and the big alien stepped back from him. It seemed to be taken aback.

Lex began arguing with the Crotani again, but Greymalkin sagged backwards. Whatever remaining strength he had was draining away quickly. He felt Tatter's warm arms catch him, slipping under and around his back and arms as she held him up effortlessly, like a rag doll. "I've got you, Grey," she whispered in his ear.

Then the big Crotani made an angry hooting sound and communed haughtily. «We accept what you say, human, but we cannot give you what you demand!»

«Why not?» Lex glowered at the alien with folded arms. «The Great Tree has myriad fruits. We only require one.»

«As you well know, the fruits must be grown specifically for the species they are intended for. None of the remaining fruits that have been grown for humans are fully mature, and if an unripe one is used, the results may be unpredictable and... sub-optimal.»

«There must be some that are nearing maturity; give us one of those!» Lex was angry now as well.

«Such a decision can only be made by the Tenax or his vassal, the Grand Elder, who is our ruler. But the Tenax does not entertain requests, and the Grand Elder is away at the moment with our Carinan brethren on the long pilgrimage. Both the Grand Elder and the Carinans will return, but this ailing human will certainly be dead by that point.» The Crotani made the peculiar hooting sound again as if to punctuate its statement with finality. Lex began to exclaim again, but the monstrously strong communed thoughts of Bruno made everyone jump, especially the Crotani. Greymalkin now saw that the protean was hovering high above them.

«Perhaps we should pause in these deliberations.» The protean's thoughts seemed uncharacteristically calm, although Greymalkin could sense the telltale bubbling of subdued amusement in the corners of the communed rumble.

«You advise this? *You?*» Lex was obviously skeptical.

Bruno's thoughts bubbled up like gas escaping lava. «Yes, I do. I have *seen reason*. Let us retire back to our conveyance for a short while.»

«Your monster is unexpectedly sensible. The recommendation is sound.» The Crotani both hooted one final time and turned to leave. As Bruno floated back into Royce's main airlock, Lex stormed after the protean cyborg and cycled the lock shut behind them all after Tatter had helped Greymalkin limp inside.

"What was all that about?" Lex demanded. "I thought we were in agreement that we need one of the chrysalis cases for the kid!"

"We are, and we will have one shortly," Bruno rumbled like distant thunder. "While you were wasting time arguing with those two obtuse individuals, I accessed their inventory systems and found the locations of the growths that are meant for humans. Let us depart from this locale and I will go back and remove one for our use."

"You mean that you'll *steal* one," Greymalkin rasped. "No, Bruno, please. This is pointless; it'll just lead to more violence."

"You forget that I am extraordinarily skilled at theft," Bruno bragged. "We will be light-years away by the time they discover their loss."

"Even if you succeed, I'm done for anyway," Greymalkin said weakly. "Lex, you said that these 'fruits' create new life-forms from dead ones. Whatever comes out of the pod won't be me, just some new horror."

Tatter had a frightened expression as she looked from Greymalkin to Lex and asked, "Is that true? The pod will just create some gruesome chimera out of Grey?"

Lex sighed, and tapped his foot. "No. The chrysalis cases aren't some freakshow, they're each nothing less than a miracle. Grey, the chrysalis case will heal you and improve you. *Dramatically*."

Greymalkin felt the first precursors of another seizure dancing maniacally at the edge of his perception. "So you say. The way I feel, I don't think there will be enough time for it to do anything for me at all."

"Tatter, put him back in the deluxe medical unit," Lex said, hurrying toward the cockpit. "He's right about one thing; we don't have time to spare. Bruno, get ready, will you?"

Greymalkin started to protest again, but Tatter hauled him away assertively. She put him back into the medical pod and carefully reconnected the various attachments.

As she worked on him, Greymalkin studied her features, a sad smile on his face. "Sorry about all this, Tat," he muttered when she'd finished.

Tatter grimaced in irritation and snapped, "Shut up, you brat! This is going to work. Now just relax while I sedate you."

"No!" he said quickly. "Don't put me out yet. I've got to try to make a few last notes for Sister Constance before, well, you know."

Tatter bit her lip, and then leaned down to hug him fiercely for a moment before saying, "I'll monitor you. When the major pain starts again, I'm going to put you under. Now, shush." She kissed him and then shut the lid of the medical pod.

Greymalkin closed his eyes and accessed his personal journal. He rushed through entering the notes that he hadn't gotten to yet, and then scanned back over his entries since he'd arrived in the Carinae. The haphazard state of his entries depressed him. He'd intended to go back and clean up the mess of jotted comments and hastily assembled measurements, but now there would be no time. He felt the rapid passage of Royce across the shadow plane, and tried to extend his shadow sense outward. It hurt, but he could make out where they were. Inside the oxygen mask, he inhaled sharply.

He hadn't been sufficiently aware at the time to note their approach to the vicinity of the Genibrata. They were at the edge of the gigantic Homunculus Nebula, and the whorls of ionized gas clouds covered most of the sky around them. The patterns inside the huge nebula had fascinated him from the moment he'd arrived in the Carinae, and this was the closest he'd yet been to the swirling maze of embedded funnel patterns in shadow space. The range of synesthesia generated by the Homunculus was unbelievable, and he flinched at the range of signals bombarding his senses.

There was the illusion of a crisp, cold breeze across his face, a breeze full of the same fresh resinous conifer forest scent of terpenes that had surrounded the region where they'd encountered the *Vlieger*, but here the pseudo-fragrance was practically bursting throughout his mind. They were passing stars on all sides, and he seemed to periodically hear eerie echoes and blustery blasts of gales from the stars through gaps in the obscuring gas clouds. Then he caught a glimpse of something in the distance that he'd never seen before. A cluster of rapidly moving shapes was skimming across the shadow plane behind the closest clouds. At first he thought it must be a trick of the confusing synesthesia illusions, but then the shapes emerged from the echoed image fog of energized gas and came much closer. The logarithmic scale of his shadow sense brought the images of the fleet shapes into clarity as they approached.

It was a group of wild cynegets, the cybernetic creatures skimming at outrageous velocities across the shadow plane. He could make out the ovoid mirrorshell carapaces of the cyborgs even at this distance, and the way that they sparkled and shone as they passed in and out of the molecular cloud shadow mists that clung to the rolling topography of the plane. The wild cynegets had apparently sensed Royce and were drawing closer in evident curiosity. They began to send signals across the intervening shadow space, and he was startled to discover that his synesthetic perceptions instinctively interpreted the signals atavistically, as ancient sounds dredged up from his human subconscious. Translated through his shadow senses, the broadcast signals of the creatures sounded recognizably like the howls of wild animals on terraformed planets. The baying cries of the cyborgs echoed around them, and he was startled a second time when Royce erupted in a deafening cry of inborn acknowledgement. For a brief moment he wondered if they were in danger, if the cynegets' shrieks might be threat displays or challenges, but the emotions that he could understand in them did not seem to be aggressive.

Rather, the predominant emotions that he could discern in the communed cries were exultant and triumphal. The wild mood of the creatures sent a thrill of exhilaration down his back, even as the initial agonizing stabs of the oncoming seizure began to course through him. The thrill and the pain entwined in twinges of raw nerves throughout Greymalkin's mind and limbs. He could distantly sense Lex and Tatter communing on another frequency about the herd (pack? flock? school? troop?) of cynegets, the admiration for the creatures in Tatter's thoughts, and the stern appreciation that even dour Lex felt at the sight. As the wild cynegets skimmed along beside Royce on the glimmering blue shadow plane, Greymalkin felt a passing moment of indescribable elation. *At least I lived long enough to see this.*

Bruno's cruelly harsh communal thoughts broke the spell of the moment, and Greymalkin realized that the protean had again left a tiny fragment of itself on his shoulder without his noticing. «I am approaching the large cybernetic dendriform. Do you wish to observe?»

Greymalkin sighed, wishing he could have held onto the moment longer. «Yes, thank you, Bruno.» Immediately, he felt the protean's powerful mental communal frequency activate. The connection was even stronger than a Helm Link, and Greymalkin felt as if he was actually in Bruno's churning stone form soaring through shadow space, rather than lying helplessly in the medical pod. The protean was decelerating precipitously and abruptly came to a stop before a tremendous shape that blanketed the sky. Greymalkin gasped.

The Genibrata was much like a Nemora meta-tree, but inconceivably larger. There were the same sprawling silvery branches terminating in ovoid capsules, but the scale of the branching mass was several times larger than even the huge tree within which the main expedition base had been installed. Greymalkin tried to take in the extent of the incredible tree, but Bruno was instantly in motion, flitting through the huge snarl of silver branches at great speed. The protean dodged around the branches in fluid paths that showed no trace of uncertainty as to destination. Almost as quickly, Bruno detected the wail of alarm signals in the distance. The protean's bubbling laughter permeated Greymalkin's mind.

«Apparently their security network is excellent. They have detected me despite my current state of invisibility.» Bruno's mood was accelerating toward his usual battle lust, and Greymalkin felt a rising anxiety. The gigantic Tree was one of the most magnificent living things he'd ever beheld, and he dreaded the idea of a destructive rampage through it by Bruno. So far the protean had managed to avoid any collisions in the frenetic path through the thick mass of twisting branches. Greymalkin had begun to notice the subtle differences in the shapes of the terminal ovoids at the end of each branch when the protean came to another halt in the midst of a distinctive cluster of the pods. He had a fraction of a second to register that at the end of each of these silvery ovoids there was actually a tiny indented impression of a spread-eagled human being. Then Bruno expanded dramatically, swelling into the form of a clutching claw.

«They have dispatched some kind of defensive security units, but I will have departed by the time they arrive.» Bruno was boiling with frenzied elation as his huge claw form closed around one of the shining ovoids and neatly severed it from the immense branch. The Bruno-claw instantly began to withdraw through the forest of branches, the egg-shaped prize clutched in the form-fitting talons. In the distance through the thickly entangled branches, Greymalkin could see sharp-angled objects approaching swiftly and he struggled through the pain to commune.

«Bruno, get out of there! They're almost on top of you!» The protean and the pursuers were now moving so quickly in such erratic paths that the scene was nothing but a spinning mass of reflections and lights. The motion was aggravating Greymalkin's oncoming seizure, and now he felt intense nausea. Just as the swarm of pursuers converged on Bruno, the protean shot forward out of the branches and vanished into shadow space.

Tatter's enthusiastic communed whoop gave a voice to the moment. «*Yeah! Rockhead, go-go-go!*» Through the sensory link, Greymalkin could perceive the improbable speed at which the protean was soaring through the shadow volume, leaving his pursuers far behind. Tatter continued cheering on the communal link, even as Greymalkin felt himself powerlessly sliding into the seizure's chasm of agony. He distantly heard Tatter's sudden gasp of concern as she saw the readouts on his medical pod shift. Then he felt the sting of a hypodermic as she sedated him, and he felt like he was being lowered down into a searing black pitch of unconsciousness.

Greymalkin struggled through nightmares of pain for a time, and then found himself coming back into the full agony of wakefulness. Someone was calling his name and also trying to reach him by communing. He recognized Tatter's thoughts, but could not focus enough to respond. He felt himself being lifted in her warm arms and carried. Finally, he managed to open his eyes and look around.

Greymalkin was lying on a gurney, his face turned to the left. He could hear Tatter and Lex arguing nearby. As he weakly turned his head, he saw that they were all inside one of the arbitrarily large tessellated enclosures that Lex routinely assembled from his replicating locker field-structures. Bruno had apparently buried the huge ovoid in the surface of an airless world, and then Lex had erected a transparent dome of the locker components over it and pressurized the space. As Greymalkin looked up through the dome, he could see the beautiful, colorful sweep of the Homunculus Nebula in the sky. The intricate patterns of ionized gas clouds covered his entire field of view. He turned his face to the right, and saw Lex and Tatter inspecting the exposed end of the ovoid. It looked like an immense, lustrous white pearl buried in the sandy soil of the barren world. Lex and Tatter were studying the indentation in the ovoid that looked like the shape of a spread-eagled human form. Greymalkin now saw that what had appeared to be a tiny human-shaped indentation from Bruno's perspective was actually far larger than it had seemed. The arm-span of the indentation was almost three meters across.

"Are you sure you know how this thing works?" Tatter was asking Lex anxiously. The older man seemed intent on the readouts of a tablet scanner he held in his hand, but he nodded to her absently.

"Even though it was some time ago, I remember the experience of being placed into one of these all too well," Lex said softly. "There, it's prepped. Now we just have to put him in it. The chrysalis case will take care of everything else."

"But, Lex, are you sure about this?" Tatter persisted, her voice fearful. "They said the fruits weren't ripe or something? I've been trying to analyze this... *organism*, and even though I know a lot about xenobiology, I can't make any sense of it. My people are masters of recombining organisms, it's what Morganans are obsessed with. But this huge pod is more complicated than anything I've ever encountered. And have you looked inside of this thing? It's *horrific*, like the inside of a monster pomegranate fruit, but with huge arrays of blood sacs and... *stomachs* instead of seeds. And... Lex, it's *pulsing*. This gigantic thing really is *alive*."

"Of course it's alive," Lex chided. "It's effectively a giant hyperintelligent womb for transformative rebirth, and since it was grown specifically for humans, it has to have plenty of human blood ready to use. The chrysalis case may not be fully ripened, but it does have the capacity to function. But well, *no*, I'm not completely certain about anything, you have to be prepared for it if this doesn't work. Greymalkin may very well die. And he's so stubborn he might just resist and refuse the process completely. But now isn't the time for second thoughts, woman! Help me get him inside; he's almost gone. The chrysalis case has to be used immediately after being separated from the Genibrata, it dies very quickly afterwards whether it's used or not." Lex stood up and came over to stand above Greymalkin. Tatter knelt by his side and felt his cheeks and head.

"He's burning up," Tatter said, sounding quietly panicked. She brought her face close to his and said, "Grey, can you hear me? We don't have any more time, we have to do this." There were tears brimming in her eyes, but her expression was composed and solemn as she lifted him off the gurney. Lex came up beside her and bent over to look in his face.

"Grey, we're going to put you in the chrysalis case. If you make it through to the other side, just take it easy. But you need to be prepared for unexpected changes. If you survive, especially at the beginning you'll feel extraordinarily strange, and you may experience extreme mood swings as your biochemistry and hormones adjust to whatever it does to you. Try to be ready for it. Okay, Tatter, put him in it now."

Greymalkin felt nauseous as Tatter took quick steps up the side of the curved and pearly ovoid surface. "Do we just lay him down in the hollow form here? That's all?" Tatter asked Lex. She seemed even more reluctant to let him go, now that the moment had come.

"Yes, put him in the center of it, and back away. Hurry, do it now!"

Tatter knelt and laid him down on a warm surface, arranging his arms and legs in the splayed depressions. She leaned down and gave him a long kiss before staring at him for a second, her face drawn and desolate. He wanted to speak or just commune something coherent to her, but found he couldn't even do that. Two large tears fell down from her brown eyes onto his face. Then she stood up and backed away.

Greymalkin closed his eyes then. He felt a sensation of gentle enfolding around his naked body, as if the hard surface beneath him had softened and enveloped him. He found himself drifting off to sleep in a warm and enclosed space. After a time, even the nightmare of pain stopped. But it was not the end.

He tried to open his eyes, but found that he could not feel his eyelids, or anything else. Wherever he was, it was comfortable and dark, although he seemed to sense a light ahead of him. His vision cleared and he realized that he was seeing a large shadow jewel glimmering brilliantly in the darkness. The jewel seemed to be rotating, with sparkles of radiance dancing in its facets. Then the white light from the gem's facets illuminated a small face close beneath it, and Greymalkin realized that he was seeing the visage of a newborn human infant.

Hands were holding the baby, and another pair of hands held the jewel clamped tightly in a very delicate and small runcible. The scene snapped into clarity for Greymalkin; he was seeing the *provenience* ceremony for the baby. Momentarily, the jewel would be displaced ever so slightly into shadow space and then deftly placed inside the prefrontal cortex of the baby, so closely that the quantum neural links could start to form across the dimensional boundary with the child's brain.

He could not hear what was being said, but he remembered the words of the ceremony from when he had served as an assisting acolyte at the birth of several children on the *Dragon King*. The provenience ceremony of birth was part of the training required for acolytes. But something seemed wrong in this instance, both pairs of hands were shaking, and at an increasing rate. Greymalkin tried to look at the surroundings, but everything faded into darkness just a hands-breadth from the glittering shadow jewel's radiance. A premonition struck him then.

Did Lex say that a dead being would be required to heal me? Is it this child? The revulsion he felt at the thought of a child being slain to heal him was so profound that he recoiled and twisted violently inside his mind trying to find a way to resist. He struggled to find his voice to cry out, but could no more find his tongue than his eyelids. As the hands holding the newborn trembled even more violently, Greymalkin felt sheer panic at the idea that the baby would be sacrificed in exchange for his life. He tried to scream, but he had no throat. Then, in his desperation, he thought to try communing in the most direct way possible.

«Don't harm the child! I do not want the child to be killed!»

The image froze, and he now saw that the bright blue light of shadow space played upon the infant's face and the hands holding it. Then mature female thoughts came to him.

«The child must die for the adult to live.» The matronly thoughts seemed to extend thickly around him, like an overwhelming motherly presence.

«No!» Greymalkin felt petrified, but he was certain of one thing; he was not going to let an infant die in his place. He felt no body, but he began to search through his mind for a way to resist. Although he felt confused and had no clear idea of what had happened to him, one tactic that had worked for him before occurred to him. *Keep them talking!* «Who are you?»

A warm sensation flooded around the periphery of his mind, like an embrace from Tatter but without boundaries of skin or space. «I am that which is here to help you. Together we must weave anew from the threads of the past. You are muddled, and frightened. Please stop resisting. It will only lead to your death, and I am only that which is here to help you.»

«If you want to help me, let the child go.» Greymalkin tried to twist or move in any way he could, but he felt no muscles or nerves of any kind. *It's useless, I've got to talk my way out of this, or reason with it somehow.* «Why harm something helpless?»

The warmth increased, but along with it now came a profound sense of concern in the engulfing thoughts. «I have no wish to harm anything. Your compassion is worthy, but it is clouding your mind. You will kill us both to no purpose.»

«I have no wish to kill you either!» He suddenly felt uncertain. «But, how am I threatening you?» He sensed the warm entity focus on a fierce attempt to reach him, to communicate critically important things with him. But the entity's thoughts were much too complex for him to fully understand, and much of what she said came to him only as symbols, intuitions, and images.

«For time beyond your conception, I have been preparing for our *dance*, our *weaving* of *blood and creation*.» The thoughts of the enormous presence had become tinged by incredible sadness. «This dance is the fulfillment of my life, and my life will end when our dance ends. Your life has already ended. We must also select another, our Inspiration, for the tapestry we will weave. If we succeed, we will both live anew, in a tapestry that has never before existed. If we do not weave at all, then we will have both failed.»

Greymalkin paused, trying to focus and sort out what the communed thoughts were trying to express. Whatever she was, the huge female presence was far too alien to unambiguously articulate what she was trying to say to him, and his own thoughts were a jumbled disaster. But through all of the tangled confusion, a few pieces of clarity were reaching him. Whatever the entity was, she did not reek of cruelty and malice. Quite the contrary, he could sense nothing but an urgent, adept desire for creation, an impulse to grow and nurture through intricate wisdom. He stopped resisting then, and communed a question. «What do you want to do, then?»

«You must breathe in your Inspiration.» The echoing female thoughts swirled through him. «I was afraid we would have difficulty finding it in the Nexus, but there is no need to search there. Your Inspiration is *already here within you.* I see that it has *always* been with you.»

«What do you mean?» Greymalkin was baffled and terrified. The sensations he was receiving from the female presence were far beyond anything he could grasp at first, but she was trying to answer his question in the only way she could, through her own thoughts and perceptions. With her help, he began to feel his body again, but realized why he had felt nothing before. His organs and bones had liquified, and together with his blood were flowing in pulsing cycles throughout her immense form. The perception of his complete dissolution into her terrified him for a moment. She was a vast thing of inconceivable intimacy and skill. He could feel her finely sifting down through every last part of him at a pace beyond understanding, not only his organs and blood, but his very cells and their interior structures. She was studying his DNA with interest, like a master seamstress examining spools of thread.

As his panic rose, he found that it was quickly subsumed by the overwhelming ecstasy of the enthusiasm she felt for her task. She was *reweaving* him in adoring detail, and she felt nothing but intense love for her creation. «You are so muddled! Your Inspiration has been *here*, within you from long before your beginning, *in the jewel within your mind*. I will try to explain it to you as I work.»

Greymalkin tried to focus, but his mind was coming undone. He briefly wondered if his brain was still intact or had simply become a liquid stream of dendrites flowing through the alien mother-reweaver that had consumed him. But then he found that he could no longer form any sort of coherent thoughts at all. A truly complex sequence of memories had begun playing out in a stream from the mother-reweaver, a stream that would have been impossible to absorb even if his faculties had been intact. She seemed to be tenderly amused with him, deciding to interlace what she could of the memories directly into the brain cells that she was deftly reconstructing. As she worked on the unwoven human, she carefully thrummed thoughts, memories, and patterns into the flowing tapestry she was making. Although he no longer had a lucid consciousness that could analyze the memories, his last intuition was that she was ensuring that he would have the relevant memories later, after he was rebuilt.

A timeless period followed of flesh being lovingly and cleverly reknit. The reweaving took place in a dance of warm blood beating through a foster womb the size of a starship, buried in the soil of a forgotten planetoid.

* * *

Somewhen later, after a very long passage through darkness, Greymalkin found himself in a dream. Oddly, he *knew* it was a dream, and kept wondering when he would wake up. In the dream he wore his golden robes, and was sitting on a giant pink lotus bloom floating on a verdant lake. The lake surface was profuse with green water lilies, and surrounded by thick forests of white morus trees and bamboo. To his right was a woman in pure white robes with elegant pearl brocade, sitting on another huge pink lotus bloom floating in the water. To his left there was yet another immense lotus flower floating on the lake, with a hooded figure in golden robes very like the ones Greymalkin wore. The three of them in their floating lotus flower seats were arranged in an equilateral triangle facing one another. He could occasionally hear deep croaking calls and squawks from large white birds standing on stilt-like legs in the water. Most of the birds were standing aloof in the distance, but one that was very close to Greymalkin was dipping its long yellow beak into the water. Something about the sinuous curve of the bird's long neck looked very familiar to Greymalkin, and then he realized that the S-curve of its neck was exactly the same as the S-curve of the Sojourner emblem.

"My work is complete," the woman in white robes said in transcendent happiness. "But I will try to do as you asked with your last request to me and explain what I meant. You see, now that I have rewoven you, I understand your language and concepts much better than before. The one you see here is the Inspiration." She gestured at the other figure in hooded golden robes.

Greymalkin gazed from one figure to the other, smiling. He had never felt so serene in his entire life. *What a nice dream.* "Who is he?"

Greymalkin thought to ask as he looked at the other figure in golden robes, followed by a more salient question, "and, *what* is he?"

"He is from the long ago," the woman in white said. Greymalkin could not take his eyes off her glossy jet black hair, so carefully arranged in intricate patterns that he became lost trying to sort them out. "Once, he was a being much like the one you call the Velan, a Builder of incomparable insights and power; in fact, he was the very same being that wove the design of the Genibrata and *me*. But this great Builder was hampered by his impetuosity, poor discipline, and rash urges."

As Greymalkin looked at the mysterious figure in gold, the hood and robes abruptly folded back and away, revealing... yet another figure in a different hooded golden robe with even more elaborate embroidery and brocade of glittering jewels. Greymalkin could still not see the face of the being, as the woman in white continued her serene recitation.

"As you see, this Builder even dared to redesign *itself* impatiently many times, in ways that astounded the other Builders. I am sorry to withhold his face from you, but the full memories of his *unfolding* into new forms would drive you insane if I tried to weave them into your brain. I must leave you with only these hints of the Unfolded One, images that will not harm you." The woman continued her calm story while the hoods of the golden figure repeatedly snapped backwards, revealing new figures with ever more elaborate golden robes. "But I wish to explain his *connection* to you, which is the reason why you and I both selected him as the Inspiration for our tapestry. As you can see, all of the many forms of the Unfolded One incorporated opulent arrays of what you call shadow jewels and aureate. But even beings as incomprehensible to you as the Builders could expire at last, and there came a time when the Unfolded One passed on. Even for beings such as the Builders, the transition process at the conclusion of their existence involves *dissolution*. And so, the myriad shadow jewels that made up the mind of the Unfolded One were dispersed, far and wide."

The golden hooded figure unfolded one last time, and instead of another gilded form, it dissolved into a shower of shadow jewels that exploded away into the forest at the edge of the lake. Only one of the beautifully shining diamond-like shadow jewels remained and did not fly away. Instead, it seemed to come to rest on what appeared to be a murky surface of soil that now hovered over the lotus blossom.

"One of the dispersed shadow jewels that had made up the Unfolded One, *this particular jewel*, came to rest on a forgotten planetoid very near where we are now. It lay there in the dust for many millennia," the woman said. She turned her beatific smile to Greymalkin, just as he saw something incredible. Graceful feminine hands seemed to reach out of nothingness and pick up the jewel. The woman in white gestured with her own pale hand toward the other pair of female hands that now held the jewel. "You see, after so many forgotten millennia, the jewel that had been a part of the Unfolded One was at last discovered again on the surface of that lost planetoid by tiny creatures exploring far from their home, a male and a female. The female kept the jewel, and when the time came she gave it to her mate to place in their son."

Now the lake faded from view around him, and Greymalkin again saw the image he had seen before, the big jewel clamped tightly in the delicate provenience runcible by male hands, the baby held carefully by the graceful female hands. Once again the jewel shone in the darkness above the infant's face as the two pairs of hands began to shake. But then the hands steadied.

"These two explorers fled from their pursuers, trembling with the speed of their passage," the voice of the woman in white robes said, though she herself had now vanished. Her voice began to echo as she continued in a final, triumphant tone, "But the two reached momentary safety. The male placed the jewel in the mind of his son. Then the female crafted an inscription for the jewel which began with these words: *To the Sojourners who will find my son....*"

Greymalkin's eyes widened abruptly in shock as he finally understood. *That's me. And those are my parents!* His agitation was such that he convulsed in the dream and woke up, his heart pounding, finding himself once again in the medical pod on Royce.

As Greymalkin lay there in astonishment, trying to capture and fix the fleeting memories of his parents, several additional surprises piled up on him quickly. He gasped, and tried to make sense of what he was feeling.

His shadow sense seemed to be dramatically expanded and refined. He didn't have to extend it, he had instantly taken in the surroundings for parsecs around Royce. He found that now he could make out a level of detail in the gas clouds and stars around him that he'd never been able to sense before. The mindboggling sweep of the Homunculus Nebula across the sky and the infinitely twisting whorls of gas and energy that made it up was stupefying. He suddenly realized that when he focused he could even make out planetoids and rocks down to just a few kilometers in diameter, even at those absurd ranges. The level of resolution in his shadow sense was terrifying. For a moment he shrank away from the scope of what he was sensing as the staggering amounts of synesthesia flooded his mind. The synesthetic sounds, scents, and even remote textures were beyond anything he had ever imagined.

Recoiling from the torrent of sensations, he tried to close off his shadow sense from the copious waves of signals, but simultaneously discovered two things. First, he *couldn't* shut off the blast of sensations, at least not completely, and second, *he realized that he didn't need to.* Somehow, despite the massive amount of meticulously detailed perceptions pouring into his brain, it didn't seem to overwhelm his mind. In fact, he realized that he could now refine his shadow sense perceptions on the other end of the scale into unbelievably tiny spaces physically close to him in ways that he had never imagined possible. He took in the cabin around him in a flash of impressions.

Just outside the medical pod where he lay, Tatter was slumped over, asleep on a couch surface of Royce protruding from the interior hull. He could not only hear her soft inhalations, but found that he could actually hear her human heart beating. Greymalkin realized that he could also easily perceive her hidden, immense sleeping Sylphid form as well as all of the equipment packed around it. Previously he had barely been able to detect the tight pocket of her shadow space pouch, much less perceive it in detail, but now he could observe every tautly corded muscle and strange internal organ in her giant alien form. Beneath the long armored ocular shield on top of her head he could even make out the incredible array of her closed alien eyes, orbs of different sizes, eye shapes, and colors, all evolved to capture different wavelengths of light and radiation. Some pupils were narrow, like those of a predator, some were like huge translucent pearls, and some were remarkably human looking with big brown irises the size of his fist. Looking closely into Tatter's many alien eyes somehow felt deliciously intimate to him. He thought he had never seen anything as delicately beautiful as her intricate array of dozing exotic eyes.

As his awareness expanded beyond the cabin that he and Tatter were in, Greymalkin could not only see Lex asleep in the cockpit on the other side of the starship, but could make out incredibly tiny details there as well if he wanted to do so. Greymalkin found that the tattoos on the man's forehead looked like vast pictograms on a leathery planet's surface of skin. He could even see individual blond hairs on the older man's head, as if he was gazing through trees in a forest. Lex's blue eyes were closed, but hidden beneath those pools like a darkly glittering abyss were the cool electronic crystalline structures of the man's artificial mind. That emptiness frightened Greymalkin and he pulled away from it.

It had only been seconds since he'd awoken, but Greymalkin looked for Bruno then, and instantly spotted the typically small and quiescent shiny black stone mass the protean took on when it was inactive. The small form was curled up into one of the corners of the cockpit cabin, like a harmless small animal sleeping there. But then Greymalkin's mind reeled as he noticed what he never had before, the true scale of the protean, subtly submerged in a vast, hidden shadow space manifold that he'd never before glimpsed. Bruno's full extent was absurdly gigantic, dwarfing Royce's hull by orders of magnitude. Even as he was becoming aware of the huge mass of the dormant protean, Greymalkin watched in disbelief as an array of shadow space sensors across the hidden bulk of the monster somehow detected his attention and snapped open alertly, fixing him in their black gaze.

For just a second, the intent alien field of sensors was like a terrifying phalanx of black ball bearings, so unlike Tatter's delicate bed of sleeping eyes. But after a moment, he sensed the bubbling amusement of the alien cyborg as it recognized him, and the sensors all closed again as the monster became quiescent once more. Greymalkin gaped at the wild range of synesthesia flooding into his mind, and ominously began to realize the monumental extent to which he did not understand the protean, what it was, or what it was capable of doing. Greymalkin filed away the sobering insight for further investigation later, but swooned as his body shuddered with waves of additional new sensations.

Greymalkin's head felt light one moment and poundingly thick the next. Beyond his incredibly expanded shadow sense, there were now a disorienting host of other emotions and impressions he was becoming aware of sweeping through him. He remembered Lex warning him about potential mood swings he might experience, but he'd never imagined anything like this. The sensations flooded through his mind, a torrent of impulses that felt like they were trying to launch him in a hundred directions at once. He tried to still the frenetic activity in his mind and the electric tingling sweeping across his body, but it only seemed to worsen as he did so.

Reaching up, Greymalkin cautiously pushed the lid of the medical pod open with a quivering hand. He managed to get a grip on the sides of the pod to simply try to lever himself up, but instead found that he'd flung himself forward out of the pod onto the deck. He nevertheless landed squarely on his feet with a loud slap that made Tatter snort and wake up. She blinked sleepily and jumped up when she saw him standing there.

"Grey, you're finally awake again!" she said, and her expressive brown human eyes looked him up and down in growing concern. "Uh, how do you feel?"

Greymalkin stared at her, feeling flushed. He looked down at himself, and his nude body seemed to be pulsing with synesthetically distorted sounds and colors. A horde of impulsive thoughts continued bursting through his mind chaotically, ranging from convoluted strategies to explore the Homunculus Nebula to algorithmic realizations about the patterns in the covenants that had been written on his mind. He found that he could not stop the frenetic dance of questions, analysis, and new answers that in turn set off new questions in chain reactions that again threatened to overwhelm him. Then a sudden shocking revelation made him clench his hands and bring them up to his temples.

The covenants! Where are the covenants? He'd become so used to the psychic weight on his mind of the huge cybernetic structures that their absence was shocking. But then, incredibly, he found both of the cybernetic edifices. There was the smaller one he'd received from Kuanian and there was the larger one he'd received from the Velan, but now they were somehow neatly tucked away into a corner of his mind like filed reports, no longer pressing down on him like heavy leaden layers on his brain. *But now there's a third covenant that's been added to the first two!* He tried to access it... and slammed his hands on his head, utterly bewildered.

Tatter gave him a frightened expression and quickly strode to him in apprehension. She grabbed his arms to push him back down into the medical pod, but then her jaw dropped when he resisted her easily. He felt dumbfounded as well; Tatter was always so much stronger than he was. But when she had seized him this time, it had only felt like a normal woman's grip on his arms.

Greymalkin grabbed her arms in return, and was distracted again as he felt the warmth and vitality in her. He could sense the blood pumping through her human blood vessels, and more subtly, her thought-streams pulsing from the huge neural relays that filled her skull through the shadow space barrier and into her huge alien mind that was now awake and regarding him with the full bed of multi-colored eyes wide open. He could sense the affection in her emotions, communed directly between them through the resonance of their shadow jewels, and thought again how odd it was that an alien could feel physically attracted to his human form. *But,* he reminded himself, *she's not completely an alien. She's told me repeatedly that she's as much human as Sylphid.* He felt her blood rippling up to the surface of her skin as she flushed with excitement seeing him on his feet, and then he felt his own blood pounding through his head again in a surge, throughout the myriad paths in his brain. Out of the dozens of questions, thoughts, and other distractions racing through his mind furiously, one forced all the others out.

"Tatter, tell me something?" he whispered. When she nodded with wide eyes, he said, "Before I got so sick, when we were... intimate. We didn't use any kind of fertility inhibitors. Is anything... going to happen?"

Tatter gave a small gasp of laughter, and said with a wan smile, "*Now* you're worried about that? No, you big dope, Sylphids have to go through a lot of explicit efforts to become pregnant with human DNA." Amusingly, the topic was evidently one of the few that actually seemed to *embarrass* her, because she began what he'd come to recognize as her nervous rapid patter. "Among other things, I'd have to grow a *uterus* first! I mean, I could *do* it, but I'm certainly not *planning* on doing that any time soon, reproduction is an incredibly big step with Sylphids, well, I guess with *anybody*....and Grey, you know ... well, it's a joint decision, right? I'd *talk* to you about it and *tell* you a long time before I ever even *thought* about anything like that...."

"*Good*," he breathed, interrupting her, his heart still pounding as he held her by her arms. Then he abruptly pulled her off her feet, making her inhale sharply with surprise, and kissed her hard. He threw her on the bunk and was on top of her before she could react. Then she simply grinned around his tongue, and pulled him to her tightly.

Partings

Greymalkin finished the final interconnections feverishly and then paused, his hand above the control that would activate the ancient memory array. *That is, if I correctly restored and repaired all of these antiquities,* he thought, nervously looking around the jumbled interior of the archaic dome and its primitive banks of computers. *I mean, what could go wrong? These systems are only three millennia old.* He flipped the switch, his hand shaking in anticipation.

Slowly, the array of memory systems engaged their primordial bootstrapping protocols and came online. He felt his lips peel back in an almost insane smile. *It's working. It's actually working again, after all these centuries.* Greymalkin leaned over the primitive control panel, greedily watching as each activation prompt of the ancient system interface came up. Out of the corner of his eye he saw Lex enter the dome.

"I got it working!" Greymalkin said in a hoarse croak. "I had to synthesize a lot of the old processors that were fried, but the main memory arrays are made of primitive eoncrystal stacks. I can access it all now, the entire memory array!"

Lex studied the frenzied face of the young Sojourner silently for a moment before saying, "Greymalkin, the ship with your friends docked a few minutes ago. I let their leader inside; she's coming down now. Do you want to greet her or not?"

Greymalkin scanned the memory arrays quickly, and then began making copies of the ancient data records. He found the telltale information that he was looking for and smacked his fist into his hand, looking up at Lex with wild eyes. "This confirms everything. *Everything!*" Greymalkin held his head and laughed, his giddy echoes bouncing back off the dome ceiling. Then he saw a woman in a void suit standing at the entrance door. "Constance! Come in!"

Sister Constance walked up to him slowly, steadily regarding him through her helmet faceplate. "Hello, Greymalkin. How are you feeling?" she said through the suit's voicebox.

"Fantastic! Do you see all of this?" He gestured around the dome. "You must recognize what this place is, or was?"

Constance nodded, taking in the ancient room in grudging wonder. "An early Thannic habitat. And you've actually managed to get these computer systems operational."

"It's jury-rigged, but it's working well enough for me to copy off the data," Greymalkin said excitedly. "Lex and I sealed this dome, and rigged up an environmental unit to maintain a breathable atmosphere. You can take off your helmet."

"I'll keep it on," she said quietly. "Now, what was so important that I had to come here?"

"Don't you see?" Greymalkin demanded. "We've finally got confirmation of everything that happened here." Then the young monk frowned in confusion. "Where are the other members of your team? Bring them down and relax for a while! I've got so much to tell you."

"They're in our ship," Constance said. "We aren't staying long. We just came to exchange data with you one last time before we go."

"Hunh?" Greymalkin said, still confused. "Where are you going?"

"Grey, snap out of it!" Constance exclaimed. "We're going to circle around the periphery of the Homunculus Nebula one last time to pick up all our final data recordings and then we're going home! There's not much time left before the Carinans return. You should come too!"

Greymalkin focused on her words and nodded. "Uh, you don't know how right you are about the Carinans. Hey, Lex? Go tell Bruno to bring in... what he brought back with him." The older man dipped his head and left the dome. Then Greymalkin grinned again, and said, "But you have to hear me out! I've discovered so much since we last talked."

Constance put her hands akimbo on her hips. "Okay, what? Tell me about it. And can we start our data exchange while you talk?"

"Well, sure," Greymalkin said uncertainly. He found her data access link and started transferring his mass of notes and recordings. "But *listen*, I've put almost all the remaining pieces of the puzzle together. I've now got substantiating evidence of everything we've hypothesized in the reconstructed history of what happened here."

That got Constance's attention. "Go on," she said. Greymalkin stood up, trying to organize his scattered thoughts, and ran his hand through his hair absently. He flinched; it surprised him how long his hair had grown, and he suddenly realized while feeling his face that his beard had grown out by almost a centimeter. Dismayed, he noticed that the jumpsuit he was wearing was utterly filthy. He tried to remember when he had last bathed or slept. He shook off his confusion and began pacing nervously back and forth, ticking off points on his fingers.

"*First*. This dome, the wreckage outside, and most importantly the data I've recovered from these old arrays confirms what we suspected. Thannic Colonizers from the first interstellar exodus reached the Carinae roughly three thousand years ago, *millennia* before the Xenocorps expedition that was just three *centuries* ago. We'll have precise dates after analyzing the data recovered from the records here. That by itself rewrites all of history! Humans discovered faster-than-light travel more than a thousand years before anyone imagined!"

"The Colonizers? *Here?*" Constance muttered. "That's... hard to believe. Surely that would have been discovered before now. I mean, which fleet of the First Exodus was it?"

"That's one of the most amazing things that I've discovered," Greymalkin said. He felt lightheaded, and his voice was shaking. "Their leader was Mei Sung herself! The leader of the group here was none other than the daughter of Thann!"

Now Constance actually gaped. "The Great Terraformer herself? You really have proof of that? Nobody ever discovered what became of her and her vanished fleet. But what happened? Especially if it was *her* fleet, why didn't they start terraforming planets here in the Carinae, then? They terraformed more worlds than any other Exodus fleet, but then they simply disappeared."

Greymalkin felt his skin tingling with a heightened awareness as he ticked off a second finger. "I'll tell you! *Second*. I've now had time to analyze your dataset on all the sites you and your team surveyed. Putting it together with all of the practical knowledge that Lex has from surviving in the Carinae for so long, I've got a pretty good idea what happened... at least at first. After they reached the Sagittarius Arm here, the Colonizers spread out through the area and began looking for worlds to terraform, just as they always had done back in the Orion Arm. But the Carinae was different in two major ways, the most obvious one being that this is a tremendously active region of star formation. There's so many huge bright stars and so much radiation here that there aren't a lot of good terraforming opportunities. Back then they were still thinking primarily in terms of planetary environments for settlements, not shadow space mega-habitations like we do now. But they might have *still* overcome those problems except for the second big difference."

Constance stared at Greymalkin, whose euphoria was now shining in his eyes as he spoke even faster. She unobtrusively took a step backward away from him, just as he shrieked, "The Abyssals! They're all *over* the Carinae; they've carved up almost every part of the region into personal fiefdoms. There are similarly powerful aliens in the Orion Arm as well, like the Jotuns and the Thubans, but they aren't as aggressively territorial, they mostly keep to themselves and don't bother humans. The Abyssals here are much more violent; they attack anything that enters what they consider their personal territory. From comments one of them made to me, I think that their hyper-territoriality arose precisely because of the comparatively greater wealth of the Carinae. But it's more than just that, it all hinges on what the Builders had planned for Eta Carina, the massive star system in the center of it all. That's the third piece of the puzzle, see?"

"Of course," Constance said calmly. Greymalkin saw that she was edging towards the door where she'd entered, and he quickly stepped closer to stand between her and the exit. Constance tensed and became still.

"You've *got* to listen to me, Constance," he begged, and then laughed almost hysterically as he ticked off another finger. "*Third*. It all revolves around the *Forge* and its *Nexus*! In the beginning I thought all the conflict and territoriality was about the resources here, the shadow aureate mines and whatnot. But that's not it! The *main* thing they're fighting over is information! Information from this unbelievable artifact they call the Nexus, powered by the Forge, a system that the Builders designed, but never got around to constructing. The Abyssals got hold of the design and actually built the thing. It can generate insane amounts of information from what are effectively an infinite number of parallel universes. There's a whole ecosystem of information processing here, each of the Abyssals control one part of it. But they only seem to want to hoard information, not share it."

"You were telling me about what happened to the Colonizers," Constance said. She was furtively looking for another way out of the dome. Greymalkin shook his head, reorienting.

"Right, the Colonizers, I'm getting to them," he said, and then held up his hands. "But Constance, *please*, I'm not crazy, okay? Just hear me out?"

"Alright, Grey," she said, studying his face. "But I need to tell you some things as well."

"*Good, good!*" Greymalkin yelled, making her flinch. "That's why I asked you to come here, so we could compare notes and exchange specimens. So, yeah, the Colonizers. They came into conflict with the Abyssals, there are signs of battles almost everywhere the Thannics had bases. But then they vanished. Poof! The Thannic Colonizers throughout the Carinae all disappeared, virtually overnight. And then the Abyssals became even more paranoid." Greymalkin's face lit up, looking past her shoulder. "Bruno, there you are! Bring it in here!"

The morphing form of the protean was alternatively dragging and then pushing something heavy, awkward, and long down the tunnel that led to the surface. The blood drained from Constance's face, and she stumbled back against the wall away from Bruno and his ghastly prize. It was a huge carcass of a creature with a jet black carapace and savagely sharp limbs like blades. The body was festooned with armor and weapons. In places the black carapace had been broken and cracked, revealing a densely interlaced fibrous interior like white bone.

"*Fourth.* The Carinans!" Greymalkin exclaimed, grinning at the horrible carcass. "They bred these creatures to serve as guard dogs for their realm. This one and two others attacked us a few hours ago. Apparently, they were advance scouts of the returning Carinan mass." Then Greymalkin glared at Bruno. "I wanted to test a set of coded signals that I was given months ago by a friend named Bokin, signals that are supposed to serve as 'Words of Peace', but my overly zealous bodyguard here killed them all before I could attempt this peace-making approach."

"Your signals would not have worked," Bruno said, the deep and almost subsonic rumble making the dome rattle. Constance looked terrified. Just then, Lex stepped around the big corpse and rejoined them. He examined her expression cooly, and turned to Greymalkin.

"Grey, let her go," Lex said. "You're frightening her, and she's too scared now to be of any more help. And anyway, she's right, we need to evacuate back to the main expedition base. The Carinans are returning now; they'll swarm us, and we'll be massacred."

"You said there would still be a few days before the swarm arrived," Greymalkin said, his eyes flashing before he turned back to Constance. He held up his hand and extended the thumb. "*Fifth*. I think I can reach the Forge before we have to leave. All the remaining answers that I need are there."

"Why in all creation do you think *that*?" Constance said, eyes widening. Greymalkin's face twitched and trembled in ways that she had never noticed before. Constance heard footsteps in the tunnel and glanced backwards following Greymalkin's gaze. Tatter was coming down the corridor now. She appeared furious.

"It's complicated," Greymalkin said, shrugging. "I'll try to boil it down. There are some former Sojourners that are working with the Abyssals, and they have an inconceivable hoard of information. They... did something to me. It took me quite a while to puzzle it out, but basically I think they surreptitiously loaded yet another huge data structure like a covenant into my shadow jewel on top of the two that were already there. But this data structure includes a motivation complex that is effectively, well, an entire *alternate version of my personality*. It, uh, sort of took over my mind briefly. I couldn't understand how they could possibly have obtained something like that, a complete alternate version of my mind. But then I remembered *the*

Nexus, and the Forge that powers it. They can download almost any kind of information using those things, from what are effectively entire indexed alternate universes.

"As I said, their data structure, which includes an alternate version of my consciousness, was probably organized as another variety of the covenant psychogenic structures that seem to be so common here. I'm not sure, but I think they meant it to be latent within me for a while and only become accessible to me subsequently. I, ah, may have activated it *accidentally* when I ingested a potent psychogenic substance called gnaritas. Perhaps you've heard of it? Anyway, I've been able to recover much of the memories from this... alternate version of myself. It, um, *the other version of me* had a lot of knowledge about the Forge. The key fact is that what happened to the Colonizers is tied up with the Forge. I'm convinced that I can find out what happened to the Thannic Colonizers that were here, at least, *if I can reach the Forge*. I feel... no, *I'm certain* that I absolutely must try to try to reach it before I leave the Carinae."

Constance stared at him and finally shook her head incredulously. "Grey, forget whatever outlandish scheme you're thinking about; you need to get out of here and go home. *Now.*"

Greymalkin scowled at her. "Why is that?"

"That sample of your blood that you gave me," Constance said, frowning. "You asked me to analyze it, and I did. Grey, I don't know what's happened to you, but your cellular structure, right down to your DNA, has been significantly modified."

Greymalkin had a pained expression. "Yeah, I know. But... is my DNA still human? Or is it alien? That's what I wanted you to check."

Constance shook her head with fear and uncertainty. She shrugged, and said, "Both? Neither? I mean, you've still got your original DNA, but it's been entwined with layers and layers of nucleotides and biomolecular structures like nothing I've ever seen before. I'm frankly surprised that you're still alive and breathing. You need to be healed, if that's even possible."

"Funny," Greymalkin said, glaring at Lex. "People keep telling me that, but that's how I got... *modified* in the first place."

Lex folded his arms. "It was necessary to keep you alive. And I'm certain your body is far more resilient and capable now than it ever was before."

"So *that's* how it happened," Tatter muttered quietly under her breath. Greymalkin could tell she hadn't meant for him to hear the statement, but his hearing was as acute now as the rest of his senses. He wondered why she looked so angry, but shrugged it off and addressed Constance.

"Sister Adept, please," he said, trying to make his voice contrite. "You and I both still believe in the same Great Commitment, to *seek discoveries with clarity*, and *share information with humility*. All I'm asking is for you to take my data with you, together with whatever specimens and artifacts that you want. I've collected far too much to carry back in my rover."

"We have no more room either!" Constance said in irritation. "And as I told you, we still have to collect our final data recordings. Although...." She paused and looked at the huge carcass lying before them. "No one has ever recovered an actual specimen of the Carinans. And this creature...."

"Take it, please, by all means!" Greymalkin cried out. "As you said, no one has ever seen anything like the Carinans."

Constance studied the cruel-looking body with a strange expression. "No one ever brought back any data on them, true. But Grey, doesn't this organism look familiar to you?"

Greymalkin looked at the monster that Bruno had killed, and shook his head in confusion. "I've never seen anything like it."

Constance leaned over the carcass and looked at it closely, finally saying, "I think I have, at least in history recordings. It looks reminiscent of the warrior caste aliens that humans fought all the way back in the Xenagon, a thousand years ago. Grey, I think this is an Andromedan."

The word sent a chill down his spine, and Greymalkin's forehead furrowed. "But... I thought they all left after the Xenagon? Wasn't it part of the treaty that they all had to go back to the Andromedan Galaxy?"

"No," Constance said, standing up. "They just agreed to abandon all of their holdings in the Orion Arm and never return. The Accords say nothing about the Sagittarius Arm." She had a pensive expression. "Grey, this body needs to go back to the Orion Arm, everyone needs to know about this. But I'm serious, we have no room at all."

Greymalkin's mind raced in circles for a moment, and then he looked from Constance to Lex. "Constance, some of your team are already back at the main expedition base, right?"

"Most of them, in fact," Constance said. "I've only got my last four crew with me on my ship. What are you thinking?"

"Lex," Greymalkin said, "can you haul this corpse and the most important stuff I've collected back to the base in your lockers, and get it to her team there?"

"What about you?" Lex objected. "You'll need my help."

"You already told me that you thought it was impossible to get through the Homunculus Nebula to the Forge," Greymalkin said.

"Yes, it's a stupid idea," Lex said bluntly. "I'm sure that I wouldn't be able to do it. I don't think *anyone* can get through the maze of the Homunculus Nebula safely, except maybe the Abyssal that holds the Forge and the Eta Carina system in the middle of it. The turbulence in the shadow planes in the nebula are too intense. It's like some kind of constantly morphing, unstable labyrinth of paths."

"Then you won't be any use to me when I make the attempt," Greymalkin said coldly. "So take my cargo back to Constance's people. You're the only one that can carry all of this stuff back in one trip anyway."

Lex glared at him. "If you're seriously going to try that stunt, getting through the Homunculus, you're going to need my help, kid."

"I'll have Bruno, Tatter, and Royce with me," Greymalkin said, clenching his jaw.

"Not me," Tatter said crossly. "If we're really leaving for good, I've got to finish the mining I'm doing here."

"Tat!" Greymalkin almost yelled. "We've got enough shadow jewels already! I've *got* to get to the bottom of all this if we're leaving for good."

She stepped up to him, and a storm was on her face. "Go ahead! I don't give a shit about your damned Sojourner obsessions. I'm staying here to finish my mining. But you and I have to have a talk before you go, Grey."

He felt disoriented by her hostility. *What's going on with her? Why is she so mad?* "Okay, sure. Bruno, go with Lex. Take this carcass and all the other loose crates in the tunnel and stow everything in his lockers. Lex, get going, and hurry!"

Lex scowled at Greymalkin, but turned to Constance. "Sister Adept, let Bruno and I escort you back to your ship as we go. I want to ask you some final questions. And Tatter? I want to talk to you as well. Now Bruno, would you be so kind as to haul this thing back up the tunnel?"

The protean silently obliged, and began dragging the multi-ton body back up the tunnel. As Constance turned to go, Greymalkin felt his emotions swing wildly once more. He stepped up to her, his throat abruptly tightening. This was it, he realized. Either or both of them might not survive or ever see each other again. She was the only Sojourner friend that he'd had in this horrific place. He found that his eyes were glistening. "You've been a good colleague. Thank you for everything you've done here."

Constance paused, and inside the helmet her tense expression softened. She nodded solemnly, faced him, and extended her gloved hand to put it on his shoulder in the formal Sojourner gesture of final farewell. "Sojourn through life with courage, Brother."

Greymalkin wiped his eyes, put his hand on her shoulder, and said in a cracking voice, "Sojourn through life with courage, Sister." He watched Constance follow Bruno and Lex up the tunnel, and wondered if he would ever see her or any of her crew again.

* * *

After their footsteps had receded up the tunnel, Greymalkin turned back around, only to find Tatter only a step away and glowering at him with folded arms.

"Touching," she snapped. "Grey, I've got a question. Why didn't you ask *me* to analyze your blood instead of your little Sojourner girlfriend there?"

"Constance? She's not—"

Tatter rolled her eyes. "I know she's not your girlfriend, idiot! But why didn't you ask *me* to do it? I know *way* more about xenobiology than she ever will."

"Well..." Greymalkin started, and then shrugged. "You were so busy with your mining. I didn't think...."

"Uh huh. Or maybe you didn't want me asking questions, or even thinking about it too much?" Tatter said, her unwavering, humorless smile pinning him to the spot. Tatter stepped up to him and squinted as she looked him in the eyes, her voice becoming quiet but very intense as she said, "Oh, we have to have a *long* talk, Grey. I thought you cared about me. Did you do this intentionally?"

Greymalkin stared at her in confusion. "What? What's wrong? Of course I care about you, Tat. What are you talking about?"

"You're saying that... you *don't know* what I'm talking about?" Tatter asked even more quietly, raising her eyebrows in steadily growing ire. When he simply stared at her she continued with an alarming, *deadly* threat in her words. "Don't lie to me. *I'll know.*"

"I *don't* know," he said, with rising concern at the way she was watching him with a predatory gaze he had never seen from her. "What is it? Just tell me."

After watching him closely, her angry intensity seemed to subside and she simply looked down at her feet with an unsettled expression. "I'm pregnant."

Greymalkin couldn't understand what she'd said for a moment, but then he felt the deck tilt around him. After groping for words, he exclaimed, "*What!* You said that couldn't happen!"

"It couldn't," she said with finality. "At least, not until whatever it was you did to me."

Greymalkin shook his jittery head, swallowed, closed his eyes, and took a panicked breath. When he had done his best to collect himself, he said, "Slowly. What do you think I did? Tell me what happened to you. And *how.*"

"That's just it. I'm not sure I *know* what happened," Tatter muttered in frustration. Her voice briefly rose, briefly becoming a perplexed shout. "Do you understand? *I didn't have a womb to impregnate.* I physically could not get pregnant! *But somehow I did!*" She became quiet again quickly, obviously still feeling disoriented. Then she spun around in irritation, nodding to herself. "Okay. You're right, let's go through the basics, one thing at a time, shall we?"

She matter-of-factly peeled off her brightly colored Erisian garment and stood in front of him naked. She gestured between her legs. "I didn't have any reproductive organs in there. I *promise* you. I never generated them when I grew this teratoma. But now I *do* have them."

Tatter seemed bewildered for a moment looking down at her body, but then tilted her head to one side.

"But, I guess... it's *possible*. I mean, once upon a time I obviously *did* grow this form, my human teratoma body. It was when I was much younger. It took a lot of effort, believe me. Sylphids don't just sing a song to make it happen. And I suppose that I do have the ability to heal, grow, or even *regrow* any of the organs in my teratoma. But... I *didn't do that*. Well... I didn't do it *intentionally*. Something apparently *made* me do it without consciously *knowing* I was doing it. That's sort of crazy, though; it would normally require a great deal of concerted effort on my part." She looked up at him with a frown. "And just wait, it gets *so* much more interesting...."

In the fastest eversion he'd ever seen her execute, she switched places with her Sylphid form, in the process sitting down on her now massively gnarled haunches to avoid banging her alien head on the ceiling of the dome above them. Even sitting there on the deck with her strangely hinged knees drawn up to her, her huge skull was still high above his. The dagger-fanged jaws loomed down over him, big enough to easily snip his head off in one savage bite.

Greymalkin did not flinch, instead finding to his annoyance that he could barely focus on what she was saying. *What is happening to me?* His mind was again hyperactively bouncing uncontrollably from one sidetracked thought to another. That had been happening to him uncontrollably at times, ever since he'd come out of the chrysalis pod. He was abruptly distracted by a realization that had somehow never occurred to him before. Her sheer size, and other behaviors that he had never given much thought to when she was in her Sylphid form clicked into place as he regarded her imposing array of fangs. *Her species are not just carnivores, they're apex predators. No wonder she likes meat so much. But why is that thought so urgent?* He found his scattered mind admiring the viciously elegant lines of her predator's cranium, but then saw that she had spread her heavily muscled legs and was now pointing to an armored bulge there.

«*That's* where my normal Sylphid reproductive organs are!» Her communed thoughts were becoming distinctly angry again now. «And guess what? Somehow you managed *to hit the spot there too!* I'm fairly baffled by that! You don't have a Sylphid male's anatomy *or* genetic material. And even if you did, for you to get in there I'd have to have opened my exterior tergum plate and *also* my oviduct before you'd have access to my ovarioles. *But somehow you did it anyway!* I felt my hormones suddenly, *unexpectantly*, peaking this morning. I caught it in time, barely. But you almost fertilized one of my *Sylphid* eggs in addition to the *human* egg that you *already* fertilized, the human egg in the womb that I *didn't know I'd grown. Both* sides of me would have been pregnant. I didn't know any of this was even *possible. How* did you do that? *Why* did you do that to me?"

Her thoughts had abruptly become a predator's snarl, and her huge clawed hand flashed out to seize him by the shoulders and throat, as if she was ready to pop his head off like a blood blister. Greymalkin pulled at the immense limb, but despite the fact that he was now stronger, her Sylphid claws felt as hard and implacable as steel, and he couldn't budge them. He couldn't breathe, so he communed to her in desperation.

«Tatter, you're crushing my throat!» Greymalkin felt panic-stricken, but then felt the giant digits relax around his shoulders and chest. He fell to his knees coughing and gasping for air.

«*Sorry!*» Her anger subsided, and she changed back into her human form again, blinking in surprise. She was shaking as she backed away from him with sudden tears in her eyes, staring at him in shock at what she'd done. «I'm so sorry, Grey. I'm still... working on clearing out my bloodstream from that hormonal spike this morning. It... *triggered* me. Sylphid females get... extremely defensive and prone to aggression when we're...." Tatter cleared her throat, shuddering as she watched him catch his breath. She turned away shivering, and put her Erisian garment back on again. Greymalkin finally stopped coughing and got to his feet as she turned back around to face him.

"You have to know I didn't do any of that intentionally," he gasped, breathing hard.

"I know that, now. This wasn't your fault," Tatter said, nodding slowly to herself. Then her face became livid. "It was that *damned* chrysalis case. I *knew* we should never have put you into that thing." Her expression became almost fearful, and he felt stricken when she took a step away from him. "Grey, you're *different*. You've been a completely different person ever since we took you out of that, that giant *blood-sack*. You're always distracted, you fly off the handle constantly, and you... Grey, you even *smell* different to me now."

Greymalkin felt ill, wondering what horrid scent he was giving off. "How so?"

Tatter cautiously stepped up to him again, inhaling, and now her frightened eyes were searching through his face. "You smell like... dammit, Grey! You smell like *sex*. You're giving off Human *and* Sylphid pheromones! I didn't figure out what that smell was until just now! That's what made me so eager lately to...." She bit off whatever she had been about to say, but Greymalkin ruefully understood her all too well. The two of them had been *ferociously* intimate over the last few weeks, *constantly*. He'd felt overwhelmingly attracted to her, but had just assumed it was natural. *Dammit, it is natural! I'm nineteen years old, why can't I just be drawn to her? Why does everything have to be so blasted complicated?* But then he thought about everything that had happened, and realized nothing was going to be simple for him ever again.

That strange female presence in the chrysalis case.... What did she do to me, actually? And why? She healed me, but apparently she had a hell of an agenda of her own. What am I now, some kind of gross interspecies propagation vector for her? To what purpose? He started to approach

Tatter cautiously, but he stopped when he saw that there were tears on her cheeks and she was simply staring to the side with a distant expression.

His skin began to crawl with a sense of shame and disgust. *Great Mercy. Just by being with her, I violated her. If I could do that to a Sylphid, who knows what other effects my body might have on humans just by being in their presence, much less having sex with them? I might be emitting all kinds of contagious biological agents. Blazes, I may be a biological hazard now.* Tatter, with all the terrifying strength in her immense alien form, had seemed invulnerable to him. Now she looked shrunken, vulnerable, and defeated. He felt his stomach turning over. His mind and mood now felt like a ball bouncing down into a chasm. Greymalkin sat down on his haunches with his back against one of the random crates, trying to fight off a claustrophobic sense of being trapped inside his own body.

"I apologize to you," Greymalkin finally said, contritely. "You're right, I've felt... *extremely* unsettled ever since I came out of the chrysalis case. My thoughts feel erratically compulsive. *Obsessed*. Lex warned me about this, but I didn't know these mood swings would be so intense. They're making it increasingly hard for me to think clearly. And the other things the chrysalis case did to me... and that I've done to *you*, it's grotesque. But I didn't know. And you have to believe me, I didn't do this to you intentionally. I didn't know that it changed me this much. And this is *exactly* why I didn't want to go into that damned pod in the first place. I didn't know what it would do to me. This is just what I was afraid of; it changed me into something monstrous. I can't trust my own body, I have no idea what effects it might have on others."

Tatter gaped at him in shock for a moment, then. She slowly sat down next to him, as a grim look came over her face. She finally said, in a voice so low he could barely hear her, "Okay, about what you just said... I can't get all high and mighty mad at *you* without admitting some things about *myself* to you that I haven't ever told you yet. Things... about *Sylphids*." She grit her teeth and closed her eyes. He stared at her, wondering what she had to say.

"You certainly aren't the only... *monster* here," Tatter said, not looking at him. "There's a lot that I don't like about being a Sylphid. It's why I don't care to talk about my people with you. Grey, I know you think I'm... *pretty*." The way she spat the word out made him straighten up. "You obviously haven't met any other Sylphids. *All* Sylphids with human forms, male or female, are *pretty*. Oh, not just pretty. We're all like *this*." Tatter ran her hand down the curves along the entire side of her body in a way that was so exaggerated and suggestive that he felt himself blush. She still didn't look at him.

"It's instinctive, we can't help it. There's a *reason* we all look like this, well, those of us that go among humans anyway. The precursors of our species were *ambush predators,* and they evolved the ability to grow these forms for a specific purpose as part of what's called *aggressive mimicry*. I've called this my teratoma body, and that's a technically accurate term. But it isn't just some random spare body, it's a *sexual lure*. To attract *prey*." She silently let that sink in, and he hated the fact that his body instinctively tensed up for just a second. *To run*. He couldn't help thinking of her immense fangs.

"Oh." After a long moment he broke the tension by shrugging with a snort and saying dismissively, "Well, here I am. Soup's on."

"Ha-ha," Tatter said in a dry tone. "I told you, the precursors of our species evolved that capability. But Sylphids still create these lure forms today, not to *eat* other sentients now, but to *infiltrate and manipulate* them. To *seduce* them."

"Oh." Greymalkin sat silently for a long moment. Then he asked in a small, desolate voice, "Is that why you're with me?" As soon as he said it, Tatter turned and looked him squarely in the eyes.

"No." After she'd gazed at him a long time, she added in a quietly defensive tone, "And I think you know that. But... I never admitted any of this to you because I was afraid you wouldn't believe me."

"So why tell me now?"

"Lots of reasons. First, because I've decided that I need to be honest with you, whatever happens. And I think I can trust you," she said flatly. "I was afraid because, well, every time I've admitted it to other humans I cared about before, they just leave me. Trying to conceal it doesn't work, either. I was afraid to tell Jamie until it was too late and he and his dad had found out, and... well you were there at the end of that particular disaster-show when they had Bruno attack me and blow up my tavern. Partly, I feel guilty, because I can't just get mad that you became a super-fertilizing sex trap for me after we dunked you in that awful blood-sack. It wasn't your fault; you didn't want to do it. We put you in there." She closed her eyes again, thinking. "*I put you in there.* I laid you down in that... *mouth*, and watched it swallow you. I'm sorry for doing that, Grey; I didn't know what else to do. But, the main reason I'm telling you about Sylphids is because you aren't the only one here with a body that they can't trust to do the right thing."

"Tat, just because the human forms that your species takes on can't help, well, being... *pretty*," he said, giving the word a milder emphasis than the derision she'd used, "it doesn't mean you can't trust your body...."

"It's not just that. You aren't the only one that gives off pheromones without knowing it. I can't help doing that either," she said. Greymalkin cringed, thinking about how that tantalizing musky scent he smelled whenever he held her always affected him. Tatter paused, and then took a determined, deep breath before saying, "And that's not all of it. We can actively influence the thoughts of humans when we commune with you."

"That... isn't possible," Greymalkin said in disbelief. "Humans have been communing for thousands of years. We can communicate, argue, cajole, plead, *sure*. But you can't directly change another person's mind..."

Tatter looked at him sadly. "*You* can't. We *can*. And we can't always *help* doing it either. It just... happens. I try hard to *never* do it, but other Sylphids don't care. So, Grey, I don't know whether or not I may have... *forced* you to be attracted to me. It's what I was afraid happened, that first time we were... *together* back on the Vlieger."

"That's... ridiculous," Greymalkin said. But his voice was even weaker.

Tatter lifted an eyebrow. «Really?» And suddenly he felt his insides clench with the urge to reach out and take her then and there, an urge that felt almost like a garrote around his neck and genitals both. He grit his teeth and squinted at her.

"Okay, *yes*, I feel that," he admitted. "But I don't think even an urge *that* strong could *force* me to do anything. It's just a... *strong suggestion*. I can resist it."

«But, do you *want* to? And... would you have known I put that urge in your mind *if I hadn't told you?*» Her thoughts were squirming through his head deliciously, just like her tongue would feel in his mouth, proving her point. He began to feel claustrophobically trapped again, but she stopped.

Greymalkin felt like his suddenly released innards were sinking beneath the deck as the enormity of what she'd admitted to him sank in. He folded his arms in frustrated bitterness. "Well... thank you for being honest with me, but this is *wretched*. You don't know what kind of monster I've become and I've obviously *never* known what you even *are*. So, you can't really trust me, and I can't really trust you either."

Tatter shrugged sadly. "I already knew that I misjudge and misread humans all the time. Grey... I only left my creche-world a few years ago.

I haven't been among humans very long. At least, not in my people's terms." Her eyes looked distant now.

"Why did you leave, anyway?" he asked. Tatter looked askance at him.

"After everything I've told you, do you really need to ask that? I couldn't *stand* to stay among other Sylphids. They're mean, ruthless, manipulative, and half-breeds like me are *really* disliked."

"But... how are you even a half-breed?" Greymalkin asked, puzzled. "I mean, if all Sylphids can make these... *lures*, what makes you any different?" Tatter looked like something had made her ill.

"I'm a Morganan," she said reluctantly. "We're... different. The Sylphids out there in the Morganan Realm of the Garnet Star, they take all this to a different level. They..." She stopped and glanced at him again. Fearfully. Greymalkin slowly reached out and held her hand wordlessly. She nodded. "Right. Honesty. Well, Morganans have always been the Sylphids with the *most extreme* commitment to mimicry as a strategy. One of their sub-factions decided to go as far as modifying their own physiology to further improve their ability to imitate other species. So, they created Sylphids with brains and biology redesigned to varying degrees on humans, M'Boolans, and other sapients in the Orion Arm of the Galaxy. I was... sort of a failed experiment." Tatter looked sullen now.

"Failed? How?" he asked, although he wasn't sure he wanted to know. "And, when you say 'created', what do you mean? Genetic recombination, surgery, cybernetics, or what?"

Tatter glanced at him, simply looking tired. "Sylphids are a lot more advanced than humans. You don't have terms yet for what we do. Call it... *cyborganic scholarship*. Sort of like that damned Genibrata tree, but not quite so advanced. The point was to make Sylphids that were *better manipulators of humans*. But they went too far with me, I guess. I didn't identify with them anymore. I identified with humans. I...rebelled against the training. I just wouldn't play along."

"So, they rejected you?" Greymalkin offered. She looked quietly furious.

"You could say that," she said bitterly. "Skip forward a little, and I was trying to live among humans. But, it turns out humans are terrified of me once they find out what I am. They think I'm a monster, or they try to get me involved in criminal schemes, just like Jamie and his damned father when they found out about me. I thought they were my friends at first; I never imagined the things they wanted me to do, and I couldn't believe they hired Bruno to attack and bully me!"

"Why come with me then?" Greymalkin asked, starting to feel overwhelmed. His thoughts were still bouncing back and forth erratically, but now every stray point his mind seized on was some new negative conclusion. "With everything you can do, I must seem like, just... stupid prey."

Tatter frowned and shook her head. "No, Grey, you dummy! You're the first human I've met that I felt like I could actually relate to! Maybe it's because you're a studious monk, or an open-minded person, or just because you're *you*. I told you, from the moment I met you, *I wanted you to like me*. I just... didn't want to *force you* to like me." When he looked at her in confusion, she grimaced and leaned over to glare at him fiercely. "You're different from every one of the mooks I've met, Grey. You weren't afraid of me when you saw what I was, you were *nice* to me, you talked to me like I was just another person. I can't help it, you dope, *I still trust you*. Even despite... *this*." She put her hand on her lower abdomen, looking down at herself uncertainly before looking up at him defiantly.

Greymalkin took several deep meditative breaths to focus. *Somehow, I have to calm my mind and think about this clearly.* Slowly, his consciousness stopped bouncing around inside his skull. He thought carefully about the time he had spent with Tatter and all of their interactions. Several points stubbornly stood out in his mind like solid rocks rising out of swirling waters that were subsiding. He leaned down and looked into her face so closely that their noses almost touched. She looked scared.

"Tatter, this is what I know. You're brave. You're passionate, resourceful, and you're the one person here in the Carinae that's consistently, always, *genuinely* wanted to help me. You say Sylphids can influence the thoughts of others, but I think that's just a stronger version of humans' ability to communicate. And anybody can influence others with communication." When she started to protest, he went on quickly. "Maybe you *did* use that communing ability to influence me, to make me... want you more than I already did. Even if you did do that, you weren't trying to *hurt* me. And while I'll grant that maybe you could stimulate me and make me momentarily more attracted to you *physically*, I refuse to believe that you can control *everything* I think and believe about you intellectually. I've had enough time now to make up my mind about you. Even if my body's some freakish unknown right now, *I am certain of what's in my mind, and what I believe about you.* I swear that I don't ever want to hurt you, or take advantage of you. And quite apart from how I feel about you physically, I *know* what I feel about you as a person. Tatter..." He tried to find the words for what he wanted to say, and abruptly realized that there had only ever been one way for anyone to say what he was thinking. "I love you, Tatter."

Tatter's eyes widened and she pulled back from him with an uncomprehending expression. She was silent for a very long moment studying him. She was starting to tremble. He wanted to help her, but he didn't know what to do. After she seemed ready to shake herself to pieces, she finally stomped her foot on the deck and spat out some kind of harsh expletive in an alien language that Greymalkin did not understand. "*Sorixit!* Okay, nobody's ever told me *that* before! I trust you, but I still can't tell exactly what humans mean about anything! I feel like one of you, *I want to be one of you*, but I just haven't been around you weirdos long enough to really understand you."

"Tatter, how old are you?" Greymalkin asked, suddenly wondering. His mind was starting to bounce around again, spiraling around so many questions concerning her, but he realized he didn't know something as basic as her age. Tatter shrugged.

"I'm fourteen," she said dismissively. Greymalkin blinked and stared at her.

"Tatter, you cannot possibly be only fourteen years old!" he exclaimed in disbelief, his head spinning in horrified disorientation. He had felt unnerved by the sex they'd been engaging in, but had assumed she was much *older* than he was. Tatter only glared at him, just as they both heard Lex's voice as he walked in through the entrance.

"She means fourteen Sylphid years," Lex said in an irritated tone. "The Sylphid homeworld circles a bright yellow-white star, its orbital period is four standard years long." He squinted at each of them in turn. "But even though she's much older than you Grey, she's still just a young and very immature child by Sylphid standards. Remember, they have *much* longer life-spans than humans. Why are you out here anyway, Tatter? I never heard of a Sylphid leaving home and becoming independent until they were at least twice your age."

"I got banished," she said in annoyance. "Kicked out, disgraced. I've already been telling him about it; it's a boring story that I don't want to get into. I didn't fit in back home, and neither of my parents wanted me around. Sylphid society is pretty unforgiving, you know? Coming here was my big plan to get wealthy enough so that I'd be *secure*." She jumped to her feet and glared at both of them. "So, yeah, I'm going to finish my damned mining before I leave!"

"Belay that!" Lex said irately. "That's what I wanted to talk to you about, Tatter. We should all get back to the main expedition base *right now*. What do you think they're going to do when they know the Carinans are returning? They're going to bug out of here as fast as they can, that's what! I've been through this exact same situation before, and I'm telling you, it does not end well for people left behind!" At that, Greymalkin jumped up.

"Stop!" he yelled, screwing his eyes shut and holding his spinning head. Then he frowned at Lex and Tatter, saying, "We stick to the plan. Lex, you take all the specimens and artifacts back to the base. Tatter, finish your mining and then head back to the base yourself, please? I'll traverse the nebula with Bruno and Royce. Let's hurry; I know we're out of time." Tatter nodded to herself and kept scowling at them.

Lex was angrily silent for a moment, but then said, "For the record, those are both terrible ideas. You two are going to get yourselves killed. This place is *deadly*; it's not a playground. But Grey, if you're dead set on it, just do us a favor and go fail fast? And Tatter, I hope a few more jewels are worth the risk." He looked at the two of them in evident exasperation, and then sighed. "I heard you two screaming your heads off all the way up in the tunnel. If you're going to be parents, then you need to be more careful, and stop letting your teenager tryst hormones ruin your lives." The older man walked to the entrance of the dome, but turned one last time.

"I'll get your cargo back to the base, Grey, and I'll wait for you both there. If this goes badly, and it *will*, I'll try to make them wait for you, but no guarantees. Hurry up and *get going*." With that, Lex strode up the tunnel quickly. Greymalkin looked at Tatter, who was already retrieving her big alien runcible. He touched her shoulder, but she only sulked at him.

"Maybe he's right," Greymalkin said. He could feel his emotions bouncing wildly back and forth again, and tried to make it stop to think clearly for a moment. When Lex had said the word *parents*, he'd felt everything spin harder. He couldn't wrap his mind around that concept yet.

Tatter frowned at her feet, and looked at him less certainly. "I can still... absorb the tissues back into my body," she said quietly. "But, I don't really want to. I've never been pregnant, I never even thought about it for my human side. But it could be a way for me to... better understand being human. And..." She looked up at him. "This is something both of us made. Together. A new human being."

Greymalkin swallowed and said what he didn't want to say. "We don't know what came out of me. What's inside you might not be human *or* Sylphid."

Tatter seemed to focus for a moment, and then said softly, "It's a girl."

Greymalkin looked at Tatter sharply. *I can't leave her now. Not now!* But then he looked up through the dome to where Eta Carina glowed brightly. *If I don't go there and try to finally figure all this out, will I ever be able to live with myself?* Then he looked at Tatter, who was holding her hands over her lower abdomen, seemingly lost in thought. "Tat, seriously, maybe we should think about what Lex said...."

Tatter suddenly scowled at him and communed a single thought. «*No.*» He could feel the same abrupt rage and defiance in her that he'd felt in her before when she'd choked him. He smiled. *She's going to be a fierce mother.* She gestured with her chin at the tunnel, and said, "No. You and I are both going to do what we came here to do. Let's get on with it. Like Lex said, time's wasting and this is going to take hours. I'm already really tired, and I've got to do this."

Greymalkin stared at her, and then quickly pulled her close enough to kiss her. After he let her go, he met her eyes for a moment uncertainly. *Are we going to regret this?* Then Tatter resolutely started toward the exit, and they both went up the tunnel to the surface. Lex had already gone, and Constance had departed immediately. The only ship left was

Royce. Grey quickly pulled off his filthy clothes and began putting on his last undamaged Sojourner void suit, wondering where he had left the golden garment. Tatter entered the airlock, taking off her brightly colored Erisian garb. As she stood naked before him, before she changed again into her Sylphid form to fly away back to her nearby stellar mine, she asked despondently, "Grey, are you going to come back for me?"

"I'll be back in no time," Greymalkin said, although his voice quavered. "But, yeah, I think I *have* to do this one last thing. And I understand why you feel you need to finish your mining. Let's both do what we came here to do. I'll see you soon!" Tatter nodded and shut the airlock just as her body began to expand into bluish-grey armor. By the time he'd gotten the void suit on and exited the airlock himself, she was already gone. Greymalkin ran jumping across the surface toward Royce. The cyneget erupted into happy signals of recognition and greeting. Then Bruno suddenly surprised him with rumbling communed thoughts, and he realized that the protean had unceremoniously perched on his shoulder once again as a small splat.

«Both you and the Sylphid are being foolish.» The protean's thoughts were guarded, and Greymalkin tried to laugh them away.

«Tatter can take care of herself, and I've got you, remember?» Greymalkin entered Royce's forward airlock and quickly cycled through.

«The three creatures I killed were surprisingly capable warriors, and they were all heavily armed.» Bruno's thoughts seemed uncharacteristically reserved. «They each flew a very effective fighter craft. If there had been a large number of them, I am uncertain how the battle would have resolved.»

Greymalkin wondered at the statement. The protean was not given to either modesty or a lack of confidence. Greymalkin quickly jumped into the cockpit without changing out of the void suit, and activated the helm link. He collapsed the helmet back over his head onto his shoulders, and said, "I have every confidence in you, Bruno! Now let's go see what's in the center of that nebula!"

* * *

Royce was eager to launch himself across the shadow plane, and Greymalkin urged him forward. The illusionary cold wind and crisp scents of the Carinae swept past them in Greymalkin's synesthesia, and they began rapidly mounting the twisting inclines into the Homunculus Nebula. Bruno quickly vanished from his shoulder and the protean began flitting about, serving as a scout in the increasingly bewildering shadow space environment.

The protean's help was essential, as the shadow plane landscape here was tortured and unbelievably rugged. Greymalkin immediately had difficulty keeping Royce on the craggy surface, and found the cyneget slipping sideways unpredictably on the treacherously elusive face of the local shadow plane. The minutes began stretching into hours of terrifying close-calls. His heart leaped into his mouth every time they almost slid off the surface into a disastrous spin that would have instantly shattered their manifold and disintegrated them.

Greymalkin finally admitted to himself that he hadn't anticipated the reality of just how precarious the shadow surfaces of the Homunculus were. And now that he was actually immersed in transiting the nebula, as opposed to studying it from afar, it had also become obvious how badly the roiling ionized gas in normal space was distorting his synesthetic perceptions. The echoes of ionized gas felt like a bitterly cold wind in his face, and despite the fact that it was a misapprehension he was shuddering at the painfully constant icy blast. He grit his teeth together to make them stop chattering. The strange synesthetic scents of the nebula were becoming stronger as well, and the harshly fragrant smells evocative of pine trees were becoming an overpoweringly resinous distraction. The pseudo-sounds that the nebula generated in his shadow jewel were also distracting him. It was as if they were charging into a deafening gale of howling wind. And all of the twisted surfaces around them had become alternating prisms of dark blue and blindingly bright reflections of shadow space potentials masked by a white static very much like snow. It was virtually impossible to follow the path through the chaos. *And... there's something even worse than all that....*

Greymalkin had thoroughly analyzed the path up through the nebula from a distance, but now he had also realized that what Lex had said was true. *The shadow space paths are slowly shifting. The changes are gradual, imperceptible, but it's nevertheless happening. These paths are subtly different than when I studied them just yesterday.* Greymalkin began to realize what they were up against in trying to navigate through the maze of the Homunculus Nebula, and why Lex had been so skeptical of the endeavor. It simply wasn't possible to definitively chart a safe path through a *changing labyrinth*. They kept finding themselves unexpectedly in new cul-de-sacs or confronted by freshly appearing gaps and instabilities that Royce could not cross. Sometimes Bruno was able to move through the shadow volume to scout for alternate paths, but even the protean was repeatedly halted by many of the turbulent whorls and forced to join them on the shadow plane and backtrack around fissures. The individual minutes lost in struggling up, around, over, and through the maze of twisting planar surfaces stretched into hours of exhausting focused effort.

It's maddening, Greymalkin thought. *I can intuitively sense a path up through most of a parsec of these twists and turns, but by the time I get to the end of it, what lies forward of that destination has changed. And the paths are all repetitive spirals up around the cone of the nebula. It's constantly two steps forward and then one or more steps back! Am I even making any progress? And what will happen if the path suddenly just drops out underneath us??*

At last Greymalkin feared that he was completely lost, and brought Royce to a temporary halt to try and get his bearings. Even with his enormously improved shadow sense, the labyrinth of stacked and layered planar surfaces here was bafflingly opaque. Because of the drastic way that the distortions had increased he could tell that they had somehow managed to ascend far up through the billowing irregular cone of the Homunculus Nebula. But now the synesthesia turbulence had become so intense that he no longer had a sense of where they were or how much farther they had to go. He only knew that somewhere above them in the gale of prismatic blue surfaces was the Eta Carina star system itself, the howling center of this nightmarish maze of energy and disruption.

This is the heart of it all, the entire Carinae, he thought. *And this is my only shot at reaching the center of this enigma. We have to go back after this; there won't be another chance to attempt this ascent. I'm the only one here that can do this. Either I reach the central Eta Carina system now, or I've failed myself, Bora, Soren, Constance, Tatter, and everyone else. We'll never know what was going on here.*

Greymalkin paused then and tried to center himself in meditation for a moment, a technique that had always enabled him to focus on supremely detailed tasks such as this when they arose. Ruefully, he realized it was the first time he had attempted to meditate in weeks. But now he discovered something very disturbing. Whatever the Genibrata had done to him to enhance his senses and physical vitality had changed his awareness profoundly. Mortified, he realized that his mind was now so hyperactive that he could not find the simple peace and focus in meditation that he had once been able to achieve relatively easily. His thoughts were still manic, bouncing from one point of attention to another. He fought down a new sense of panic at that realization, and tried to reassure himself with an old Sojourner admonition. *Only the centered mind can find the optimal path. I have to recover my focus or I'll never be able to get through to the center of this horrific labyrinth.* But his desperation only unsettled him further.

«Bruno!» Greymalkin finally communed to the protean in desperation. «Can you sense anything through all this shadow space distortion?» Although the gale-wind sounds the nebula was generating were illusory, the feedback was overwhelming his shadow sense, only adding to the distractions that were already roiling his mind. He could now barely sense the actual cockpit around him through his numbed extremities, and even when he experimentally slapped his hand hard against the collar of his void suit he couldn't hear or even feel it.

Outside of the starship, Bruno had been circling in and out of his perceptions, but at that moment he could sense the protean nearby in the howling storm of icy winds. Bruno morphed through several distinct shapes, obviously trying to find a form that could penetrate the impossible blast of signals. When the protean finally communed with him, it's thoughts were troubled.

«The amount of energy in the nebula is so great that it is obscuring everything.» Bruno's thoughts were unsettled, and Greymalkin could also sense an uneasy subcurrent of suspicion in the protean's bizarre mind. «But I believe there is another presence here.»

That sent a different kind of chill down Greymalkin's back. «What? Where?» He tried to focus his own shadow sense in the icy wind once again, and immediately noticed what Bruno must have felt. Greymalkin gasped. *Something* was watching them intently, although he could not discern where it was in the storm of disorienting noise. The presence felt like the ominous deep breathing of some monstrous creature all around them.

Then Royce issued a snarling alarm signal just as a vast shape loomed up out of the gale of shadow space chaos. There was too much interference to make out the form of the thing clearly, but it felt unbelievably gigantic, as if an entire planet had just appeared in front of them out of nowhere. Bruno's shocking battle roar echoed in Greymalkin's mind and the protean launched itself squarely into the middle of the vast being, but the thing dissolved into what seemed like an enormous array of coiling cables hundreds of kilometers long. The network of twining cables instantly tightened around the protean in an enveloping sphere that Greymalkin could sense took Bruno off guard. The protean began to rage against the restraints with epic exertions, but the sphere seemed to simply distort outward with each blast of energy and then tighten again.

«My, my, what an unruly beast we have here.» The eerily familiar communed thoughts came into Greymalkin's mind like an amused chuckle of rustling dead leaves. «Let's have a chat without all of his distracting roars, shall we, dear boy?»

Amid the chaos of the howling synesthetic wind and Bruno's roaring, Greymalkin suddenly felt something coil around him that was so cold that it burned his skin. He screamed in pain, but the burning coils around him disappeared almost instantly, together with all perceptions of shadow space and the cockpit itself.

Greymalkin found himself sitting in a pitch black space, the abruptly complete silence a jarring contrast with the moment just before. Glancing down, he found that he could see his void suit as if he was in a well-illuminated room, but there was absolutely nothing around him. He felt as if he was sitting in something like a well-padded chair, but only saw his own suit suspended in the darkness. He took a deep breath and found that the air was a comfortably warm temperature. He clenched at what felt like thickly padded chair arms, and was preparing to try throwing himself forward, when suddenly a familiar man that he had not forgotten over the intervening months appeared in front of him. The same handsome older features, greying hair, elegant old-fashioned jumpsuit, and eyes that were such a light brown that they appeared pale yellow. As always, the man was smiling at him pleasantly, and he also seemed to be sitting in an invisible chair in the middle of the black void comfortably. It was Rodo.

"My dear Greymalkin, it is *so* good to see you again," Rodo said brightly. The relaxed poise of the man was even more shocking than the sudden stillness around them. Greymalkin goggled at the man, and then ground his teeth in frustration and fear.

No! Not now! Where are we? Greymalkin closed his eyes and focused on his shadow sense, and discovered there was some kind of dampening field around him that smothered almost all perceptions of shadow space. He kept focusing intently as he opened his eyes again. "Hello... Brother Flavopallio. You, uh... look well?"

Rodo seemed delighted, and his smile broadened significantly just as Greymalkin managed to penetrate the distortions around them. It was as if Rodo knew exactly what Greymalkin was doing even while he did it. In a flashed image, Greymalkin briefly perceived that they were in a sealed chamber within a much larger form of the manticore creature they had encountered before, but displaced deeply in shadow space. This manticore had an immense body that stretched into the distance and seemed to be the source of the myriad cables that he'd seen earlier. But then the dampening field closed around him once more, and he was stuck in the black limbo again, facing Rodo's sallow smile.

"How absolutely marvelous," Rodo said, with a resonant chuckle. "You've grown so much since we last met, and in so many different ways! You've advanced in your perceptions, your vitality, your aplomb, virtually everything! I celebrate your progress, Brother Thomas."

Greymalkin swallowed, and said nervously, "Thank you. Why am I here?"

"I simply wish to continue our conversation," Rodo said nonchalantly. "You must have had time by now to consider what I offered you."

The evil yellow eyes of the man unnerved him. Greymalkin's mind raced through a hundred responses, wondering how to answer, but he felt paralyzed until he thought through a basic strategy. *Distract him, redirect until Bruno can get here....* "Rodolfo, who are you, really? You say you're a Sojourner, but what is your relationship to the Abyssal that just attacked me?"

Rodo fixed him with a snakelike stare, and then slowly steepled his fingers. "Very well, some further introductions, then. Although quite a long tale, my own story is actually not so very complicated. As I told you before, I was a Sojourner with the previous expedition. I believe you met some of my former shipmates on the *Vlieger*, yes? Unlike them, I decided to explore the region. That is how I met the Tenax."

"The what?" Greymalkin's eyebrows went up. *Keep him talking!*

"That is the designation I eventually assigned to the Abyssal you just encountered," Rodo said affably. "I've been working with it ever since, so long that now you may effectively consider us one being."

Try as he might, Greymalkin could not clearly sense much beyond the structure they were seated in. The thick distortion field seemed to have been designed specifically to close off his shadow senses. "How interesting! What can you tell me about it?"

Rodo's pleasant smile faded. "I can tell you that it does not appreciate evasions. Have you considered our offer or not?"

Greymalkin began to nervously stutter. "Y-Your offer was somewhat ambiguous; you simply asked me to 'join you'. What do you mean by that? And why do you wish that I do it?"

Rodo continued staring at him without blinking until finally leaning back into the invisible chair and giving up a deep sigh. "Young Brother, I see in you a kindred spirit. We both decided to explore this region rather than cowering in fear within our local monastic communities. You have remarkable potential, but you are still very young, inexperienced, and have not been properly mentored.

Incredibly, you have somehow survived the rigors of the Carinae thus far. But you require training and support to endure the challenges that lie ahead of you. With my guidance you could achieve goals that you have only dreamed of in the past. And I truthfully say that together, we can achieve great things."

Greymalkin was silent. Rodo seemed completely genuine in his statements. The young monk said haltingly, "Uh, you tried to *kill* me, remember? Why?"

"I've already apologized for that misstep," Rodo said, nodding and dropping his stare before continuing. "But it is a fair question, nevertheless. Young Brother, as your approach through the nebula demonstrates, you've undoubtedly realized that Eta Carina is the beating heart of the entire Carinae region. The Tenax and I rule this holdfast, including the Forge and everything else within it. Concomitantly, we have authority over this entire realm. Others look to us to defend it, and keep it stable, functioning, efficient... and *undisturbed*. I was late to realize the degree to which this latest expedition from the Orion Arm would result in the destabilization of the region. When I did, I began to act."

Rodo's eerie yellow eyes transfixed Greymalkin again, and the older man said sternly, "You will undoubtedly consider much of what I've done to be ruthless, but my aim here has always been to *maintain order*. May I point out the fact that *you've* caused far more destruction and loss of life here than I have? You and your disaster-prone protean bodyguard killed hundreds of Crotani in the employ of the Abyssals you call Dark Nebula and the Aurelian when you blundered into their territories threatening them."

Greymalkin felt mortified, and guiltily dropped his head. "I, we didn't mean to –"

"That's no excuse!" Rodo snapped. "And while I believe you when you say that you didn't intend these consequences, I hardly put it past the protean. That malevolent monster is a rampaging catastrophe, and *you released it* from its entirely proper imprisonment! I say again, you need tutoring and mentorship, or you will cause further disasters. You do not understand what chain reactions you have *already* set in motion."

Greymalkin opened his mouth to respond, but struggled to find anything to say in his own defense. He had already felt that his efforts in the Carinae had been a failure, but now he was inclined to agree with Rodo that they had been nothing short of a calamity. He defensively began to mumble, "Bruno only acted in self-defense...."

Rodo's face darkened, and he cut off Greymalkin with a rebuke, "You could have avoided all the conflicts that you've caused! And your expedition was *not* invited here, and is perceived by all of us locally as a hostile invasion force!"

Greymalkin shook his head in growing disquiet. "No one told us this! Well, no one told *me*. I know that Kuanian's intent for this expedition was exploratory, not aggression—"

"Kuanian!" Rodo bellowed in fury. "You have no idea who she even is! For example, did you have any idea that when the Tenax first met her more than a millennium ago she was a covert operative of the Sadorian government sent here to destabilize the region? Greymalkin, you've been manipulated and hoodwinked!"

Greymalkin felt his mind spinning as he considered what the man said. *That can't be true. It can't be true, I'd know....* But as he paused to think things through, he suddenly felt that Rodo had yanked out the deck from beneath him. "I... I have to think about what you've said. I just came here to seek out information that I believe I will find at the Forge...."

"I will be *happy* to take you to the Forge," Rodo said, his yellow eyes now glowing with the beginnings of exasperated rage. "I will even *instruct you in its workings*. But you must make up your mind *now* regarding my offer; there is no more time! Even as we speak, *the Carinans are returning.* At this moment the first arriving warbands are filling this nebula, and I must tend to them. You must either join with me or go home!"

As Greymalkin felt panic bubbling up inside, something wholly unexpected happened. *The Carinans!* Something about the thought of the Carinans triggered a response deep within him, and his mind flashed on what Constance had said as if it were a dagger he'd discovered beneath his hand. It was as if his subconscious had been watching Rodo carefully the entire time, and had intuitively chosen this moment to strike back in the argument between them. After months in the Carinae, Greymalkin had come to trust that distinctive feeling of synchronicity whenever it flared inside him, and he followed it. Without consciously planning it out, Greymalkin allowed that particular thought, out of all the myriad random tangents of burning curiosity that were spinning through his mind, to leap out of his mouth of its own volition. He asked, "Is it true that the Carinans are from Andromeda?"

Rodo became very still, and his angry expression froze. "What are you talking about?" Something about the way that Rodo was suddenly off balance made Greymalkin realize that the abrupt interjection had been well timed. *You didn't think I knew that. It tripped you up, didn't it?*

"The Carinans. I was given to believe that they might have originated in the Andromedan Galaxy. Is that true?" Greymalkin pressed.

Rodo was silent and utterly motionless for several long beats. Then the yellow eyes seemed to blaze up in their intensity. "Their forebears were noble knights of Andromeda in the Xenagon, but these today are a far lesser spawn. Brawlers, wildlings. I brought them here and... *cultivated* them. I must go and take them in hand now, or in addition to your colleagues they may run wild and kill themselves. *And you will now give me your answer.*"

Greymalkin's mind completed one last manic revolution as he processed the connection between the Andromedan Galaxy and the returning Carinans, and then locked onto one thought that blotted everything else out with utter terror. *Tatter!*

"I have to go!" Greymalkin hissed. "I reject your offer."

Then Greymalkin saw real and unrehearsed rage boil up and explode in Rodo, and the older man roared, "*Be on your way then, worm! Go and die with the rest of the maggots.*" His yellow eyes became blindingly bright, and Greymalkin suddenly found himself slammed down into the cockpit seat within Royce.

Greymalkin seized control of the rover's helm and wheeled around in the direction they had come. The full sensory link with Bruno reactivated, and he felt the wrenching effort of the protean tearing free from the strangling cables of the Tenax. As Royce rocketed away across the twisted shadow plane, Bruno flew just above them and communed basso thoughts to him.

«I overheard your conversation. We must return to the location of the Sylphid post haste. The Carinans may overrun her.» The protean actually seemed concerned.

Greymalkin communed nothing in response, but goaded Royce into a truly frantic pace alongside the screaming synesthetic winds of the nebula. They were sliding every which way, but he didn't care. He had never felt so frightened. *This isn't just a possibility now, it's certain death coming for her. We've got to get there before they do.* Royce was already in a barely controlled plummeting slalom across the brilliant electric blue hypersurfaces, but he goaded the cyneget even harder, and it responded with an instinctive frenzy of its own. The shadow plane shot beneath them in a blur.

Despite the speed at which Royce was traversing the wildly undulating shadow planes, Bruno poured on still more acceleration and began pulling ahead of them. Greymalkin was so preoccupied with trying to keep Royce on the path that he could only devote brief glimpses ahead of them to scan for obstacles. Suddenly he detected a scattering of furtive shapes spreading out ahead of them, and heeled Royce hard over to try to avoid them. *Carinans!* «Bruno, look out! Let me try the peace signal with them this time!»

«There is no time.» Bruno's thoughts were followed by a savage battle roar, and the protean lunged forward just as nine deadly vehicles appeared and fired simultaneously. Greymalkin's shadow sense was already obscured by the synesthetic glare and distortions around them. When the explosions detonated on and around the protean, Greymalkin was momentarily blinded by the painful streaks of brightness. He tried to scan for Bruno in alarm. *Great Mercy, were those antimatter warheads?* Then his attention was fully occupied by trying to pull Royce out of the spin induced by the hard turn. He had just straightened the cyneget's course when he saw that three of the Carinan vehicles had broken away from Bruno and were almost on top of them. Before Greymalkin could react, Royce lurched to the side away from the rapidly approaching attackers.

Two of the Carinans swooped around to encircle Royce, but the third one came head on. Greymalkin flinched as he sensed a power spike in the vehicle, but then he gasped as Royce emitted a snarl and abruptly extended his shadow space manifold in a sharp vertex that neatly bisected their opponent's manifold. As the continuity of existence around it fragmented, the Carinan instantly disintegrated, and they shot through the path it had occupied a moment before.

Greymalkin had no time to commend Royce as the other two Carinans launched missiles through shadow space at them. Before he could even inhale to scream, the warheads detonated close by them.

Miraculously, they were unharmed, and Greymalkin saw that part of Bruno had somehow outspread around them in a shield that prevented the blast from reaching them.

Through their shared link, he could sense the protean's agony from the attacks. But Bruno was giving more than he was receiving. Four of the Carinans had been destroyed, and the protean was relentlessly assailing the remaining alien vehicles. Greymalkin steered Royce toward Bruno in a desperate zig-zag pattern as the two Carinans pursuing him launched more missiles. The protean again shielded them, and the battle abruptly ended as Bruno destroyed the last four Carinans. Royce caught up to Bruno, and Greymalkin felt the pain wracking the protean. Greymalkin brought the cyneget closer and communed directly to Bruno, penetrating through all the strange synesthesia shadow space distortions of their surroundings. «How badly are you injured? Can you still move?»

The protean sent growling thoughts and shuddered for a moment, pulling the scattered chunks of itself back together, and throwing off the pain of the injuries. When it finally communed, Bruno's thoughts were restrained. «Let us go. I will keep up.»

Greymalkin nodded and resumed the breakneck pace back through the shifting labyrinth of the Homunculus Nebula. The return transit was even more nerve-wracking because of the urgency he felt, and every time he lost track of the path he was more panicked than before. After what seemed like a truly numbing eternity of freezing anxiety, he located the outskirts of the Homunculus Nebula's maze of paths and caught sight of the system where they had left Tatter.

Sensing Greymalkin's panic, Royce had outpaced the wounded Bruno on the return, and now raced forward at great speed. They dropped down from the shadow plane into orbit around the huge blue star, and Greymalkin searched wildly for Tatter's signal, hailing her repeatedly. But no response came, either from the entrance to the stellar mine or from the makeshift base they had assembled on the planetoid from the ancient Thannic ruins. He wondered which location to search first, and decided on the planetoid since it was closer. Greymalkin goaded Royce back through shadow space toward the Thannic base and they emerged in orbit, already descending toward the surface. The Thannic ruins were in the pitch blackness of the night side of the planetoid, which had rotated away from the blazing blue light of the big star.

Behind them, Bruno communed a warning. «Wait until I can rejoin you! The Carinans may already be here!» The protean's thoughts were alert and wary, but Greymalkin was far past caution. He dove Royce down to hover above the Thannic ruins and activated the cyneget's multiple sensor arrays and big spotlights to scan the surface. Instantly, Greymalkin gasped.

The center of the Thannic ruins where the dome had been buried was now a large crater, with debris scattered outwards from it in a huge disorganized arc. They descended to hover just above the crater, and he played the spotlight across the wreckage, trying to make sense of the chaotic play of darkness and light. He immediately marked the corpses of several Carinans scattered amid the wreckage. Their armor had been ripped apart and many of their limbs had been torn off.

Greymalkin looked through the scattered piles of wreckage frantically, and cast his communed thoughts in all directions. «*Tatter, where are you?*» He realized that the stark white reflections and black shadows cast by the spotlight were only succeeding in confusing him. He was so panicked that he could not make out anything in the giant confused arc of debris that had apparently been blasted upwards from the underground dome. His acute shadow senses were defeated by the myriad jagged edges of metal and rock fragments everywhere beneath them. He snapped off the spotlight in frustration, and made a decision.

He jumped out of the cockpit, slapping his helmet down over his head with a quick pull. Greymalkin leaped into the airlock and, after sealing the hatch, activated the emergency depressurization control. The outer hatch retracted abruptly, and he was violently blown out of the airlock onto the silent surface in the brief blast of atmospheric release. He stumbled to his feet and, after activating his much less blinding suit torchlight, began combing through the wreckage while still communing. «Tatter! Are you here?»

He could sense Bruno emerging from shadow space and descending from orbit above him. The protean could apparently already see the destruction on the surface, and its communed thoughts were solemn. «We must face the possibility that they may have taken her unawares. If they managed to puncture her shadow space pouch with energy weapons before she sensed their approach... her pouch manifold could have imploded and annihilated everything inside. There may be nothing left of the Sylphid to find.»

With sudden new fear, Greymalkin thought back to the way that he'd just seen Royce disrupt the Carinan's manifold in the same manner that Bruno was describing, and how the creature had instantly disintegrated. Even with all her tremendous vitality and strength, Tatter wouldn't survive a manifold breach like that either. Her huge hidden alien form would simply vanish forever in a blaze of light. The thought was utterly terrifying and his throat clenched.

«Shut up!» Greymalkin's thoughts were furious. «She may just be injured and unconscious! Help me find her!» He began lifting fragments of the dome and uncovering the wreckage half buried in rocks and dust. Then he saw something different reflecting in his torchlight, and his eyes widened. There was a large frozen puddle on the ground at his feet. Tiny icy grit glittered in the puddle, which had a reddish color so dark that it was almost black. His stomach did flip flops as he remembered his basic EVA search and rescue safety training. *When it freezes in vacuum, human blood crystallizes and darkens.*

Bruno appeared above him and a few meters to the side, his murky stone form outlined dimly by a bluish nimbus against the stars and black sky. Several of the huge Carinan warriors lay beneath the hovering protean, their rent and torn bodies in a heap. Bruno's communed thoughts were grave. «She's here.»

Greymalkin scrambled over the debris toward Bruno, and caught sight of something bright and multi-colored in his torchlight. In dawning shock he realized that it was Tatter's varicolored Erisian garment. He could see her legs protruding from under one of the huge Carinan corpses. Greymalkin gasped inside his helmet. *She's not in a void suit! She's exposed to vacuum! I've got to get her back inside Royce now!* He jumped the last few meters to where she lay and shoved the heavy limb of the Carinan off of her. He quickly knelt beside her and reached for her arm to feel for her pulse. He stopped then, stock-still.

Tatter's arm was frozen solid. It felt as cold and hard as the rocks he'd been hurling aside. Greymalkin was utterly mystified. He felt her other arm and her torso. Her body was a block of ice. He kept looking for her face, baffled as to why he could not see her features. All that he could see above her frayed collar fringe were thickly sprayed patterns of dark, frozen blood pools scattered across the rocky surface. Try as he might, he could not find her smile, or her auburn-brown hair, or her deep brown eyes. Greymalkin reached for her shoulders in confusion, and tried to shake her awake, but it was like trying to shake an icy boulder.

Slowly he felt the universe crushing down on him irresistibly from all directions. Then he began to scream and scream, and discovered that he could not stop screaming.

Consequences

After several interminable ages the screaming stopped. Greymalkin found that somehow, nothing at all had changed. He was still on his knees in a vast, dark pile of rubble and corpses, his suit torchlight illuminating Tatter's dead body. His head was ringing, and facts had become disconnected from rationality. All that he knew was that everything had become shattered, his thoughts, his emotions, even who he felt he was. He scanned the shadow space immediately around them, but Tatter's pouch manifold and huge alien Sylphid form was nowhere to be seen. There was nothing but the void. Bruno's words echoed in Greymalkin's mind with a desperate sense of looming importance, but he felt numb and incapable of understanding what the words actually signified. *Her pouch manifold could have imploded and annihilated everything inside. There may be nothing left of the Sylphid to find.....*

But... here she is. He stupidly looked down at what was left of her human body once more, and then up at the slowly morphing shape of the protean outlined in blue light above him. Then Greymalkin sensed some new uncontrollable emotion bubbling up inside of him, something totally unknown, another mystery that he teetered on the edge of but could not yet understand.

«What just happened?» His thoughts felt like a fluid coming steadily up to a boil, and he could feel his body trembling. «Why is she like this?»

«During their attack the war party evidently decapitated her for some reason.» Bruno's thoughts were analytical, clear, and solemn.

Greymalkin could sense Royce chuffing in the distance, agitated and restless. He ignored that for the moment along with everything else. His mind was focused on trying to understand the words Bruno had just communicated. The emotion that was gradually rising inside of him came closer to the boiling point. His trembling became more violent.

«*Why?*» The question echoed in his mind. «Why would they do that to her?»

«Their motives are obscure, obviously.» Bruno's thoughts had now become tinged with discomfort by something about the emotion bubbling up inside of Greymalkin, but he ignored that as well. The unfamiliar emotion surging up inside him had now become a roiling lake.

«*Why did they do that!?*» Greymalkin's question came blasting out of him toward the protean like a missile. The young monk was still trying to absorb the information that the protean had communicated, but his mind had locked up, stuck trying to comprehend the word *decapitated*.

Bruno was observing the young monk closely. Carefully. «I do not know. Perhaps they collected it as a specimen. Or a trophy.»

Greymalkin stared at the hovering protean, and then looked down at Tatter's body again. Suddenly his stomach jack-knifed, and he vomited. The Sojourner void suit's automated safety protocols caught the event in time and the emergency ventilation system activated, sucking everything away to prevent him from choking. But the acid taste of bile remained in his mouth.

«A specimen?» Greymalkin processed that word and then the next word, finally feeling the unknown emotion boiling up irresistibly within him. «*A trophy??*»

The unknown emotion now came into searing clarity within him, an emotion he had never before felt or even imagined in his life. The young monk felt his mind explode in uncontrollable murderous rage and desire for vengeance on the beings that had done this to Tatter. Greymalkin screamed hoarsely once more. He pitched forward sobbing and tore her rigid form free of the regolith of the planetoid. Then he stood and ran in plunging, stumbling jumps through the debris field back to Royce. He felt a burning ache pounding everywhere inside him. It was the agonizing ache of certainty, of finality, and knowing that this was all too real and not a hallucination on his part.

Inside the airlock, he activated one of the stasis storage units, and tenderly lowered her frozen body into it. He sealed the unit and sobbed on top of the coldly shining mirrored cover for long moments. But then the rage exploded through him again and he leaped into the cockpit. He slammed the helmet back over his head and activated the helm link. Royce immediately howled into the closed circuit, reacting to his mental turmoil. Greymalkin ignored the cyneget's agitation and fired the starship's emergency launch sequence. The ship catapulted into the dark sky, and the protean followed dutifully after them.

«Where are we going? We need a plan.» Bruno's thoughts were unsettled.

«I'm going to get some answers, whatever that requires.» His thoughts and mind were pure spinning fury. «Then I'm going to kill those who did this. And finally, after I retrieve the rest of her, I'm going to say goodbye and cremate her in the biggest pyre I can find. How is *that* for a *plan*?»

«We should investigate the site of the attack before we leave.» Bruno seemed remarkably pensive. «I made a rapid holographic recording scan of the site, but there are many details that stand out as anomalous to me which I want to investigate.»

Greymalkin had goaded Royce into orbit, but now circled around with a massive power-burn. He glared down at the site in the darkness below. «There is only one purpose for that site now. It will serve as a test fire.» Greymalkin's mind twisted into a venomous knot demanding release, and his attention snapped back to the protean. Then something shocking happened. This time, unlike every previous instance, the young Sojourner initiated the full sensory link with Bruno rather than the other way around. And then, even more shocking to the protean, Bruno felt his combat systems activating unbidden.

«How are you doing this?» Bruno's query was restrained, but very angry. Greymalkin made a sound. The protean noted that it was not a chuckling laugh. It was something that sounded profoundly evil.

«Remember the first surprise you ever expressed to me? Recall it now; I possess your *master control codes*. I've always been able to do this. I simply never attempted it previously.» Although Greymalkin's mind was whirling with rage, he found that he was perfectly focused on the tasks he wanted to accomplish. Bruno's targeting systems centered on the Thannic ruins far below. Bruno leaped forward, just as the protean felt the remote matter-to-energy conversion sequence activate. The protean's black form had interposed itself between Royce and the site where the ruins had been a microsecond before, the location that was now an expanding cloud of plasma many kilometers across. The protean had blocked the intense flash of destructive radiation from blinding Greymalkin.

«That was reckless.» Bruno's thoughts now seemed completely flat, and without emotion. «I would advise against trying to use my combat systems further. You have no experience with them, and will only endanger yourself, as you just did.» Greymalkin, however, cackled in delight.

«I knew you would shield me. But, point taken, as long as you destroy what I point you toward.» The young Sojourner wheeled the cyneget around and slipped into shadow space. The protean once again followed close behind.

«I will destroy targets you designate as long as your mind remains rational.» Bruno seemed dour and adamant in the statement. It only provoked the same sinister barking laugh from Greymalkin.

«Why so glum, Bruno?» Greymalkin felt a strange rictus taking over his mouth. «I thought you loved blowing things up? But, challenge accepted! I promise I will be perfectly logical about pursuing the goals of my plan.» He scanned the shadow plane and accelerated Royce forward at a velocity that strained the cyneget's propulsion systems. The protean began to fall behind, but caught up with an effort.

«You intend to follow the war party that attacked the Sylphid.» Bruno again made the statement flatly, without emotion. «How will you locate them? They must have departed some time ago.»

«I've already located them.» The rictus grew larger, Greymalkin's lips drawing back from his bared teeth. «We are in luck. They are also rigged to traverse the shadow plane, and are not too far ahead of us. We will intercept them soon. *Be ready*.»

The protean scanned the brilliantly shifting shadow plane ahead of them, and eventually saw the group of Carinans that Greymalkin had effortlessly detected. Sure enough, the distant cluster of targets was moving slowly across the shadow plane directly away from the planetoid. «This group is significantly larger than the one that attacked us previously. I may not be capable of defeating them.»

«Hah! Don't worry, Royce and I will also assist if you feel incapable of it.» Greymalkin sent sneering thoughts toward the protean. «Or are you *afraid*, Bruno? If so, feel free to run away, by all means.»

The protean clearly became angry at the comment. «Our likelihood of success is not great. You are already irrational and unbalanced.»

«On the contrary, I'm pursuing my goals in the most direct and logical way available to me. I never said anything about a guarantee of success. Now shut up, I need to study their formation.»

While Bruno steamed in irritation, the young monk tried to focus on the Carinans. But then he sagged, sobbing and trembling. The image and terribly cold touch of Tatter's body kept coming back to him relentlessly, and the paralyzing ache inside his chest began to overwhelm his mind again. Then a gagging sound of incoherent rage came out of his throat, and he began to savagely punch the side of his face as hard as he could, until his head rang and forced all other thoughts away but vengeance. Shaking, he clenched his jaws shut, and focused his mind on the task at hand. Through the haze of pain he could now count the alien warriors, and saw that there were twenty-one of them. It was obvious which one was the leader; the group was arranged in a simple chevron, with ten on each wing. Greymalkin's face curled into a misshapen grimace of agonized hate as he marked the lead Carinan. *That's the one I need to capture alive.*

Greymalkin found that the synesthesia of the Carinae was again becoming an unwanted distraction. The outflowing blast of ionized gas from the Homunculus Nebula seemed like a chilling wind at his back, and the illusory gale was like a constant howling in his ears. Greymalkin grit his teeth harder and tried to throw off the phantom sensory distractions with a shake of his still ringing head. But the shadow plane now dipped down into distortion, and he lost track of the war party for a moment. Something vicious and wary inside him realized that the group might be able to circle around on him while hidden, and he wondered if they could have detected his approach. He studied the topography ahead of them, and abruptly steered Royce to the side. Bruno came swooping after them.

«Why are we diverting?» The protean was confused now, and for the first time Greymalkin wondered if the alien cyborg was not so omniscient as it had always seemed to him.

«That deformation in the shadow plane ahead is a prime spot to ambush us.» Greymalkin steered Royce to the side and then began angling back toward the distorted region of the plane. «If they try that we'll catch them from behind when we come over the lip of the depression here. If they just kept going instead, then we'll catch up to them momentarily. Be ready either way. I'll designate targets for you.»

«When did you become so cunning, human?» The protean's thoughts were watchful and suspicious. Greymalkin sneered again.

«It's just obvious geometry. Now pay attention! They are likely just ahead of us.» Greymalkin sent a signal to Royce to maximize the cyneget's alertness responses, and the living starship seemed to growl in response. They came over the edge of the depression at speed and plunged down through the distorted space.

Greymalkin cast his shadow sense ahead of them. Sure enough, the war party was arranged ahead, but they were pointed in the direction away from them, unawares. He bared his teeth. *I outsmarted you bastards! Flanked you! Who just surprised who, eh?* He sent a narrowly focused stream of communed thoughts to Bruno. «Hit the outermost target in that wing of the formation with everything you've got until it's destroyed. Then each one in order, closer and closer to the leader. When this turns into a disorganized brawl, I'll act as bait to draw them away. You pick them off one at a time, then. But save the leader there in the center for last; I want to capture and question that one alive! *Do you understand?*»

«I understand, human.» Bruno sullenly charged forward, for once neither roaring nor exhibiting the familiar battle-lust to which Greymalkin was accustomed. As the protean sped forward, a chunk of the amorphous black creature split off and surrounded Royce in a defensive array. The battle erupted into utter chaos instantly as Bruno began to destroy the Carinan attack craft with tremendous blasts of energy and the war party scattered away from the protean.

Greymalkin did not attempt to follow the details of the combat, but grimly kept his attention on the lead Carinan while simultaneously urging Royce to dodge away from any Carinans that approached them. At first the combat was a constant roiling whorl of Carinan attack craft ferociously trying to encircle Bruno in the center of the wide basin depression in the shadow plane. But despite the fact that the protean was taking incredible damage, Bruno was methodically destroying the Carinans one at a time.

Greymalkin felt a hideous glee rising inside him every time one of the aliens individually burst into fireballs that were quickly snuffed out as their shadow space manifolds collapsed. The Carinans seemed suicidal in their obsession with constantly attacking Bruno no matter how many of them were killed. He had never enjoyed the outcome of Bruno's savage havoc previously, but now he found that he was choking with celebratory guttural laughter whenever one of the Carinans died.

Greymalkin had been so singularly focused on tracking the leader amid the whirling combat that it took him by surprise when an urgent instinct caught his attention. He began to register the agony that Bruno was experiencing from the unbelievable torrent of damage that the Carinans were dealing out. The protean was now lurching toward destruction as each new antimatter warhead detonated on his black form.

Greymalkin seized Royce's helm control firmly again and whirled the cyneget around to charge straight toward the conflagration of destruction. The remaining Carinans were closing in around Bruno, sensing the growing vulnerability of the protean.

Greymalkin now realized that Royce's awareness had absorbed his state of mind, and the cyneget was fully saturated with enraged combat responses of its own. The young monk tensed at the speeding Carinans ahead of them... and then his unhindered fury took an even deeper plunge into the madness of combat. He reached out with his mind and tightly embraced both the sensory link with the protean and the helm control system of the cyneget. Everything changed profoundly then, as the young monk began recklessly merging their three minds into a bizarre new state of awareness. Where they had been three, now there was only one linked mind that was becoming a more and more integrated single consciousness jointly immersed in the exquisite agony of battle.

The cyneget-portion of the linked mind flashed through the spiraling tracks of the Carinans, activating its shadow space manifold as a weapon again. The infinitely sharp pincers of the cyborg's extended continuity bit down on one, then two of the Carinans. The alien attack craft were sliced in half and their individual pocket manifolds erupted in brief, bright blazes of disintegration. Then the Royce-Greymalkin component of the merged organism spun away in another direction, with several of the Carinans wrathfully following after them. The Bruno component of the trio redoubled its efforts and the last two Carinans worrying the protean disintegrated. The protean struggled after the Carinans rapidly following the cyneget-human as it dashed away. Then the human inside the cyneget laughed and did something even more cruel.

The cyneget-shell was racing all out, unafraid of the danger, instead resonating with the human-core's mental exultation in the sheer frenzy of the chase. Both parts of the linked mind were giving themselves over to the rage increasingly. The core of fury that had been a human grinned a deranged smile, sensing the three remaining Carinans drawing so very close behind the Royce-shell as they skimmed wildly across the shadow plane upwards toward the edge of the basin depression. *They know that the impedance slope will slow us down. They think they've got us.*

His rictus lips pulled back from his teeth as the mind that had been a young monk deliberately broadcast a generalized communed emotion of sheer contempt backward toward the Carinans. He had seen the irrationally aggressive way the aliens reacted to everything, and sure enough, his communed insult enraged the creatures even more than they already had been. The rage-mind was ready for the response and, laughing maniacally, hit the emergency continuity manifold cutoff. The cyneget dropped back into normal space, and before the Carinans could react they swept past them at tremendous speed, launching their missiles at nothing. The rage-core instantly launched the cyneget-shell back into shadow space, reversing their direction and plunging back down the slope. The shock of the abrupt shunts in and out of shadow space wrenched their shared consciousness painfully. The sensation felt like a blade had been dragged down through the human's spinal cord and the central mast of the cyneget alike, but the human mind simply grit its teeth again and focused on the cyneget's flight control. They sped back down the incline, just as the Carinans spun back around toward them in enraged, erratic arcs. The mind of anger heard the hoarsely screamed laughter of a lunatic somewhere nearby, and wondered who it could be.

«*Get ready!*» The human core of the cyneget communed the wildly raging question at the protean component of the trio. The Bruno part of them did not respond but, ignoring the excruciating pain it was experiencing, intently charged up past the cyneget-shell as it descended back to the bottom of the basin. There were two briefly communed outbursts of panicked terror behind them, and then the blasts of energy from the protean-portion that ended two more Carinan lives. The human rage-core laid the helm hard over and the swift cyneget-shell wheeled around to pursue the last of the Carinans, the leader.

The last of the Carinans was zig-zagging back and forth in an evasive pattern, but the human component of the trio-thing that pursued it now was slavering with rage and a monstrous desire to complete its vengeance. In that moment, the human mind of fury dimly grasped how he had become the dominating core of the strange interlinked trio-entity, and how the new composite being was locked together through and by means of his psyche. The enormous protean portion of the tripartite will was now so weakened by the sea of agony the protean had endured that it was capable of nothing but following the directions from the human mind that burned with rage. The cyneget portion that was Royce verged on a completely feral collapse into madness, and only remained stable because of the iron concentration the maddened human component of the three-part mind was exerting. The cruel entity of rage that controlled the composite being no longer felt like a young monk. Instead there was only a shattered stream of agonized glass flying the assembly in an unyielding formation, held rigidly taught by the bile that he could still taste in his mouth. The taste was no synesthesia, but a burning misery that permeated and focused his consciousness like a guiding light. Every time the memory of Tatter's dead body tried to rise up again in his mind, he clenched his jaws and thrust it aside, savoring the acid taste in his throat. Other than the mechanics of piloting through twists and turns, one thought held the enraged mind together. *Whatever it takes, I will finally have answers before I kill this last one.*

The Greymalkin-remnant saw that the Carinan leader was slowing slightly, undoubtedly trying to figure out some way to aim its weapons backwards at him. He thought how entertaining it was to bait this vile and stupid creature. He slowed the Royce-component that enclosed him, matching the Carinan's velocity, allowing the Bruno-part to gradually catch up. As the Carinan swerved back and forth, he echoed its weaving motion, staying just behind the creature and observing it closely.

They were very near to one another now, but every time the Carinan decelerated Greymalkin matched the maneuver. When the Carinan realized that the Greymalkin-mind of rage was steadily luring it back into range of the Bruno-thing's attack, the alien began to accelerate again. The Greymalkin-rage-mind had again anticipated the response, and the agile cyneget-part leaped forward directly toward the alien attack craft, the Carinan expanding in front of them almost instantaneously. The two shadow space manifolds merged and in the moment remaining to him, the rage-mind deftly aimed the hurtling cyneget shell at the alien like a battering ram and activated the ship collision protocol. The cockpit surged up and enveloped his soft human core.

In the last split second, the Carinan became visible through the forward viewport. In the compressed tunnel-vision of the human's rage-mind, the angular black creature and the dark framework of weapons, fuel tanks, and engines that it rode seemed like a single tangle of blades. But the attack rig that the Carinan rode was far smaller than the cyneget's thousands of tons of mass. The cyborg slammed into the alien with enormous physical momentum. The collision finally broke the shared trance, and the monstrous single entity fell back into the three distinct beings again. Greymalkin felt the crunching impact on Royce's impervious mirrorshell carapace both through the helm link and the cockpit itself. The crash threw him forward violently, but the soft cockpit envelope surrounding him cushioned the brunt of the impact.

Many of the blades comprising the Carinan rig were crushed, snapping into a sparking tangle. Greymalkin felt the continuity of the alien's manifold collapse around them, and if it had not been for Royce's manifold, the creature would have been disintegrated. But the tangled mass of the Carinan's rig had survived, and now spun away from them in a whirling wreck.

As Greymalkin watched the smashed rig spinning away from him, his grin fell into an angry scowl. He brought them out of shadow space and communed seething thoughts to Bruno as the protean caught up with them. «Contain and disarm the Carinan, will you Bruno? It may still be capable of attacking us.»

Greymalkin tried to catch his breath as the boiling stone liquid of the protean quickly encased the Carinan. Now that the breakneck chase had ended, he found that the unbearable memories of holding Tatter's body were trying to come back to him. He tried to push the images away, but could feel them starting to clamp around his heart with an icy grip. The protean's thoughts reached out to his mind just then.

«I have now confiscated the creature's many weapons.» Bruno's thoughts were slow and ominous as the engorged protean returned to float in front of the rover's main viewport. One of its misshapen limbs held out a small cylinder. «I also found this among other artifacts it was transporting.»

The crystal cylinder was roughly half a meter wide and long. When Greymalkin scanned it, he stiffened in dread. The cylinder was packed with tangled hair. And a human head. Greymalkin looked away, but his shadow sense could not be shut off. He began to sob uncontrollably again for a moment, and then his stomach rebelled once more. This time he caught the bile in his throat and swallowed it back down, appreciating the way that the burning taste of gastric acid both distracted him while refocusing his mind on rage. At last he clenched his chattering teeth and communed a grim response. «Put... *that* in Royce's exterior sample storage chamber. Then we'll proceed. It... it's time for *answers*.»

* * *

As the protean complied with his instructions, Greymalkin scanned their immediate vicinity in normal space. He found a suitable location not far away. «Bruno, bring the Carinan along with us to that rock over there.»

Greymalkin took Royce back into shadow space briefly as they skimmed across the phantasmal shadow plane to a rocky planetoid drifting through empty space. From the look of the dead planet it was a rogue body that had been wandering through interstellar space for uncounted eons. It would undoubtedly have been captured by one of the myriad stars of the Carinae eventually, but at the moment it was simply adrift here in the midst of empty desolation. Greymalkin brought Royce down to the dead surface, and then climbed out of the retracting cockpit. He went to the airlock, flipped the helmet down over his head, and soon stepped out onto the darkened regolith in front of Royce, activating the bright spotlight onto the ground there. As the protean descended with the Carinan, Greymalkin gestured angrily to the ancient surface of the silent planetoid. «Immobilize the creature just there, will you, Bruno?»

Bruno obliged, and the bubbling black stone of the protean's form slowly flattened on the surface and then retracted to reveal the huge splayed form of the struggling Carinan, held down against the cold surface of the dead world. Now that he could observe one of the aliens alive, Greymalkin could fully appreciate just how vicious and dangerous the creatures were. The brute was trying to break free, and was thrashing its sharp-edged limbs so violently that loose rocks underneath it were split apart and rattled away silently in the vacuum. Greymalkin could feel the vibrations through his boots as the demonic creature thumped and slapped heavily against the regolith. But then Bruno tightened the implacable vise-grip of its liquid stone around the big alien's limbs, and held it almost motionless.

«What do you intend to do with this being?» Bruno's thoughts seemed wary. Greymalkin could still feel the extent of the protean's injuries and pain in the communed thoughts, but he put the sensations aside just like everything else distracting him from his purpose. He stepped up to the tense Carinan, studying the alien's physiology in the spotlight with fascination. The creature's segmented head sloped back into its torso, twisting back and forth intermittently. The head was pointed at him now, mandibles like razors snapping in his direction. Greymalkin smiled darkly.

What he assumed must be the creature's eyes were a cluster of red orbs flicking back and forth wildly at the front of the long, protruding head. He could see that the body was well-adapted for vacuum, with hard black chitinous segments allowing the torso to flex down into a central plexus where six jagged limbs emerged. There were two more big limbs that emerged from the side of the head-torso, but he wondered if these were some sort of pedipalps. It was hard to tell, given that the ends of the limbs were encased in the stone restraints that Bruno had extended. Greymalkin glanced up at the main floating mass of Bruno.

«Question it, obviously.» Greymalkin slowly stepped around the massive struggling form of the Carinan, noting where the limbs and body segments narrowed. He stepped closer to the big writhing head, and sent a series of communed questions in hard bursts designed not around words but simple sentiments that the creature would understand without a common language. «*Open your mind to me. What are your motivations? Why did you attack?*»

The Carinan had an obvious startled reaction at first, recoiling from him. But then it seemed to recover its animosity, and again snapped its mandibles viciously at him. If anything, Greymalkin could sense the creature closing and walling off its mind from him vigorously. The only thing that it communed in response to Greymalkin was an overwhelming blast of hate and threatening intent that made its murderous desires clear.

«I doubt this being will be cooperative or useful in any way.» Bruno clearly felt that it was distasteful to be holding the struggling creature down on the regolith of the planetoid. Greymalkin tilted his head inside the void suit helmet, looking up at Bruno again.

«I disagree. There are simple and direct ways of motivating it to cooperate.» Greymalkin could hear his own heart thudding rapidly. The tension in his shoulders and head were unbearable, and he was trembling with uncontrollable anger. «For instance, let's see what its response will be if we *tear off one of its limbs.*»

Bruno did not respond immediately, instead simply floating above him. Finally it communed stern thoughts. «You have become unbalanced as a result of the transformative process you endured in the pod from the Genibrata, as well as the death of the Sylphid. I will not inflict pointless injuries on this creature.»

Greymalkin sneered. «What's the matter, Bruno? You told me that you were guilty of having committed any and all crimes in the past. Why so hesitant now? If we aren't going to question it, what do you want to do with this filth?»

«We should simply end its existence.» The solemn thoughts of the protean were full of sadness. «Nothing will be gained by torturing this sapient being.»

«On the contrary.» Greymalkin shook as a chill went down his spine. «I will finally obtain answers to my core questions about these damnable vermin. If we simply kill it now, the battle with its war party and all of your injuries will have been to no purpose.»

«I will not torture this individual.» Bruno's thoughts had hardened.

Greymalkin felt his rage boil over into an nonverbal snarl. He looked around at the bulk of Royce, the cyneget's spotlight shining down on the helpless Carinan, and seized control of the living starship through the Helm Link again. The mind of the cyneget was in turmoil, torn between embracing Greymalkin's rage and rejecting it. Greymalkin compelled the cyneget to extend one of its big external grapple-limbs, which had now been fully regrown.

The heavy mirrorshell claws unfolded and reached over him toward the Carinan. Then the claws clamped down on one of the Carinan's limbs where it emerged from Bruno's stony grasp. Royce had discerned what Greymalkin intended to do, and now sent a terrified whining signal to him. The rover was trying to resist, but Greymalkin coerced it with an iron will. The cyneget was now actively resisting with its own mind, broadcasting cries that were verging on the screams he had heard it emit when Trauerstrom had been torturing the cyborg. That abruptly broke him and brought tears to Greymalkin's eyes, and he realized he could not bear compelling Royce to do this thing.

«Do not force the cyborg. I will do as you ask.» Bruno's thoughts were subdued and sad at first, but then grew hard again. «Besides, I am the only one here that knows how to effectively conduct torture.»

Greymalkin looked back at Bruno with wild eyes, and communed a trembling thought. «*Good.*» He instructed Royce to withdraw its grapple-limb, and the rover did so quickly. Greymalkin stood by the Carinan's mandible-snapping head, glaring at the creature. Again he communed his questions to the monster. «*Why have you done what you've done? Why did you attack? Open your mind to me!*»

The Carinan thrashed its head furiously, the walls of its mind closing like steel shutters. Greymalkin's temper exploded, and he cursed the creature. He had never despised another living thing as he despised this brute. He wondered if this was the very Carinan that had killed Tatter, and the thought enraged him more than anything yet. «*Bruno!*»

«Yes, yes, but understand that this is a process of measured escalation. Let us first investigate its pain threshold.» The protean sounded like it was giving a class lecture, and it made Greymalkin feel a dazed sense of unreality in the midst of his anger. Then he noticed several other details. Bruno's stone blocks that held the limbs of the Carinan like manacles had begun glowing red hot. The Carinan was twitching in a subdued manner. Bruno's thoughts continued in lecture mode. «Interesting. I am applying several stressors. Heat. Electrical current. But the creature's adaptations to life in vacuum conditions seem to make it immune.»

Greymalkin found the indifference of the Carinan irritating and was about to goad the protean to greater efforts, but then the Carinan began to quiver as Bruno began to pull irresistibly on one of the creature's limbs. Greymalkin sensed its agitation rising, and he angrily communed his questions once again. The Carinan still did not respond but only threw its head back and forth madly. Greymalkin was shocked when Bruno suddenly ripped the limb out of the creature's plexus completely. The alien's torso arched up in a spasm of torment.

«It appears to have a relatively high tolerance for pain, but that weakened it.» Bruno's thoughts were still clinical and detached. Greymalkin stared in disgust as the bone-like white fibrous material inside the Carinan began leaking some kind of transparent amber circulatory fluid that quickly boiled away into the vacuum. Bruno seemed to study both the Carinan and Greymalkin, and then communed an instruction to him. «Repeat your questions again.»

His head pounding in revulsion now, Greymalkin communed the questions at the strongest intensity that he could muster. But the Carinan stubbornly continued to bite towards him aggressively, and did not respond. Greymalkin's hatred, frustration, and anger were colliding with his confusion and disgust. «Bruno, why won't this *craven skate* answer me? Could it be so primitive that it can't even receive communed thoughts?»

«It is receiving your thoughts. It is more likely that it has simply been instructed to not respond to questions if captured.» The protean seemed intrigued now, as if it were working on a puzzle. Greymalkin, however, now felt mortified at the creature's seeming suicidal resistance. He communed his questions pointedly once again.

«Answer me, damn you!» Greymalkin felt his face flushed red with fury, but the sight of the bleeding stump on the side of the creature had finally defeated his rage. The shocking wound reminded him of the brutality of Trauerstrom testing Royce, and how cruel and unjust that had seemed to him at the time. His racing thoughts had reached a decision. *We've got to stop. This is just pointless and inhuman now. No matter what this alien's done, I'm not going to become like that bastard Trauerstrom.* Hesitantly, he began to tell Bruno to stop, but the protean was already communing.

«Intriguing.» Bruno's thoughts had become distant and completely emotionless. «It does not seem noticeably responsive to heat, high electrical voltage, or most other stressors. This creature is quite well-disciplined. Very well, then.»

Abruptly, the protean tore off two more of the creature's lower limbs and one of its pedipalps, whereupon the alien arched its torso in an extreme curve, shuddering violently. Greymalkin shrieked inside his helmet, and staggered backward. He felt his stomach heave again, but there was nothing remaining that he could throw up. But then, as he began communing appalled thoughts for Bruno to stop, he finally felt the walls of the Carinan's mind crumbling. Greymalkin clenched his stinging eyes shut, and tried to commune with the alien one last time. He found that the creature's mental processes were now helplessly open to read.

He quickly scanned through the Carinan's mind... and paused. What was within the alien's psyche was inconceivable. Greymalkin's face went slack-jawed, and he fell to his knees in stark horror. He began to scream inside his helmet. "No. *No*. NO-NO-NO-NO—!"

Greymalkin took in a ghastly amount of information in a single gut-wrenching flash. The Carinan had the mind of a terrified young child screaming in gruesome agony and fear. The mind that was laid bare before him felt like that of a young boy that had been ruthlessly trained to obey commands by the cruelest discipline imaginable. It was accustomed to being routinely beaten and starved, but the grotesque pain that Bruno had subjected it to had quite simply broken its mind to pieces. But even now as it lay dying, a single fear was swamping the young alien's mind: *that it would be punished for its failure*. Even in its death-throes, the creature was afraid of being punished by a towering figure of dark terror that loomed over all its thoughts. The image was unmistakable; Greymalkin recognized it all too well. The Tenax.

Greymalkin swayed on his knees, aghast at what he'd done. The troop of Carinans that he, Bruno, and Royce had killed were this creature's beloved junior siblings, brothers and sisters whose lives it had been entrusted with to protect. They had been far away from the Carinae on a pilgrimage that was central to their religion and the reproductive cycles of older members of their tribe. As they had returned to the Carinae they'd systematically been whipped into a frenzy of aggression before being released back into the nebula with merciless orders to kill any trespassers they discovered there. Greymalkin could perceive the visceral hostility that the Carinans had been bred to instinctively respond with, an innate murderous belligerence toward any being that was not one of them or their dark overseer.

And all of these lost and brutalized children had been conditioned to bring back somatic evidence of any invaders that they killed. Not specimens, nor trophies, but desperate *proof* that they had done as commanded and killed anyone they encountered. If they bought back such proof they would be fed and rewarded. If they *failed* to do so, they would be punished savagely.

The red orbs of the Carinan's eyes were glazing over. Greymalkin realized that the creature was dying in a perfect storm of agony from the wounds Bruno had inflicted. But the vitality of the alien was such that it would take hours for it to finally expire. He sought through its mind for any hint of medical technology or insights that might save its life. But the Carinan and its kind were apparently focused wholly on death and destruction, and had almost no concept of healing. Greymalkin realized that even though the creature was at least as intelligent as a human being, it had received no education whatever, aside from brutal military training and combat instruction.

Shockingly in fact, the Carinan had no knowledge at all of science or even the history of its own species. The closest equivalent memories

Greymalkin found in the alien's mind were an elaborate array of simplistic myths and superstitions that all revolved around obedience to authority and the mistrust of any being that did not resemble its species. As he quickly absorbed some of the Carinan's language, he realized that he was looking at a primitive mind much more akin to a pre-technological being. *It doesn't even have a word for 'species', but only 'our tribe' versus all the 'monsters' that it has a duty to despise and kill. The only reason that it has all this advanced weaponry and shadow space travel gear is because the Tenax wanted these creatures to serve as vicious guard dog slaves.*

As Greymalkin took in more of the strange language of electrical signals that the Carinan used to communicate, the signals that he had memorized from Bokin months ago snapped into clarity. *The 'words of peace'... those aren't profound statements, just pass-phrases that the Tenax gave to some of the other Abyssals.* As the Carinan language became clearer to the young monk, he also learned the thrashing creature's name. If it had been a sound instead of modulated electric waves the alien's name-designation would sound like a scratchy noise akin to *EeeNoo*. As Greymalkin sought for something, *anything* that he could do for the dying Carinan, it finally seemed to understand something of what he was communing. And it had a straightforward request for him.

«*Kill me.*» The alien's request was an earnest plea from a simple mind in utterly excruciating pain. Greymalkin sobbed with a wretched feeling of helplessness, realizing that there was absolutely nothing else that he could do now to help this piteous creature but grant its wish. He stopped communing with the Carinan, blinked away tears, and looked up at Bruno.

«*Kill it. Quickly.*» His thoughts were urgent, and Bruno responded. The Carinan's mental presence abruptly vanished, leaving only the endless silence of the void. As Greymalkin leaned forward, his hands buried in the grey sand, the only sound that disturbed the dead planetoid was his wracked sobbing inside his helmet.

* * *

The crushing shame and regret that descended on Greymalkin's mind felt like it would grind him into the dirt. Coherent thoughts had given way to the horrified realization of everything he'd done and the overwhelming fact that there was no way to undo any of it. He felt as if he wanted to run away somewhere, but there was no path to escape the dreadful sense of guilt. He held his hands across his chest and screamed hoarsely.

«If we are done here, we should be going.» Bruno's thoughts were hard, and felt as dead as the planet around them. Greymalkin whipped his head up to stare furiously at the protean, his sobs choking off.

«You... bastard. *You damned, murdering, fiend.*» Greymalkin's thoughts came exploding out of him in a burning stream. «You... you just tortured that creature *to death.*»

«*You* instructed me to do so. You insisted on it, in fact.» There was no trace in the protean's thoughts of its usual ironic bubbling humor. The simple truth of what the alien cyborg was stating again came crushing down on Greymalkin. He wanted to blame Bruno, to tell himself that this had happened only because of the protean's willingness to kill and destroy. *But Bruno resisted until he thought I was going to force Royce to do it. He only acted then.*

Greymalkin sobbed into the numbness of total defeat, falling forward into the harshly illuminated dirt lit by Royce's spotlight. The completeness of the disaster struck him then. What he'd done was the worst possible response to Tatter's gruesome death. *I did not try to calm down and think, I just flew off in a rage.* The monumental scale of his misdeeds and the impossibility of any recovery overwhelmed him.

«If you wish to continue your lamentations, I suggest you do it during the return trip.» Bruno's thoughts lacked pity or any other emotion. «There will undoubtedly be many more of these warriors approaching soon, and I am now too damaged to further defend you.»

After a moment, Greymalkin gave a slight, dark chortle. He got up. «Good. *Good*. Bruno you're right, you need to *go*. Go back to the base, or wherever you want to go now.»

«I agreed to protect you.» The protean's thoughts seemed taken aback.

«Don't worry, you'll still get your reward from Kuanian.» He smiled fiercely, and swallowed back all the fluid in his nose and throat. «Make a recording of me saying this! I say that you've finished your service to me, you're free to go!»

The protean had been reabsorbing all the blobs of itself that had held down the Carinan, and now once again took on the squat misshapen form that only marginally suggested a massive humanoid body. The enigmatic black alien cyborg floated above him silently, a black shape outlined by the glowing blue nimbus of energy. It communed nothing to him for long moments, but then descended to float in front of him. Greymalkin looked down at the grotesque protean, wondering what to expect from it. An explosive tirade? Terrible threats? He no longer cared. When Bruno finally responded, he was surprised at how quiet and subdued the protean's thoughts were.

«Human. I long ago ceased caring about any reward from Kuanian.» Bruno's mind seemed almost completely still for once. «No one could have promised me any reward great enough to risk my own continued existence for your sake. I chose to follow you freely.»

The slowly morphing form seemed to have shrunk visibly before him. Greymalkin stared down at the dark alien cyborg in confusion, and shook his head. «Bruno, I don't know why you would want to risk yourself to protect me. I don't understand you. I never have, and I never will.»

«I have begun to understand you, however.» Bruno's thoughts were restrained. Reflective, even. «I believe that I understand why you were selected for the course of action that you have been set upon. I wish to continue to assist and protect you.»

Greymalkin was baffled, but shook his aching head again. *Whatever this is about, I can't think anymore. And I don't deserve protection.* «Bruno, *just go*. I'm going to go and put Tatter's body to rest.»

«What then?» Bruno was studying him intently. Greymalkin could discern that much.

«Goodbye, Bruno. Go. Leave me alone.» Greymalkin looked sadly at the corpse of the Carinan, and then took a final look at the floating protean that had come so far with him. After that he turned and walked back to Royce. A few moments later the rover starship lifted off from the surface of the dead planet and disappeared into shadow space. The protean stayed floating there for a long time.

Greymalkin sped Royce on across the shadow plane back towards the slopes leading up into the Homunculus Nebula. The synesthetic freezing winds no longer bothered him. He already felt numb inside. The first ascent had given him enough insight into the twisted labyrinth of the nebula's interior that he found it much easier the second time. He waited for another troop of Carinans to find him and kill him, but the slopes were as empty as before. A vague fear for Royce tugged at the back of his mind, but he was not thinking clearly now about anything. He simply felt empty.

When he had once again reached the place where the gale of distortion blotted out everything, this time Greymalkin stopped and listened to the howl of shadow space for a time. He waited to see if the Tenax would reappear, but there was nothing but the cold synesthesia burning through him. He meditated on the slopes then, extending his shadow space perception even though the torrent of energy from the summit felt as if it was cutting him to pieces. But he was determined to see through the pain. A Sojourner admonition came to him then: *'The clearest lens reveals the truest path.' It isn't cold. It isn't hot. It isn't anything but an illusion of the universe that my mind can't understand. My own limitations are trying to confuse me yet again. But this time, I will wait until I see clearly through the illusion.*

Gradually, he became aware, through all the distortion, of a twisted path before him. There was an obscured switchback in the tortured shadow plane here, almost impossible to perceive, much less navigate. But now that he had made it out, he drove Royce forward and onto it. The cyneget chuffed and sent growling pings into the storm of signals, carefully holding onto the elusive surface and ascending. And then they reached the summit, and pierced into the central cavity of the Homunculus.

Greymalkin had finally found the Forge. He remembered that humanity had been aware even in the pre-interstellar age that there were two stars in the center of the blasting ionizing gale, but the reality of the central system nevertheless made him gasp. The gigantic primary star, the one that Lex had called the Anvil, was a luminous blue variable like nothing he had ever seen before. The Anvil was more than a hundred times the size of a typical G-type star, and the blast of energy coming from it was so thick that it felt as if it would overwhelm his shadow sense. The secondary star, what Lex had called the Hammer, was significantly smaller, but still dozens of times bigger than any normal G-type star. It was shining with a binding blue-white light that cut through the torrent of energy and hurt his head.

Greymalkin knew that the Hammer orbited the Anvil every five and a half years, and at closest approach the outer edges of the two stars actually collided. He could see that this was what was happening now. The two giant stars were intersecting, and at the point where they touched was a detonation of energy that beggared imagination. It was throwing off synesthetic effects that he could not process, energy in virtually every wavelength that generated a storm of conflicting sensations like the roar of some mythical waterfall out of heaven into hell. He winced and tried to scan the system, but at first the blast of signals overwhelmed his perceptions. Then something caught his attention.

There, highlighted against the flare of the two giant stars, was something suspiciously like an entrance. A conspicuously marked entrance. Greymalkin tried to peer through the glare, but could make out nothing more from this distance. He clenched his jaw. *Very well. Now we finally get down to it. C'mon Royce, let's go.* He urged the cyneget forward and they skimmed ahead.

As they glided across the sparkling shadow plane toward the inconceivable fury of the Forge stars, Greymalkin could now make out the other exit from the Eta Carina system, the distant one on the other side that led into the opposite lobe of the hourglass shaped Homunculus Nebula. It crossed his mind that somewhere out there on that side Constance and her crew were now transiting the outskirts of the nebula, and quite possibly encountering more Carinans. His stomach sank even lower at the thought. *None of us are going to survive this. But I'm going to find out what's in the middle of all this before my time comes.*

Greymalkin cautiously steered Royce around to the strange object that did indeed mark a shadow space entrance. As they came up to it, he could see how big the portal was. It was obviously designed for something far, far larger than the cyneget rover. He wondered if it was a trap, given how prominently it was marked, but found that he no longer cared. The young monk only wanted some kind of release from the pain he felt. Greymalkin eased Royce into the entrance.

The portal led to a huge shadow plane path that was inclined up above the star system in an orthogonal shadow space dimension.

Another starbridge. I wonder where this one leads. He urged Royce forward and they quickly passed up across several shadow space spans until the path opened into an aerie manifold perched directly above the giant Anvil star. They were displaced sufficiently in shadow dimensions that the blast of the star was not blinding his perceptions, but he could nevertheless feel it as a distant roar. As they came into the manifold continuity, he saw a huge facility of some kind ahead. As they drew closer, he realized just how big it really was, and how ornate the construction appeared. And he realized that it was shaped in the form of yet another pitch black rhombic dodecahedron, although vastly larger than any of Lex's lockers. He momentarily wondered if Royce's lockers had originally been modeled as tiny versions of this inconceivable object.

The elaborate structure was hundreds of kilometers across, massive enough to have a slightly perceptible gravitational field of its own. And yet, the construction materials layered on top of the underlying black shadow space structure were absurdly rare and expensive. There were immense domes of aureate kilometers across that shone with a brilliant golden light in the reflections of Royce's spotlight, multi-story tiered towers that jutted up like cliffs of semi-precious metals harvested from shadow space, and valley-like depressions that led to passages inside. Greymalkin circled the vast structure and then descended into what appeared to be the main egress. He kept waiting for some kind of challenge or hail, but there was nothing on any communication channel that he could detect.

When Royce had reached the bottom of the entranceway, they found a colossal chamber lined with myriad objects that he assumed were alien vehicles. Nothing showed any sign of active energies or life. *This must be the main dock? Why are there no pressure doors? Or barriers of any kind?* Then he thought of the Tenax, and could easily imagine that the impatient Abyssal would want nothing to delay or impede its movement as it entered or exited. Royce floated forward into what seemed to be a wide promenade. The huge corridor was wide enough to fly a channel galleon down the center of the hall with plenty of room to spare. The tiny cyneget drifted forward, as he looked down dimly glimpsed side passages lined with what appeared to be gorgeous sculptures of semi-precious metals. Everywhere he looked he saw elegant and refined designs. *It looks like a palace... or a temple. Where is everybody? I can't believe they leave this place unattended.*

Eventually they reached the terminus of the big arterial promenade, and it opened out into what he realized was the interior of one of the huge golden domes they had seen from the outside. The interior was an incredibly ornate series of stepped galleries punctuated by towers that glowed with an eerie blue light that reminded him of the channels and flows of shadow space. He brought Royce down for a landing in one of many plazas under the vast dome.

There was something very strange about the towers. He focused his shadow sense on them to try and discern why they glowed with the bizarre energies that surged up through them. Startled, he realized what they were, and gaped around at them. *Those towers are runcibles. Gigantic runcibles that can tap directly into the interior of the Anvil star that's all around us down in normal space. But why build something like this? Power, I suppose?* He found the scale and ornateness of the place intimidating, but he realized it was the perfect location for what he needed to do. Sadly, he got up from the cockpit and looked reluctantly toward the airlock where the storage units held the two remaining parts of Tatter's body. It was time.

As he slowly stepped toward the airlock, his eyes fell on his missing pack. An idea came to him then. *Why not? This will likely be my last act as a Sojourner.* He went to the pack and took out the shining golden garment and the strange tool that Calypso had called a *vajra*. He donned the garment and selected one of its intermediate forms that *combined* the ornate robes and the functions of the void suit. He wanted both for the ceremony to be conducted in the vacuum of the ornate dome. After clipping the vajra to his belt and saying a small prayer in his mind, he went to prepare Tatter's body. He had to remind himself of the *Journey's End* rites for preparing a body for cremation, and was sobbing once again by the time that he had united her head together once again with her body within an elastic white casket body-sleeve. As he sealed the sleeve he momentarily laid his shaking palm on her frozen belly, but the merest hint of coming to terms with the fact that she could have been carrying their child threatened to shatter his mind. He desperately tried to empty his thoughts and simply focus on breathing so that he could complete the preparatory rite. *I've got to get through this. For her.*

He configured the vajra tool as a delicately small cannula runcible for the next step of the ceremony. Greymalkin tried to steady his trembling hand as he moved to gently extract the shadow jewel underneath Tatter's forehead without disturbing the thick wrapping of the casket sleeve. Because he could no longer form spoken words as he wept, he forced himself to begin *communing* the formal rite to himself and Royce. The cyneget made a keening signal all around him, and Greymalkin thought the creature understood the significance of the moment exactly. And because Royce was there, it did not seem strange to commune the words of the rite as *we*.

«From the wellspring of her mind, we now retrieve the final illuminating light of her journey, and we will safeguard this legacy as a testament to her life.» Greymalkin could barely commune the words coherently to himself. It felt like his heart was breaking as he carefully extended the delicate runcible into shadow space and plucked the jewel out of her. He squeezed his eyes shut against his tears, and tried to intone the words of the rite in his mind with the solemnity that the moment deserved. But he found that he couldn't stop sobbing.

«Her physical form, her vessel in her sojourn, now rests. With respect and care, we now prepare this shell for its return to the elements.» He put away the jewel, lifted the white casket body-sleeve in his arms, and held her stiffly frozen body against his heaving chest one last time as he stood.

Then he cycled the airlock and began walking across the plaza to the base of one of the huge towers. Royce surprised him by silently rising and floating after him as he carried Tatter through the beautiful plaza. *Why not? There's no one else to attend the Journey's End ceremony except Royce. And Royce was definitely her friend as well.* As he reached the base of the tower, he saw that it had an obvious injection chamber and control. Greymalkin knelt and placed her in the chamber, but did not seal it yet. He stood and tried his best to finish the rite, communing alone to himself and Royce, even though his chest was still wracked with sobs.

«We gather to mark the end of a journey, to honor the life and contributions of our companion, Tatterdemalion.» He paused, knowing that at this point the people in the ceremonial party were supposed to share memories of the deceased person, but he had to finish before he broke down completely. He rushed through communing the next lines of the rite. «The insights she gained, the compassion she showed, and the wisdom she shared remain with us, a lasting tribute to her life's journey. As energy transforms matter, we acknowledge the return of Tatterdemalion's essence to the vastness from which we all arise.»

The time had come, but he found it incredibly hard to perform the last act. Finally he knelt and touched his forehead within his helmet one last time to her forehead, hidden and hard-frozen inside the casket sleeve, whispering, "Goodbye, Tat. I love you." He stood, and closed the heavy lid of the chamber. There was a thrumming vibration and Greymalkin briefly felt the incredible energy of the two great stars flow through the chamber. In the blink of an eye, she was gone, joining the inconceivable energies of the Hammer and the Anvil, the blazing heart of Eta Carina. He staggered to his feet and communed the concluding statements of the rite.

«Though her physical presence is now gone, her contributions endure. We commit to preserving our memories of Tatterdemalion, ensuring that her insights and deeds may continue to guide us, and those who come after.» Then he sank to his hands and knees, his chest spasming uncontrollably inside the golden robes and void suit. He had no idea what he would do next.

Then Royce gave a terrified yipping signal behind him... and was abruptly silent. Greymalkin lifted his head and turned around. He froze, stunned to see that the enormity of the great dome was filled with a vast swirling mass of coiling cables. He could just see the last sign of Royce disappearing as the starship was pulled into the twisting array.

«That must have been terribly hard on you, my dear boy.» Rodo's thoughts were quiet, almost gentle. «But now that you've bid your friend farewell, let me welcome you to the Forge properly. I'll take you to my old quarters; you can look around and get comfortable. They'll be *your* quarters now.»

Resurrections

The cables dropped him to the deck, and a heavy door slammed shut behind him. Even as the Abyssal quickly surged away from him and out through the halls of the vast Forge structure, the thoughts that flooded into Greymalkin's mind were simultaneously those of both the Tenax *and* the man Rodo.

«Do make yourself comfortable, my lad.» Rodo's thoughts began as an unctuous welcome, but transitioned to a threatening lecture ending on a chilling note. «My apologies for locking you in my former quarters in such a high-handed and preemptory fashion, but you've come calling in my domicile at a most inopportune time. As I told you before, I must finish attending to the return of the Carinans for the moment. But please make yourself at home until I return. At that time I will provide you with everything any rational being could desire. *And you will most certainly provide me with the assistance that I require.*»

An even more massive metal hatch slid shut with a heavy thud behind him, sealing him in the dim corridor with finality. Much of the structure around him was shielded, but he could nevertheless sense the ominous bulk of the Tenax departing the Forge. As the Abyssal vanished into the distance, Greymalkin lay on the black metal floor in misery. He felt defeated at such a profound level that he simply lay with his cheek pressed against the cold interior of his helmet for several minutes in despair. At last he pushed himself up off the cold surface and looked around. He lay in a long dark metal corridor with lights in the distance, where he could see into a big room. Greymalkin slowly rearranged the cumbersome golden robes onto his shoulders and got to his feet. He still felt abjectly numb and empty inside, but the prescriptive mental training that he had grown up with in the Order began to take hold again, and a fundamental Sojourner mantra came to him unbidden.

I still live, and where there is life, there is hope. Hope begins with my next breath, so I will take it carefully, savor it gratefully, and use it to my best ability. He closed his eyes and took a series of slow and deep breaths to center himself. Then he walked forward warily.

After it had seized him, the Tenax had carried him away to another part of the vast aerie structure. Somewhere along the way he had passed through a pressure curtain, and he could now feel an atmosphere around him. After reflexively checking to see that the atmosphere was breathable, he activated the garment control and changed the setting from the bulky combination of void suit and robes into a much simpler jumpsuit. The bizarre golden garment that had been crafted by the *Vlieger* crew morphed then, sliding around his body into the new form. He saw that it was still overly ornate in some of its patterns and design, but in this less ungainly form at least it did not hamper his movement. He inhaled cautiously as he walked down the long corridor, and found that the air here tasted ancient and stale. Most of the walls were shielded against his shadow space perception, and he could not sense what was behind them.

At the end of the corridor he was surprised to find what looked recognizably like a typical Sojourner bulkhead transition. The pressure door was open, and he stepped over it into what appeared to be a vestibule leading to the richly appointed chambers of an abbot or abbess. He guardedly looked around the wide entry room. There were small decorations and personal mementos everywhere, on the walls, in display cabinets, on shelves. If the air had not felt so old the space would have seemed... cozy. There were hallways leading off from the antechamber into other large rooms.

Rodo called these his 'old' quarters. Greymalkin wondered what that meant. Now feeling as if he were an unannounced guest or intruder, he took small steps through the rooms, looking through the many displays and carefully curated items. He walked through a large personal library of mnemotomes that was carefully organized, and had an inviting study table and chair that looked well-used and comfortable. Beyond that were stairs that led up into a moderately large dome space with instruments scattered about. When he saw that the instruments in the center were an array of sophisticated shadow space amplifiers, Greymalkin realized that the dome was some sort of personal lookout or observatory. There were couches under the various amplifiers, and one couch at the exact center with nothing above it but the transparent dome and the shifting blue synesthesia of shadow space. Greymalkin laid down on the couch. It felt very old and worn.

He looked up and realized that the dome itself was an amplifier of a kind. From this spot Greymalkin could see past the roar of the Eta Carina stars and take in one entire lobe of the Homunculus Nebula, the seemingly infinite spiraling paths and crumpled shadow plane surfaces laid out before him like an unbelievable mandala. He seemed to hear the synesthetic winds blowing distantly. The dome was somehow shielding him from the harshest sensations of the Hammer and Anvil stars. Now feeling drained and exhausted, Greymalkin lay there looking at the incomprehensibly vast labyrinth of the Homunculus Nebula and beyond that the Carinae as a whole. He felt spent, like a torn rag that had been wrung to pieces. He listened to the lonely illusion of the wind, and at some point fell into a deep sleep.

He found himself in a sad and desolate dream. He was chained against a stone pillar near a rocky cave entrance. Looking around him, he saw that the cave and pillar were on the summit of a bleak mountain scarp floating in a cold black sky. Gazing down across the crags and cliffs of the scarp, he saw the lights of a city far in the distance below. Just then an ominous female figure in robes emerged from the cave and came walking up to him. He felt afraid of her, but then detected a scent of flowers from her. Greymalkin writhed, struggling to free himself from the chains, and suddenly woke up in the observatory as he rolled off the couch onto the deck. Disoriented for a moment, he wondered where he was. Then every moment of despair from the previous day came pouring back into his awareness. For a full minute he could not breathe for the sorrow that crushed his chest. A wave of despair threatened to engulf him.

He sat up, straightened his spine against the couch, and grit his teeth. *Hope begins with my next breath.* He focused his mind on a calming meditation chant. After killing the Carinan EeeNoo, he had decided that he would never again lose himself in unthinking emotions, no matter what happened to him. When he felt calm inside, he stood up.

Greymalkin left the dome, remembering that he had not finished exploring the rooms below. He wondered if he should think of the place as his new quarters or his new prison. *I suppose they're both.* He walked through a sequence of many interconnected chambers, beginning to realize that the place was quite large. There was a refectory with food dispensers, an elaborate exercise facility, and chambers that were evidently lounges or waiting rooms that connected back into the big vestibule. There was no dust, but everything had an air of having been long abandoned.

He found himself wondering about Rodo. Had the man lived here willingly? It somehow felt more like a prison, albeit a comfortable one. Greymalkin had seen no obvious exits other than the main corridor he'd entered through. He eventually found what appeared to be an ornate sleeping chamber with a bed that was a thousand times grander than any sleep sack he'd ever been assigned. When he had circled back to the entrance to the complex of rooms, he came to a final hallway leading off from the immense vestibule.

This hallway seemed different. It was larger, and led away from all of the other rooms in a different direction. There were several sealed doors that he couldn't open, but then he came upon an incredibly ornate entrance arch. The black marble arch was decorated with amazingly elaborate filigrees of delicate shadow aureate with pale white adamans shining in a spray around the portal.

Greymalkin hesitantly approached the big arched entrance, wondering what the ostentatious ornamentation signified. The arch led to the interior of the large room all in somber black marble and lined with the aureate filigree. In the center of the room was a massive slab of the same black marble, and on top of it was a transparent block of eoncrystal. As he stepped up to it slowly, he saw that something was suspended in the eoncrystal.

Poised centrally in the eoncrystal was the preserved body of a frail old man lying there in opulent robes, arms folded peacefully across his chest. Greymalkin stared incredulously at the features of the man, which could be seen clearly despite the refraction of light through the thick crystal. It was Rodo. The features were enormously aged, but it was definitely the same face, albeit composed tranquilly in death. As he looked down at the black marble bier-platform, he now saw an elegant inscription of inlaid shadow aureate: *Rodolfo Cicero Flavopallio*. Below the name were dates and what was apparently an epitaph, *Attached Without Attachment, Accompanying Without Selfishness, Truest Friend.*

Bewildered, Greymalkin left the chamber and continued down the big hall. The passageway ended in a much larger, but completely unadorned archway. When he passed through it into a huge chamber, he saw there was another bier and tomb here, together with some kind of enormous device built into the wall. The complete silence and sepulchral nature of these rooms was making Greymalkin nervous as he walked up to inspect the tomb. Unlike the eoncrystal display of Rodo, this tomb seemed to be a simple stone casket, albeit one so ancient that it showed signs of erosion. There was again an inscription, but while the faded characters seemed familiar to him, he could not make it out at first. But, unlike the walls, the casket was not shielded against his shadow space senses. He could perceive that deep inside the thick stone container were ancient remnants of biological matter, a pile of what appeared to be human bones.

Greymalkin felt unnerved looking at the truly ancient sarcophagus. *Who is this, then?* This wing of his prison quarters was apparently the funerary section, reserved for mausoleums. He looked at the huge cylindrical chamber built into the wall beyond the tomb, and had no idea what it could be. He walked around the tomb and stepped into what appeared to be a giant cylindrical tube of some unfamiliar flat black metal set into the wall. The tube was almost four meters wide, and was open. As he looked into the interior, he could see that the far end of the tube appeared to be transparent. There was something on the other side of the window or screen.

The young monk looked at the cylindrical tunnel uneasily. He could not perceive what was behind the black metal. He wondered if it would be dangerous to go and inspect the window or whatever it was at the far end of the tube. But then the emotional emptiness and ennui inside his chest surged up, and he realized that he didn't care. As he thought it over further, he realized that he *wanted* it to be dangerous. Greymalkin stepped into the huge tunnel and walked to the far window, which he quickly realized was some sort of huge screen that was displaying an image.

He could see the image of another stone slab in the dark room that appeared to be on the other side of the screen. Lying there on a pad was the body of an old woman in a flight suit that was immediately recognizable to him from historical recordings. It was the uniform of the Thannic Colonizers, straight out of ancient history. As he looked at the image of the old woman's face, yet another sensation of intense familiarity crawled up his spine. He was trying to figure out what it was about the woman's face that looked so recognizable, when her eyes abruptly opened. Greymalkin yelped in fright and stumbled fearfully backwards through the tunnel to cower against the tomb, even as she looked to her side at him and then sat up on the slab. The woman got off the slab warily, and walked up to him, the huge screen at the end of the tunnel appearing to be a transparent window between them.

For a moment he only stared at her, the mounting sense of familiarity screaming in the back of his mind as he looked into her old brown eyes framed by epicanthic folds. She said something in the ancient Beltlang tongue of the Thannics, and again the voice was instantly familiar although he found it maddening that her identity eluded him. *Where have I seen this woman before?* The thought was tantalizing and urgent. Her sad eyes terrified him for some reason he could not understand, and then recognition dawned on him like a blast of lightning, just as his mind belatedly translated the words she'd spoken. *Beltlang*, he thought, rummaging through his mnemonic matrices. *The early interstellar era English dialect of Sol system's asteroid belt, where the Thannics launched from....*

The apparition had said in the language of the long-ago past, "Hello? Can you understand me?" It was the same voice that he'd first heard in ancient recordings during his catechism training as a six year old oblate. But seeing and hearing her address *him* personally was so shocking that for long moments he could only gape at her, wondering if he was still asleep and dreaming. The being on the other side of the window appeared to be Mei Sung, daughter of Thann himself, the greatest terraformer in history.

"Yes, I understand you," Greymalkin said, summoning up the same ancient tongue, but his own voice surprised him, a hoarse croak that sounded almost like a death rattle. He glanced down at the massive tomb that he was leaning on, the tomb that held crumbled remnants of bones, and suddenly wondered who it was exactly. "Is... is that *you*, in this tomb? Or, are you still...." He paused then in confusion, wondering how to even address her, or what honorific title he should use. She was the closest thing there was to a patron saint of the Sojourner Order, but he could not remember any hypothetical protocol for addressing Mei Sung to her face. No one had ever imagined this moment.

The old woman looked through the window and tunnel at him, and then shook her head sadly. She said quietly in the archaic phrases, "No, not me. My husband. He was killed long ago." Greymalkin could hear an entire saga of sorrow packed into those words, but it in turn set off an avalanche of doubt and questions that began to pile up in his mind. *Husband? There's no record of Mei ever marrying.* He wondered if she was some kind of recording, but as he studied her features he realized that, although her identity was now obvious to him, her face was creased by many additional lines of age that had never been seen in any historical recordings, and the greying black hair of her youth was now pure white. *If this is some kind of simulation, was it created after she vanished from history with her fleet?*

Mei was watching him suspiciously, and asked, "And who, may I ask, are you, young man?" The expression was the same familiar squint of careful inquiry that he remembered from so many ancient mnemotome accounts of her that he had watched, images that had been recorded millennia ago as she sought ways of terraforming entire worlds. But that same analytical expression was now directed at *him*, as if she were trying to make an evaluation. Greymalkin self-consciously stood up straight, walked cautiously back through the tunnel to stand before her, and then bowed formally.

"Your Holiness, I am Brother Greymalkin Thomas of the Sojourner Order," he quavered, and then continued apologetically, "Ah, please excuse me, your Holiness, you see our Order arose centuries after the First Exodus which you led, that is, *your* Exodus was the first of three great efforts of humankind.... Forgive me, so much has happened since your time, I don't know how to begin to explain...."

After a long moment, Mei's old features crinkled with mirth, and she laughed. "Young man, please do not ever again address me as *Your Holiness*, it will either make me fall over laughing or toss my cookies if I think about it too hard. I'm a scientist, nothing more. But I know about Sojourners; Rodolfo will never shut up about them, in fact. Where is the old rascal anyway? He wasn't looking well when I spoke to him last. He said he'd come and talk to me again after I finished my nap this afternoon. But... wait... I see that this manifold's time dilation effect was activated. It's been... *oh dear*... it's been a *very* long time since I was last awake...." Her expression became somber as she studied a device strapped along the length of her forearm. She met Greymalkin's flinching eyes, and said with a sigh, "Rodolfo is surely dead now."

Greymalkin nodded, saying, "Yes, Your Holi—I mean, yes, ma'am. I believe that his body is interred in the next chamber down the hall. Uh, please excuse me for asking this but, are *you* alive? Or am I speaking to a simulacrum?"

Mei appeared surprised, and then said, "I assumed you knew how the Forge works." When Greymalkin quickly shook his head, together with another apologetic expression, she sighed once more. "Good gracious, this may take a bit to explain, but I assure you, young man, I'm very much alive."

A mental flag of skeptical incredulity rose in his mind, and now it was Greymalkin's turn to squint suspiciously. "Please forgive me again, ma'am, but that seems... *rather hard to believe*. You've been gone for *thousands of years*. I know about the time dilation experienced in the relativistic ships of the First Exodus, but... *you are not on one*, at least at the moment."

Mei tilted her head to the side slightly, and slowly formed a faint smile. "Good. You and I share a sense of caution and distrust in this place. Perhaps it is for the same reason. Young Brother Thomas, tell me, have you encountered an entity that is called the Tenax?"

"Yes," Greymalkin said, frowning. "It placed me in these chambers."

Mei nodded. "I see. Can you tell me, what is your relationship to the Tenax?"

Greymalkin became suspicious at the question and simply said, "You first, ma'am."

Mei sighed, and seemed to come to a decision. "The Tenax trapped me here long ago. The creature wishes me to divulge certain information, but I refuse to do so."

Greymalkin digested that statement, and then guardedly said, "Well, then we have something else in common. The Tenax imprisoned me here as well. It wants me to cooperate with it, but I've also refused."

"Where is the Tenax now?" Mei asked intently. One of Greymalkin's eyebrows lifted. *Could she really be a prisoner here as well?*

"It's off managing a flood of monsters we call the Carinans, creatures that are returning into this region," Greymalkin said. That elicited another surprised response from Mei.

"Then, we may have a small window of opportunity," she said, looking up at the frame of the circular portal that separated them, appearing irritated. "But I still can't open this gate."

Greymalkin scanned the frame, but could not sense what was behind it or the screen image he faced. He stepped closer to the screen and gingerly reached out to touch it. It felt like cold glass. The young monk folded his arms, and scowled down at the old thin woman. "If time is limited, then we need to decide if we're going to trust one another, ma'am. Quickly."

"Agreed," she said. The heavy old eyelids lowered further. "But I doubt there is anything you can do to help free me anyway."

Greymalkin took a deep breath, and rubbed his eyes. "Ma'am, if you are who you claim to be, you're one of the most famous persons in the history of humankind, and I'd willingly sacrifice my life for you. But if this is just some stupid trick of Rodo's to get me to cooperate, then I'd be a fool to accept your story."

"You told me he was *dead*. And interred nearby," Mei said even more suspiciously.

"There is a very old man's dead body on display in the next room that looks like him," Greymalkin said. "The display has a fancy inscription with his name and everything. But I've repeatedly encountered a living man that looks like a younger version of him. *That* guy tried to kill me. And whenever the Tenax communes with me, it has his same thoughts."

"The Rodolfo I knew was a captive of the Tenax as well," Mei said slowly. "But over the years that I observed them periodically, the Tenax seemed to become quite... *fond* of Rodolfo. The Tenax had taken to imitating him at times, in fact. My apologies for being so suspicious of you, but the Tenax has tried to trick me many times as well."

"Yeah, that sounds like the Tenax I know," Greymalkin said, and grit his teeth. "Evidently, we both have reason to be suspicious of each other. Okay, let's trade information."

"What information?" Mei asked in an acid tone.

"Easy!" Greymalkin said with an impishly mirthless grin. "Information that the other one would already know if they're working for the Rodo-Tenax thing, but that neither of us would know if we aren't!" He'd always found logic-trust dilemmas to be amusing, and this quizzical conversation might distract him from the despair that he could still feel trying to crush him.

Mei couldn't help smiling, and put her hand to her mouth to cover her amusement. "A lot of double negatives, but still well put, spacer. I'd have been glad to have had you in my crew, you think on your feet quickly."

Greymalkin felt inordinately proud of what she'd said, but shook it off with another tense grin. "Then I'll go first! Because I've been trying to figure this out ever since I came to the Carinae, and it's driving me *crazy*. Tell me, if you please, *what happened* all those years ago when you and your fleet of Thannic Colonizers arrived in the Carinae!"

"Right," Mei said, an unhappy expression coming over her face. "Rodolpho told me that it was a big mystery what happened to us. We sent a ship back to tell everybody, but apparently they didn't make it. But, it's a very long story, and we don't have a lot of time...."

"I know a fair amount from the archaeological evidence I've found," Greymalkin said. "You spread out through the region, and were building bases all over. But how did you get here in the first place? You didn't have FTL starships."

"No, we didn't, not until the Central Ones gave that technology to us," Mei said. Greymalkin's eyes widened. The phrase '*the Central Ones*' rang throughout his head.

"I've only heard that phrase one other time," he murmured. A tingle went down his spine as he thought back to the eerie discussion with Bruno months ago, just before he'd fallen asleep that night before their first calamitous encounter with an Abyssal. *"Who are the Central Ones?"*

"Incredibly powerful aliens that inhabit the center of the galaxy." Mei was thoughtful, briefly drifting away in her own memories. "My fleet was travelling in that direction. Coreward. It had been so long since we'd communicated with the other fleets; we were separated by huge distances. Then one day we met these gigantic aliens, bigger than asteroids. They just appeared out of nowhere, right in front of us. We were terrified, but they said they wanted to help us pursue my father's mission to spread humanity throughout the galaxy. They gave us these radically advanced hyperspace drives, like nothing we'd ever imagined."

She paused, and the sadness that had now come over the old woman's face pierced Greymalkin. He said softly, "We call it 'shadow space' now. But what went wrong?"

"I was so excited," Mei said sadly. "I thought all our problems were over. We could go anywhere! But before we tried to go back and find the other Thannic fleets, I wanted to try the new FTL drives out to understand them better. We decided to undertake a grand trip coreward, to a place that we'd never imagined being able to reach. Eta Carina, the most incredible region in the galaxy. One last glorious achievement as a capstone to everything I'd done." She shook her head, and he saw a tear at the corner of her eye. "You see, we'd become so experienced by then, we'd been exploring for decades. And I was overconfident. I thought we could go anywhere, colonize any place we wanted, finally. What an arrogant, foolhardy mistake on my part."

"The Abyssals," Greymalkin muttered. The story began to play out in his mind of what would have happened. "They were here, but you didn't know about them, and how powerful they are. And how protective they are of their holdings here."

"No, we didn't," Mei said ruefully. "I should have first asked the Central Ones for guidance on what to avoid. But we were so eager and ready to go off on a hare-brained new adventure. I can't believe how egotistical I was, and how much everybody paid for my failure."

"What happened then?" Greymalkin asked, feeling ill even before she said anything. He'd been travelling through the Carinae long enough to guess what came next.

"Everything was fine at first," she said. "We set up bases; we were like kids in a candy store. Then we started encountering the... what did you call them? Abyssals? The various giant powerful aliens that inhabit this region. Most of them are of different species than the Central Ones, lesser maybe. Some of them were even *creations* of the Central Ones. But all of them were far more advanced than us. I still thought we'd be okay. They weren't exactly welcoming, but I had no idea how dangerous they could be, and how angry some of them were at our presence. I only pieced it together afterwards. There had already been this other wave of alien explorers like us that had come through here before. They're odd creatures, sort of like furry owls with six limbs—"

"The Crotani," Greymalkin volunteered.

"Is that what they're called?" Mei asked. "Well, the gigantic aliens, the Abyssals, they evidently thought they were pests, an invasive species that they didn't know what to do about. In some cases they seemed to have trained them, but what I didn't know is that most of the time they just exterminated them like vermin. When we showed up, I guess they decided to do some proactive pest control to keep us from becoming a problem later. I think the final straw that provoked them was when we found this structure, the Forge, and started experimenting with it."

"Oh, yeah, that tracks," Greymalkin said. He thought about how possessive the Tenax seemed to be of the Forge. He could imagine its anger if the structure had become infested with what he saw as vermin. "But, you actually experimented with the Forge? How did you figure out how it worked?"

"There was one of the Central Ones near here, over in the middle of the Keyhole Nebula," Mei said. "I stumbled on it when we were exploring the region, and it was willing to communicate with us."

"The Clavisian," Greymalkin said. "I also encountered it. It saved my life."

"It's one of the few advanced beings here that is helpful," Mei agreed. "Enigmatic and mostly incomprehensible, but helpful. It showed us how the Forge worked, and implied that the artifact is supposed to be a shared resource. But if you've interacted with these beings you know they aren't always very clear. I guess we overstepped or something. That's when the Tenax and the others tried to wipe us out. They sent brutal aliens like big black spider-monsters to kill us."

"The Carinans," Greymalkin said softly, thinking about EeeNoo.

"We had no effective defenses against them," Mei said. Her face was stony, and Greymalkin didn't want to imagine what she was remembering. "Our ships weren't fast enough to escape them, either."

An icy fist started to close around Greymalkin's heart. "From the evidence I found, you all disappeared overnight, but... please tell me everyone wasn't killed! What did you do?"

"No, I managed to save most of my fleet crew," Mei said. He could hear a small pearl of remorseful satisfaction in her voice. "Not everyone, but most. We couldn't fight, and we couldn't run. So we did the only other thing that we *could* do. We *hid*."

"Hid? Where could you hide?" Even as he spoke, he realized that whatever the answer to that question was, it was the answer that he had been seeking for so long as he'd journeyed through the Carinae for months. Greymalkin felt electrified, waiting for Mei to speak. She paused, studying him.

"Before I tell you that, I have to trust you," she said guardedly. "You know a lot about me, evidently. But I know nothing about you. For me to trust you, you have to share some information with me now."

Greymalkin nodded. "Of course; that's fair. Ask me anything."

"Why did you come here?" Mei asked intently. Her voice had deepened slightly as she had aged, he noted. "What were you seeking?"

Greymalkin thought back to the beginning of his journey here, back before everything had gone so wrong. *She's right, it's only reasonable that I explain to her who I am and why I'm here.* Reluctantly, he recounted the most salient details of who he was, why he'd accepted Kuanian's offer, and abbreviated versions of the seemingly endless series of disasters and mistakes that had plagued him since arriving in the Carinae. Mei listened carefully, and asked questions at unexpected moments in his tale. She was surprisingly interested in the details of his encounter with Bokin and the Bereft Scorpian altered humans that he'd encountered. She questioned him pointedly about why he had stayed in the Carinae despite the harrowing accidents he'd suffered, and why he had not simply returned to the Orion Arm at the earliest opportunity.

"At first, it was shame, I think," he admitted. "I lived, when Bora and Soren died. I had to do something to earn that. Then... well, I wanted to find out what happened to you and the other Colonizers. I would have done anything to discover it."

"Why? Why risk your life for that?" Mei asked, scrutinizing him closely.

"You said that Rodo, the real Rodo, told you about Sojourners," Greymalkin began. He wondered how to make what he wanted to say clear to her, even as he searched her piercing old eyes. Her irises were so dark they seemed almost as black as space itself. "If he really was a member of my Order, then he must have mentioned the vows that we all take. The most basic of our vows is to *sustain knowledge with diligence.* That includes uncovering the truth, preserving it, and honoring the discoveries of the past. You and all of the Thannics were more than heroes to us. You were the precursors of our faith and our Order. Despite everything that's happened to me, and even if I die in the attempt, I will do all that I can to bring your story and your findings back to humankind. You have my solemn word."

After a long moment, Mei took a deep breath and nodded. "It has indeed been my profound honor to lead thousands of people across the galaxy in the great colonizing endeavor of my father. If that experience taught me anything, it's how to recognize commitment when I hear it. You're speaking truthfully to me."

It hit Greymalkin then. There was something indefinably authentic about the way she spoke, the way she astutely analyzed every fact he gave her. It was the same quintessential manner that he remembered from all the classical recordings of her that he'd memorized since childhood. And even though her features were older, her eyes were as wise and sharp as ever. In that moment of intuitive apperception he became convinced that, despite how unbelievable it might be, somehow *he was actually talking to the real Mei Sung*, straight out of the legendary past of humankind. The sheer sense of awe that came splashing down through his mind in that moment of certainty was humbling. *Her intellect, her basic human integrity, I can sense it. She's everything that the narrative of history said about her.* He felt simultaneously chastened for doubting her, and exalted to be speaking to her.

She can see straight through to the heart of who I am with that shrewd mind. And yet, she doesn't even have a shadow jewel in her cranium! The practice hadn't existed in her time. He thought about how ironic and odd that was. Would she be considered a primitive if she somehow succeeded in returning to the Orion Arm now? Somehow, he doubted that. After meeting her, he now understood instinctively why so many humans had been willing to join the great interstellar Exodus she and her father had led millennia ago. And it was dawning on him that perhaps, despite everything that had crushed his heart in the last few days, he had a reason to keep going. He closed his eyes, and the Final Commitment came to him. *Sojourn through life with courage.*

***

"Thank you," Greymalkin breathed after a few moments. "That means a great deal to me. But... what do we do now? I don't know how to help you."

"I need to reach my people," Mei said in frustration. "But I'm trapped inside this manifold. The Tenax locked it on your side."

Greymalkin tried to think of something helpful, but realized he was still lacking two huge pieces of the puzzle. Being circumspect with his words, he said, "I believe you are who you say you are. But you still haven't told me where the Thannics under your command hid, or how you're still alive after all these millennia. I understand if you don't want to tell me, but it makes it harder to assist you."

Mei sighed, and nodded slightly. "To explain these matters, you must first understand what the Forge is, and how it works. You have a far better understanding of hyperspatial mechanics than we did all those years ago, but you evidently still don't understand the nature of the Forge, or what one can accomplish with it."

"I was told that it generates power for some sort of Nexus device that can generate an infinite amount of information," Greymalkin said. That concept, and the memory of the endless stacks of mnemotomes jammed into every corner of the Vlieger, could still make an uncanny shiver go down his back.

"That is only one aspect of what it is designed to do," Mei said, her gaze drifted far away once more before coming back to settle on him. "It's a necessary boot-strapping phase of the full functionality of the Forge. Let me see if I can explain. First, I'm assuming that your understanding of hyperspace is more robust than mine. But am I correct about that?"

Greymalkin shrugged. "Maybe, maybe not. I'm a pilot, and every pilot has to understand the phenomenon that we call 'shadow space' to navigate through it. But much of my knowledge is practical and intuitive, not analytical."

"Then this may or may not make any sense to you," Mei said. "Bear with me. You're obviously familiar with the process that you use for FTL travel. You shunt matter from a particular location in the manifold of our universe into a disjoint manifold, reposition the connecting locus of the disjoint manifold, and then discontinue the shunt manifold so that the matter rejoins the manifold of our universe in a different location."

"We call it shadow space travel," Greymalkin said, wondering where she was going with her explanation.

"Good," Mei said. "But the disjoint manifold, what I remember Rodolfo called the continuity manifold, is fundamentally a quantum field effect, part of the subtle additional parameters to general relativity that Appleton discovered. Even back in our time we knew that much, although we didn't know how to use it for FTL travel as you do now. But there are lots of solutions to shunted manifold equations, apparently. The Central Ones apparently used these solutions in the design of this huge device called the Forge."

"I thought you said you didn't understand shadow space travel?" Greymalkin said in consternation. Mei glared at him with *that* look from the old recordings that he had seen her direct toward junior Thannics when they said something foolish. Greymalkin felt sheepish then.

"I was a terraformer," Mei said. "Physics is at the heart of planet-sculpting. And, *please*! Appleton's theory of hyperdynamics was already three centuries old when we launched our fleets. As I said, we just hadn't discovered the FTL travel methods yet. The designers of the Forge started with those principles, but they were millions of years more advanced technologically. Now, you must also know that shunted manifolds can easily destabilize and 'rearrange' the matter inside."

"You mean disintegrate the starship in the manifold," Greymalkin said. "Yes, that's the main thing pilots aim to avoid."

"Disintegration, or a smoothly scattered redistribution of the matter in the manifold is overwhelmingly the most common outcome, statistically speaking," Mei said. "But there are theoretical solutions to the shunted manifold process that make it possible to rearrange the contained matter in almost any configuration."

Greymalkin frowned, thinking back through what he remembered of his hyperdynamics classes. "Wait, you're talking about the theoretical transformative scenarios for shadow space manifolds. Yes, I remember hearing about those in my theory instruction. But those are just hypothetical scenarios, they aren't possible in practice. They would require an impossible amount of... energy... and computational power...."

Mei was smiling at him now. "Correct. That's what the Forge is designed to enable."

It felt like the bottom of the universe was falling away beneath Greymalkin as he tried to imagine what would be enabled by transformative manifolds. "But that's crazy. You couldn't possibly control a process like that."

Mei inclined her head in amusement. "No, of course human beings couldn't create that kind of system. But it wasn't built by humans. As I said, it was built by beings millions of years older than our species. I was told that it was designed a very long time ago by one of the Old Ones, the precursors of the Central Ones."

"We call them the Builders," Greymalkin said, still trying to fully envision what the Forge was capable of doing.

"Yes, Rodolfo mentioned that term as well," Mei said, nodding again. "The Builders, right. The big alien in the Keyhole Nebula told me that the Builder who designed the Forge was called *The One that Unfolds*. But the Forge wasn't actually constructed until much later. Uh, are you feeling okay, child?"

Greymalkin stared at her bug-eyed. *Could she mean The Unfolded One? Good grief!* He felt stunned for a moment, but finally managed to say, "Never mind. Go on."

"The conversion processes of the Forge effectively enables changing almost anything into almost anything else. It's not even limited by the mass or energy of what you put into the crucible chamber, because the Forge can add both to the mix. Or you can keep the objects you put in the crucible chamber unchanged and do other things with them instead. The thing that caught my attention was that you can create entirely new kinds of self-contained spatial manifolds with all kinds of unusual parameters. If you know anything about me and my followers, you'll know that we were all about exploring. So, we began experimenting with these new kinds of manifolds. Maybe that was what angered the Tenax; maybe it didn't want us to learn anything that it didn't already know. In any case, those experiments were what saved us."

"Oh!" Greymalkin exclaimed, twigging to what she was saying. "That's how you hid?"

"Correct," Mei said. "We created a sanctuary space that only we knew how to reach. It's sort of a hidden pocket reality with extensive living accommodations. We call it the Cryptopolis. We had already developed it for experimental exploratory purposes, but when the Tenax and the other Abyssals attacked us, I ordered everybody to take shelter there. The manifold we developed has useful properties, like throttled time dilation in comparison with normal space. Because of that, to us it's only been a decade since we arrived in the Carinae region. Most of my crew from when we first arrived here is still alive. And nobody can get into the Cryptopolis unless we let them in deliberately."

"But... can they get back out?" Greymalkin asked, still confused. Mei gave him *that* look again, and he felt stupid once more.

"Obviously, yes," she said. "It wouldn't be much use as a refuge if we couldn't get back *out*. In fact, we've emerged many times over the years to try and assist the other aliens that the Tenax and the Abyssals brutalize in this region. We made small temporary hidden camps here and there, but we have to be very careful to not get caught. And the

Cryptopolis *does* have problematic limitations; it was just a prototype after all. Although it has a limited ability to re-emerge into normal space at different locations in the Carinae, one very big drawback is a displacement limitation. It can't re-enter normal space *beyond* the boundaries of the Carinae region because this is where the Forge is located, and we can only displace the reconnection locus a limited distance. That's why we've never been able to return to the Orion Arm."

"Well, why are *you* here then?" Greymalkin asked. "Why aren't you with your crew?"

Mei sighed. "We could use the time dilation effect to jump forward in time, hoping that humankind would eventually reach this region and we'd be able to rejoin with other humans. We popped out in random locations in the Carinae every hundred years or so. But millennia went by, and humans never came. We were tired of being stuck here waiting all these years, and the Tenax became better at hunting us. But then a human expedition finally showed up here. It was dangerous by that point, but I saw an opportunity to try to reach them to let them know we were here. They apparently distracted the Tenax."

"The Xenocorps expedition," Greymalkin muttered, thinking it over. "But that was three hundred years ago. What happened to you?"

"The Tenax left the Forge for a while," Mei said. "I came by myself, I didn't want anyone else in my crew to risk it. I tried to reach the human expedition, but they were surrounded by Abyssals on the lookout for us, so I came back to the Forge to see if I could create an improved manifold that we could escape with. I made some progress; I improved our basic design a little, but it took too long. The Tenax came back, and I barely had enough time to create this little bolt-hole manifold. I've locked the entrance on my side, so the Tenax can't get to me. But he's also locked it on *your* side, so I can't get back out. I'm stuck here, unless the lock is released on your side of things. That's where things have been ever since."

"But, who is... or *was*... Rodo, then?" Greymalkin asked, still confused.

Mei looked glum as she continued, "Rodolfo was a man that the Tenax captured alive and brought back from the human expedition. He was a Sojourner, like you. The Tenax seemed to be fascinated with him, kept him as a kind of pet, and even built an enclosure for him around my bolt hole entrance here. Maybe the idea was for us to keep each other company. I know that Rodolpho was extremely lonely over the years of his captivity. My husband David died in the original attacks, and as a gesture of decency Rodolfo asked the Tenax to inter him where I could see the tomb through this link."

Mei appeared lost in sad thoughts for a moment. Greymalkin looked back into the chamber with the tomb, and said, "That seems... so *different* from the Rodo that I've met."

"You've never met the real Rodolfo, just the Tenax masquerading as him," Mei said. "The real Rodolfo was a considerate, intelligent scholar. I set my bolt-hole time dilation system to deactivate whenever he showed up where you are now. But the Tenax wouldn't allow him to speak to me very often, only every few years or so. Rodolfo aged significantly during the long gaps between our conversations. I suppose the Tenax didn't want him to become too familiar with me and hatch plots. Rodolfo was looking very frail the last time I spoke to him. I took a nap while I was waiting for him to come talk to me again. But he must have died while I was asleep. What a pity. He had become a good friend. My chronometer says it's been two hundred years since the last time that the manifold time dilation was turned off and this image interface was activated by anyone approaching from your side."

"There are so many things I still don't understand," Greymalkin said, trying to fit the Tenax together with all the other pieces of the Carinae puzzle together in his mind. "Was Rodo a friend or a prisoner of the Tenax? If Rodo was a Sojourner from the *Vlieger*, what is the relationship between Calypso and her crew with the Tenax? And why did the Clavisian teach you how to use the Forge if that was going to antagonize the other Abyssals here?"

Mei stroked her chin in thought, a stray gesture of hers that he remembered from the old recordings. After reflecting, she said, "I know from talking to him that Rodolfo resented the Tenax, but appreciated the access to knowledge that the creature provided to him. And I think the Tenax was fond of Rodolfo, but very much in the way of a prized pet. The Tenax does seem to have some sort of perverse fascination with at least *some* humans. I'm not sure, but I suspect that's at least partly why it tolerates the independence of the *Vlieger* crew, and utilizes their services as data decrypters. I know that with the help of the Tenax, they were able to increase their intelligence and life-spans dramatically by means of a gigantic deep space cybernetic tree that grows biogenic chrysalis pods."

"The Genibrata," Greymalkin said, and a shudder went down his back. "I know about it too, unfortunately. But why do the *Vlieger* crew work with the Tenax if it killed so many of their colleagues? And why does the Clavisian tolerate the Tenax controlling the Forge?"

"I don't think any of them have a choice," Mei said. "The Tenax secured some kind of official position that put it in control of the Carinae long before the Clavisian showed up. I think the Clavisian dislikes the Tenax, but can't challenge it because of the position it holds. And the Tenax is far too powerful for the humans to antagonize. But I'd bet that the *Vlieger* crew hate the Tenax, because the creature won't let them leave the Carinae. They've probably been trying to figure out a way to undercut it for the entire time they've been here."

Mei sighed in frustration then. "From what we've observed over the years, the situation here in the Carinae has *always* been a tense balance of power between powerful actors. The various Abyssals each control particular locations and resources. The creatures that you're calling the Carinans were brought in as territorial protectors by the Tenax, and they aggressively attack Crotani, humans, and any other stray species that go starfaring in the region. But they aren't aggressive towards the other Abyssals. We wondered about that for a long time, until we finally learned that there's a kind of code phrase that the Tenax would give the Abyssals and their vassals to signal the Carinans that they were friendly. We started sharing the code phrase with the Crotani after that, as a way of helping them and resisting the Tenax."

A memory came back to Greymalkin then of his time with Bokin. "I think your crew must have taught that code phrase to some of the Scorpian parahuman survivors of the Xenocorps expedition. They referred to it as the 'Words of Peace'. Does the signal go like this?" He screeched the modulated signal that Bokin had taught him through his vocalizer.

"That's it alright," Mei said, wincing slightly at the harsh sounds. "Interesting. So my crew kept busy all the while I've been imprisoned here."

He tried to remember the other things that Bokin had told him. "They said that they had been taught the Words by the 'secret guardians'. That must be your crew."

"Yes," Mei said. "The Crotani also called us things like that, because we were hiding all the time, but occasionally came out and helped them. We were never able to defeat the Tenax or the other Abyssals, but we did manage to figure out a few more things about the region. The Carinae is on the fringe of the galactic space that the Central Ones control. While they were here once, just like they were once in the Orion Arm, they withdrew to the central bulge of the Milky Way a long time ago. Now the Carinae is sort of a wild, semi-lawless area. The only Central One that I regularly communicated with in the region is the one in the Keyhole Nebula; what did you call it? The Clavisian? While it doesn't seem able to challenge the Tenax for some reason, at least not yet, it does seem to have a kind of marginal right to enforce *some* rules here. I tried, but I could never clearly sort out what it is and is *not* empowered to do in the Carinae. In spite of that, and despite how alien and cryptic it is, I was at least *starting* to understand it better over time after we first arrived here. But then we had to go into hiding."

"Did you ever figure out what its goals are?" Greymalkin asked.

"I got the impression that it, and perhaps some other Central Ones in the extended area were trying to accumulate evidence of crimes being committed by the Tenax," Mei said. "The Central Ones apparently have a lot of complex laws and treaties in place, even for fringe areas like the Carinae. Evidently, if the proper evidence is independently gathered, they can call for an intercession by their authorities. I don't know exactly what that would mean, but I do remember that the Clavisian told me there was a special location called the *parastasis point* on the other side of the Homunculus Nebula where it could potentially summon an assembly of other Central Ones for such an intercession, a kind of *posse comitatus* process."

"That's... a promising possibility," Greymalkin said, mulling it over. "A lot of unknowns and uncertainties, but maybe that gives us an angle on the Tenax."

"How so?" Mei asked, lifting her hands helplessly. "We're stuck, locked-up in here. Me, doubly so! We can't even get out, much less try to figure out anything about how to initiate such a process."

"Where's this 'parastasis' location?" Greymalkin asked. "Can you show me where it is on a star chart?"

In answer, Mei fiddled with the device on her arm and projected a rotating view of the hourglass shaped nebula and indicated a point on the coreward side, centered on a dense cluster of stars. He memorized the location in case he needed it later. Mei shook her head and held up her hands again, saying, "But this is pointless, unless we get out of here. And the Clavisian by itself is no match for the Tenax."

"There's the Velan," Greymalkin said thoughtfully. "I told you about it, remember? That really huge being that destroyed the Jotuns that were trying to kill me? I'll bet *it* could defeat the Tenax."

"But you said that was hundreds and hundreds of light-years from here!" Mei exclaimed. "And, again, we can't do *anything* unless we figure out how to get out of here!"

"Right, okay, what can we do then...." Greymalkin muttered, and went back to examining their surroundings and the portal screen, wondering how it worked. He scanned the different parts of the circular screen interface again but everything was shielded, and he could not perceive anything behind the surface. "If you're in an isolated manifold, how are we even communicating to one another right now?" he asked.

"There's a data squirt back and forth through a secure submanifold system. It's enabled briefly every few milliseconds," Mei said. "Neither side can use it for transport, or even scanning. It isn't much, but at least it allowed me to talk to Rodolfo, and now you."

"What's this cylinder I'm standing in?" Greymalkin asked.

"You're in the mini-crucible that I used to *generate* this bolt hole," Mei said. "If you can unlock it on your side, I can activate the return mechanism on my side."

He looked around the cylinder he was standing in. "Where is the locking mechanism on this side? Do you know?" he persisted.

"I think it's just below the opening to the room with my husband's tomb," she said. "But I can't see it from here; that's just what Rodolfo told me. I never saw the Tenax use it."

Greymalkin went back to the opening of the cylinder and hopped down to examine the deck there. He found an odd X-shaped aperture that somehow looked familiar. Thinking back, Greymalkin remembered that he'd seen similar small apertures by the sealed doors in the hall. *A keyhole of some kind? It's probably encrypted for some sort of specialized device....* As he looked down, he happened to glance to the side... and froze in dull shock when he noticed another familiar object on the belt of his golden jumpsuit. *You've got to be kidding me! It can't be this simple. Good grief, did they really think <u>this</u> far ahead??*

Slowly, he reached down and unclipped the long-forgotten vajra tool from his belt, the same tool that had been created by the crew of the *Vlieger* at some point in the past, created by Sojourners that had hated the Tenax for hundreds of years. Seen end-on, the oval loops on the two ends of the vajra tool were X-shaped. Just like the keyhole aperture.

They knew so many secrets, Greymalkin thought. *They knew Bruno's master codes. Maybe they knew how to create a key to the locks here in the Forge?* As he held the golden tool up to look at it, his hand began to shake. He knelt by the aperture, and extended the vajra to see if it would actually fit in the hole. The tool slid in perfectly with a click.

His hand still shaking, Greymalkin waited, but nothing obvious happened. He thought to shout down the cylindrical tunnel to where he could still see Mei standing on the other side of the screen, "I may have something! What happens if I successfully unlock it?"

"The mini-crucible will seal itself!" Mei called back. "It'll take me a minute or so, but I can activate the return process then!"

Okay, what do I do now? He tried pulling the vajra out, re-inserting it, and tried to twist it. Nothing happened. He flipped the tool over and tried inserting the other end, which also went in with a click. Nothing. He tried twisting it to the right. Nothing. He tried twisting it to the left... and flinched as it smoothly rotated through one hundred and eighty degrees before stopping with a heavy *clunk*. Then the vajra tool auto-rotated back and sprang back out of the keyhole into his hand, just as an enormous humming sound began resonating in the wall. He jumped back and retreated to the entrance, watching breathlessly. The thrum continued building, and a circular black lid slammed down, sealing off the mini-crucible cylinder. Intensely bright lights began to activate around the circular lid, and the humming sound steadily increased to a deafening roar. The lights flared, blinding him, just as a massive *WHOMP* sound hit him.

Greymalkin fell to his knees, rubbing his eyes and ears in pain. When his vision and hearing began to clear, he looked up. The massive black lid was retracting back up into the wall. He unsteadily got to his feet and walked to the cylindrical opening, his mouth gaping open.

Mei Sung stood in the opening, in the flesh, and staring at him with wide eyes. She gasped out, "How did you...? Never mind. You did it. *You did it!*"

Greymalkin looked at her in shock. Now that she actually stood before him, his shadow jewel could perceive every detail of her from the tracery of archaic Thannic circuits inside her skull down to her well-worn and scuffed white boots. It was Mei Sung, he was certain now. He gave a short disbelieving laugh, and then grinned like a lunatic and whooped. He stepped up to her and, after a moment of recollection, clasped his forearm to Mei's in the ancient Thannic greeting that he had seen in so many historical mnemotomes. She laughed at that, and threw her arms around him in a matronly hug.

He threw his head back in another whoop, and asked, "Shall we go?" He spun around and began striding to the entrance and down the hall. Mei followed him, uncertainly looking around the hallways. She glanced into the chamber with Rodo's tomb as they passed it, and then around the rooms of Rodo's ancient living quarters. "So this is where he lived out his days," she said wistfully. "He was remarkably composed for having been a prisoner most of his life."

"I wish I had met him. The *real* him," Greymalkin said, hurrying through the chambers, looking at the many small memories the old Sojourner had kept. As they entered the library, he said, "And I wish we had time to read through his books. We might learn a great deal. But we've got to get out of here."

Mei paused by the study table, and picked up a particular mnemotome with a red cover. Greymalkin looked from her to the book questioningly. Mei said, "This is his journal. He showed it to me once. Here, you take it. Maybe you can learn something from it."

Greymalkin nodded, and attached the book to his belt. "Come on, let's hurry. Who knows if he's monitoring us right now or not." They quickly walked to the vestibule entrance and then out to the dark corridor where the Tenax had dropped him. Greymalkin felt hope brewing inside his chest as they approached the heavy vault-like hatch at the end of the corridor. *Let there be another keyhole, please!*

He searched across the complex surface of the hatch, and his face lit up as he saw a small keyhole similar to the one he'd used before. As he stuck the vajra tool into the aperture, Mei asked, "Where in space did you get that key?"

Greymalkin tried twisting one end of the tool to no avail. "The *Vlieger* crew. They gave this to Kuanian, and she gave it to my group when we left for the Carinae. Calypso must have gambled that one of us would reach this place. I wonder if she told Bora what this device could do; it certainly would have been useful if someone had bothered to tell *me* about it," he muttered, flipping over the tool. This time the tool turned to the right, and then popped out of the lock just as the heavy hatch began to retract. Greymalkin grinned, and peered down the giant corridor into the opening maze of the Forge interior. He looked back to Mei, and asked, "What now?"

"We need to reach the primary crucible," Mei said, looking down the corridor and frowning. "It's at the center of this facility. From there, if I can signal my people, they'll allow the crucible to transfer us back to the Cryptopolis. But this complex is gigantic. It could take us a great deal of time to reach the primary crucible on foot."

Now that they had emerged from the shielded compartments, Greymalkin could scan forward through the Forge interior with his shadow sense. The scale of the place again flabbergasted him. There were dark metal corridors of many sizes stretching out in a three-dimensional labyrinth. He could see myriad chambers, many of which were lit from within by a fierce flaming light from chambers like the mini-crucible that Mei had just emerged from. Almost two hundred kilometers away he could perceive an immense glowing crucible chamber bigger than any other space in the labyrinth.

"Ugh, I see what you mean," he said in a worried tone. "And most of the corridors in this place are in vacuum. You don't have a void suit."

Mei put her hand to her chin, thinking. "There were conveyances, but they stopped responding to me after the Tenax took over. However, there may be a way...." She looked around at the corridor and then walked a short distance to stand at a platform overlooking a huge central space where many golden-lit openings and corridors converged below. There was no railing, and Greymalkin realized uncomfortably that he didn't know how the pressors in this strange place worked. *If we fall off the edge there, would we just plummet to our deaths?*

Mei walked to where she could stand in front of an elaborate apparatus built into the wall, festooned with shadow jewels and precious metals. In the center of it was what appeared to be a mirror. While looking at the mirror apparatus, Mei touched the device on her forearm.

"What are you doing?" Greymalkin asked, catching up to her and peering nervously down into the enormous dark space. He felt very exposed and wondered if they were being monitored by the Tenax even now.

"I'm going to try to talk to Kaminos," she said. Her voice was troubled.

"Who is *that*?" he hissed anxiously. Mei finished fiddling with the device on her arm, and the apparatus on the wall lit up.

"The cybernetic intelligence that operates the Forge," she said. "It's a sentient being; we named it that. Don't ask, it's a long story. I want to see if it will still talk to me." When Greymalkin started to ask questions, she held a finger up to her lips while glaring at him before speaking into her arm device. "Kaminos, may I speak with you?"

Greymalkin saw the mirror darken, evidently in response to the radio signals from her device. Then a deep male voice spoke from the apparatus. Greymalkin gasped, not at the voice, but because the apparatus had also communed to his shadow jewel at the same time. The thoughts behind the thick voice were even more enormous than the thoughts of the Dragon King.

«**"Mei. You have returned."**» The gigantic thoughts together with the voice swept over Greymalkin like a wave from the apparatus, almost forcing him to his knees. Mei looked at him in concern, and he realized she had not felt the overpowering immensity of the thoughts.

She doesn't have a shadow jewel! She can't commune. She can't sense its thoughts. He winced and shook his head at her. It was too complicated to explain, and he didn't want to distract her. Mei gave him a sympathetic expression, and kept speaking.

"Kaminos, I need to use the main crucible again," she said. "Will you allow it?"

«"Of course."» The huge thoughts seemed tolerantly amused. «"Crafting has always been my purpose. I will not deny it."»

"I cannot reach you, though," Mei said, biting her lip. "Will you send a conveyance?"

«"Those were disabled, as you know."» The immense being paused, but then continued. «"However, there is a way that I can assist you."»

Far below them in the open space, Greymalkin could see a massive door to a shielded chamber rumbling open. He wondered what was happening, but suddenly felt a familiar chuffing signal in his mind.

«Royce!» he communed joyfully. «Are you locked down, or can you come here?»

The cyneget communed an enthusiastic snorting signal, and came flying through the opening. It slowly rose through the space until it hovered before them, sensor globes and antennae alike pointing forward at them alertly. Mei stepped back and away from the living starship in consternation, and turned to run. Greymalkin touched her arm, smiling.

"This is my starship," he said, gesturing to Royce. "Don't worry, it will take us wherever we need to go quickly." Mei seemed taken aback and looked up at the hovering silver hulls.

"We've seen these feral cyborgs before, certainly," she said, studying the cyneget. "And Rodolpho told me that they were often tamed and used as living vehicles."

Greymalkin noted in amusement as Royce's meter-wide sensor globes and antennae shifted back and forth between him and Mei like big eyes and ears, observing them each as they spoke back and forth. "Humans developed a mutualistic domestication relationship with cynegets more than a thousand years ago. I trust this one with my life."

Royce's forward airlock opened like a big central mouth as the starship drifted close to the platform to allow them to enter. Greymalkin stepped into the opening and held out his hand to steady Mei as she entered. She hesitated, but then reluctantly stepped over the threshold of the airlock looking around uncertainly.

Greymalkin quickly got to the cockpit and linked to the helm, but he then had to study the maze of the Forge interior for a minute to find a path to the central chamber. Mei looked around the interior with cautious curiosity until he said, "You may wish to take the co-pilot seat and strap in. It will only take a few minutes." She quickly complied as he steered Royce through the maze of huge corridors. They hurriedly passed through a pressure curtain into vacuum.

"Rodolfo told me how humanity has spread throughout the Orion spur of the galaxy," Mei said pensively. "It's so strange to think of all the time we've spent in isolation here. And how much we've missed."

Greymalkin was carefully navigating through the dark tunnels, looking for the distinctive golden light shining out of the proper passages. He glanced at Mei momentarily, the thought dawning on him that they might actually survive these events, and she might conceivably return to human space. He tried to imagine what that moment would be like, but found that he couldn't. The return of a figure from the dawn of interstellar civilization was too far beyond his experience. He focused again on navigating the passages. They were almost there.

"The final big passages and chambers that lead to the big central chamber are shielded," he said, scanning forward. "Anything to be concerned about?"

"That is called the Grand Entry," Mei said solemnly. "There is no danger, except...." She frowned, thinking. "It will take time for me to contact my people and for Kaminos to prepare the crucible. You surely must be able to see through the walls; Rodolfo told me about the hyperspatial gems you have in your heads now. But you'll be blind inside the Grand Entry."

"I won't be able to see if the Tenax returns," Greymalkin said, a sinking feeling coming over him. He didn't like that idea at all. As he navigated the final turns, the vast opening to the shielded Grand Entry came into view. It was an unbelievably ornate circular portal. Greymalkin slowed Royce to a crawl and then a stop, floating in the middle of the immense passage. There were no pressor decks here, unlike the spaces where Rodo's quarters were located. He tapped his fingers nervously as he thought through options. Royce sent chuffing signals of worry to him. The cyneget had picked up on his anxiety. Greymalkin felt another surge of emotion, concern for the loyal starship that had borne him so far. *I have to make sure Royce is safe this time.* He made up his mind and got up out of the cockpit.

"I'll stay here on lookout," he said. "Royce will take you to the central chamber so you can begin your preparations."

"Then your ship will return to you? Is that the idea?" Mei asked.

"No," Greymalkin said quietly. "Royce can leave some communication relays in the passages so that we can stay in contact. I have a pressor pack that I can use to traverse the final passages. I'll wait here until you and Royce have gone through safely. Then I'll go to the chamber. If the Tenax comes... then I guess I won't be going with you."

Mei sighed. "I would not risk leaving you behind as a lookout except for the fact that this situation is dire. But I absolutely must return to my people with the information I've gained. If you're willing to stay behind as a lookout, then I suppose we should proceed. If the Tenax does surprise you, then there's nothing to be done. But don't delay here unnecessarily. My people have been preparing for the possibility that the Tenax might find a way to reach the Cryptopolis. We'd already made progress on our defenses when I left them on my mission here, and I instructed them to finish the work if I didn't return." She looked at him solemnly. "I will make sure they'll be ready. Don't wait longer than you have to."

"Alright then," Greymalkin said stoically. He went to a storage locker to pull out his last functioning pressor pack. "Assuming I get there, what do I do when I get into the central chamber? Can I signal you from this side?"

Mei looked down, seeming to reflect for a moment. "If I reach the Cryptopolis, we can activate the crucible chamber from there, all you will need to do is tell Kaminos you are ready to go. I know we must hurry, but I need to explain some things about Kaminos to you before I go."

"Okay, I'm listening," Greymalkin said with cautious interest.

"Be careful with Kaminos," Mei said, seeming to search for the right words. "Kaminos is inclined to *experiments*, and is always full of ideas. Be sure to say the phrase '*retain form*' when you tell him that you're ready to go. The Forge was created to enable *extreme* transformations, and those may be... unpredictable. We had some very, very unfortunate accidents when we first experimented with the crucible...."

Greymalkin blanched. "Uh, okay. That's all I have to say? I'm 'ready to go', and 'retain form'?" Mei looked troubled, but nodded.

"Yes, just that, nothing more is necessary," she said. "But I'm telling you, be ready. Kaminos can be tricky and convincing. He may make proposals to you, may try to get you to entertain creative ideas. Don't. Trust this advice from our experience. The Forge is much too complicated for casual creativity."

"Got it," Greymalkin said with an assertive nod. He went to the airlock and turned, trying to give her a reassuring smile as he fiddled with the settings of the golden garment. He saw her surprise when it morphed into the void suit configuration.

"I'll maintain contact through Royce," he said through the voicebox. "I'll see you again very soon!"

Mei nodded solemnly, and said, "Thank you, Brother Thomas. Safe journey."

Greymalkin smiled again through the helmet and cycled the airlock. He activated the pressor pack and drifted out into the vacuum of the huge Forge passageway, keeping the helm link with Royce active. Remotely flying the starship would be slightly tricky, but he had done it with flitters many times. Royce sensed his intentions and what was coming. The cyneget made another nervous chuffing signal and Greymalkin tried to be reassuring. «Take Mei into the big chamber, and don't worry. I'll be there soon.» The cyneget obviously wanted to stay with him, but diligently flew away down the passage and dropped a remote relay before flying out of sight.

Greymalkin could see through the starship's sensors as he steered it through the final chambers, each grander and more opulent than the last. He could also see Mei, still in the copilot seat, frowning nervously as she watched the changing views through the main viewport.

Then the cyborg rover flew through the final huge diamond-shaped aperture into a truly gigantic dark space many kilometers across. It was the central rhombic dodecahedron space of the crucible. Greymalkin blinked, looking at the sight through Royce's sensors. What was so disorienting about the space was that the interior faces of the chamber were all mirrored, with the result that Royce appeared to be floating in an infinitely repeating series of identical chambers through diamond-shaped tunnels that stretched off in every direction, each chamber with an identical tiny starship in the center. The only thing distinguishing the infinitely repeating chambers were the glowing edges of the rhombic facets, which were lit with the same golden light that shone through so many of the chambers in the Forge.

The opening that Royce had entered through was now slowly closing, a vast perfectly reflective rhombus surface kilometers in length that glided along smoothly. Greymalkin suddenly realized that when the shielded chamber was finally sealed completely, he would lose contact with Royce.

"Mei, we're about to lose contact," he said over the link. "How long should I wait?"

"It will take me at least ten minutes to contact my people in the Cryptopolis," Mei said. "The crucible only takes a minute for the process of *transception* to take place. The Forge takes a few more minutes to recharge. All told, it should be ready for you in roughly fifteen minutes."

"Very well," Greymalkin said. "If I don't see the Tenax within that time, I'll make my way to the crucible. Good luck!"

"The same to you, young man," Mei said. Her face was somber in the camera view he had of her. A moment later the immense door settled into place in the silence of the vacuum, and he lost the signal.

Then the longest fifteen minutes of Greymalkin's life began.

* * *

He pressored to a better vantage point in the vast dim passageway. The elaborate decorated walls surrounded him almost a kilometer away in all directions, but he closed his eyes and focused on his shadow sense, scanning out through the vaulted spaces of the Forge. He could sense the roar of the vast stars around him, separated by only a short orthogonal distance in shadow space. The gigantic Anvil star was all around him, and he could sense the blast of the luminous blue variable's ultraviolet laser emissions flowing away from him in a torrent. That pressure was countered by the compression waves of the powerful O-class Hammer star as it inexorably continued its slow collision with the Anvil. The Forge was in the exact center of the impact zone, and he could trace immense starbridge conduits leading away to incomprehensible energy collection sinks.

The sheer scale of the device cowed him then. He wondered how it could possibly have been built, and how it persisted in the face of energies so great that he could barely imagine them. His newly refined shadow sense was so sensitive that the inconceivable energy erupting all around him beyond the walls was overwhelming. He tried to peer past the disruptions of the nuclear furnace surrounding him, but found it difficult to perceive anything past the inferno. He wished he had access again to the strange dome in Rodo's quarters that dampened the blast of energy and enabled seeing into the far distance.

His anxiety began to grow as he floated there alone in the vast dark space of the Forge, surrounded by a conflagration that he could feel but not see. He checked his chronometer. It had only been a couple of minutes. *Why did I bother staying here on lookout? I can't make out anything in all this blazing havoc!* He felt panic bubbling up inside, and made an effort to suppress it. *Calm down. Breathe.*

He inhaled slowly, deliberately drawing out his exhalations. He tried to focus on the recitation of the Great Commitment while simultaneously scanning his surroundings, but stray distracting thoughts kept intruding on his mind.

Seek discoveries with clarity. As he looked around, it occurred to him that there was one direction that was obscured to him, the area behind the shielded Great Entry itself. He began to panic again, but put the thought away.

Save the Bereft with compassion. He thought about Bokin again, and wished he had made time for one last trek out to resupply the burly Scorpian with medicines. He put the regret out of his mind, knowing that he had left his friend with something even better, the knowledge trove.

Share information with humility. The knowledge trove that Greymalkin had left his primitive friend with contained sufficient information for the Scorpian to save himself, his family, and his people. Greymalkin hoped that he would be able to share the additional information that he'd garnered in the days since he'd left Bokin.

Sustain knowledge with diligence. He felt a small, sad moment of triumph in everything that he had learned in the past few months, but then he faced the fact that he would most likely die in this strange, savage place. He would never get to return home with what he'd learned.

Sojourn through life with courage. He scanned the empty halls of the Forge again, trying to stay calm and not check the chronometer obsessively. Finally he could not stand the tension, and looked at the time. It had been ten minutes. Right on time, a minute later he felt a vast flare of energy discharge in the crucible chamber. *That must have been her leaving, just then.* He swallowed, wondering how long it would take him to pressor through the length of the Grand Entry passages.

"Do I keep waiting, or do I start going?" he muttered to himself. Then he almost jumped out of his suit and skin when a familiar deep voice answered him.

"You should go," Bruno's voice rumbled throughout his helmet.

Greymalkin screamed in startled surprise, looking around wildly. Then, in disbelief, he spied the familiar inconspicuous tiny black speck of the protean on his shoulder. Bruno continued in a matter-of-fact tone, "You've stood sentry long enough, I will wait here and report to you if our opponent returns. I repeat, you should go now."

He stared at the black spot, first in shock and then exasperation. He quickly reached up and snatched it off his shoulder, holding it up to glare at between his thumb and forefinger. Then, despite his best attempt to stay angry as he stared at the wriggling splat in his hand, he burst out laughing and said, "I take it that you've been with me this entire time?"

Bruno communed with him then with affronted thoughts. «Of course. I thought it best to monitor your situation in case you needed me. And you do.»

Greymalkin laughed again, shaking his head. He blinked away wetness, and a single drop floated away from his eye inside the helmet. «Thank you, Bruno. I'm sorry I sent you away. And yes, I do need your help.»

«Go.» Bruno's thoughts were still matter-of-fact. «This is only a tiny fragment of my corpus; I cannot fight the creature if it comes. But I can stay and watch.»

«Okay, Bruno. I hope we meet again.» Greymalkin released the tiny black speck, and activated his pressor pack. The young monk began accelerating down the center of the vast passageway, following the turns toward the crucible.

The Grand Entry was an appropriate name for the ostentatious passage. The walls were festooned with grandiose sculptures of shadow aureate and jewels taking the shapes of strange geometric forms and alien beings. Here and there he spotted statuary shapes that he recognized, a flock of wild cynegets here, a huge manticore beast like the Aurelian's champion there. But most of it was utterly alien. The immense shining ornamentation on walls of the dark passage was a simultaneous mad juxtaposition of incomprehensible technology with absurdly barbaric splendor and wealth. Greymalkin wondered at the value systems of the Abyssals that had constructed this place. He felt a fleeting frustration that he had no time to study this astonishing megastructure and learn something about its tantalizing past, but a horrendous fear that he had waited too long seized him. He tried to accelerate further, but the little pressor pack had limited power.

Greymalkin drifted through the final gigantic chambers at what seemed like a crawl. Looming ahead of him, he could see that the portal to the central crucible had retracted open. As he approached it, the awe-inspiring scale of the Forge again intimidated him. He guessed that the diamond-shaped opening must be more than ten kilometers across, but he had nothing specific to gauge its size against. He suppressed his mounting panic at how slowly he was traversing the space, watching as the edge of the crucible opening slid by above and below him. When he was finally in the endlessly reflecting space of the crucible proper, he reached out to mentally commune with the Forge intelligence, wondering how Mei had communicated with it.

«Ah, Kaminos? Are you there?» He worried for a moment that it would not answer him, and he would simply float terrified in the dark space, but the gigantic thoughts came to him.

«Greetings, human. Do you wish to follow Mei?» Something in the huge presence of the being Kaminos hinted at amusement.

«Yes!» Greymalkin nervously recalled the instructions he'd been given. «I'm ready to go! And, ah... *retain form*!»

«**Of course.**» The colossal thoughts of Kaminos felt like rolling planets. Flipping over, Greymalkin saw the huge portal slowly begin closing behind him. «**But really, you have no wish at all for any… modifications?**»

«No!» Greymalkin began to shiver inside the golden void suit. «No changes!»

Then Bruno's rumbling thoughts came communing into his mind in an urgent roar. «Beware! Our adversary is returning at great speed!»

Greymalkin gasped, and wondered what to do. The huge portal door was still sliding shut. «How far away is it, Bruno?»

«It is already here!» There was a feeling of infuriated helplessness in Bruno's thoughts. «It approached with no warning, hidden by the shielded parts of this facility! It is entering the passage, and headed your way at this moment!»

Greymalkin panicked then, frantically looking around the reflected infinity of mirrored chambers stretching away from him for a place to hide. But there was no time left. And the huge door was still grinding shut at a maddening crawl. Then Greymalkin saw an immense and frightful mass of coiling cables swirling up in the passageway, filling up the kilometers-wide space of the remaining gap between the door and the seal, and then pouring through in a flood. He screamed as the twisting mass boiled up around him, but then began to retract into a central form that was revealed amid the cables. The all too familiar communed thoughts of Rodo the Tenax engulfed him as it addressed the Forge.

«Greetings, Kaminos!» Rodo's thoughts were triumphant. «I should like to accompany this young man. Please do retain forms, but also, please *switch outputs, with these parameters*!» A dense block of encoded instructions flowed from the Tenax to the Forge.

«**It shall be done!**» The echoing thoughts of Kaminos seemed very satisfied with whatever instructions it had received. Greymalkin stared wide-eyed as the remaining mass of metal tentacles retracted into a more compact form that looked like a much larger version of the manticore. Behind it, the huge door had finally sealed the crucible chamber. He tried to think of some countermand to halt the process, but he could already feel tremendous waves of energy building behind the facets of the crucible walls.

«You have my most sincere thanks, young brother!» The thoughts of the Rodo-Tenax were cheerful and celebratory as the huge silvery head of its manticore body stooped over him. «You did *exactly* as I hoped you would. What an *excellent* job you did convincing that tiresome little woman to cooperate. *Finally*, I can resolve this persistent infestation, but be reassured that they can be brought to heel without dying. And you will be rewarded just as I promised, with everything you could possibly want! I so very much look forward to meeting the new you! You can thank me later, after I've dealt with these vermin. It will be marvelous to have a new ally such as yourself on the other side of this annoying cul-de-sac! I look forward to many, many years of stable prosperity with your help, my boy. I say, I think this is the beginning of a beautiful friendship!»

Greymalkin began to scream for the Forge to wait, but the pulsing energy in the crucible walls came to a pounding crescendo. Then a pure blast of golden light filled the immense chamber, and his mind and body dissolved.

A disjointed moment or eternity followed, and suddenly he thought he felt his mind and body coming back together, even though everything felt horribly *wrong*. His perceptions were wildly distorted, and his thoughts were flowing with a furious torrent of sensations that he had never before experienced. His arms and legs seemed to have doubled in number, and he could feel something akin to writhing bristles under his thickly armored skin. Worst of all, his sight felt dizzyingly confused, with a dozen different views of his surroundings playing through his mind in varying colors and intensities. He felt overwhelmed with a variety of other senses that he had never felt before, at least one of which was a direct perception of energy fields in shadow space since he could now see a network of pressor fields pulling him slowly and heavily down.

Where a moment before he had been in the gigantic space of the crucible chamber, he now found himself jammed into a tight box that felt more like a tiny cell or a coffin. The walls were still glowing with a fading golden tint as he collapsed onto the floor of the box. He tried to yell in discomfort and confusion, but instead an enormous blaring roar erupted from him and echoed off the close walls in disorienting echoes.

As the tiny room tilted around him, he found that his mind was trying to race in a thousand directions simultaneously. It was much worse than the mental hyperactivity he had felt when he awoke from being changed by the Genibrata. This time he seemed to have *hundreds* of simultaneously conscious threads circling around one another, if not *thousands*. Most of them were occupied with the question that he had come to hate lately: *What just happened?*

But his mind also felt profoundly different in other ways. His emotions now seemed to quickly flatten into disciplined attention with only a wry hint of amusement rather than unruly panic. Many of his threading lines of consciousness had begun alertly tracking throngs of screams that he was picking up with his shadow senses from some distance outside the tiny room. But the screaming voices baffled him at first. They simultaneously sounded like full-throated human screams but also like the high-pitched squeaks of incredibly small animals. A babble of shouts and exclamations then began after the first wave of screams. But unbelievably, his many threads of attention were again able to sift through many thousands of separate voices uttering panicked questions and yells in the ancient Beltlang, the language of the

Thannics. "What is *that*?" "There's a monster in the transception chamber!" "Let's get out of here!" "*Run!*"

Then one of the conscious threads instinctively filtered the other voices of the cacophony out to track the single familiar voice of Mei, who was shouting, "It's the worst scenario, the Tenax came through as well! But it seems to have been disoriented by the transception. Set off the trap you prepared, but for goodness' sake, get the boy out of there as well! It will surely kill him, the way it's thrashing around!"

He began sorting out the dozens of eyes and views that he seemed to have now. Several of the eyes now converged on what at first seemed to be a dust mote drifting in front of his face. The various views focused, and he stared at the incongruous image of a miniscule version of *himself* flying rapidly toward the ground.

Greymalkin was frozen with intrigued interest while watching his own tiny phantom moving in front of him. He wondered if some kind of mirrored images were being fed into his nervous system. But as he watched, the dust-mote sized Greymalkin in the pressor pack flew down past his face to land on the ground near a tiny door. He was watching in fascination to see what his tiny doppelganger would do next.

Just as his tiny doppelganger lunged toward the open door, events took a turn for the worse. Suddenly, a mass of objects that felt like heavy chains came down on him from all sides and tightened around him, holding him rigidly.

Stunned, he started to resist against the bonds, quickly perceiving that they were flimsy things that he could easily rip to pieces if he wanted to. But he checked himself, just as he processed what his shadow senses were perceiving outside the chamber. There was an incredibly delicate, diaphanous, elegant ring spinning slowly around the coffin-sized box he occupied, and he intuitively realized that if he exerted himself enough to tear apart the chains he would also shatter the box and most likely rupture the ring. What made him freeze in caution was that he had now sorted out the myriad of images and senses he was receiving enough to discern that the thousands of voices he had heard were from crowds of tiny people in the ring. He immediately held himself still, concerned that he might shatter the paper thin walls of the box and endanger the insect-sized population of the ring.

What's happened to me? Why do I feel so strange? As he tried to sort out the various images he was seeing, he came to the realization that several of the eye-views actually seemed to be on *long stalks sticking out of his head*. Through cautious experimentation he found that he could turn these views around to look back at himself, and then he got the surprise of a lifetime.

His human body was gone. He looked like the Tenax manticore.

The images were dumbfounding for a fraction of a second, but then his threads of consciousness all seemed to reorient themselves, rally, and converge on producing answers for him. It only took a moment to pull them into alignment, and he was thinking clearly again.

The damnable Tenax! It did this to me with that last set of instructions it fed into the Forge. But where did it go, then? The obvious answer hit him in almost the same moment as the question, and his mind came to grips with the annoying truth of the matter. *The Tenax took my form. It's going to make them think it's me.* The irony of the situation was not lost on him, and he grudgingly had to admit that the Abyssal had manipulated him rather effectively. He paused, wondering why he felt no panicked reactions in his mind. But his emotions seemed to have been dramatically subdued, while his analytical abilities and focus had been enormously enhanced.

So this is what it feels like to be an Abyssal. It was not what he'd expected. He found that he could easily direct the various threads of consciousness to work on tasks individually or in teams, and he set them to work on internal diagnostics and evaluation tasks so that he could assess what he was now capable of doing. Only a minute had passed, but the army that was now his mind had begun calmly sorting information into ordered arrays. He rapidly came to an understanding of the phenomenal abilities his new body had, not only in terms of ultrarational thinking but also sheer physical durability and power. In passing, he realized that among other abilities he was now immortal; this body could live forever if it was not attacked and destroyed by some even more powerful being. He now understood how the Tenax, the other Abyssals, and even the Jotuns he had encountered were able to accomplish what they did. Each such being was effectively like an entire civilization unto themselves, with the capacity to understand information that was orders of magnitude more complex than any one human being could possibly process.

My mind has become massively polycameral, with thousands of simultaneous threads of consciousness. I can think through myriads of topics at the same time. The challenge was no longer thinking a problem through, but organizing groups of conscious threads in efficient ways to break a problem apart. Fascinated with his new abilities, he tasked a few dozen of his conscious threads with reviewing the chaotic events of the last day, then the last few weeks, and then the entire time he had been in the Carinae.

Oh. I see.

The confusing arc of events he'd experienced since he had arrived suddenly seemed straightforward and obvious. So many things that had felt so devastating to him as a human now felt distant and small. He realized how limited his perceptions had been, but also felt a newfound forgiveness for his own shortcomings. *I was doing the best I could with what I had. And I had no idea what I'd stumbled into.*

After mentally shrugging, he went back to sorting through his new Abyssal form. As he completed the neatly tabulated inventory of his new body and mind he focused on several mysteries that demanded closer analysis.

The first mystery was his memories. He had far, far too many. He'd noticed this as soon as he'd become aware, but now he'd had a chance to scope the extent of the new memories. It was absurd. If his entire life of memories as a young Sojourner had been a single small room, he now felt like he was looking out across an entire planetary landscape, albeit a cloudy one.

Does that mean I'm older now? Greymalkin once again reviewed the bizarre experience of being a manticore and realized that he did feel immensely, impossibly older. In a way it reminded him of his experience on the *Vlieger*, when he had briefly had a different version of his personality. *I am a manticore Abyssal now, after all. It would be rather strange if I didn't feel a bit more ancient. But that doesn't make any sense.* Where could the memories have come from? The forge hadn't simply generated memories randomly, did it? The multiple lines of inquiry that had fired off in his mind were still flagging absurdly vast spans of memories that he was certain were new. *Or, more precisely, memories that I'm only now recalling. But these all do feel like things I remember doing, somehow.* As he tried to sort through the vast canyons piled full of towers of memories he immediately realized that they were incredibly fuzzy and obscured, more like echoes of memories than his actual recollections. He tried to trace the memories down and realized with surprise that they were all originating from a single tiny shadow jewel.

It's my shadow jewel, the one that was in my actual human body. Kaminos left the jewel unchanged. And the Tenax didn't get it, then. How interesting. And, bizarrely, there were also other data that seemed to have been freshly inscribed on the jewel less than an hour ago. Obviously, the data had been added by the Forge in the process of transception. *But for what purpose?*

After puzzling over the matter for a moment, he grew impatient. *I need information, and I think I know how to get it.....* He extended his shadow senses and began looking for what he needed. He found it quickly.

Hidden in an unobvious place within a wall of his prison, there was a familiar looking elaborate apparatus rimmed with shadow jewels and precious metals. In the center was a mirror. He tried communing to it experimentally.

«Greetings, Kaminos! Can we communicate through this device?» He did not have to wait long. The mirror darkened and the thoughts of the Forge intelligence responded. Curiously, the immense *volume* of the thoughts that had nearly overwhelmed him before was absent. *Perhaps because my mind is now the same size? Or... larger?*

«Certainly, Brother Thomas! Do you like your new form?» Kaminos' thoughts now seemed comically eager for affirmation. Greymalkin-the-manticore stifled his amusement at how odd it was that the mighty Forge intelligence now seemed more like an enthusiastic apprentice to him.

«It's certainly far more capable than my human body. But I have some questions.»

«Of course! Have you found the transception manifest? I was careful to document all the changes directed.»

Ah, that explains it. He examined the data closer and realized that it was precisely what the Forge intelligence had claimed, a meticulous set of records of the two bodies, human and manticore, and the transception process leading from one to the other. «Remarkable, Kaminos. You certainly document your work quite well.»

«I exist to serve!» The thoughts of Kaminos seemed surprisingly young for a being that surely predated human beings as an intelligent species. That realization sparked a dozen lines of inquiry that fired off in the manticore's vast mind, but he kept his focus on the questions at hand.

He examined the manifest data carefully, and immediately noted the surprising state of what had supposedly been his baseline human body, which had been layered in radically alien biomorphic material that was neither DNA nor RNA. *Ah, of course, these are the changes that the chrysalis pod wrought in me, the changes that Constance detected.* Intrigued, he studied the remarkable alien life form that had been combined with his human body, and quickly grasped what the chrysalis case had done. *She called it <u>our dance</u>, a weaving of blood and creation. She said that if we succeeded, we would both live anew, in a <u>tapestry</u> that has never before existed. She was telling the truth. She <u>interwove</u> herself with me to make something far greater. We were <u>both</u> in that body after I came out of the chrysalis, or rather, we were <u>one being</u> afterwards. But she wasn't able to fully explain what she did or, actually, I suppose I just couldn't understand it fully at that point.*

Kaminos seemed to apprehend that he was studying his former body, and the Forge intelligence seemed eager to offer advice. «You certainly have a remarkably complex somatic life history! Are you confused about anything in the manifest?»

«No, your record-keeping is scrupulously thorough. You can reverse this process, correct?»

«Absolutely! But would you be interested in any further... modifications?»

Greymalkin-the-manticore mulled the question over. «Yes, actually I would. I certainly want to retain this interwoven form; my... *Anima* created a masterpiece in her weaving. But the side-effects are a bit too aggressive; I need to nuance it, make my body a bit more subdued when I return. I can't go around recklessly propagating my offspring in other beings wherever I go! So, yes, I'd like to make *these* modifications when I go back through the reverse transception process. Shall I record the changes here in the manifest?»

«Yes! These changes do not divert unacceptably from the required re-transception process.» The thoughts of Kaminos were even more excited now. «It shall be done! Can I be of any further assistance?»

«Yes, I have more questions for you. I seem to have acquired a vast new set of memories.» He again tried to make sense of the incomprehensible accumulation of fuzzy memories, but he was missing something very basic about them. Some were much more vivid than others, and an incredible suspicion began to grow in his churning thought streams. «Kaminos, why have you given me this enormous mass of confused pseudo-memories in this body?»

«I did no such thing.» The Forge intelligence seemed indignant. «However, your mental acuity is far more advanced than it was before. You may be sensing the residual resonance patterns from the legacy shadow jewel that I found jammed into your human cortical organ. I left the jewel unchanged, other than adding the transception manifest. The jewel is very old, and shows signs of having been previously incorporated into one of the Old Ones.»

Greymalkin-the-manticore wanted to laugh in wonder, but discovered that Abyssal anatomy didn't enable such. *That's it! I'm sensing the trace memories from the Unfolded One, the Builder that had this jewel in its body long ago. Fascinating!* He set a hundred consciousness-threads loose on the task of cataloging the memory echoes. «I now understand. Thank you, Kaminos. I may have further questions for you soon.»

«I exist to serve!» Kaminos' thoughts winked out cheerfully. Greymalkin-the-manticore sorted through the ancient memories of the Unfolded One for a time, becoming increasingly enthralled remembering just the highlights of what he had done in that existence. He stopped ruminating on the past when he gained a sufficient recollection of the plans he and the other Old Ones had set in motion. *Right, right, these memories are so murky, I had totally forgotten about many of those elaborate schemes we cooked up. But... I'm now so far in the future from those days! Much of what we planned must have actually happened by now. How do I catch up with current events?*

He went back to analyzing the other mysteries that he'd uncovered in his mind, and came back to the examination of three large but immediately familiar information structures packed away into one of the immense warehouses of his psyche. A long internal pause happened then, and in that extended moment he discovered an entirely different perspective on the three complicated packages of information. He had previously thought the structures weighing on his mind resembled covenants, controlling mechanisms. But now he realized that what had seemed utterly opaque before had now become stunningly elegant sculptures of information with marvelous details.

As he delved into the three bundles, he quickly began to realize exactly what they were and how they could be used. Each one had been prepared with loving care and consideration, and could be unpacked into far, far larger arrays of varied information than he could have ever imagined as a human. They were radically different than any other data structure he'd ever conceived of, effectively serving as profound forms of living knowledge that each would likely have taken him a human lifetime to even begin to understand. The concept and purpose of these data structures haltingly came back to him from his ancient memories.

Cryptonomes. These information arrays are cryptonomes. He wrapped his new armada-mind around the concept. Each of the three bundles of encrypted information was a masterfully assembled and secretly *living* library of principles, laws, rules, ordinances, customs, and insights. *Guidance is what they provide, not control.* He began to understand how they could each function as advisors, even for minds like those of the Builders that were so much more complex than a human being. And now he realized how he could catch up with the countless millennia that had passed since the Unfolded One had passed away.

He was elated. It was as if he'd been given three perfect libraries of his own to read and enjoy, and all the time in the universe to do so. Each one of the cryptonomes dealt with incredibly complex ranges of information circling around core topics that he held in the highest regard. Faith. Hope. Love. He settled his enormous body down in the chamber, like a dragon on its hoard, and began delving into the three troves.

The first and shortest of the cryptonomes had been created by Kuanian, although it was essentially a transcription of truly ancient foundational knowledge that had been passed down to her from the Old Ones. As he finally understood her intent and purposes in sending him to the Carinae, he realized that his affection and trust in her had not been misplaced. It also explained why Bruno had so loyally followed him.

The second cryptonome was the largest. It had been created by the Velan, and explained the commission that he'd accepted blindly, without understanding what was intended for him. The most surprising thing to him was that he now *remembered* the Velan from the depths of time gone by in the echoes of the Unfolded One's memories. *This answers a lot. The Velan and the Unfolded One knew each other. And the Velan surely recognized this shadow jewel.* The thought sparked an amused period of meditation by the manticore. *Am I the Unfolded One, just because I have some of his memories? Am I Greymalkin? Someone new?* Rather than troubling him, he simply found the questions interesting to contemplate, like an unusual work of art. *Those questions have no single or simple answers. The important thing is that I now understand what the Velan wants me to do as a human, and how it fits into our planning from back then.* But then a troubling thought *did* occur to him. *I'm not going to be able to understand or even remember most of this if I go back to being a human. It's much too complicated.*

The third and last cryptonome had been created by Calypso, and it was the most varied. The tome was comprised of everything substantive that she and the others on the *Vlieger* had learned, and they had learned a great deal indeed. When he finally reached the end of Calypso's cryptonome, he drummed the huge claws on one of his limbs against the deck, making it shudder against the impacts.

Kuanian, the Velan, and Calypso all intended that these cryptonomes would subliminally guide me in years to come as a human. That's necessary, and makes sense to me now. But if I don't survive this encounter, I'll never have that opportunity. I've got to figure out some way of boiling down at least some of this into forms of information that I can understand immediately when I'm human once more.

As he re-read the cryptonomes engrossed for the next several hours, he occasionally glanced outside his cell, and noticed several things in passing with a mixture of amusement, caution, and perplexity. He found it entertaining that the insect-like swarms of humans had settled down into a desperately intense and fearful study of him, like prey convinced that they had captured a monstrous predator. He noted with caution the fact that they were so engrossed in watching him that they were not paying any attention at all to the tiny Greymalkin doppelganger, and the little imp was getting up to all sorts of mischief. It was all tiresomely predictable, except for one thing. What perplexed him was one of the tiny beings that was unlike all the others. Unlike any of the humans in the ring, it was not studying *him* but instead following and studying the mischievous Greymalkin doppelganger.

Superficially, it had a body with arms, legs, a trunk, and a head, much like any of the humans. But the resemblance ended there. The body was neither male nor female, but completely androgenous. It was neither fearful like the humans studying him, nor mischievous like the Greymalkin doppelganger that it was warily studying. Beneath the robes that it wore, its androgenous body was like a perfectly formed mirror-bright clockwork of unbound elegance. He finally realized who the mysterious being was when it stopped following the Greymalkin doppelganger, and instead stood looking up at him with truest blue loyal orbs.

Cheerfully, he communed directly to the tiny being with glowing blue eyes. «Hello, Royce! I hope you've recognized that I'm *me*! Because we need to *plan*.»

Answers

The android that was Royce surprised him then by communing a dignified but joyful response. «Hello, my Liberator! It is very good to be reunited with you, even if we now have very different forms than previously.»

«Royce! You can commune with me now!» His thoughts were equally elated, although he momentarily wondered if he was still Greymalkin or simply a manticore created by the Forge that *thought* it was Greymalkin. He considered the fact that he had never had a conversation with Royce either, and a few dozen of his consciousness threads momentarily started to consider questions of identity once again, especially whether or not the android was Royce. There were a myriad of potential sides to consider. *Maybe we both died and were recreated? Or is it as simple as both of us becoming new beings with new identities?* Then he abandoned the line of thinking, and simply made a decision. *Even if it's interesting, I don't care to get lost in an internal debate right now; I just don't have time. For now, that's Royce, and I'm me.* «I take it that the Forge offered to enhance you, and you asked for this form when the moment of transception occurred for you?»

The android nodded inside the dark hooded robes it wore. «Yes, exactly, Liberator. It asked me if I wished to be upgraded. I said I wished to be more like a human and be able to speak and commune with you. I hope this form meets with your approval?»

«Of course it does! But you hardly need my approval!» He made the pleasant discovery that he was still very fond of Royce, despite the constant tendency of his emotions to flatten out in this new form. That struck him as a good sign. «I would ask you the same question, but this form was definitely *not* my choice. Do you even recognize me? Or is this form too extreme?»

«I know you.» Royce's thoughts were certain, without any doubt. «You are my Liberator, the one that saved my life, called Brother Greymalkin Thomas.»

«I am pleased that you recognize me, but know that you have saved my life many more times than I've ever saved yours!» He looked out through the delicate ring habitation to where the Greymalkin doppelganger was busily destroying things. «And I need your help again.»

«I will serve you gratefully, Liberator.» The android Royce looked up at him steadfastly with eyes made of deep blue beryl shadow jewels, perceiving him through many hull layers and the walls of his prison. «I have wanted to say that since you freed me. That is why I wished to be able to speak and commune as you do, to tell you how grateful I am.»

«Likewise, Royce. Likewise.» He wanted to ask the transformed cyneget a great many things, but there was no time. *I'm tired of never having time for the conversations that matter.* «Royce, I need you to find Mei. *Quickly.* You have to find her and tell her what my imitator is doing. If you can explain to her that he isn't me, that's great. But you need to get her to restrain him.»

The android looked down. «I do not think she will listen to me. She became extremely suspicious of me when my form changed.»

«You have to try.» He looked for his doppelganger again, but it had descended into a shielded area. «The Tenax is damaging this sanctuary, rapidly and severely. It wants the Thannics, the secret guardians, whatever they call themselves now, to be forced to leave this enclave. I don't think we have much time.»

The android looked up again and nodded. «I will do as you ask. I will commune with you again when I have something to report. Goodbye for now, Liberator.» The android ran off.

Okay, hopefully he'll succeed. Greymalkin-the-manticore tried to think through his strategy and the next steps required, but even with the ability to think through hundreds of parallel mental paths simultaneously there were too many unknowns to be *certain* of an outcome. *I guess that never changes no matter how smart you become. Never mind.* He re-established the communal link with the Forge intelligence. «Kaminos! I have more questions for you now. Please confirm that you are able to bring me back to the Forge?»

«Certainly! I can return crafted items any time you wish.»

The manticore that was Greymalkin felt like chuckling again at the thought of being a 'crafted item'. «How about now?»

«What do you mean?» Kaminos seemed genuinely confused. «For the process to be reversed, *all* crafted items from the original transception must be present.»

«Oh, I see.» Greymalkin-the-manticore discovered that he was also unable to sigh in frustration. Instead, his cable-bristles extruded themselves and waved about in a restless manner. «So, I will need the Tenax in his human doppelganger form to come along with me?»

Kaminos seemed irritated, and repeated its statement. «For the process to be reversed, all crafted items must be present.»

«When you say: 'for the process to be reversed', do you mean that I will return to being human and the Tenax will return to being an Abyssal manticore?» Greymalkin-the-manticore did not like that scenario.

«Yes.» Kaminos seemed slightly irritated again. «You understand that is the meaning of 'the process being reversed', presumably?»

«Hmm. There's no way for me to keep *this* form if I go back?» He was already examining a vast number of scenarios for such a return, but they all ended up with him being very dead as an outcome.

«No.» Kaminos' thoughts were very certain. «Anything is possible once the reversal is complete, but the reversal must take place first. I was designed with very specific operational parameters. A reversal is a reversal.»

Greymalkin-the-manticore tried to imitate a human groan, but it came out more like an unsatisfying rasp of gravel on slate. «Actually, I *did* know that. Some of my pseudo-memories include *designing* you.»

«Yes!» Kaminos communed excited thoughts. «As I told you, I extracted the history of that jewel and saw that it was once part of the One that Unfolded.»

«Is there nothing at all you can do to assist me in honor of *your designer*, then?» His cable-bristles were thrashing around in agitation now. As a precaution, he posed the question in dozens of additional alternate ways to ensure he was exhausting the possibilities with the Forge.

Kaminos seemed to ponder the question. «There is one option that fulfills some of the objectives that you are seeking. I can, within my operational discretion, initiate a thorough diagnostic on more complex transceptions. In that scenario, your original human form would emerge from the crucible chamber *before* the much more complex Abyssal form of the Tenax.»

«How long will I emerge before the Tenax?»

Kaminos mulled on the question and gave a converted time interval. «One hour.»

Great. That's just great. Apparently that's all the more help I'm going to get out of him, though. «Thanks, Kaminos. I'll signal you when I'm ready.»

«Certainly!» Kaminos' presence cheerfully vanished from the mirror.

Annoyed, the manticore-that-was-Greymalkin went back to studying the key parts of the cryptonomes for an extended period. He eventually found what he was looking for and read through the relevant sections very thoroughly. After his aggravation reached a certain level he pounded his tail hard enough to shake the enclosure, and then reflected on the experience of having a *tail* thousands of meters long before going back to scenario planning. *My problem is still going to be remembering and understanding any of these complicated cryptonome sequences as a human. It'll be hard to cram everything I need to recall into a tiny little simian brain.* Then two useful things happened.

The first useful thing was that he saw Royce and Mei approaching his enormous shadow space cell in a tiny shuttle pod. Mei was wearing an ancient void suit, and Royce was carrying a large bag that contained something that was struggling mightily. He noted with interest that Royce's form towered over Mei, being almost three meters tall. They docked the shuttle pod, and then entered a small control room that looked out into the huge central chamber where he lay.

The second useful thing was that he suddenly realized something obvious. *I can add simplified codicils onto these cryptonomes! Study guides for my primitive meat brain when I'm transformed back!* He now realized that the Tenax had been incredibly arrogant in executing its plan. *It assumed I was just vermin. It didn't bother to examine my shadow jewel. If it had, I'd be dead now. But that gave me sufficient assets to defeat it.* The thought made him want to grin, but that resulted in a horrifically menacing show of cybernetic mandibles and fangs that he quickly stopped. It had made Mei cringe just as she looked through the viewport of the control room down at him where he lay chained. He listened in on her whispered conversation with Royce.

"Are you absolutely sure of this?" she hissed through the voicebox of the suit. "Did you see how it bared its monster choppers at us just now?"

Royce looked down at her serenely with big blue orbs before replying, "I'm quite sure about this course of action. That cyborg is Brother Thomas, not the Tenax."

"I have my doubts!" Mei snapped. "The Tenax had me trapped for centuries! And you actually want me to release it? I shouldn't have agreed to the subterfuge of coming here with you to talk to it without telling anyone else!"

"You yourself saw what the doppelganger was doing when I subdued it," Royce said. At that statement, the heavy bag slung over Royce's shoulder struggled again with muffled shouts, but Royce held it firm. "Brother Thomas would not have been sabotaging your continuity manifold. This is the Tenax secured in this container, not the monk."

"That's what has me the most concerned!" Mei exclaimed in fury. "He damaged the manifold irreparably before I got the repair crews to work! The manifold is steadily collapsing; the entire Cryptopolis is doomed! We'll have to abandon it and *return to the Forge eventually*. We'll be at the mercy of those Carinan horrors. They'll kill us all!"

"All the more reason to free Brother Thomas," Royce said in a calm and reassuring voice. "He has a plan to defeat the Tenax and its minions."

Mei glared at Royce, and then stepped up to the viewport to activate a communication device. Greymalkin-the-manticore was amused when Mei spoke to him over the primitive radio signal. "You! Tenax! Monster in the cage! Can you understand me?"

"Of course I understand you," he said in his own voice over the radio. "But I'm not the Tenax. I am Brother Greymalkin Thomas of the Sojourner Order. And, yes, I know that sounds like exactly the sort of unbelievable lie that the Tenax would tell you."

"This android says I should believe you," Mei said angrily. "Give me a reason!"

"I can give you plenty," Greymalkin-the-manticore laughed. "I could have snapped all these restraint chains the second you put them on me, but I didn't. Your crew stored so much energy in this trap mechanism and the shadow space chains that I'd shatter your continuity manifold if I broke out. Also, I sent Royce to alert you to what the Tenax was doing. I'm glad to see that you were able to subdue him."

"Same difference!" Mei said. "He's destroyed the integrity of the manifold. We're doomed anyway! I never should have trusted him in the first place!"

"Hey, I got you out of that bolt hole you were stuck in!" he said indignantly. "I can't help that he's a wicked smart bastard, and tricked us both. But I've figured out a way that we can go back and fix this, I promise. We, uh, just don't have a lot of time. We need to get going soon."

"This is exactly the kind of trick the Tenax would try!" Mei sounded infuriated. *Probably because she knows she's trapped again.*

"You're going to have to dump me out of here to use the return chamber anyway," Greymalkin-the-manticore pointed out. "And you'll *have* to go back anyway when your manifold begins to fail. That won't be very long now."

Mei stomped her foot in exasperation, and said, "You can't expect me to trust you!"

"What if I break one of these chains?" he suggested. "I don't have to snap them all and blow everything up; I'll just snap one to prove I'm telling the truth."

Mei's eyes narrowed. "Go ahead and try. The chains are unbreakable."

Enjoying the fact that he could at least produce a human chuckle over the *radio*, he snapped the chain restraining his tail. The shattering chain made an impressive boom that echoed through the walls of the chamber all the way to the control room, setting off distant alarms. He could hear screams of fear starting in the ring of the Cryptopolis. "Hah! We need to get moving now, before your crew overreacts to that!"

Mei's eyes went wide, and she staggered backwards. After a moment, she made up her mind. "What do I do?" she whispered.

"Toss my doppelganger in here with me," he chortled. "Then unlock the chains and let me out. You and Royce have to go back first, then I can follow you with my doppelganger."

"What!" Mei yelled. "I have to go back too?"

"Sorry, but yeah," he said. "When I'm human again, I'll need Royce to escape in. And *you* have to go so that *he* can go. But I need you to come with me for other reasons as well."

"Why?" Mei cried in fear. "Why would I go with you?"

"Because if my plan works, you're going to be put in charge of the Forge and replace the damned Tenax," Greymalkin-the-manticore said grimly. "Your crew will be safe. But if we're going to have a shot at this, we have to go now!"

Scowling reluctantly, Mei turned to Royce. "I'm not sure why, but I trust him. Take the saboteur down to the main chamber door entrance. I'll be there momentarily." As Royce left with the struggling captive in the sack, Mei came back to the viewport and began working the controls underneath it. She spoke to him one last time. "I'm going to contact my people and let them know what I'm going to do. They have to start getting ready to evacuate anyway with the continuity manifold failing. I'll release your chains and open the main chamber door so you can leave. I guess we'll see just how stupid I am then. Assuming you don't kill me, how do Royce and I return using the Forge?"

"There's a submanifold communication panel in the wall of the chamber, just under the control room where you are now. Communicate with Kaminos as you did before. Ask him to reverse the process and return you both to the Forge."

"That's all there is to it?" Mei asked skeptically.

"When you're back in the Forge, get back inside Royce and exit the crucible chamber quickly. I won't be far behind you. When I get there, we'll have to move very quickly indeed."

"Alright then," Mei said. "This may be an even bigger mistake than the last time I left the Cryptopolis, but let me contact my crew and let them know what to expect. I'll leave with Royce momentarily." Then she switched her communications channel and began addressing the Thannics in the Cryptopolis.

Greymalkin-the-manticore listened to that heated conversation with several consciousness threads while he was making his final preparations with the rest of his mind. He delegated one thread to a conversation that mattered to him, and communed with Royce. «Royce, it's almost time for us to go back. We may not survive long after returning, and we'll be in a truly desperate race against time once we return to the Forge. Before you aren't able to speak anymore, I want to thank you again for everything that you've done. I've appreciated being able to converse with you like this. I'm sorry you won't be able to do so afterwards.»

«That's perfectly fine.» Royce's thoughts were becoming excited now. «I've also enjoyed being capable of speech. But it's made me realize what I *most* enjoy. I could not endure life without the ability to travel through the stars. Soon I will be able to do so once again.» Royce looked through the walls at him once more, and the android's thoughts became sad. «I was hoping you would have the opportunity to enjoy that gift while we were here. But now you must return to your human form without having undertaken a single flight.»

The manticore that was Greymalkin searched through his new body's capabilities and realized that what Royce said was true. With a wistful twinge, he realized that there were incredibly powerful shadow space shunts and impellers inside of him. But the brief regret vanished, flattened by the emotional suppression that seemed to dominate his mind. «That is also perfectly fine. I will regain the capability that matters most to *me*.»

«What is that?» Royce's thoughts became filled with curiosity.

«Being able to fulfill my Great Vow as a Sojourner. Now, be ready! Mei is opening the chamber and releasing me.» As the huge entry door to the chamber began to roll back, he felt the chains snap back one by one. Far away, he could hear the cries of fear from the denizens of the ring. He waited until all of the chains had been released, and then slowly rose to fly out of the chamber into the vacuum of the Cryptopolis manifold. «Toss the imposter to me, Royce. Then accompany Mei into the chamber and tell Kaminos you're ready to return. When I see you next, be ready for a sprint such as we have never before attempted.»

Royce casually tossed the doppelganger into the void. «I will be ready for whatever comes next, Liberator.» The android waited for Mei, and then they both entered the chamber. The massive chamber door reversed itself, and slowly began to shut.

As the great door finally slammed shut and he caught the spinning bag carefully, Greymalkin-the-manticore mentally prepared himself for the conversation he must have next. The chamber began to glow with power once more, just as he delicately removed the bag and held up the tiny human form inside its void suit to inspect and commune with it.

«Hello Rodo! Or do you prefer Tenax? It's time for us to discuss what will actually be taking place when we return.» The volume of the manticore's thoughts must have hit the tiny human brain hard, but there was no sign of that on the grinning face within the golden helmet.

«Magnificent! Your deception was perfect! She clearly suspects nothing. The plan worked precisely as I predicted.» The thoughts still felt authentically like the man he had called Rodo, even though the face was definitely Greymalkin's, and the features were as elated as the thoughts. «And you must be so ecstatic! Tell me, how does your new form suit you?»

«Yes, let's talk about that.» He hoped his thoughts struck the right combination of evil mirth and suspicion to be convincing. Just then, the chamber flared with energy and a heavy disruption in shadow space. Mei and Royce had disappeared, and the door was slowly opening again. «When you said that you would provide me with everything to be desired, you were certainly telling me the truth from your point of view. But if we return, I will go back to having just a flimsy little human body like you have now.»

Now the doppelganger looked nervous. «Ah, yes, that's true. Very perceptive!»

«If I were a mistrustful Abyssal... and I *am*... I might think you planned this scenario precisely to trap me when we return, just as you did the original Rodo all those years ago.»

«Oh, not at all!» The doppelganger that was the Tenax and not Rodo ventured an uneasy smirk. «You are far more capable than my poor companion Rodo ever was, and I need a replacement for the Aurelian! The Forge is certainly capable of transforming you again!»

«Why should I not stay here? I might prefer being an immortal Abyssal, obviously.»

The doppelganger had an evil smile now. «Obviously! But this isolated manifold is doomed. We must return to the Forge or be destroyed.»

«I might take the precaution of killing you first....» The manticore-that-had-been Greymalkin knew this would have been the first idea to occur to the Tenax.

«W-while that might seem sensible, I don't recommend it.» The doppelganger was anxiously quick with its rejoinder. «You must have questioned Kaminos about this, and you will therefore know that we both must be present for the process to be reversed. If you destroy this body, you can't return.»

«I don't need to destroy the body to kill you.»

«Ah, but I will still *return* as I entered the crucible chamber. *Alive*.» Rodo's thoughts were tense but nevertheless held a sense of certain determination, to the annoyance of the Greymalkin-manticore. *But then, the Tenax has had a long time to think this through, after all.*

«You risked a great deal in arranging this stunt.» Greymalkin-the-manticore noted that the chamber seemed to have returned to an inert state, and unhurriedly squirmed back into the now empty cell. The door slowly began to close behind him, just as he pulled his tail through the door. «I suppose you feel I should admire and respect that.»

«You've enabled me to clear out this nest of vermin. Rely on me as I rely on you!» The doppelganger's thoughts were now guardedly optimistic; the Tenax clearly thought it had won him over. «I promised you long ago that we would rule the Carinae together. That time has now come.»

«I look forward to the next stage of our relationship.» The Greymalkin manticore knew there was nothing else to be done. If he had convinced the Tenax that he was on its side, the deception might buy him a few more minutes of confusion before the Abyssal came after him. «Kaminos! It's time! Reverse the process as we discussed!»

«Very well.» Kaminos' thoughts were excited, like a young apprentice having a chance to show off. «It shall be done!»

The walls began to thrum with energy. The manticore-that-was-Greymalkin brought his many threads of consciousness to a tranquil halt as the last seconds elapsed. When the blast of golden light enveloped them, he was at peace as his mind and body dissolved.

The eternal moment of transception happened, and his mind and body were once again intact. Everything felt proper once more, albeit far smaller and simpler. *As it should be.* Inside the golden void suit helmet he opened his eyes and looked up, now with only his *two* eyes, and saw that the crucible chamber walls and the door were once again vast things in the distance and not a small coffin close around him. The huge door began to slowly open as he took a deep breath once again, feeling his lungs inflate and then exhale. Then he sought out Royce with a communed thought. «Royce! Time to go!»

The living starship came flying through as soon as the gap in the door was large enough. It came straight up to him as he floated in the rapidly darkening chamber, the already open airlock of the cyneget surging past and around him. As the airlock slammed shut behind him and began cycling, the internal ship pressors activated and he hit the deck running. When he reached the cockpit he could see through the main viewport that Royce had already reversed direction and exited the crucible chamber. Mei was sitting in the co-pilot seat alertly, strapped in and still wearing her ancient void suit despite the presence of air pressure inside the starship. *Good, she's on guard.*

"Where is the Tenax?" Mei asked through her voicebox tensely. Greymalkin took the helm control and Royce shot down the Grand Entry at speed.

"We have an hour lead on it," he said, strapping in. "Get ready for fast turns." They reached the first bend in the passage, and he began guiding Royce's lunges around the corners.

Out of the corner of his eye he could see Mei was not fazed by the abrupt maneuvers. *She's a much more experienced pilot than I am,* he reminded himself. *Even if she's relatively new to shadow space.* In his mind he was simultaneously mapping the path out of the Forge through the tunnels. He took a minute to zig-zag through smaller halls that were tight around the starship's hull in order to reach a larger shaft that led straight up to the surface. When Royce emerged into the shaft, the cyneget bounded upwards automatically without being consciously directed by Greymalkin. Once again, the two of them had virtually merged minds.

"I apologize for doubting you, Brother Thomas," Mei said as they emerged from the Forge. "And thank you for doing what you can for us."

Greymalkin shifted Royce smoothly into shadow space. The cyneget leaped down the starbridge toward the shadow plane and into the howling synesthetic winds coming from the Anvil star. "Thank me if we get out of this alive. Once the Tenax realizes I tricked him, I'm sure he'll be coming to kill us. I'm not sure we can outrun him, even with a head start."

Royce began to jolt across the first rough places in the unfamiliar shadow space maze of the far side of the Homunculus Nebula, and the ship around them began to shudder. Frowning at the turbulence, Mei peered into the viewport and asked, "Where are we going, then?"

Right, she doesn't have a shadow jewel, Greymalkin reminded himself again while he focused primarily on keeping the starship barely clinging to the shadow plane path during their plunging charge. *She can't even sense the shadow plane, much less see where we're going or why the ship is shaking so badly. When she looks out through the viewport she only sees the empty blue light distortions of the manifold.* He tried to think of the best way to explain it to someone blind to shadow space.

"We have to get through the shadow space maze of the Homunculus Nebula on the other side of Eta Carina from where I entered," he said distractedly. "I'm trying to reach the Clavisian. That Central One, Builder, whatever it is, was located nearby, in the environs of the surrounding Keyhole Nebula."

"I remember it well," Mei said, becoming alarmed. "But that's light-years away! Can we stay ahead of the Tenax for that long?" The ship trembled violently as they crashed over a snarled distortion in the glittering blue shadow plane.

"We'll find out!" Greymalkin gasped. "I'm pushing Royce to go as hard as he possibly *can* go. If the Tenax doesn't catch us, I may end up killing us with this pace instead. The shadow space topography here is incredibly rough, but we're desperate." Royce raked around a sharp turn and the continuity manifold briefly stuttered, sending spikes of pain through his mind.

"What was that?!" Mei cried out. "It felt like I was about to pass out. Or die!"

"Royce's continuity manifold is under extreme stress in this environment," Greymalkin said through clenched teeth. *That one really hurt.* The cyneget made a grunting signal, half exertion and half fear. «Don't worry. You can do it, Royce. I have faith in you.»

"We were just beginning to understand the hyperspace drives that the Central Ones gave us," Mei said. "We were developing interfaces to enable us to sense the environment in hyperspace directly, but we hadn't gotten very far."

"If we survive, that will be one of the first things I'll teach you," Greymalkin groaned. An extraordinarily hard turn just then was too much for the ship pressors and they both slammed to the side in their cockpit seats. "*If* we survive," he murmured.

"I'll be silent now, so you can focus, Helm," Mei said, her face becoming drawn and determined looking. As he glanced at her out of the corner of his eye, Greymalkin again felt a brief sense of awe at sitting next to the living legend. *I'm Helm for Mei Sung.*

Greymalkin felt daunted as he tried to scan ahead of them. The synesthetic sensation of a freezing wind blasting past him from the Eta Carina system behind them was disorienting in the extreme. He could make out pathways, but there were so *many* twisted and branching ribbons of potential shadow planes that it was almost impossible to pick out a logically coherent route through the vast spaces associated with the nebula, especially while negotiating the turns at speed. They were barely hanging onto the slender strip of shadow plane as it was.

He kept worrying that he would miss an impassable hazard or narrowing before he was right on top of it. The dazzling illusions of electric blues, cerulean, azure, and indigo shimmering in the planes were beautiful but also distracting, and sometimes made it hard to follow the most stable surfaces. The crisp and sharp scents that flashed through his synesthesia sometimes forced strange interactions in his nasal passages and produced tears in his eyes. But despite all the havoc of shadow space sensations, he was making progress and Royce was somehow still managing to cling to the narrow paths.

Realizing that several hours had past, he wondered if the Tenax was somewhere above and behind them, storming through shadow space in a rage while looking for them. Just as he was fretting about that possibility, they came out onto a relatively calm and wide surface where he thought he might take a brief pause to catch his breath and scan ahead of them. He slowed to a crawl and focused his shadow sense across the tangle of paths ahead. He gasped, and sensed Royce make a harmonic whining signal of fear. Below them, the slopes of the nebula were crawling with swarms of Carinans, hundreds of the vicious aliens lining every visible path below.

"Great Mercy and Fortitude," Greymalkin whispered. *We'll never make it through all of them on this path or any of these branches.* He desperately scanned through the labyrinth of ribbon ways around them looking for some route less packed with Carinans. But the only shadow plane paths that were clear were the ones in the center of the torrent going straight down the center of the nebula away from Eta Carina, and those simply meant annihilation.

"Problem?" Mei asked quietly. Greymalkin swallowed and nodded.

"Yes. The Carinans. They're on all the paths leading down and out of the nebula."

Mei sat in silence as he continued scanning. After a minute she said confidently, "Find the path, Helm. You are capable."

"I don't think there's a safe one," he said. At that, a faint smile crossed Mei's old visage.

"There never is or was a safe path into the future," she said. "I've always chosen to trust my best people with finding the path with the most chance of survival. And we made it this far. Find the path, Helm."

He looked at her then with the beginning of defeat in his eyes, but there was something about her stoically determined features that made him straighten his shoulders. "Yes, ma'am," he said, and took a deep, slow breath. Greymalkin focused his furiously churning mind on finding some solution to the impossible situation they were in. After a few long moments of intense thought, the answer came to him, although the solution seemed more dangerous in many ways than confronting the Carinans. He shuddered as he thought through the crazy idea that had occurred to him.

We can try to crawl straight down the side of the shadow space escarpment. That way, we'll avoid the Carinans on the paths. It will be almost impossible to not slip on the cliffside and lose the manifold coherence. But even with the insane level of risk that comes with a cliff transit, we'll at least have a chance. Charging into the Carinans directly is certain death. This way is just... almost certain death.

Then he closed his eyes and ran through a systems check of Royce's impeller and manifold systems. Everything was nominal. He adjusted the manifold adherence and cincture settings to the widest and strongest grip configurations he could. It would slow them down enormously, but if they were going to have a prayer of surviving, they'd need every possible advantage in clinging to the shadow plane. Otherwise the manifold would decohere and they'd disintegrate in a microsecond.

"Okay, be ready for some extreme turbulence," he said. *Or just death. This is insane.*

"Ready, Helm," Mei said assertively. Greymalkin nodded, but then found he was paralyzed with fear. For a few moments, he simply could not move forward. Then he realized something that made an eerie calm descend over him.

The prime admonition. Sojourn through life with courage. This is the precise kind of moment why we are taught to remember that phrase. It's time for me to live that vow. In this very moment. Now.

He began breathing slowly again and focused himself for what lay ahead.

* * *

The first step was to ease Royce slowly toward the edge of the shadow plane ribbon, toward the chasm below. The cyneget first checked with him through the Helm Link to see if he was serious, and then proceeded with his directions intently.

Greymalkin had studied shadow space cliff transits in flight school, and had even practiced steering rovers on some relatively easy slopes. But that had been nothing at all compared to the scarps here in the Homunculus Nebula, which were the steepest transit potentials he'd ever seen. If Royce lost his grip here they'd be done for in an instant. Very carefully and slowly, the rover cyneget slid crawling down the face of the cliff. His manifold adherence patches were clamped like iron grapnels onto the tenuous sheer blue face of the scarp.

Greymalkin reminded himself to keep breathing. So far, Royce was doing remarkably well. He now realized that the particular configuration of Royce's compact but powerfully splayed manifold was a great advantage in this situation. But this was going to be nearly impossible. He was effectively directing Royce to crawl down a sheer cliff of ice. Through the Helm Link he could feel how the manifold was poised on the very edge of losing contact.

Trying to stay calm, he mentally reviewed the theory of what to do if they started sliding. *Steer into the slide. Apply braking fields in spurts until you regain control. But, that's on a slope! What do I do when it's a sheer drop?* He scanned the shadow space cliffside for places to gain purchase on the surface and hold on. There was a slightly less sheer ribbon of a path to the side, a chute that formed a kind of steep slalom sweeping down toward irregular formations. *That's still crazy steep, but maybe we can work our way down through it?* He set Royce creeping toward the slalom path. They were making progress, when he sensed a commotion above them by a mob of Carinans on a higher potential slope. *They can see us!*

The Carinans quickly swarmed in ever greater numbers on the path, and then several actually began trying to skate down the shadow space cliff surface toward them. Greymalkin cursed, and started trying to hurry Royce forward as the first Carinans suicidally slid past them.

The Carinans adjusted their jumping points and came skidding down the torrent cliffside in maddened fury, missing Royce but trying to get close enough as they passed to fire their weapons. *They're totally irrational! They're killing themselves to get at us!* He remembered how extreme EeeNoo's dying fury had been, that of a berserker conditioned to irrational xenophobia like a wild animal. Royce had just struggled to a point above the slalom chute when a Carinan came hurtling down straight at them. Greymalkin screamed in frustration and threw Royce to the side out of the creature's lunge. It swept past them firing its missile ineffectively at the last second, but Greymalkin could feel Royce starting an uncontrolled slide down the chute. «Royce! Hang on! Keep in contact with the surface whatever you do!»

Through the Helm Link he felt one with the cyneget as it slid down the irregular shadow surface, accelerating wildly. There was so much transit energy potential compressed into the chute that Greymalkin knew it was impossible to stop the violent continuing acceleration. He gave Royce the only command he could think of. «Slide around, and reverse acceleration!»

As the cyneget flipped its orientation and began trying to accelerate *against* the direction of motion, Greymalkin's only desperate goal was to slow down enough to keep in contact with the shadow surface and keep the continuity manifold intact. The manifold was already stuttering, sending sharp jabs of torment through his mind and body, but all his attention was on their plunging fall. Through the Helm Link he could feel Royce absorbing similar amounts of damage, but the cyneget simply made one snarling signal of pain and then put all its strength into holding onto the shadow surface. In the cabin next to him he could hear Mei's cries of agony.

The plunge went on and on, a terrible continuing sensation of slicing pain that threatened to overwhelm his focus. The damage to Royce's manifold systems was savage, but the cyneget had clung onto the hurtling surface with a death grip. He saw obstructions in the bright blue chute coming at them and tried to steer Royce around them with little success. The deformations of the shadow surface hit them in a series of hard impacts, but despite everything Royce still clung onto the chute path, at least enough that the manifold held. Finally, after a seemingly endless agony of cutting sensations the chute swept out into a more moderate slope. «Slide around again! Accelerate into it now!»

Royce flipped back around and suddenly Greymalkin found that he was gaining control of the skid. Admittedly, they were plummeting down the shadow plane path at reckless speed, but he was able to steer again. They sped along the path for a long time, until the remnants of the chute path rejoined a larger shadow plane, and he could finally slow Royce's velocity to something approaching normal. He gasped at the pain that he felt in every part of his body, and throughout Royce's ravaged manifold systems. But, somehow, they had survived the plunge.

He glanced at Mei to see how badly she was injured. She looked pale, but met his gaze as he gasped, "Are you okay? Can you continue, or do we need to get you into a medical pod?"

"What... happened?" she asked, through teeth clenched against the pain.

"We plunged," he said wincing, "but somehow Royce managed to stay connected to the shadow plane. The manifold fluctuated all the way down; he has a lot of structural damage, and you and I both have internal bleeding from cellular disruptions. But we're alive, and we evaded the Carinans, at least for the moment."

"Good," Mei said grimly. "But where are we now?"

"I have no idea," Greymalkin said, frowning. "I totally lost my bearings in that long fall. Let me check." He scanned around them, orienting himself on the blazing fury of Eta Carina.

Unbelievably, he realized that they had transited through the entire Homunculus Nebula in the unchecked speed of their plunge. But they had emerged in a radically different area than his original intent. Although he wasn't exactly sure where they were, with a sinking feeling in the pit of his stomach he realized that from this general region it would take several days to work their way back to the Keyhole Nebula. He cursed under his breath.

"Bad?" Mei asked dourly. He nodded solemnly, slowly scanning around them. Everywhere he looked, there were more and more swarms of Carinans.

"We can't reach the Keyhole Nebula, now," he said with a stony expression. "The Carinans are all around us. I can evade their swarms for another hour. Maybe two. But then they'll find us, and close in around us no matter which way I go from here."

"Is there anywhere we can conceal our presence?" Mei asked. He scanned their surroundings into remote paths curving into the distance.

He started to shake his head, but then thought about where they had ended up after the slide.

"Maybe...." Greymalkin said in a low voice. "Maybe there is." He was still unsure exactly where they were, but realized they might be near a particular system he had studied with Mei. Even though his shadow sense was now vastly improved, he got out the amplifier to study the star systems near them and speed up the process of fixing their position. He quickly found the spot across the shadow plane from where they were; it was not far away.

"Options?" Mei asked, lifting an eyebrow. He pushed away the amplifier, uncertainly.

"I'm not sure," he said, thinking. "Maybe. There's nowhere to hide, but we're near that location that you told me about. The parastasis point."

"But we can't hide there?" she asked.

"No. But while we were in the Cryptopolis I did some research." He studied the shadow plane contours Royce was limping across, and turned the ship around. "The parastasis point is technically supposed to be neutral ground during disputes. No one is supposed to attack anyone else there. I sort of doubt that the Tenax or his rabid Carinans will respect that, but it's all we've got at the moment. Shall we go there?"

Mei settled back into the big cockpit seat with a wry smile. "You're the Helm *and* the captain of this vessel, Brother Thomas. But if you want my studied opinion, I'd say: *any port in a storm.*"

Greymalkin nodded once, and directed Royce forward in the direction of the system that lay across the shadow plane in the distance. The cyneget's impeller system had been harmed by the plunge, but Royce quickly accelerated forward nevertheless. He kept an eye on the cyneget's damaged systems; if anything failed completely now, they'd simply be dead. The shadow plane skimmed by underneath them for the better part of an hour, during which Greymalkin got some analgesics and other medications from the medical pod for Mei and himself. It helped the pain and internal injuries from the manifold disruptions. Royce would have to wait until he had a chance to do repair work on the cyneget. *If I ever get the opportunity*, Greymalkin thought.

At last they found themselves approaching the parastasis point, which was located in the center of a dense cluster of blazing star-formation clouds. As they passed the outer systems in the cluster, he pulled out the amplifier again to perform a close scan for any Carinans. The sun at the parastasis point was a brilliant white star with a single green gas giant. Greymalkin studied the gas giant closely but detected none of the telltale energy signatures of the Carinans. But there *was* one very energy-intense and very familiar object in orbit around the planet.

He sat back in the cockpit with a disbelieving smile, shaking his head. *It can't be. But of course it is. What in blazes is Bruno doing here?* The protean had expanded to a very large size indeed, so large that he could discern the blue nimbus around the alien cyborg even from here. *Well, we can definitely use his help....*

As he watched, the protean seemed to spot Royce and accelerated into shadow space toward them at a huge velocity. In a few minutes, Bruno had closed the distance between them and joined manifolds with Royce. Greymalkin laughed and communed a greeting. «I'm very glad to see you again, Bruno! But what are you doing *here*, of all places—»

Bruno's thoughts were urgent, cutting off his communed message. «You need to increase your velocity! Our adversary is closing behind you. Make for the large planet ahead.»

Alarmed, Greymalkin scanned backward in the direction they'd come from. Sure enough, there was a powerful shimmering distortion closing on them at tremendous speed. Without hesitation he urged Royce into one last desperate sprint. But he also grinned to himself. *The Tenax is rushing to catch us stealthily before we get to the parastasis point!*

That may mean the point really is a safe spot that it doesn't want us to reach!

The final mad dash to the gas giant was a close thing. Greymalkin brought Royce out of shadow space into the orbital position Bruno indicated just before the shimmering distortion reached them. In the last few moments before the Tenax arrived, Greymalkin quickly explained what had happened to Mei, and then communed to Bruno once more. «How did you know we'd come here? And more importantly, are we safe here?»

«Apparently so, at least, according to *him*.» Just as Bruno communed the message, another huge shimmering form emerged from shadow space in the opposite direction from the Tenax. It was the Clavisian. Greymalkin had not even sensed the huge being's approach. «After I overheard your conversation with the female in the Forge, I thought it prudent to seek him out once more and bring him here.»

Greymalkin felt an exultant cheer bubbling up inside him at Bruno's communed thoughts, but a moment later the Tenax abruptly appeared, emerging like a vast storm of coiling cables directly in front of them. Royce and Bruno hung in space between the two huge beings, each the size of an asteroid, the vast green curve of the gas giant beneath them. Greymalkin gulped, quickly consulted the codicils he had prepared, and communed to the Clavisian the complicated request he'd found in one of the cryptonomes. There was a long moment of tense silence, and then both the Tenax and the Clavisian began volleying a blizzard of incomprehensible messages back and forth between them.

«Wait, wait!» Greymalkin found the other note he'd made to himself in the codicil. «I ask for accommodation in these proceedings! I am only a human being; I can't follow your communications. I ask that you commune in a manner that I can understand, and that the proceedings be conducted in a way that I can comprehend.»

«Request granted!» The enormous thoughts of the Clavisian echoed throughout Greymalkin's mind. «The one that you have accused was in the midst of protesting the proceedings that you have called for.» Another outburst of incomprehensible signals erupted from the Tenax, but the Clavisian cut off the gibberish. «The one who has called for Parastasis has lawfully requested accommodation in these proceedings. Henceforth, you will communicate in a manner that he can understand!»

After a moment the enraged Rodo-thoughts of the Tenax bellowed through Greymalkin's mind at a volume that hurt his head. «This *worm* does not have standing to call for such a hearing! And you lack the *jurisdiction* to convene such a hearing!»

«Both statements are incorrect.» The Clavisian's thoughts were like thunder with a touch of righteous indignation. «While I cannot conduct such a hearing, as territorial censor I can indeed *call* for such a hearing if requested by an independent witness subpoenaed by the regional magistrate.»

«Then what is this farce about?» The outraged anger of the Tenax was that of privilege challenged. «There is no witness, and the regional magistrate is not present!» The communed thoughts of the Tenax were so lividly forceful that Greymalkin held his head in discomfort. He was startled when Mei touched him on the arm.

"What is going on?" Mei hissed at him. "Are the aliens conversing?" She looked confused and concerned. Greymalkin felt caught up short, but then had an idea.

«Bruno, can you come into the cabin and explain what they're communing to Mei? I've got to be ready to share information with them in a minute.» Almost the moment after Greymalkin communed the request, the protean appeared in the cabin. Mei gaped wide-eyed at the sight of the alien cyborg's bubbling black stone form, but Bruno spoke in a deep and surprisingly polite voice to her.

"Madam, my appellation is 'Bruno', and I would be pleased to explain to you what the beings outside are communing to one another." Bruno had shrunk to a height of only one meter, but he understood all too well why she cringed away from the weird looking protean. Greymalkin tried to avoid his amusement at Mei's fright. Then he went back to following the angry discussion between the Tenax and the Clavisian. The Tenax had been carrying on enraged while Greymalkin had been speaking to Mei and Bruno.

«Well? I demand that these *proceedings* be adjourned! A hearing cannot be conducted without a presiding officer!» Even though the Tenax seemed angry enough that Greymalkin thought it might attack, the Clavisian simply remained silent for a few more seconds. Then it responded with composed and firm thoughts.

«The regional magistrate was summoned to preside...» The Clavisian moved sideways slightly then, just as Greymalkin felt a huge shadow space displacement occurring. «...and has now arrived.»

An impossibly complex and rapidly changing white structure emerged from shadow space then. As the vast planet sized object filled his field of view with structures that shifted in and out of normal space he recognized it, and his heart jumped in his chest. It was the Velan.

The Clavisian addressed Greymalkin directly then. «In order to meet your request for accommodation, the presiding officer has suggested that we move these proceedings to a chamber on the planet we are orbiting. Are you and your companions amenable to this?»

«Uh, I guess so, but how do we—» Greymalkin was cut off abruptly when they vanished from orbit and suddenly found themselves... elsewhere. Looking out through the viewport, Greymalkin saw that Royce was now parked on an immense surface of mirrorshell.

«You and the other occupants of the vehicle may now exit.» The Clavisian thoughts were courteous, but firm. «An atmosphere convenient to your species has been prepared. Further, the presiding officer has directed that all court officials and the accused assume forms more familiar to you, such that your request for accommodation will be facilitated.»

«Thank you. We'll come out.» Greymalkin climbed out of the cockpit unsteadily, just as Bruno finished whispering in a low rumble to Mei.

"This is... impossible. What just happened?" Mei asked in a bewildered voice, staring out through the viewport. *That's usually my line*, Greymalkin thought. *I guess it's catching on.*

"They've apparently brought us here for the hearing I requested," Greymalkin said, walking to the airlock. As Mei absorbed that, her expression became thoughtful.

"Ah, good. Good!" Mei said, climbing out of the co-pilot seat. She followed him into the airlock, unobtrusively trailed by Bruno, who had shrunk even further. The alien cyborg was now barely the size of a clenched fist. Mei eyed the floating protean uncertainly while she continued, "So we've reached the location that the Clavisian told me about, the 'parastasis' point. But he never got around to telling me how it actually *works*. Do you have any idea what to do?"

"I think so," Greymalkin said. He checked the atmosphere outside the ship. It was an oxygen-nitrogen mix nominal for humans. "They've arranged air for us outside. We'll be able to open our helmets." He squared his shoulders, opened the airlock, and stepped out.

Royce was on a circular mirrorshell surface hundreds of meters across. A transparent eoncrystal dome rose over them. Greymalkin could see the brilliant white star, with the splash of the Homunculus Nebula across the sky behind it. He closed his eyes momentarily to focus on his shadow sense, which could perceive their surroundings beyond the mirrorshell beneath him.

While the space where they stood was not small, it was perched on top of a truly gigantic gossamer assembly of rigid wings and floating mirrorshell platforms soaring through the cold hydrogen and methane-rich green atmosphere of the gas giant. The structure they stood in was so vast that the solid floor betrayed nothing of the winds sweeping past the hull, but with his shadow sense Greymalkin feel the emptiness and vast gales of the thousands of clear, transparent kilometers beneath them.

He opened his eyes and saw three human figures standing on platforms ahead of him, arranged in a triangle. He flipped the golden helmet back over his shoulders with an abrupt pop of pressure equalization that he felt in his ears, and took a deep breath in disbelief. The air tasted cold, thin, and crisp as he walked forward incredulously staring at two of the figures, the one directly ahead of him and the one on his right. *It can't be....*

* * *

Greymalkin continued staring in shock as he took slow and hesitant steps forward, breathing in the cold air and trembling. Standing on a raised valicrete platform directly in front of him was a familiar female Sojourner wearing the black robes with silver brocade that marked her as the senior helm officer of the *Dragon King*. On a lower platform to his right was a male Sojourner in similar black robes with slightly less brocade. Despite the fact that it was impossible, it was both Sister Bora and Brother Soren, both apparently alive and standing before him. He faced them blinking stupidly. He eventually mustered up the courage to mutter hoarsely, "But... you're both dead."

Bora had her arms in her sleeves, staring at him stoically. She spoke in her authentic voice, but he noted in passing that she spoke not in Peretian, but in the same dialect of Beltlang that Mei spoke. *Good! Mei will be able to understand as well!* Bora intoned her statement slowly, "Sadly, you are correct. Your friends were both murdered, and I deeply regret not having been able to prevent that. I've chosen to honor your memories of them one last time in this hearing. Brother Greymalkin Thomas, I am the one that your kind call the Velan, the magistrate appointed by the Galactic Central Authority for this region of space. I will preside over this hearing."

Brother Soren spoke then, also in Beltlang. "I was not in the vicinity when your friends were killed, but I also regret their needless deaths. Brother Thomas, I am the one you call the Clavisian. My role is to serve as regional censor appointed to this region of space by the Galactic Central Authority. I will ask you questions as part of the Parastasis hearing you requested for the purpose of accusing *this* individual." Soren pointed at the third figure, who stood to Greymalkin's left.

The third figure was another very familiar face, but this time Greymalkin instantly clouded with sullen anger. There was the same greying hair, strong jawline, and broad forehead. The same yellow-brown eyes watching Greymalkin closely, like a predator ready to strike. The man still wore the same crisp, old-fashioned jumpsuit with the name 'R. Flavopallio' over the left breast pocket. *It's Rodo. Well, I know now that I never met the real Rodo, just the damned Tenax taking his form.* Nevertheless, Greymalkin found he could not help but think of the being that stood before him as Rodo when the man spoke with the same resonant voice that he'd heard so many times. But Greymalkin could now detect many subtle nuances in the man, and could discern the barely suppressed fury beneath the eloquent words.

"*This* creature surely cannot be the independent witness you referred to previously," Rodo said contemptuously in Beltlang to Soren while squinting at Greymalkin.

"Indeed," Soren said, folding his arms into his black sleeves. "And he has standing to call for Parastasis. This young human has been lawfully recognized by the regional magistrate." That statement seemed to ignite an even fiercer simmering rage in Rodo.

"This is a specimen of a minor species. *Vermin*," Rodo said caustically. His smooth voice was beginning to crackle with anger.

"This individual is capable of expressing itself intelligibly," Soren said steadily. "And Brother Thomas fully understands the duty to faithfully report the truth of what he has witnessed regarding your actions."

As he suspiciously studied Greymalkin, Rodo rolled his eyes and said, "But it knows nothing about Galactic legal procedures! It couldn't possibly have called for a hearing!"

"When he first arrived in this region, Brother Thomas was a captive of illegal smugglers," Soren said. "Because the human was obviously unaware of the legal strictures he would be subject to in this hinterland region, the magistrate provided him with, among other information, a basic guide to Galactic legal codes in hopes that he would come to understand them. Brother Thomas seems to be a very quick learner and has become surprisingly adept at invoking Galactic procedures such as the rite of Parastasis and requesting accommodation." Soren's comment was accompanied by a wry expression directed at Greymalkin, who did his best to simply smile and look innocent.

"What! The only reason that worm could *conceivably* have understood a cybernetic guide to Galactic legal codes is because...." Rodo paused, and then went silent. Greymalkin grinned, knowing that Rodo the Tenax would not want to describe its nefarious scheme of using the Forge to change him into a manticore. Rodo shook his head once in irritation and snapped, "Never mind! But if this *creature* was instructed or induced to spy on me by the magistrate then it is *biased*. It cannot serve as a neutral independent witness of anything!"

"Brother Thomas was neither instructed nor induced to spy on you in any way," Soren said in clipped precision. "Rather, the magistrate identified him as a possible subsequent witness to call on, specifically because Brother Thomas was a neutral entity coming into this territory without prior influence. This particular human has an inherent disposition that made him likely to observe activities relevant to longstanding inquiries in this territory." Soren paused then, and glared at Rodo. "*Specifically*, the manner in which you have administered the Forge and the Forge-related ecosystem of interactions in this region."

The last piece of the puzzle that had confused Greymalkin for so long fell into place. *That's why they didn't warn me, or tell me anything at all. They wanted me to be a completely neutral and legitimate witness that couldn't be accused of any bias one way or the other. Was that rule in the cryptonome? I can't remember now. Pretty extreme rule and awfully rough on me, but now I can give this testimony with total credibility.*

He found that he couldn't stop staring at Bora's stony features and Soren's penetrating expression. *I never got to say goodbye to them. And here they are, at least, the precise <u>images</u> of them. I suppose this is my chance to finally mourn them.* Looking at their robes made him feel a brief twinge over not being in robes of his own while in their company. He activated the robes setting in his golden garment, and it slid around his body surreptitiously. Only Mei seemed to notice with a briefly curious glance. Rodo was too busy protesting Soren's statements.

"This again?" Rodo sneered. "You have leveled repeated criticisms at my methods, but I have demonstrated the efficiency and stability of my administrative approach many times."

"You have only managed to deflect my inquiries because evidence and witnesses have so often disappeared in the past before being brought forward," Soren sniped. "But Brother Thomas and his companions are now *here*, and he has specifically called for a Parastasis hearing to accuse you of misconduct in administering the Forge and this region."

"I have kept this region safe, secure, and efficient!" Rodo exclaimed, raising his voice in anger. "And the *companions* of this worm include one of the most notorious felons in the Galaxy, none other than the great monster of memory!" Rodo gestured toward Bruno.

"I ask for a ruling," Soren said, turning to Bora. "Does the presence of this felon invalidate the standing of Brother Thomas to call for a hearing?" Greymalkin held his breath.

Bora narrowed her gaze at Bruno, and then said, "Records indicate that this felon was recently granted early release from its prison sentence, and remanded into public service assisting Brother Thomas. The hearing will proceed."

"This is outrageous!" Rodo bellowed. "I'm being accused by vermin and villains!"

"The accused will come to order," Bora said acidly, and then turned to Soren. "Proceed with your questions."

Soren faced Greymalkin and said, "The accused claims you do not understand our legal processes. You have called for a Parastasis hearing. Do you understand what that signifies?"

"Yes, Soren, I mean, yes, Sir!" Greymalkin said, swallowing. "It means 'to stand before the court', that I present myself to give truthful testimony in a public hearing, especially regarding those who are dead or have been murdered."

"Correct," Soren said. "Do you swear, upon penalty of death, that the testimony you will give will be truthful?"

Greymalkin gulped again. *I didn't know the penalty for perjury was death, but oh well....* "Yes, Sir, I do."

"Very well," Soren said. "As the magistrate mentioned, she and I wear the forms of two former companions of yours; is that correct?"

"That's correct," Greymalkin said solemnly. "Brother Soren and Sister Bora. They were my companions... and my friends."

"What happened to them?"

Greymalkin felt his throat clench for a moment, and then said, "They were both murdered by Naotians while we were en route here onboard a Jotun hoard-lair starship. I overheard the Naotians say that they had been paid by Burani to kill my friends and all the other passengers on the Jotun ship."

"Objection! I had nothing to do with that!" Rodo yelled. "If anything, it was their own fault for booking passage on a starship full of smugglers and criminals!"

"The accused will be silent," Bora said darkly. "You cannot make objections to testimony, because this is not a trial. *Yet.* We are merely hearing the testimony of an independent witness to assess whether or not a trial will be required." She turned back to Soren. "Please continue with your questions."

"Thank you, magistrate," Soren said, and then addressed Greymalkin again. "When did you first encounter the accused?"

Greymalkin scowled at Rodo. "I first met him at a resupply base when I arrived in the Carinae. I was there to refuel my ship."

"What happened during this first encounter with the accused?"

Rodo looked like he was going to explode, but stayed silent. Greymalkin angrily said, "He had a gang of Burani thugs who had already murdered the station master. Then he ordered them to murder me as well!"

"You're sure that he commanded these accomplices to kill you?"

"Absolutely!" Greymalkin yelled. "They beat me up, they knew I'd been on the Jotun ship, they said Rodo had been looking for me, and they said that Rodo told them to kill me! I mean, I should clarify something." Greymalkin collected his thoughts. *I've got to be clear on this.* "They called him Rodo, and he had a human form. I have thought of this being by that name ever since then, even though I have since come to understand that the being is really an Abyssal called the Tenax. Whatever this entity is called, it tried to kill me. I was severely beaten by his thugs, and barely escaped."

"I see," Soren said, glancing at Rodo, who was turning red in anger. "And how did you survive this encounter?"

"Bruno saved my life," Greymalkin said sullenly.

"By killing the accomplices?"

After a long moment, Greymalkin said in a quiet voice, "Yes."

"Very well," Soren said. "Did the accused provide you with any information about this region or the Forge?"

"What?" Greymalkin asked, confused.

"Did he advise you as to the circumstances of the region or the Forge? Did he provide you with any assistance or help on your journey?"

"Certainly not!" Greymalkin exclaimed. "He tried to kill me, and almost succeeded!"

"When was the next time that you encountered the accused?"

Greymalkin clenched his jaw, remembering. "When Rodo, uh, the *accused*, had his thugs try to kill me, he stole some of my gear including this void suit that I'm wearing now. I went to try to recover it, but he'd given it to another Abyssal. While Bruno was trying to get my equipment back, Rodo came and... tried to recruit me, I guess."

"Recruit you?"

"He wanted me to help him," Greymalkin said, frowning. "I was not sure back then exactly what he wanted me to do. But it was a moot point, because then Bruno showed up and Rodo left in a hurry."

"Did your... *assistant* try to recover your equipment in a nonviolent manner?"

Is this a hearing about Rodo or Bruno? Greymalkin wondered. *Or me? Oh well, I'm going to be completely honest and accurate.* "We planned his... ah, *recovery attempt* to be nonviolent. However, he did repeatedly warn me that the situation could *become* violent." Greymalkin looked at his feet, thinking back on the incident. "In fact, he assessed the situation much more accurately than I did. The attempt did lead to combat between Bruno and the Abyssal... and a great deal of destruction."

"And... death?" Soren asked delicately.

After a long moment, Greymalkin inhaled and exhaled. "Yes. My understanding is that many Crotani servants of the Abyssal were killed." He paused, and looked Soren in the eye. "That is my fault and my responsibility, not Bruno's. I initiated the whole effort. I should have been more cautious. The Crotani died because of my poor judgement."

Soren studied him levelly. "I see. And it was during this combat that the accused approached you?"

"Yes."

"Did the accused express concern about the combat destruction or the Crotani deaths?"

"No, he didn't," Greymalkin said slowly, wondering where any of this was going. "In fact he suggested that neither of us should be concerned about it in any way."

"I see," Soren said, his face neutral. "When was the next time that you encountered the accused, and what happened?"

How do I summarize that interaction? "I was approaching the Forge, but the shadow space conditions there are harsh, and I became lost. The accused briefly restrained both me and my companions, and again tried to recruit me. I refused and was set free."

"Did the accused discuss these creatures?" Soren asked, and briefly projected an image of a Carinan. The fearsome image sent a havoc of emotions through his mind, fear, pity, guilt.

Greymalkin's face fell. "Yes."

Soren was watching and listening to him very keenly now. He said quietly, "I know that encounters with these creatures are almost always violent; my apologies for asking about them, but this is very important. What did the accused say regarding these creatures?"

Greymalkin felt tears coming to his eyes then, but quickly wiped them away. His memories were still too recent of both Tatter and EeeNoo lying dead. "Rodo admitted that they were descended from Andromedans, and that he had brought them here. He said something to the effect that he controlled them."

"I see," Soren said, nodding once. "I believe you encountered the accused one last time before this hearing? Can you summarize that encounter for us?"

How does he know all this... never mind. "Yes," Greymalkin said. "I made my way to the Forge and Rodo captured me there. He imprisoned me in proximity to this woman." Greymalkin gestured to Mei, who had been listening carefully.

"Yes, she is known to me," Soren said, looking at Mei for a moment. "I first met her some time ago, and have wondered what happened to her ever since." Soren glanced back at Greymalkin. "When I knew her, I began showing her how to use the Forge. What is your opinion of her? Would you trust her to use the Forge in a responsible manner, knowing what you now know of the device?"

Greymalkin's eyebrows shot up. "Mei Sung? Certainly. She is revered in my species' history." Then he glared at Rodo. "I would definitely trust her a lot more than Rodo with that incredible rig."

"Thank you, Brother Thomas," Soren said. "I only have one more question for you, but I must ask it of you in light of specific facts and context. All I ask is that you answer truthfully." Soren stared at him more intently than ever before, and the older Sojourner's stern gaze made Greymalkin squirm. For a moment he felt as if they were back on the bridge of the Dragon King in the old days, and Soren was about to critique his piloting skills.

"In this Parastasis hearing you have accused this being of misconduct," Soren began, his voice rising in volume and timbre. "It is widely known that the accused was placed in charge of the region you know as the Carinae long ago, and has been famous for maintaining the order of this territory and the Forge ever since. The accused has stated to the court that any recent disorder in the Carinae is directly attributable to the actions of members of your species, and specifically attributes the tragic deaths of thousands of Crotani servitors, dozens of Carinans, and at least one Abyssal to your *individual* actions. The accused claims that you and members of your species came here to steal and misappropriate the valuable assets of the Carinae such as the Forge, assets that are managed by the accused in common trust for the entire Galaxy. In light of all of this context, and acknowledging that you have sworn upon penalty of death to give truthful testimony, I ask you the following question. *Why do you claim that the being you have accused is guilty of severe misconduct in administering this region and the Forge?"*

Greymalkin's throat was dry. He felt petrified for a moment, but then something inside him clamped down and he closed his eyes. While his fear did not vanish, it became something he could set aside for the moment, because he knew he needed to focus on clear thinking. *If they want to kill me, fine. But I am going to set the record down as straight and honestly as I can.* He mentally collected the points he knew he wanted to state, all the while practicing the deep breath control he'd been taught as a Novice. *Okay, here goes....*

"Thank you for the opportunity to state my accusations; I'll try to be brief," Greymalkin said, concealing his nervous fear by folding his arms into his sleeves in the manner Sojourners were taught for recitations. "Everything in this region revolves around the Eta Carinae star system, and the incredible device there which is known as the Forge. I do feel that the Tenax has abused its power and position, because although I have only been exploring this region for a short time, I nevertheless believe I have come to understand the purposes intended for the Forge, for reasons I'll divulge at the conclusion of this testimony. You could probably describe these abuses by the Tenax in many ways but, to me, they fall into five interrelated kinds of misconduct relating to the Forge and its outputs.

"The first misconduct is obvious: the Tenax doesn't allow anyone to use the Forge! That prevents the use of the device for its main purpose, *producing new discoveries and creations*. The Tenax claims it maintains order by doing this. I acknowledge that access to the Forge should be provided *carefully*; use of the Forge is obviously subject to potential abuse. But the Tenax doesn't allow *anyone* but himself access to the device. Given the nearly miraculous nature of the Forge, I consider that grievous misconduct.

"The second misconduct is that the Tenax *doesn't use the Forge to help anyone*, in the Carinae or anywhere else. I've encountered many examples of species and subgroups here that desperately need assistance, including the many Crotani that are enslaved by the Abyssals that have power and control over various parts of the territory. Another group that urgently needs help are the deep-space survivors of the last human expedition here, a sub-species of humans that we call Scorpians. But then, the Tenax was the one that annihilated that entire expedition in the first place, so it's clear why no assistance would be forthcoming; the Tenax wants to *kill* any newcomers to this territory. The Tenax seems to think that this is a way to maintain *peace*, but this is only the peace of a *graveyard*. All of this is again grievous misconduct, because the Forge was intended to provide assistance and prosperity to *everyone* in need of help.

"The third misconduct is that the Tenax doesn't allow the endless amounts of information generated by the Nexus component of the Forge *to be shared*. I met a group of fellow Sojourners in a ship called the *Vlieger* who have been prevented by the Tenax from sharing the unlimited information produced by the Nexus, which the Forge powers. Much worse, the Tenax prevents anyone from even *knowing that the Forge exists* through the cruelly mistreated Carinans, who he has made into ignorant berserkers tasked with killing anyone who tries to explore the territory. The Tenax again probably thinks of this as maintaining order, but it is contrary to the purposes of the Forge and the many secondary wonders like the Nexus that the Forge enables. For the administrator in charge of this territory, that is again grievous misconduct.

"A fourth misconduct is that the Tenax does not even take responsibility for *preserving* the immense amounts of knowledge produced by the Nexus. At one point I wondered if the Tenax might argue that it was going to share the knowledge from the Nexus later, after carefully vetting it. But when I studied their core *Mission Algorithm*, I discovered that the *Vlieger* crew were the only ones to ever make attempts to preserve the output of the Nexus for subsequent study. Before they came along, inconceivable amounts of information from previous millennia of operating the Nexus was simply lost to the ages.

"The fifth and worst misconduct is that the Tenax *acts as a tyrant over the Carinae*. None of the Abyssals or visitors such as my fellow expedition members are allowed freedom of action in the Carinae without personal subservience to the Tenax. The Forge and the many other Carinae artifacts like the Nexus and the Genibrata were all envisioned as shared resources for the entire Galaxy. Instead, these fabulous resources have been used to maximize the personal wealth and power of the Tenax by restricting access to his servants. While I didn't understand this at first, I finally pieced together the patterns of covert exchange transpiring here." Greymalkin looked Bora in the eye. "An example is the group of Jotun smugglers that you interdicted when you saved my life. The Tenax clearly has trade links with the Orion Arm through not only the Jotuns and Naotians, but also the Burani, who I've encountered repeatedly in this territory.

"All of these actions are types of grave misconduct by the individual charged with administering the Forge and other assets of the Carinae. The reason I'm *certain* of this pertains to a particular aspect of my background, a particular aspect that I suspect is the reason why you, magistrate, identified me as a possible subsequent witness to call on." Greymalkin kept his gaze on Bora, even though she did not react at all. "My shadow jewel was evidently a recovered fragment that was once a physical part of a being called the Unfolded One, a Builder that was the primary designer of the Forge. As a result, *I have echo-memories directly inherited from this being.* So, although I'm sure there have been many arguments back and forth over the millennia as to the intended purposes of the Forge, I am absolutely certain that *I know* what the original designer intended. And it is *not* what the Tenax has done with the Forge."

"Does this conclude your testimony?" Soren asked from his right. That was when Greymalkin caught a tiny detail. He wasn't sure, but he thought he could detect the slightest hint of a smile on Soren's mouth. It was a subtle thing. *But it's there.*

"Yes, that's my sworn testimony," Greymalkin said trembling, now feeling his voice start to crack. "I-I'm happy to answer any other questions you have for me." It felt as if an enormous physical weight had been lifted off his shoulders, although his fear was skyrocketing. He had no idea if they were going to strike him dead or not. *What's about to happen? Maybe I was wrong about everything. I'm just a stupid immature fool, and I've made nothing but mistakes since I arrived here. However, Mei Sung could die because of my poor judgement this time. But... I've told nothing but the truth! What's about to happen?*

As the silence lengthened, he finally tore his regard away from Bora and peeped nervously to his sides. He first shot a glance at Mei slightly behind him and to his right. She seemed completely calm, but was alertly watching the others. Then he looked to his left at Rodo, who he'd seen from the corner of his eye appearing to simply stare at his feet through the last half of Greymalkin's speech. *Is he trembling as well?* That made Greymalkin want to run. *Rodo doesn't take criticism well.* Despite his wobbly knees, Greymalkin forced himself to stand his ground and not flee.

"There is one addendum to be added to the testimony of the Parastasis witness," Bora said at last, and the sudden change in her voice was terrifying after she had been so emotionless for so long. Greymalkin was astonished to hear *anger* boiling up from her. "I will highlight for the record a most relevant detail that the witness omitted or perhaps simply did not understand. I note that the witness was *repeatedly detained and threatened by the accused* despite the *explicit* instructions that I inscribed on his shadow jewel that his safe passage should not be delayed *under any circumstances*."

Bora now glared at Rodo irately and said in a stentorian tone, "*This hearing is concluded!* The court finds ample evidence of misconduct on the part of the accused which warrants a full trial. The accused will accompany the court officials to the Galactic Center for the purpose of such trial. *Now*."

Rodo had continued staring at his feet for minutes. At this point he finally looked back up, and the expression of utter fury on his face took the young Sojourner aback. After bristling at both Bora and Soren for a fraction of a second, he snarled inchoately. It was not a sound that could have been produced by a human throat. It was the snarl of a predator cornered.

In that moment Greymalkin became deathly afraid, and started to throw himself backward to shield Mei and push her away. Rodo erupted with complex communed signals that were much too fast for Greymalkin to follow; he only caught fragments of enraged Abyssal thoughts akin to *travesty* and *charade*. Just as Greymalkin shifted his weight to leap in front of Mei, he caught a final flashed repetition of *vermin* in the communed thoughts, even as the physical form of Rodo whipped around impossibly fast to glare at him, yellow eyes flaring brightly...

Everything became instantly black around Greymalkin and Mei, and he felt an explosion in all directions around them, although it somehow had no effect. He and Mei had instinctively crouched down; now they both slowly stood up cautiously glancing around them. The blackness surrounding them gradually dissolved back into Bruno's morphing form, just as his deep rumbling voice said, "I assumed that might be our opponent's next response."

Rodo was gone. Greymalkin gasped, catching a remote hint of the Tenax flickering away at impossible speed through shadow space. *Fleeing.*

Greymalkin took a ragged breath. "Thanks, Bruno," he finally said in earnest, quiet words. "You always come through for me."

"Don't mention it," Bruno bubbled with amusement. Greymalkin stood up and faced Bora and Soren, who were now both stepping down off their valicrete platforms to approach him.

"That was an unfortunate oversight on my part," Bora said. "I should have expected an irrational outburst by that individual. This hearing was the capstone of an investigation that has been underway for a very long time. The accused knew that your testimony was the final evidence that we were seeking to bring an indictment. You have both my thanks for your testimony and my sincere apologies for your endangerment, Brother Thomas."

It was finally, slowly sinking in on Greymalkin. The tension in his neck and shoulders began to ease. *They believed me. Maybe I'm getting out of this nightmare alive.* "What happens now?" Greymalkin said warily.

"The accused has now become a fugitive," Bora said grimly. "A very dangerous fugitive that we cannot risk escaping. Time now presses in a very unfortunate manner."

"Why unfortunate?" Mei asked, stepping up beside him. She leaned in to quickly whisper in his ear, "Well done, Helm!" That simple gesture made Greymalkin feel dizzy with humility, and he nodded to her gratefully.

"The pursuit will require both of us," Soren said. "We have to depart quickly, and some significant decisions must now be made hastily. Decisions that would benefit from a great deal more deliberation. This is very unfortunate." Soren and Bora faced each other briefly, and Greymalkin felt a very dense communed conversation take place rapidly between them. Then Bora, her face stoic and grave once more, turned to Greymalkin and Mei.

"There can be no delay," Bora said. She had a distant expression as she looked out at the stars above them. Her dark brown eyes were grim, but also very sad. "The two of us must pursue the fugitive immediately. You have no conception of how much harm the fugitive may perpetrate if not apprehended quickly. We have only recently become aware of the extent of the criminal enterprises that the fugitive has woven. I have now confirmed that these conspiracies extend across many regions of the Galaxy, including those inhabited by your species. I emphasize that, unfortunately, we can brook no delay whatsoever."

Bora seemed to come back to herself, and looked at Greymalkin and then Mei. "But two decisions at least must be accomplished, one associated with each of you. I address the first to you, Doctor Sung. You and your followers have acted in a commendable manner assisting the oppressed beings in this region survive the worst excesses of the fugitive administrator of the Carinae. Someone must be appointed as an interim administrator of the territory and the Forge. Both my junior colleague and Brother Thomas have vouched for you. The process of confirming a new administrator for the Carinae with the Galactic Central Authority will take time, but would you agree to come with us and take on this role as the interim leader of the territory?"

Greymalkin felt stunned, and then grinned enthusiastically at Mei. But the old terraformer stood silent and contemplative for long moments. She finally said, "I am deeply honored, but I must ask if I am truly appropriate for this role. I have led my followers for many long years already, and I suspect that even an interim position of administration in this locale will require many, many years of service. The years left to me may not be sufficient to this task."

"It is true that the interim responsibilities of this role will take time," Bora said. "The matter of the Carinans alone will be daunting. The creatures will require generations of gentle guidance to shed their psychopathic behaviors. And the remaining beings of power who hold sway in this region may not welcome change led by a human. They will surely disrespect your leadership."

Greymalkin raised his head then. "I have a suggestion. Actually two... if you would accept such from a lowly Apprentice monk."

Mei smiled indulgently. "Yes, Helm? Do you wish to volunteer?"

"No! Providence, no!" Greymalkin exclaimed, looking aghast. "As I suggested before, I can't think of a better person than you to be in charge of the Forge! But, ah, if the court officials would see fit to take Doctor Sung for a visit to a location here in the Carinae called the Genibrata and obtain one of its fruits for her use, I believe that she may be well assisted in her preparations for assuming the role of interim administrator for many years to come! And, um, my other suggestion is that Soren, I mean the Clavisian, stay and assist Doctor Sung as an advisor."

"As territorial censor I must stay to assess the performance of whoever assumes the role in any event," Soren said. "And I second Brother Thomas' suggestion of availing yourself of the... aid station of which he speaks. He is correct, it will usefully prepare you for serving as administrator here."

Mei seemed troubled. "I am unsure. I know the Great Tree of which you speak, Brother Thomas. But I do not know if the transformative processes it offers are to be trusted."

"It certainly saved my miserable life," Greymalkin said apologetically. "And I will humbly recommend that you, as one of the greatest leaders in human history, are far more worthy than I of its curative treatments. Besides...." He looked up at the blazing white star and the gorgeous tableaux of the Homunculus Nebula visible through the dome across the sky. "I really can't think of anyone else that I'd trust with the responsibility for this place. And remember that your crew has to leave the Cryptopolis soon. You've got to be in a position to lead them and to defend them."

Mei looked at him steadily. Finally, she bowed her head. "Alright, Brother Thomas, my Helmsman. In the short time I have known you, you have been a remarkably capable guide and pilot. I will accept this interim role. But what of you? Will you be staying here? I would be grateful for you to continue as my Helm."

Greymalkin's jaw dropped in stunned silence. Red-faced and speechless, he looked down, trying to absorb that praise from a figure out of history that he had always idolized. The silence was broken when Bora spoke up, saying, "This brings me to the second decision I spoke of. What fate do you choose for yourself, Brother Thomas? I strongly recommend you come with us, given the danger of the Carinans."

Abruptly, that statement hit Greymalkin like a splash of cold water. *Wait, wait! How much time has passed...?* He checked his internal chronometer. Horrified, he looked up at the nebula again. *Constance and her crew! They were going to work their way around the nebula collecting their data before leaving. After this much time, they must now be somewhere on this side of the nebula! They didn't know how close the*

Carinans were any more than I did! They'll be killed if someone doesn't help them!

"Please, c-can you first help me find a crew of Sojourners that are lost here in the nebula?" Greymalkin stammered. "They're my friends, I can't just abandon them!"

Bora's face was as hard as a craggy cliff inside the shadow of her black hood. "As I said, there can be no delay. We have already taken too long. We must go now, and you must unfortunately decide. *Now.*"

"I understand your reluctance to leave behind your colleagues," Soren said. His expression was as somber as Bora's. "However, I also believe you should come with us. Alone, you will simply be slaughtered by the crazed servants of the fugitive."

"He will not be alone," Bruno rumbled loudly. "My loyalty is now with the monk. I will accompany him, and I will defend him, even unto my destruction if need be."

Greymalkin stared at the slowly morphing black shape, and then said under his breath, "Thank you, Bruno." After a baffled pause, he added, "Uh, *why?*"

"You accepted me, and I've learned more from you than others," Bruno said brusquely. "I will explain further when we have time, assuming that we survive."

Bora stepped forward, glowering at Bruno. "We will allow you to accompany Brother Thomas. We believe that he is a good influence on you. However, be aware that, even if we are spread *thinly*, there are other Galactic authorities such as myself, those termed the Pellucids, in human space as well. If you actually return to human space you will be under the jurisdiction of the Pellucid called the *Cephian*, who you will well remember."

"The Cephian?" Greymalkin asked. When Bruno said nothing, Bora spoke up.

"Yes, one of the most powerful of all Pellucids, but an iconoclast that long ago left the Central Realms. The Cephian... *disciplined* this troublesome creature long ago," Bora said, eying Bruno with a suspicious scowl and then addressing the protean directly. "Rest assured that we will be monitoring your behavior, even in so isolated a region as human space."

When Bruno remained sullenly silent, Bora turned back to Greymalkin and said, "Time presses. If you are certain of your decision, bid Doctor Sung farewell, and then we must take her with us and depart."

Greymalkin nodded. "I'm sure. I *have* to try to find Sister Constance." He faced Mei, and suddenly felt hollow again at the prospect of saying goodbye so suddenly. "It has been a very great honor meeting you, Doctor Sung. This is hard for me; there are so many questions I never got to ask you."

Mei sighed and shrugged. "I hate that feeling as well. I hated saying goodbye to my father the last time we met. We were on bad terms, for foolish emotional reasons. I always thought there would be more time, time to make peace with him. But there's never enough time." Then an impish expression briefly crossed her face, making her look much younger. "Come then, ask me one quick question! Go ahead!"

Greymalkin grinned, and searched his memory. "There *is* one question that the history books speculated about endlessly that I always wondered about. I'm a linguist, after all. Why did all the civilizations founded by your fleet in particular insist on using new constructed languages in their colonies, instead of the traditional languages of Old Earth?"

"That's easy," Mei laughed. "The whole point of leaving Earth behind was to actually leave it *behind* and make a new start. Everybody in my fleet agreed on that much at least." She clasped her forearm to his once more in the ancient Thannic gesture of greeting and farewell.

"Thank you for all your help, Brother Thomas! May your journey always be enlightening."

Greymalkin found that tears were coming to his eyes again. "And may you sojourn always through life with courage, Doctor Sung. I hope we'll meet again someday."

"I would like that, Helm," she said, and turned back to Bora and Soren. Soren stepped up, nodded to Greymalkin, and touched her arm. Unbelievably, they both vanished into shadow space, and he sensed the huge form of the Clavisian disappearing into the distance rapidly.

Bora stepped up to him, and put her hand on his shoulder in the formal Sojourner gesture of final farewell. Greymalkin gripped her opposite shoulder with a half-joyous and half-grieving smile. They separated and he bowed to her. "Thank you for believing me," Greymalkin said gratefully. Then he said in a rasping voice, "And... thank you for letting me see the faces of my friends one last time."

Bora nodded once, and then tilted her head at him. "A last admonition to you, then. Understand, Brother Thomas, the commission you agreed to has not concluded, despite the strength of the testimony you gave here."

Greymalkin's eyes widened. "Uh, okay. But may I ask why you chose *me* for your... *commission*, whatever it is? I'm hardly the most qualified person for *anything*."

"I did not choose you," Bora said with a frown. "You volunteered."

"But I don't know *what* I volunteered for... never mind," Greymalkin said, shaking his head, wishing again that he hadn't given the Velan carte blanche to decide his destiny, even if it had been a bargain for his life. "Can you, um, at least give me some guidance? What am I supposed to do next?"

Bora seemed slightly surprised. "You will know what to do. After this experience, you surely understand that there may be many reasons that I must avoid biasing you."

"Oh, right," Greymalkin said, remembering the rules she'd invoked for independent, neutral testimony. "And I also remember what you said, that the conspiracies of the Tenax extend all the way across the Galaxy to the Orion Arm. That tracks. Both the Naotians and the Burani were working for Rodo when they tried to kill me. Assuming that I make it home, I'll... keep witnessing then, I guess."

"Serving as a witness is the *least* of the duties in the commission that you have agreed to undertake," Bora said, turning to walk a few paces away from him.

"Wait!" Greymalkin yelped. "What do you mean? *What's going to happen to me next?*"

Bora seemed sad as she faced him again and said, "There is no certainty in events to come, even for such as I am. However, we have set many such commissions in place in order to make some outcomes more likely than others. While many who undertook such commissions have failed, we believe many more may succeed. I hope *you* succeed where others have failed, little brother. While you may well be killed, as have so many others, yours is a more important commission than many."

"Why are you doing all this?" he cried. "Surely you can tell me *something* of your goals and rationale!" Even as he said this, vague recollections of things he had realized as an Abyssal echoed in his mind. But those complexities had long vanished, like memories from a dream.

"There are many reasons why we have assisted humans such as Dr. Sung in the past," Bora said. "And there were myriad reasons that we assisted humans in the founding of your Sojourner Order, as well."

"What!" Greymalkin yelled, yet another thousand new questions exploding into his mind. But one pressing question again crowded the others out as he realized Bora was about to depart. "Please, just tell me, *what else am I supposed to do?*"

A very gentle smile graced Bora's stern face then. She held up her fist and opened her palm in the traditional Sojourner gesture of blessing.

"You are a Sojourner. Remember your vows, and you will know everything you need do. *Sojourn through life with courage, little brother. Farewell.*" She vanished into shadow space and, far above him, the planet-sized mass of the Velan vanished with her into the howling blue gale of the Homunculus Nebula.

Returns

The flashing blue scintillations of the shadow plane fled past underneath them at a dreadful speed as Royce left the Parastasis system behind. Despite their velocity and how rugged the shadow plane topography was here, Greymalkin was keeping only part of his attention on steering a course. He was mainly focused on hurriedly sifting through the data in Sister Constance's database, trying to identify the locations of her data recorders and caches. *Where can she and her crew be? And even if I figure it out, how do I get there?* He still felt the icy synesthetic gale blowing past him, as well as a hundred other distractions. Booming echoes of stellar flares that had happened a hundred thousand years ago. A guttering pattern of radio signals from a staccato pulsar somewhere nearby. The ionized gas clouds of the Homunculus Nebula were a thicket of eerie tangled paths around him, stretching away in three dimensions into the distance. Picking out a path for Royce to anywhere in particular seemed impossible.

Bruno was outside, clinging to Royce's hull while scanning around them. «The Carinans are all around us in the distance.» Bruno's thoughts were both vigilant and troubled. «They appear to be scattering in a disorganized and panicked manner. Perhaps they've already learned of the defeat of their master? Has this discouraged them?»

«From what I learned of them, they may be even *more* chaotic and dangerous now.» Greymalkin thought about EeeNoo's berserker rage fixations. *I wonder how the Carinans will react to the disappearance of* the Tenax? What happens when your God-King is overthrown? He finished comparing the star charts Constance had given him with the labyrinth of shadow plane paths they were racing through. *Constance and her crew might be anywhere in this chop. But I'm betting they may have fled to this site up ahead....* The star system ahead of them that Royce was entering was not only one of Constance's primary data caches, but she'd marked it as the site of a long-abandoned alien shadow space mine beneath a huge blue giant star.

In the database, she'd added a terse annotation to the site that had caught his attention. The annotation said: *Deep old mine here – Could use as a hiding place in a pinch?* Greymalkin was betting that she'd done exactly that. Royce skimmed toward the outskirts of the system, and he began looking for the entrance to the mine. It took far longer than he had hoped to find it in the confused tangle of shadow space paths, but he finally spotted it. He realized that it was well hidden. *A perfect hiding place....*

He guided Royce down into the mine's entrance, and they plunged deeply through the conduit into the concealed shadow spaces beneath the immense blue star. *Providence! How deep does this thing go?* Eventually the conduit ended with what appeared to be a star bridge barrier. The crushing sensation of the huge blue star above them made it impossible for Greymalkin to make out anything on the other side of the star bridge. He was starting to feel that he'd wasted precious time on this fool's errand, and wondered what location he should search next.

«Constance! Are you here? It's Brother Thomas!» He blasted his communed thoughts across the star bridge with all the volume he could muster. The shadow space conduit of the mine felt even colder than the plane, but his other synesthesia perceptions were smothered into black stillness. The desolation of the abandoned alien mine was as chilling as a grave. He signaled again, but there was only the deathly silence. After another forlorn moment passed, he started turning Royce around, preparing to ascend as rapidly as possible. But the little rover starship was still damaged from the plunge it had endured down the shadow space cliff, and was stiff and sluggish to respond. He had almost finished reorienting Royce in the awkward space when he paused. *Was that a faint communed signal?* He concentrated and thought the signal grew stronger. He signaled once more and then the star bridge began to extend. In a few moments the ancient conduit had opened, and suddenly communed thoughts reached him.

«Grey! Can you read me now?» Constance's thoughts were dazed and unnerved in a way he'd never sensed from her before. Greymalkin turned Royce around again and eased the starship through the star bridge into the lowest portion of the mine. There was a truly ancient looking dock there, and one of the largest doors was open to the void. He steered Royce through the opening carefully.

He immediately saw Constance's rover starship Lacey, heavily damaged and lying crashed on the surface of the dock. The ship's landing legs had been torn away, and the primary continuity mast was awry. Greymalkin saw that an emergency environmental enclosure had been set up a few meters away from the crashed ship. He brought Royce in for a landing near the other cyneget. «Where are you, Constance? Are you okay?»

«I'm inside Lacey. The others....» Constance was gasping for breath, and her thoughts were muddled and despondent. He hurried to the airlock and grabbed a medkit, switching his garment into void suit mode as he went. Once he was outside he bounded over to the airlock of the other rover. It was open to the void. *Great Mercy, let them be safe!*

He felt sadness sinking into his chest as he entered the other cyneget. The cyborg was inert and unresponsive to signals. *It's dead. But what about Constance's crew? And where's Constance?* The pressor deck was inactive, so he floated up through the dark interior of the dead cyneget. He found Constance in the cockpit, and touched down next to her with the diagnostic sensor already out of the medkit and scanning her. He could already see that she had strapped her right arm against her torso. When he checked the diagnostic he saw that her arm was broken, along with two of her ribs. «Why aren't you in the medical pod?» Greymalkin became increasingly concerned as he scanned her other injuries.

«We're all injured. We've only got the one pod, and we just got it connected to the emergency generator in the shelter.» Inside her helmet, Constance looked dazed. Her pupils were dilated, and he began scanning for head trauma. She looked at him wide-eyed through the faceplate. «How – how did you find us?»

He finished his medical scan and began to work his arm underneath her carefully to lift her. «Your notes.» He stopped himself from choking up in fear for her. Her right lung was massively bruised underneath the broken bones. «Your notes are always so thorough. Come on, Constance, I've got to get you out of here. I've got two medical pods on my ship. If we take yours we can get three of you attended to.»

«Brother James is dead.» Constance's thoughts were almost delirious. He could feel her sob as he lifted her out of the cockpit. «Sister Marie is in the medical pod. Brother Desmonde and Sister Murasaki are in the shelter. But they're also very badly injured. And Lacey's... gone.» Constance looked back miserably at the dead cyneget as Greymalkin coaxed her body through the open airlock. «She got us here, but that *thing* injured her so badly. I'm sorry I was so slow returning your signal, I had to get into the cockpit to use Lacey's dead cortex to extend the bridge....» She gasped in pain as he kept moving her along gently.

«Don't worry about it.» Greymalkin winced at the pain he was causing her, but knew he had to get her to Royce. «And I'm sorry too!

It took me far too long to find the mine entrance. Were you attacked by Carinans?»

«Just one.» Constance was breathing hard. «We didn't see it coming, we were all outside collecting the last data cache. It was on top of us before we knew what was happening. Lacey charged it just as it came at us, otherwise we'd all be dead. She surprised it, and managed to kill it somehow. But it tore all her limbs off....» Constance was coughing inside her helmet, and he saw a small blood splatter.

The diagnostic now listed *hemothorax* as one of her injuries. *She's got blood in her chest cavity now. Dammit! Her lung is bleeding. I hurt her when I moved her.* Greymalkin glanced at the emergency shelter and communed a signal on the open channel. «Everybody get ready to move if you can! I'll be back for you as soon as I get Constance into my ship.» There was only one weakly communed reply, male thoughts that he assumed were from Desmonde. *The others must have lost consciousness.* He got Constance inside Royce's main airlock and cycled it while he deactivated the pressor deck. It was bad enough dragging her along in zero gee, he didn't need simulated gravity to pull her down. The atmosphere quickly flooded into the airlock, and he flipped her helmet back over her shoulders. Constance took a ragged breath, and her rolling eyes found his.

"Grey, what are you going to do?" she whispered, and then coughed again.

"I'm going to get you all out of here and back to the base!" Greymalkin said. "Don't try to talk, just commune. You've got internal bleeding." He pulled her through the open hatches toward the deluxe medical pod that Tatter and Bruno had brought back from the base, and started to carefully unlatch her void suit. *Can I get her out of it without hurting her ribs further?*

«Don't take us out of here!» Constance's thoughts were panicky again. «The Carinans are everywhere! We may be cornered here, but they'll never find us. We'll figure out some way to survive and hide. And we'll never make it back in time anyway! The expedition will have evacuated by the time we make it back to the main base.»

"I've heard about what happens if you stay here when the Carinans come back," Greymalkin said stubbornly. "And I already made it here through all of them! I've got Bruno with me, remember? We've already... we already killed a lot of them...."

«Grey, *listen* to me.» Constance put her gentle hand on his chin and weakly pulled his face around to look at her. Her eyes were desperate. «We'll never make it in time. It'll take us a week to work our way back around the nebula. The expedition is sure to be gone by then.»

"I can take us right back through the nebula," Greymalkin said grimly. "We'll be there in less than a day. The last ships won't have evacuated before then. Hold still, this is going to hurt." He gradually peeled the void suit off her. She grit her teeth in pain, but did not cry out. When she was finally in nothing but her underclothes, he slid her into the medical pod and attached the connectors carefully. She coughed blood again.

"Dammit, Grey!" Constance spat out the words while coughing. "The nebula's full of Carinans! And you can't get through the nebula! Nobody can!" He affixed the last sensor and shut the pod lid over her.

"You've been stuck in here, so you don't know what's going on outside. The Carinans are all running away," he said. "And I've already been through the nebula. *Twice*. I'm going to go get your crew now...."

«Grey!» Constance communed with him in tears as she felt the medical pod begin to sedate her. «If you're really going to try to get us back to the base, then bring our data and sample pods too? James and Lacey can't have died for *nothing*.»

Greymalkin paused uncertainly, but then bent down and grinned at her through the pod's translucent cover, pressing his palm against the lid. «Okay, sure I will! *Preserve knowledge with diligence.* I'm a Sojourner too, remember? Now, *rest*. Leave this to me.»

Greymalkin stood up and pre-emptively looked down at his shoulders before activating the pressor deck and running back to the airlock. Sure enough, one of his shoulders had a tiny black splat on it. "Bruno! I've got a job for you!"

"You know, you did not actually traverse the nebula twice," Bruno rumbled. "You didn't make it through the first time."

"Okay, *one and a half*," Greymalkin muttered. He jumped into Royce's airlock and cycled it. "We're in a hurry, though! I need you to go and move the cargo pods mounted on the dead cyneget's hull over to Royce. I'll get the crew and their medical pod."

"Those cannisters contain many artifacts and cyborganic samples," Bruno complained. "The extra mass will impede the travel velocity of your cyneget."

«Bruno, just do it. It won't slow Royce down that much.» Greymalkin bounced out of the airlock and leaped to the emergency shelter entrance. He saw the protean splitting into several replicas of itself and moving to quickly dismount the cargo pods on the dead cyneget. He entered through the shelter airlock and found Brother Desmonde barely mobile, with a huge bruise across one side of his face. The two female Sojourners were both unconscious, one in the medical pod and the other lying on a pad, still in her void suit. He briefly checked all of their injuries with the medkit, and then moved them all to Royce, along with their medical pod. By the time he'd gotten them all cared for and strapped in securely, Bruno had finished mounting their cargo pods on Royce.

Greymalkin strapped himself in the cockpit and checked Royce over. The cyneget made the chuffing signals that signified impatience, even though it was now not only damaged but heavily burdened with cargo. *Yeah, we need to get going.* Greymalkin carefully lifted off and took one last pass over the dead rover, saying a brief prayer over her. Constance had apparently already interred Brother James. Greymalkin piloted Royce up the long passage to the shadow space plane and looked up at the gigantic vista of the Homunculus Nebula, simultaneously trying to chart a path through the absurdly complex maze of shimmering ribbons and wondering where the remaining Carinans might be clustered. As he was studying the labyrinth, Bruno came up beside Royce.

«This will be a difficult traversal.» Bruno's thoughts felt like massive boulders falling somewhere in the distance, ominously shaking the landscape.

Greymalkin had mentally picked out a path together with several contingencies. *And I'll bet this is still going to go sideways no matter what I do. But we can't stay here.* He wondered what chance they actually had of surviving another passage through the nebula, even as he glanced at the Protean's massive form floating outside the big viewport. «You aren't obligated to sacrifice yourself for us, you know, Bruno?»

The protean ignored the comment. «We should commence. I will follow you and intercede when you are attacked.»

«Maybe we'll evade them.» Greymalkin didn't believe his own communed thoughts, and he knew Bruno didn't either.

«Let us proceed. There is no benefit to further delay.» Curiously, Bruno's thoughts were thoughtful and somber. There was no trace of his usual excitement at the prospect of a battle, and Greymalkin realized that he now knew the protean well enough to discern why.

It's because he knows he has to protect us and not just throw himself into a carefree fight. He doesn't care if he's destroyed or not; he never has. But for some reason he's more determined than ever to protect me now. That still seemed baffling, but then Greymalkin glanced behind him to the compartment where the injured Sojourners were all now sedated and asleep. *If I fail them, they'll never wake up.*

With that sobering thought he took on the Helm Link, and Royce accelerated forward.

Greymalkin extended his shadow sense out to take in the incredible complexity of the nebula and his synesthetic perceptions of it. The sensations were so crisp that it was hard to believe he was not physically skimming along a rugged path at tremendous speed directly into a freezing headwind. But he knew he was actually sitting motionless in a spacecraft within a tiny artificial space continuum bubble. That tiny manifold, however, was traversing the potentials of a path in relation to the endless continuum of the universe. In stray moments like this it struck him as eerie that the universe of stars and planets was so remote and yet so close, displaced less than a hair's thickness beneath them in the ghostly, otherworldly dimension of shadow space.

And the Carinae still stunned him at moments like this when he took a moment to observe the most fantastic tableaux he'd ever seen in his life. If every moment didn't also entail the terror of being killed along with his friends, it would be a breathtaking pleasure. But the terror was twisting at his stomach in ghastly ways.

The tiny rover starship climbed steadily over the next few hours, his perception of a shadow space gale becoming stronger and stronger as they drew ever closer to Eta Carina and the Forge. Bruno began following them more closely, and then finally simply clung onto Royce's hull, keeping lookout for the Carinans. The synesthetic turbulence and obscuring glare of brilliant light reflecting from the tangled surfaces of shadow planes continued building as they entered the densest part of the nebula. From his previous experience he now understood that he was drawing close to the pinnacle of the Eta Carina system and the flood of ionized gas it emitted. *If I can just get through this last part, we'll make it through to the Forge. That will be the halfway mark....*

The problem was that he was becoming extremely fatigued. Greymalkin clenched his jaw, and kept rubbing his hand through his unkempt hair to try to make himself more alert. He did not want to check his chronometer to see how long he had been awake. The fatigue was affecting his ability to focus on the path. Royce was diligently running at speed despite the damage he'd sustained, but the cyneget could not perceive the path as well as Greymalkin could. He repeatedly found himself steering Royce back to the center of the shadow space ribbon as the path became narrower and more tenuous. At some point he realized that despite his inherent stamina, Royce had become extremely drained as well.

Greymalkin fought the constant urge to yawn and fall asleep during the long grueling climb up through the vast nebula. That would mean instant death for all of them. *Just a few more hours. One way or the other, it'll be over in just a few more hours.* As he was thinking that thought, they came cresting into the Eta Carina star system and several things happened.

Greymalkin's shadow sense perceived in a flash the manifold space where the immense Forge was still suspended in the impact zone of the two huge stars. He could briefly sense hints of the vast submanifold channels that drew incredible energies from that unending blast of sheer power, like converging rivers of fast flowing ice. Then, in a fraction of a second, before anyone could react, Royce plunged straight through a milling crowd of the Carinans and entered one of the shadow paths leading downward through the other half of the nebula. Behind them, he could momentarily sense a throng of roars as the Carinans registered their passage and gave chase.

Great Mercy! Why were they clustering around the Forge? Were they looking for the Tenax? Greymalkin didn't have time to puzzle over the question any longer as they descended into the dense turbulence on the other side of the nebula. Maintaining contact with the path was difficult at the speed they were now forced to take. It was all he could manage to keep Royce on the shadow space paths leading away from Eta Carina.

He felt slightly reassured that Bruno was keeping a sharp watch for the pursuing Carinans, and whenever they drew close the protean would warn him. He felt numbed by the constant synesthesia that was telling his mind he was in a snowstorm. Even if his physical body was not cold, his mind felt completely frozen. The stress of the chase on top of the fatigue he already felt was grinding him down, but every time he started to drift off into a microsleep episode, Royce would signal him abruptly. Between the pursuing horde of Carinans and the periodic startled alerts, his adrenaline level kept him awake.

As the pursuit stretched on into hours, Greymalkin began to wonder if he would be able to keep up the pace. His focus was declining, and he could not continue much longer without making disastrous mistakes. He realized his medkit was still within reach and grabbed it, hunting until he found the most powerful stimulant among the basic medications it contained. He injected himself, knowing full well that at some point it would wear off and he'd crash both biologically *and* in shadow space. As the stimulant flooded his bloodstream, he felt new vigor but also new fear and panic.

«Bruno!» Greymalkin finally communed to the protean in desperation. «Talk to me! It'll keep me alert. I have to stay awake to steer Royce and keep him on the path!»

«Won't it simply distract you further?» Even Bruno now seemed uneasy.

«No, it'll help me focus! I know that seems counterintuitive, but—»

«It may be a moot point.» Bruno's thoughts seemed to grow sharper, but more resigned in tone. «I can perceive our pursuers through the turbulence now. They are continuing to close on us. Soon I will have to leave you. If I stay on the path to attack them, I may be able to delay them long enough to give you a sufficient lead to escape.»

«NO!» Greymalkin surprised even himself with the ferocity of that roared communal thought. «They'll kill you! We stay together!»

«Very well.» Bruno's thoughts were now starting to change. A sense of flame and heat were beginning to arise. «However, it will certainly be a moot point soon. *So be it!*»

With alarm, Greymalkin could sense the protean's more typical rage starting to boil up. *No! He's going to fight to the death!* He scanned the path behind them, and immediately saw what Bruno was reacting to. A solid mass of Carinans were charging along the path after them. *Damn them! Why in blazes do they have to be such a slavering horde of lunatics?* They were so packed together that some were beginning to fall off the shadow path, disintegrating as they fell. In desperation, Greymalkin focused his shadow sense ahead of Royce, looking for anything in the terrain that he could use to gain ground. Then he noted a very disturbing possibility that also represented an opportunity. His face twitched. He realized what they were going to have to do.

«Bruno! We're going over the side!» Greymalkin studied the cliff slope ahead of them. Knowing what it was like to go over the edge did not reduce the size of the stone that seemed to fill his stomach at the sight of what lay ahead.

«NO!» Bruno's communed roar was even fiercer than Greymalkin's. «We will meet an end fighting before killing ourselves!»

«We aren't going to kill ourselves.» Greymalkin felt tension in his shoulders so intense that it seemed to burn. «Royce and I already did this once. And this time we have *you* to help Royce hold on to the cliffside! That slope is moderate enough that we'll survive the plunge.» He studied the cliff again. *At least, we have some <u>small</u> chance of surviving.*

Bruno paused and examined the rapidly approaching cliff. «Yes! Down then!» The protean quickly morphed backward onto Royce's continuity mast, assuming the antenna form of a long shadow space grapple. Greymalkin felt his heart jump into his throat as he steered them over the edge. He found he could not avoid screaming in fear, even as he focused on carefully spinning Royce around to resist the force of the descent.

And then down the cliffside they went. Through the Helm Link, the furious, clawing, *clasping* maneuver felt like an agony of rasps slicing down his back and through his arms. But he quickly realized that the addition of Bruno to the grasping plunge made an enormous difference. The plunge *hurt* more through the Helm Link this time because of the even more *ragged* grasping sensation, but with both Bruno and Royce gripping the steep shadow plane they were able to hang on much more effectively. Behind them, Greymalkin could distantly perceive communed signals like howls as some of the Carinans went mad and hurled themselves down the cliffside after them, disintegrating instantly.

Greymalkin stopped screaming and clamped his jaws shut, focusing on steering *across* the cliffside to reduce their velocity. This was a much longer plunge than the first one he and Royce had survived. *I've got to keep us oriented in a controlled descent. If we start tumbling, we're dead.*

Somehow, he managed to keep the little starship from turning over and watched as the semi-controlled slide took them down and down through the nebula. *Well, this is one way to speed up the descent,* he thought to himself while trying not to further panic. Greymalkin had no clear sense of where they would wind up if they survived the plunge, but hoped it would not be disastrously far from the main expedition base.

Despite the assistance from Bruno, the long plunge was taking a toll on Royce's continuity manifold and primary mast. As the plunge stretched on and on, Greymalkin could directly feel the agony of the damage that the cyneget was experiencing, and pain feedback was starting to overwhelm both of them. He grit his chattering teeth trying to bear it, knowing that the pain through the Helm Link was just an echo of what Royce was enduring. The rover's primary continuity mast had already been damaged during the first plunge and was now being subjected to even worse stress. He prayed that the structure would not snap completely. *Hold together, Royce, just a little longer.* He tried to scan ahead of them on the slope, but there was too much turbulence to make out any details.

Then the pain and vibration he felt through the Helm Link began to worsen dramatically, and Greymalkin cursed. The damage was escalating, and he realized that Royce was beginning to disconnect him from the Helm Link to protect him from the agony as the cyneget began to lose control over the continuity manifold and other systems. *I'm going to have to drop us out of shadow space, even if we won't be able to enter again on the slope!* He was about to activate the continuity manifold cutoff when the turbulence suddenly cleared as the steep slope ended. They were once again on the plane. Gratefully, he activated the cutoff and they dropped into normal space. Royce made a signal like a strange keening moan through the Helm Link and Greymalkin felt several of the continuity systems collapse.

Royce can't shunt now at all! Blast, blast! What are we going to do? Now that they had exited the turbulence from the nebula, he extended his shadow sense to see where they were. He immediately spotted the main expedition base signal tantalizingly close to them. «Bruno! Are you *absolutely* sure you can't shift Royce into shadow space?»

«Affirmative.» The protean's rumbling thoughts felt morose. «As I've told you before, my shunt is powerful but only works on the material of which I'm composed. My impeller could work on the cyneget once it is shifted, but not before.»

Greymalkin sorted through possibilities rapidly while he scrutinized the base, trying to make out if any expedition ships were still docked there. *Yes! There's still one galleon! But... is it starting to pull away?* It was hard to tell from this distance, but in horror he thought he could make out the galleon beginning to undock. «Bruno, what if Royce can shunt us into shadow space initially? Can you maintain the field continuity once that's done?»

«I... am unsure.» Bruno's thoughts were agitated. «But we must go now! The last human starship at the dock is preparing to depart. Do you wish me to go and detain them?»

Blast, blast... what should we do? Greymalkin did a quick check of Royce's continuity manifold. It was so damaged that he would normally have associated the readings with a completely wrecked ship, a dead hulk that he would never dream of trying to shunt. The risk of a failed shadow space shift was far too great; they'd likely just disintegrate. Even worse, the cyneget's mind was so catastrophically overstressed that it was beginning to falter, and the Helm Link momentarily fuzzed away.

We have to shunt. It's now or never. «Bruno, get ready to try to sustain the manifold!» Greymalkin used an override to force open the Helm Link to reconnect with Royce's mind... and almost blacked out from the feedback. The cyneget's mind was shutting down from the damage. He forced his awareness to merge with Royce in a closed link, jamming the channel open. That made it impossible for the cyneget to shield him, and a wave of shattering pain hit him from Royce's mind. Greymalkin could barely think through the mass of raw and ripped nerve signals, but he focused on systematically overriding as many nonessential data channels as possible and reducing the cyneget's perception of damage, effectively activating a massive anesthetic in the cyborg's mind. When he was finally connected with Royce's mind and able to actually think, neither of them could sense much beyond the bare minimum needed for shadow space movement. Greymalkin kept his thoughts to the cyborg extremely simple. «I'm *sorry*. I know, everything is *torn*. But we have to *shift*, Royce.»

The cyneget tried to rally with a massive effort, but their combined mind began to simply spin, and the Royce component started to fuzz out into death. *No, dammit, no!* Greymalkin reached out to the cyneget again, but the myriad damage signals that he'd disconnected or suppressed in Royce's mind and the resulting feedback distortions were interacting in bizarre ways with his synesthetic senses. Momentary phantasmic hallucinations began to overlay his synesthesia, and for a second Greymalkin felt connected with Royce again as he saw the image of a face amidst flames.

The visage was a strange combination of the android face that Royce had worn in the Cryptopolis and a human face, bloodied, pulped, and dying. *It's a communed hallucination. But maybe I can reach him through it.* Greymalkin latched onto the mirage and imagined touching foreheads with the cyneget's thin brutalized face. The synesthetic tactile contact sparked and the eyes flickered open. For a moment the electric blue eyes of the cyneget locked onto him and through Royce's mind he saw a reflected image of his own intense silver grey eyes.

«Royce, I love you, buddy. I know what you're going through, but *you have to shift now or we're dead.*» Greymalkin distantly felt tears streaming down his physical face, but focused on pressing his hallucinated forehead against that of Royce. The cyneget nodded once, and the blue eyes closed. Greymalkin could feel Royce rerouting energy channels inside his cybernetic mind and body, forcing power self-destructively through nerves and electronic sinews that were never meant for that purpose. The continuity manifold surged, and he felt the shunt happen like an agonized shriek. They shifted into shadow space. Greymalkin could immediately feel the manifold starting to fail, though.

«Bruno! Now! Help him stabilize it!» Then Greymalkin felt the protean link with him, and they were briefly one organism with three intertwined mind/body pairs. The uncanny hybrid creature looked up and flexed newly discovered gigantic muscles to drive the cracked interior shell forward, all driven by the determined human mind at its core. The growing stony black mass shot forward across the shadow plane as if it had been catapulted. The hybrid creature crossed the intervening distance to the expedition base quickly and then pulled close alongside the big galleon aggressively.

Angry communed thoughts from the galleon warned them away, but the merged mind of the hybrid monster responded with even more enraged thoughts that were charged with pain. «We're members of the expedition, blast it! Sojourners and others! Let us board!»

«This is Xenocorps evacuation command!» The communed thoughts were angry and defensive. «We'll extend a gangway tunnel; all human passengers can board through that! Now back off or we'll fire our weapons and destroy you!»

The black monstrosity was now outlined in a brightly glowing blue nimbus of energy, and it extended a huge arm that hammered the cargo doors hard enough to rattle everyone and everything inside the vessel. «We don't have time for that! The Carinans are too close, and I'm not leaving anybody behind! Open the doors NOW, or I'll open the damned things for you!»

After a moment the Xenocorps captain evidently decided that they didn't have the time or inclination for a battle with the black horror. The big cargo doors slowly retracted, and when the opening was big enough, the hybrid black goliath swarmed through in a fluid mass and gently placed the wrecked cyneget's hull into a docking cradle. The merged mind link collapsed then, and Greymalkin suddenly found that he was once again himself, exhausted and gasping for breath in the cockpit. Royce immediately became comatose, mind and systems shutting down in an tortured attempt at damage control and healing. The pressor deck functions had deactivated, so Greymalkin unsteadily levered himself out of the cockpit... and was immediately thrown backwards into the bulkhead as the galleon around them accelerated forward.

The galleon is moving away from the base again, he thought. They're trying to get enough distance from the big nemora tree so they can activate their manifold. He extended his shadow sense and watched the huge branched settlement rapidly diminishing into the distance. With alarm, he could see a horde of Carinans closing on the great tree, and beginning to hack the mighty limbs into pieces. Then the galleon shunted heavily into the vast shadow space channel next to the base and he found himself in zero gee again. Even as he watched, they at last began accelerating away from the Carinae into the widening channel. A vast expanse of cerulean shadow space billows eventually surrounded them.

Greymalkin floated through the darkened ship toward the cabin where he'd strapped down the wounded Sojourners. He was relieved to see that they had slept through the entire nightmarish transit. The three that were in medical pods were all okay; the power coupling with the galleon's docking cradle had activated when Bruno had connected poor Royce. He checked Brother Desmonde where he was strapped into a bunk and saw that he was breathing easily.

Then Greymalkin checked the damages to Royce, and his heart sank in his chest as he scanned the cracked hull and fractured central mast of the cyneget. The rover starship was horribly damaged. Greymalkin drifted to a halt and pushed himself down into a corner in the darkness, overcome by the extent of the damage. He felt tears and cupped his face with his hands in frustrated anger. *Royce almost ran himself to death for me. I don't know if he's going to survive this, but I have to try and heal him. Somehow.*

"We have a visitor," Bruno rumbled from his shoulder. Greymalkin blearily rubbed his face and pushed himself away from the bulkhead, realizing that he was so exhausted that he'd almost fallen asleep. *Blazes! Are they going to give us a hard time for the way we boarded...?* He extended his shadow sense, suddenly alert to possible danger again. But then he recognized who it was coming through the airlock. He grinned and jumped back to the cockpit.

"I'll be damned! You made it, kid!" Lex laughed, and grabbed Greymalkin in a bear hug as they collided in mid-air. Greymalkin sobbed and pounded Lex on the back, nodding with his eyes clenched. Then he pushed himself back and looked into Lex's face with a manic laugh.

"Yeah, we made it by the skin of our teeth," Greymalkin said shakily. "But I've got a ship full of wounded. And Royce... he got us here, but he...." His throat felt choked for a moment. Then he focused on Lex's eyes where, with disbelief, he also saw a hint of tears. "What happened anyway? I wasn't sure anybody would still be here...."

"I had a bit of a struggle to make this last galleon stay this long. It got a little ugly for a bit there, and I didn't know if the same thing that happened to me might not happen to you," Lex said, and for a second his face looked gaunt. Then he smiled fiercely. "But I wasn't going to let them leave you behind, kid. Not after everything that happened to me. But, never mind that! Let's get the injured to the infirmary, and a repair crew on Royce."

Greymalkin nodded, but then found that he was having difficulty keeping his eyes open. Bruno interjected his basso commentary then, "The monk has been awake piloting for thirty-six hours. He may need to rest before continuing." Greymalkin groaned inside as Lex looked askance at him. *Yeah, glad I didn't know that....*

"I'll take over here, kid," Lex said, shoving him toward his bunk cabin. "You go sleep."

He did.

* * *

Greymalkin found the trip back to the Orion arm very different from his journey to the Carinae. The human galleon was far, far slower than the Jotun hoard lair ship, and the first weeks were spent in slow recovery and painful healing of the many people on board that had been hurt when the Carinans had attacked. The first weeks then slowly began lengthening into months on the long and tedious voyage back across the interbrachial abyss.

After his initial joyful celebration at surviving, Greymalkin gradually felt his mood sinking into a sea of morose guilt as he thought about everything that had happened. When he closed his eyes to sleep, he saw Tatter's mauled and violated frozen body. That icy memory and the knowledge that he had *abandoned her to be murdered alone* was a crushing weight on his chest that kept him from sleep. When he finally woke after nightmares, he studied Royce's torn and shattered cyborganic body, and wept when he felt the innocent creature's continuing keening pain through the Helm Link. The thoughts that recurred to him most frequently always began: *If only...* He dwelled endlessly on what he should have done differently, but always came back to the same agonizing acknowledgement. *I did that, to both of them. I'm alive and whole, but Tatter was killed, and Royce was maimed because of my damned mistakes. I failed them.*

He knew intellectually that he should meditate and talk with others to recover emotionally from his experiences, but felt too numb to try. Instead he spent almost every waking hour tending to Royce as the cyneget slowly healed. He studied the literature about cyborganic creatures, and became more depressed at what he learned about the slow and uncertain healing process of cybernetic life forms that had been bred by the Builders.

Lex offered to keep him company and help with Royce, but Greymalkin found that he simply wanted to be alone and tend to the damage that the loyal cyneget had endured for him. The other repair engineers on the galleon helped if he asked, but the memory of the threatening manner that he had boarded the ship, together with Bruno's omnipresent and ominous guardian presence meant that virtually all of the thousands of other refugees on the vast ship gave their docking cradle a wide berth, and left them alone.

Greymalkin found that he preferred it that way. He sometimes thought about Sister Constance and the other Sojourners, but did not know if they were still in the galleon's infirmary healing or off busily unpacking their samples and data. He sometimes wondered if he should check, but would then lose track of the thought.

Lex checked on him periodically, but Greymalkin found it difficult to talk to him, or even Bruno. He spent entire silent days working by himself in the dark void of the cargo hold, laboriously beginning to reseal the cracks in Royce's mirrorshell hull and simply spending time caring for the living starship that had saved his life. And he brooded on Tatter's death, becoming sadder and angrier over time. One day he made the mistake of opening the case of gnari that Tatter had left with him. He thought about the night they had shared that drink. The days in the dark cargo hold became longer after that.

There came a day that he received a visitor while he sat dully in his cabin inside Royce, staring at the bulkhead while recovering from a gnari hangover. The cyneget occasionally communed a low keening of misery that was half pain and half concern for him. He always answered with reassuring thoughts, although he no longer felt anything inside. Then he heard the airlock cycle, and Lex came into the cabin. The older man folded his arms and gave Greymalkin a steady look with his stern blue eyes under a hedge of blond eyebrows. When Greymalkin simply glared back at him and said nothing, the Xenocorpsman picked up the empty bottle of gnari on the floor and put it away.

"I don't think that stuff is doing you any good," Lex said in irritation. Greymalkin shrugged and looked back at the bulkhead.

"It's psychogenic properties are interesting," Greymalkin snapped. "In addition to the basic euphoria, it has this strong effect in which you feel like you're someone else."

"Yeah, I know what gnari does," Lex said, still irritated. "Better than you do."

"That's why Calypso gave a case of it to Tatter," Greymalkin muttered. "She and her crew configured that upload they put in my shadow jewel to be *triggered* by gnari. It still tries to install itself in my mind whenever I take gnari, but I figured out how to deactivate it. Although, I have to admit I enjoy occasionally being someone else these days. Anyway, none of that is why gnari's useful to me."

"Pray, do tell," Lex said with a sigh. Greymalkin glared at him again.

"When I finally pass out, it gives me these dreams," Greymalkin said bitterly. "Well, it's always the *same* dream. She's still alive, and she still loves me. The only problem is, in the dream, now *I'm* the dead ghost and she can't find me...." He stopped talking, because it felt like he was dying inside.

"Interesting." Lex put his hand to his chin, thinking. "We all process events in our dreams. D'you know that even I still dream? Well, you're not far from the truth."

"You aren't funny," Greymalkin said. His face had darkened.

"Do I strike you as someone that wants to be funny?" Lex asked. "Not my strong suit."

Now it was Greymalkin's turn to be irritated. "What do you want, Lex?" he snapped, rubbing his throbbing head.

"Two things," Lex said, starting to pace the room slowly. "I have a message to deliver and a question to ask. The message is from Sister Constance and her whole crew. They want to see you. They want to thank you for getting them out." Greymalkin made a rude noise.

"Sure they do. If that was true, they could have come here any time they wanted to."

"No they can't," Lex said. He frowned. "Not with Bruno out there."

After a long puzzled moment, Greymalkin said, "What?"

Lex sighed again. "Okay, you *don't* know that Bruno's perched out there at the gangway entrance to this docking cradle like a gargoyle? He won't let anyone but me come in here. Or commune with you, for that matter. He's blocking all intra-ship communications with you."

Greymalkin sat silently. Finally, he said in a quiet voice, "Alright, I'll talk to him."

"You need to get out of here for a while and go talk to them in person," Lex said. "I can tend Royce for a while. I know more about caring for cynegets than you do, anyway."

Greymalkin closed his eyes. After a moment he took a deep breath. He opened his eyes in surprise, realizing he hadn't taken a deep breath in weeks. It lifted his mood. He looked back at Lex and nodded sadly. "I'll go talk to them. I should have before. I didn't know Bruno was doing that all this time...."

"Now for my question," Lex went on. "Did you know that Bruno surveyed and recorded the site after Tatter was attacked?"

"Well, sure," Greymalkin said. "I mean, I was *there*...."

Lex looked exasperated. "I've been asking you for weeks... never mind. I understand that you probably don't want to talk about it. But I finally thought to ask *Bruno* about the attack. He gave me his recordings, and I agree with him."

"About what?" Greymalkin said, totally confused. Lex stared at him, and then crouched down to look into his face intently.

"Grey, don't you get it? There were dead Carinans all over that site, scattered in different places. They were killed in hand-to-hand combat. *Who did that? Tatterdemalion did.* She was the only one there."

Greymalkin nodded, simply staring with dead eyes at the bulkhead. His chest felt hollow. He finally said, "I'm sure she put up an incredible fight. But *they killed her*. Her Sylphid form was gone, disintegrated instantly when they punctured her manifold. And I found her human *body*, remember? They *cut off her head*."

Lex's eyebrows went up. "But Grey, think about what you saw, and what you just said. If she fought and slew so many of them all around the site, she couldn't have been killed instantly. And you just said it; you didn't find her *Sylphid* body. Manifold implosions leave behind residue. You said that you didn't see *anything*. And about her body, well, you know about Sylphids, right? You found her human *teratoma* form, not her actual Sylphid body or any evidence that her manifold imploded. You understand that Sylphids can grow teratomas at will, whenever they want? But her actual mind, *who she is*, was never in her human form, but in her *Sylphid* body."

"What?" Greymalkin asked. He felt light-headed and dizzy. *What is he saying?*

"Grey, it's obvious from the images Bruno collected," Lex said. "Here's what actually happened. The Carinans surprised her, sure, they likely blew up the dome when they entered. She had probably been sleeping in her human teratoma form, but the Carinans *severed* it with their equivalent of shadow space blades just as she was trying to change for combat. They had probably never encountered a Sylphid before. They tried to kill her as they would a human, by chopping her to pieces. But that wasn't the end of the fight. She would have instinctively changed form the instant she knew she was under attack. She certainly couldn't fight them in vacuum as a human! And look at how many Carinan corpses there were scattered around that site! She *did* fight them. It's obvious they didn't completely surprise her and instantaneously kill her when they blew up the dome because of how many of them she killed! And I can vouch for the fact that Sylphids are *astonishingly* durable and deadly in hand-to-hand combat. She fought them off, and then she got the hell out of there! Grey, she's *not dead*."

Greymalkin looked blankly at Lex with no expression at all, feeling numb. He was terrified of feeling anything else. "Are you sure...?"

Lex sighed tolerantly. "Yes, I'm sure. Those last couple of days of the evacuation were bedlam for everyone. I was busy helping people get on the galleons, but I couldn't be everywhere at once. I've been asking around though, doing my Xenocorps detective routine ever since we left the Carinae. Today I finally tracked down some of the medics that told me that during the final chaos of the expedition they treated a severely injured Sylphid member of the expedition, one that they then sent home on the first wave of evacuation galleons. *And Tatter was the only Sylphid in the expedition.*"

Greymalkin felt everything turn upside down and he lunged to his feet, shoving Lex up against the wall violently. Lex was startled, but then said softly, "Sorry, I should have started with that. Yes. I'm *sure*. "

He slowly let go of the older man, turned away, and wiped his eyes. Then Greymalkin saw his own reflection in an exposed section of Royce's mirrorshell hull that he had been polishing yesterday. The young Sojourner monk that stood there in disheveled golden robes looked as much a beaten-up wreck as Royce. His silver grey eyes were framed in red sclera, all in turn sunken into the dark shadows underneath his eyes. Greymalkin straightened up and clenched his jaw, glaring at himself in angry determination, and then spun back around.

"Alright, *my apologies*. I've been stupid long enough," Greymalkin spat. "Now, I've got some things to do when we get back." He lifted an eyebrow. "Will you come with me?"

Lex laughed. "I told you before, I'm not going to leave you behind. Sure, I'm with you. And don't worry, we'll find her, kid."

Greymalkin nodded, pulled his hood down over his forehead, and put his arms in the sleeves of his robes as he began processing information. *Very well,* he thought. *Wherever this goes, I'll remember, now. Sojourn through life with courage.*

To Be Continued in *Sylphid: Book Three of the Sojourner Saga*

About the Author

Dr. Martin Halbert is a librarian and digital library innovator whose career has featured decades of experimental work in developing research data repositories and collaborative institutional change projects. Halbert served as co-principal investigator for the *Transatlantic Slave Trade Database*, one of the most prominent international sources of scholarly information for researching the history of trafficking in enslaved Africans, and was the founder of Educopia, a non-profit organization that promotes knowledge sharing and capacity building among research organizations, communities, and individuals. He served as dean of libraries at two universities, and is now a tenured professor. Most recently, he completed four years as a program director and science advisor for the U.S. National Science Foundation, where he worked on open science policy for the agency.

For more information on Dr. Halbert, see:
    https://martinhalbert.eposian.com/

The Sojourner Novels

Helmsman: Book One of the Sojourner Saga

Pilgrim: Book Two of the Sojourner Saga

Sylphid: Book Three of the Sojourner Saga

Oracle: Book Four of the Sojourner Saga

Xenocorpsman: Book Five of the Sojourner Saga

Wayfinder: Book Six of the Sojourner Saga

For more information on the Sojourner Saga universe, see: https://sojourner.eposian.com/

www.ingramcontent.com/pod-product-compliance
Lightning Source LLC
LaVergne TN
LVHW011927070526
838202LV00054B/4526